"How many times have you been
made to feel that
your beauty is a sin?

. . . That taking pleasure in your natural gifts is depraved?"

Fidelity's lowered eyes told him he had hit home.

"The Puritan way of life is an unnatural one," he continued. "Its notions were created by and for ugly people."

With one hand holding her firmly at the waist, he used the other to sweep the silvery curls from the back of her neck as he lowered his head to kiss her. She tried to break away and heard his low chuckle.

"So, my little Puritan has not a heart of ice. That's lesson number two in your education for life."

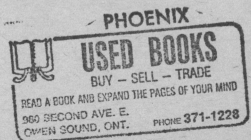

# FLAME OF FIDELITY

## SANDRA DUBAY

LEISURE BOOKS   NEW YORK CITY

A LEISURE BOOK

Published by

Dorchester Publishing Co., Inc.
6 East 39th Street
New York, NY    10016

Printed in the United States of America

# Part I

---

## Fairfax House
## 1660

# Prologue

## 1649

The bloody Civil War raged throughout England. A king had lost his head; another his father and his throne. Families were divided, friendships which had endured for generations were torn beyond repair.

The Parliamentarians, or Roundheads as they were called because of their shorn hair, were in control of the country and Oliver Cromwell ruled in Whitehall Palace as Lord Protector.

Fidelity Fairfax was six years old. Too young to remember the glittering, gorgeous Court of Charles I. Too young to know that England hadn't always been a somber place of grays and blacks and whites; that ladies hadn't always hidden their hair beneath starched white coifs and meekly done their best to appear demure and completely without humor or sensuality. She'd never seen paints, powders, or patches accentuating flirting eyes, or gold, silver, and jewels shining on exposed breasts. She'd never watched fops and gallants pass by on their way to the playhouse. She didn't know that Sunday had not always been spent in church listening to fearsome accounts of hellfire and brimstone. Her father was a Parliamentarian and a strict Protestant God-fearing man who believed that sin and degradation lay in laughter, wine, and the arms of a beautiful woman. Her father was Richard Fairfax.

Richard Fairfax had immediately declared for the Parliamentarians when the country divided into factions. He did so only partly because of his disgust with the monarchy and the threatening Catholicism of Charles I's French Queen. For the rest he did so because his cousin, Henry Fairfax, was a Royalist and he hated Henry Fairfax.

Henry Fairfax was the Earl of Wyndham. Richard and Henry shared a paternal great-grandfather, but Richard was descended from a younger son of the old earl and Henry from the eldest son—the heir. No politics can compete with the bitter frustration that comes of fortune lost by an accident of birth. Richard Fairfax was satisfied with the conditions that had forced his cousin to flee from the country. The estates of the earl had been sold by Cromwell but Richard, through his loyalty, had retained ownership of Fairfax House and, as a prosperous gentleman farmer, now saw himself as the heir of the Fairfax heritage. His sons and daughters could grow up proud—though not irreverently so—Prostestant, and Parliamentarian, without the taint of the aristocracy.

# 1

Oliver Cromwell was dead. His son had lasted only briefly as his successor, having all of his father's faults and none of his abilities. Charles II was coming home to claim his kingdom.

If there were some who grumbled over the fall of the Protectorate and the return of the monarchy, they were unheard, their complaints far overshadowed by the joyful singing and cheering of the masses. Englishmen, or at least the vast majority of them, had grown tired of the dull, pious, and sober atmosphere of Cromwellian rule. They longed for the Maypoles and plays, the intrigues and excitement that come with the gorgeous spectacle of the aristocracy at play.

Nowhere was this more apparent than in London for Londoners were not, by and large, a quiet or restrained people, and the dashing Cavaliers who came bustling into the city were a welcome sight.

Fairfax House stood far enough outside London to be surrounded by lush green pastures, sweet meadows, and growing fields. Built a few generations before, it was an imposing structure that did not reflect the Frenchified tastes of the homes occupied by the fashionable nobility and those wealthy enough to copy them.

The house stood near enough to the road to allow a clear view of those who passed and vice versa. A circular drive led up to its oak-paneled entrance. It was built of thick gray stone three stories high and stretched to the east and west of the center front with large windows spaced symmetrically along all three floors. From its slate roof innumerable chimneys revealed the presence of many large fireplaces. Its furnishings were tasteful and of quality materials, most in the solid, massive style which was even then giving way to the fragile elegance being made fashionable by Royalists returning from the exquisite Court of Louis XIV of France.

Fidelity Fairfax stood near the large, beveled glass windows of a front parlor gazing wistfully out at the continuous stream of velvet- and satin-clad Royalists who rode past on their way to the capital. Time and time again she glanced down at the dark gray wool of her dress. It had a full skirt, a modestly fitted bodice, and a white linen collar at the base of her throat. Her long sleeves ended in white linen cuffs and her feet were encased in low-heeled shoes of gray buckskin.

"They're so handsome!" she breathed as Sarah, her younger sister, came to the window.

"They're evil and degraded," Sarah disagreed.

Only a year apart in age, the two girls were as unlike as nature could have made them. Fidelity was, at seventeen, a beautiful young woman. Beneath her demure white cap her hair was the silver of moonlight across a lake. Her eyes were dark blue, a sapphire blue, set off by heavy lashes and sweeping black brows which stood out starkly on the pale ivory of her perfect complexion.

Sarah, sixteen, was gawky, an overgrown child who, although garbed almost identically to her sister, had none of the grace that marked Fidelity's every movement. Her hair, although once as blond as Fidelity's, had darkened and coarsened. Her eyes were a pale blue fringed with blond lashes and brows which might as well have been nonexistent. Their looks were nearly as much an issue between them as had been the Earldom of Wyndham between their father and his cousin.

"Oh, you don't know what evil and degradation are!" Fidelity scoffed, her eyes never leaving the pair of elegant horsemen who had stopped at the trough in front of the house to water their horses.

"I do too!" Sarah argued. "Anyone who indulges the pleasures of the flesh by dressing up in such luxurious materials and carrying on like the Royalists do is evil and degraded."

"Jealousy will get you nowhere," Fidelity smiled.

"Humph!" Sarah snorted, and then muttered, "I wish Father would move that water trough from in front of the house. I know those men are staring at me!"

Fidelity stifled a derisive laugh and glanced through the window once more. Her heart gave a little leap as she found the two gentlemen, one as blond as she and dressed in mulberry satin, and the other as dark as his companion was fair, in russet velvet, gazing toward the window in which she was framed. Instinctively her hand flew to her throat and her cheeks flamed red. Glancing around, she ascertained that she was alone, unobserved. Hesitantly she smiled, tentatively at first and then broadly, her full pink lips parting over even, white teeth. She caught her breath as the two men returned her smile and bowed, sweeping their plumed hats in graceful homage.

"Fidelity!" She whirled to find her mother, Elspeth, frowning from across the room. "Get away from that window!"

"Yes, Ma'am." Fidelity reluctantly left the window and moved toward her mother, a tiny nondescript woman who ruled her household with a firm hand.

"Do you want to be forced to confess your sins before the entire congregation?" Elspeth asked sternly.

"But, Ma'am!" Fidelity protested. "I wasn't . . ."

"Don't add lying to your burden, miss," she cautioned. "Your sister has already told me how you've taken to amusing yourself by flaunting your looks before those heathen Cavaliers. You must come to terms with your vanity, minx, and realize that it's not Christian for a woman to take pleasure in the curve of a lip or the color of a strand of hair. You'll do well to remember that if you expect to have any God-fearing man be willing to marry you."

"Yes, Ma'am." Fidelity looked at the floor, abashed. But in her heart of hearts she had to be true to herself; and if the Cavaliers who passed by were heathen and evil, emissaries of the Devil, and the dull young men in their parish were good and Christian, she thought she might rather be a heathen.

# 2

"The impudence! The colossal impudence!" Richard brought a fist down on the gleaming surface of the great oak dining table. Flatware and china rattled, crystal goblets teetered threateningly. Servants carrying trays of food and pitchers of beverage into the room stared.

Sarah, Fidelity, and their younger siblings—Nathaniel, fourteen, Jonathan, twelve, and Joshua, ten—kept their eyes studiously downcast and only Elspeth dared venture an opinion of her husband's outburst.

"After all, sir, they are family."

"Family! I'm ashamed to admit that we are of the same blood!" Beneath his hand, resting on the table, lay a piece of paper, its wax seal broken, its surface covered with spidery handwriting. "They follow the king into exile—they are driven into exile—and now they return. They bring their unholy ways back to sully the good works of Cromwell and think to stay in my home!"

"It would be un-Christian of us to refuse them shelter," Elspeth persisted.

"Un-Christian," Richard sighed. "Un-Christian to ban filth from one's own home." He surveyed his

family seated at the long table. They were a homely
people, Fidelity standing out among them as a rose
must in a field of weeds. Her beauty was a trial to
him; it seemed too vivid, too blatant. It seemed as
though she must be a foundling child, the offspring of
some painted and gowned product of the aristocracy.
He was worried that her convictions might not be
strong enough, worried what the result of her contact
with his cousin's party would be. "Un-Christian to
want to protect one's family from the taint of the
Court?"

"When will they arrive?" Elspeth asked, and the
children, who were supposed to be minding their own
affairs, the conversation of their elders being none of
their business, strained to hear their father's response.

Richard consulted the offending letter. "In a
fortnight," he read. "But the letter was mailed from Le
Havre days since. It shouldn't be too long now."

Elspeth supervised the preparation of rooms and
the planning of meals. The earl, according to his
letter, was to be accompanied by his countess, Divina
(at whose very name Richard cringed), a few man-
and maidservants, and one Baron Pierrepointe and
his attendants.

"He's bringing strangers into my home. Who can
tell what sort of man this Pierrepointe may be? For
that matter, who can tell what sort of people these
relatives about to descend upon us may be?"

But heathen or not, there was no denying that
the imminent arrival of the earl and his party had
caused a great stir among the Fairfax family. Fidelity
was excited about the opportunity to examine the
nobility at close range. Sarah was eager to find fault

and reason for added disgust, and the boys could not help but be anxious to learn more about battles and adventures in which the earl and baron might have participated.

Henry Fairfax, Earl of Wyndham, arrived at Fairfax House on a stormy evening in early May shortly before dinner. While their visitors were dismounting in the small front courtyard, grooms were dispatched to see to the horses and Richard lined up his wife and children, according to age, in the dark-paneled entry hall. In the dining room beyond, servants were laying a sumptuous buffet for the refreshment of their guests.

Fidelity gave a surreptitious brush to stray wisps of the silver hair which escaped from her immaculately white cap. Her dress, Sarah had noted with malicious satisfaction, was a dark blue, the sapphire color of her eyes. Sarah had accused her of vanity and flaunting herself but, as their guests were already arriving, there was no time for her to be sent back to her room to change.

Sarah, Fidelity noticed, looked even more plain than usual. She'd donned her most unbecoming dress, a dull brown which made her dark blond hair seem mousy and lusterless. It was as though she sought to insult the visitors by refusing to put on her best appearance. Between her sister and her mother, Fidelity was set off marvelously.

At last, after what seemed an eternity, the double oak doors opened and Richard entered the room with his cousin.

Henry Fairfax handed his dripping cloak and

hat, its bedraggled plumes soggy and limp, to a manservant. Straightening his clothing around him, he waited for his wife to shed her rain-wet outer garments.

The Baron Pierrepointe was nowhere to be seen, although Fidelity could have sworn she saw three central figures among the party that rode up to the house, but when she caught sight of the Countess of Wyndham all thoughts of the elusive baron were driven from her mind.

Divina, Countess of Wyndham, was obviously some years younger than her husband whom Fidelity estimated to be about forty-five years old. She probably was no more than thirty-five; she looked closer to twenty-two. Her hair was light, not the silver blond of Fidelity's but a golden blond, the color of ripe wheat. Her skin was pink, a flawless light blushing pink which heightened to a darker rose on her cheeks. Her eyes were dark, the lashes and brows of deepest black, and her eyelids, Fidelity realized with a start, were the same deep brown of her eyes. Her lips were a bright red—she had paint on her face!

Fidelity's eyes widened. She had never seen what her father called a painted woman at such close quarters. It was fascinating! The countess's gown was of burgundy satin with a dull rich sheen; it rustled when she moved. At the elbows, where the satin sleeves ended, ruffles of a gauzy écru material trimmed with lace billowed out and a matching ruffle of the material puffed out over the neckline of the gown which was scandalously low, revealing the swell and cleft of her breasts.

Fidelity's eyes never left he wickedly fascinating

creature as she waited for the earl to make his introductions among Richard, Elspeth, and his countess.

"Fidelity?" her father's voice sounded in her ear. "This is your cousin, the Earl of Wyndham."

If the earl noticed the tinge of bitterness with which Richard pronounced his title he made no sign of it. He took Fidelity's hand and, for the first time, she turned her attention to him.

The Earl of Wyndham was a man of middle age, slightly taller than Richard, perhaps five foot nine or ten, with graying brown hair. His features were not unlike her father's, although there was an indefinable air of adventure and a lifetime lived to the fullest that was missing in the countenance of Richard Fairfax. The earl's eyes were dark and lively and Fidelity noticed the look of surprise in them as he compared her with her sister and brothers.

"You must have been in a better mood when you made this one!" he called to Fidelity's father, ignoring the disapproving expression his comment evoked in his cousin. "She's as lovely as a spring morning." He motioned for his wife to join him and Fidelity was aware of a delicious aroma emanating from the person of the countess—she used scent!"

"Isn't she lovely, my dear?" he asked, turning Fidelity toward Divina by the hand which still lay imprisoned in his own.

"Beautiful!" Divina Fairfax agreed generously. "She'd have been a sensation at the Court of Holland."

"Perhaps she'll still have a chance," the earl stated thoughtfully. "After the king's come back."

"Not likely," Richard interjected, moving force-fully between the earl and his elder daughter. "Shall we go into the dining room? We have refreshments."

The adults moved away from where Fidelity and her siblings stood and Sarah whispered conspiratori-ally. "Have you ever seen such a harlot?"

Fidelity turned to her. "So much for your vaunted charity, Sarah Fairfax. Judge not—it says so in the Bible!"

"She's showing her body!" Sarah reasoned. "And her face, all painted, and she's showing her underwear!"

"Her underwear!" Fidelity was certain her sister had lost what little reason she'd ever had.

"It's true! Those frills at her neckline and arms, it's called a chemise—it's like a shift."

Fidelity was about to tell Sarah what she thought of such a statement when her sister turned on her heel and stalked off in the direction of the dining room and the rest of the family. Fidelity stood alone in the entry hall, her brothers having followed the earl and their parents. She was about to go there also when the great oak doors flew open and, in a swirl of rain and wind, a man entered the hall.

He was enveloped in black from head to toe, from the dark plumed hat pulled over his face to his black voluminous cloak to the heavy, mud-spattered boots which were even then leaving a dirty puddle on the shining wooden floor.

Fidelity stood perfectly still; she was faced with this menacing figure who towered over her by at least a foot. She dared not cry out to anyone for it seemed that the devil himself must have come out of the that the devil himself must have come out of the storm and entered their house. They stood so for several long, silent moments until a manservant strode up and the man pulled his hat and cloak off.

Baron Schuyler Pierrepointe stood before Fidelity, amused at her gaping amazement. He was a large man, his massive, muscular frame matching his above-average height, and broad shouldered, his body tapered down to a narrow waist and slim hips. His skin was tanned, which accented the almost white blondness of his hair and moustache. His suit, like his outer clothing, was black. His open velvet coat showed a cream linen shirt unfastened halfway down the front, its broad collar extending over the collar of the coat. The breeches were tucked into high leather riding boots which, Fidelity noticed, were silver-spurred.

"I am the Baron Pierrepointe," he said. His voice was low and velvety with an undertone that matched the amused light in his green eyes. "I am with my Lord Wyndham."

"Yes," Fidelity spoke slowly. Her eyes followed the long, lazily curling waves of his hair which, unlike the short styles affected by the young men of her acquaintance, was Cavalier in fashion. "They've gone into the dining room."

"I see," the baron flicked the ruffles at the end of his sleeves into place. "Nice of them to leave a pretty maidservant to show me in."

"Maidservant?" Fidelity's senses were bemused and his comments confused her. "Oh, you mean me? I'm not a maidservant!" She lifted her chin haughtily.

"I'm Fidelity Fairfax. The earl is my father's cousin and you happen to be in my father's house!"

Pierrepointe's laugh was deep and throaty. "Excuse me, my lady Fidelity. It seems I've only been back in England a few days and already I've an angry Parliamentarian looking daggers at me!"

Fidelity watched as he bowed his apologies and, with an air of what she hoped would pass for grudging forgiveness, she turned toward the dining room motioning Pierrepointe to follow her. With a few long strides he overtook her and, extending the velvet-covered arm, offered her his company on the short walk to the dining room.

Hesitantly, Fidelity raised one hand and placed it shyly on the velvet-encased forearm of the baron. Her fingers felt the soft nap of the beautiful material, the first time she'd come into contact with quite so rich a fabric. As they made their way silently across the wide entrance hall, Fidelity became aware of another facet of the arm upon which her hand rested. Beneath her hand, and through the thick velvet of his sleeve, she could feel the play of muscles; even with the arm held ostensibly still the movement was there in his effort to hold it in its outstretched position. Fidelity shyly glanced at the face of the baron but her movement was betrayed by the fact that she had to look up to see his face. The top of her head barely came to his shoulder. With the movement of her head, Pierrepointe looked down into her eyes and one corner of his full-lipped mouth curled up beneath his carefully shaped moustache. Hurriedly, Fidelity looked away, her cheeks flaming. Reaching the dining

room door, she took her hand from the baron's arm
and entered the room ahead of him.

# 3

Fairfax House was a study in contrasts as the Earl and Countess of Wyndham and the Baron Pierre-pointe settled in. The earl had sent some of his staff ahead to London where, by some small miracle, he had been able to regain possession of Wyndham House, his mansion in the fashionable Strand near Whitehall Palace. As soon as the house was habitable, and he had no way of knowing what condition it was presently in, he and the countess would move there and the baron would become their house guest until he could decide about his future plans.

Fidelity, although she tried to retain the upright disapproval which was expected of her, found herself fascinated by the laughter and glamour of her cousin and his wife.

Dinners were extraordinary affairs, the family of Richard Fairfax ranged like plain pigeons along one side of the table while the earl, countess, and baron seemed like peacocks. The countess appeared in a new gown every evening; reds, blues, greens, silks, satins, and velvets. Her hair was in ringlets, loose graceful waves, or piled into a chignon at the back of her head; often it was interlaced with pearls, sapphires, and even diamonds. The earl was as colorful;

only the baron retained the more somber shades of black, brown, dark green, and burgundy. Even he, however, wore lace-trimmed shirts as well as great jewels which glittered on his fingers.

The young brothers of Fidelity were fascinated with the earl's stories of the Civil War which were all carefully worded to avoid conflict with his host, and Sarah seemed to delight in watching the countess for character flaws of which she managed to find multitudes. Fidelity spent a great deal of time in silent pondering, comparing her life with those of her father's guests and looking for bona fide reasons to reject the life of the nobility for her own. It was difficult to condemn people who, with the possible exception of the Baron Pierrepointe who seemed in some way threatening to her, had never been anything but kind and complimentary.

On the morning of the fourth day of the earl's visit, she found herself alone in a parlor of the house. Sarah had gone, along with her two youngest brothers, to the nearby home of a fellow parishioner to discuss the delicious scandal of the guests, and her father, oldest brother, and the earl were far out in the fields and pastures discussing crops and animals.

"Penny for your thoughts." The voice of the countess singsonged behind her.

Fidelity blushed. "I wasn't thinking anything of importance, really," she murmured.

The countess joined her on the window seat, her delicately printed taffeta morning gown mingling with the austere muslin of Fidelity's brown gown. "You should wear blues and roses, my dear," she commented. "It would enhance your complexion and bring out your lovely eyes."

"Well, I don't really think . . ." Fidelity broke off, embarrassed.

"I see," the countess patted her hand. "I understand. But frankly, I think it's a sin to waste such beauty. Beauty is as much a gift from God as anything else. It shouldn't be treated as a curse."

"Really? A gift?" After so many years of reproachful looks and suspicious glances Fidelity was eager to hear her looks praised.

"Mother! Mother!" Sarah's voice came suddenly from the entrance hall.

Elspeth's footsteps hurried from the sewing room. "What is it?" she asked.

"Mrs. Wickham . . ." Sarah paused, catching her breath in ragged gasps. "Mrs. Wickham's time has come; she's having her baby!"

Elspeth stuck her head into the room, too preoccupied to make anything of her elder daughter in so intimate a conversation with the countess. "I'm going to the Wickhams'," she instructed. "Check on the cooks and see that dinner is ready if I'm not back in time."

"Yes, Ma'am," Fidelity answered. Through the window she could see her mother and sister hurrying down the road toward the nearby Wickham home.

"Well, it would seem that we've been abandoned," the countess remarked.

"Yes. No, I thought the baron was still here."

"No. It seems our magnificent Schuyler has ridden off into London for some reason or other." The countess lapsed momentarily into silence and a slow sigh escaped her. "Ah, the Baron Pierrepointe. He has relatives at the court of Louis XIV, you know. But his family came to England with the Conqueror. Very old and very distinguished; I daresay Schuyler is the finest blossom of that ancient family tree." She paused and then roused herself from whatever paths her thoughts had taken. "How would you like to do something totally wicked for once in your life?" Her eyes sparkled.

"What do you mean?" Fidelity asked, eyes wide.

"We are about the same size, although I have to admit that you are more slender than I. How would you like to go up to my room and shed those dull garments to shine for one secret moment?"

"Oh," Fidelity felt her heart would stop. "I shouldn't . . ."

"Who would know?" the countess persisted. "There is no one here save you and I. I would keep our little secret."

"Well," Fidelity paused but the racing in her blood told her that, should she decline this opportunity, she would always regret her hesitance. She was destined, she knew, to marry one of the dull young men with whom she had grown up. She would spend her life in exactly the same manner as she had thus far, growing eventually into a copy of her mother. Could a brief moment of sin blot out a lifetime of devotion to the principles of the church?

She fairly ran up the stairs with the countess and, entering the room set aside for the earl and his wife, was amazed at the change that had taken place there. Not that the furniture was any different, the great four-poster still sported its plain forest-green damask hangings and the drapes at the window were still held in place as usual, but there was an air of excitement that seemed to tingle in the very air. The dressing table supported a large mirror, of which there were only two very small ones ordinarily in Fairfax House (the better, so Richard Fairfax said, to discourage vanity), and the table's surface was covered with jars and bottles containing an assortment of paints and powders, perfumes and creams. The armoire stood open, packed with gowns and discarded apparel, and accessories lay scattered negligently about the room.

"The first thing we will dispense with is that cap," the countess decided. Pulling the linen cap from Fidelity's head, she took up an ivory backed brush and brushed her hair to its full, waving length. It fell in a silvery cascade to her hips, curling over on the ends.

"How beautiful!" Divina exclaimed, stroking the brush through its bouncy, thick lengths. "It's wonderful hair!" She spread Fidelity's hair around her shoulders in a gleaming mantle. "There. When we are done with the cosmetics I shall do your hair. But for now," she picked up a few pearl-headed bodkins from the tabletop and, with expert twists, skewered Fidelity's hair atop her head. "Now for the clothes."

Fidelity stood still in the center of the room as the countess moved behind her and unfastened the back of her bodice and skirt. Slipping out of the clothes, Fidelity carefully folded them and draped them over the back of a chair.

"The shoes, the shoes," Divina prompted, and Fidelity slipped them from her feet. "The shift, the shift."

Reluctantly, Fidelity slipped the loose shift over

her head and stood uneasily in the center of the room.
She was unaccustomed to being naked, even when
alone and here, with another person in the room, she
felt as though she should run and hide.

"Don't be shy, Fidelity," Divina comforted.
"Your body is not something to be ashamed of." She
rummaged through a trunk and emerged with a
chemise of almost transparent white linen, its low
neckline and full sleeves trimmed with delicate lace
threaded through with ribbon of a glittering silver.
"Slip into this." She held the garment out to the
shivering Fidelity.

Gratefully, Fidelity pulled the light garment over
her head and its long skirt fluttered down around her
legs. She glanced into the mirror as the countess
directed her into the dressing table chair and noticed
that the thin chemise was so diaphanous that her skin
was clearly visible through it. "Oh!" she cried,
holding her hands protectively before herself.

The countess, looking up from her position on
the floor where she was busily rolling green silk
stockings onto Fidelity's legs, laughed. "No one will
see it except you. Don't be overly modest."

Fidelity watched as the countess, opening various pots and jars, darkened her already black lashes
and outlined her eyes with kohl. She dusted a light
blush into her cheeks and colored her lips a delicious
apple red. As for her hair, the countess decided that a
simple style would suit her better than something
more sophisticated. With a green ribbon she pulled
the shimmering masses of Fidelity's hair up to the
back of her head where she tied the ribbon into a
graceful bow. The result was that the silver hair

cascaded into curls from her shoulders to her waist. With a tiny comb Divina pulled a few short strands from in front of Fidelity's ears and curled them onto her cheeks. Doing the same around her forehead, Fidelity's face was framed in minute curls.

"Now, let's see about the dress." Divina pursed her lips and then reached into the armoire and pulled out a gown of bright green watered silk. The bodice, its rounded neckline edged with rows of silver lace, was tightly fitted with elbow-length sleeves. The skirt was full and over it floated a skirt of silver lace. The countess lifted the heavy gown over Fidelity's head and, pulling it into place, arranged the lace of the chemise over the edge of the neckline and out of the ends of the sleeves.

"It is your underwear!" Fidelity exclaimed, remembering Sarah's comment on the night of the earl's arrival. "You do show your underwear!"

The countess laughed and ran a brush through Fidelity's hair where the gown had mussed it. She returned to her trunks and came back with a pair of green and silver gloves and a delicate silver lace fan. "You don't have to wear the gloves, just carry them," she instructed.

At last they were finished and Fidelity turned before the large dressing table mirror. "Oh, it's beautiful!" she breathed.

"Yes," the countess agreed. "I'm sorry to say that it looks better on you than it ever did on me!"

Fidelity was bemused by the feel of the cosmetics on her skin and the soft yet tightly fitted gown clinging to her figure. So wrapped up in herself was she that she didn't even hear the door open behind them.

Schuyler Pierrepointe stood in the doorway, negligently slapping buckskin riding gloves into the palm of one hand. His blond hair, tousled by the wind, lay on the collar of a charcoal jacket, his breeches were gray buckskin. The cream linen of his shirt lay against the lapels of his jacket and the ruffles of his cuffs were barely visible where he had tucked them into the sleeves of his jacket to facilitate his handling the reins.

"May I have this dance?" He spoke from the doorway, his voice carrying its ever-present undertone of mockery.

Fidelity whirled toward the door, aware of the low neckline of the gown which revealed her shoulders and most of her bosom. The countess watched, amused.

"Do you have to barge in?" Fidelity cried, forgetting that this wasn't her room and the man in the doorway was her father's guest.

"Tut, tut," the baron scoffed, entering the room and striding toward her with fluid, feline grace. "Don't imagine that you are the first young woman to appear thus attired. In fact, compared to many young women of my acquaintance you are completely covered."

"Then I hesitate to imagine the kind of young women with whom you keep company!"

"My," he laughed, with a wink toward the countess. "It seems to be getting decidedly colder in this room."

"Only in your direction," Divina replied.

Fidelity felt a warm blush rise into her cheeks. "I

should be changing back into my own clothes now," she told her cousin's wife.

"No, not yet," Divina coaxed. "Let me find my maid to give you her opinion." Turning before Fidelity could stop her, the countess was out of the room in an instant leaving her alone with the Baron Pierrepointe.

Fidelity's eyes followed the countess out of the room and then turned back to Pierrepointe who had moved closer to her. She watched him warily.

"Ah, Mistress Fairfax," he smiled. "Do not look at me so. Do you imagine that I would ravish you in Lady Wyndham's absence?"

"Truly, my lord," she replied, attempting a haughtiness she didn't feel, "I don't know what you would do. People such as you . . ." She left the sentence unfinished.

To her surprise, the scorn in her voice made him throw back his head and laugh. "Spoken like a true Parliamentarian! I hear your father's influence clearly!"

Fidelity sighed. It was true, the words were her father's and she supposed Pierrepointe had sensed the lack of conviction in her voice. She felt the blush rising warmly into her face once again.

"It's nothing to be ashamed of," the baron told her. "But the Puritan way of life is an unnatural one."

"Sir!" Fidelity prepared to defend her family.

He waved aside her objections. "How many times have you been made to feel that your beauty is a sin? That taking pleasure in your natural gifts is depraved?" Her lowered eyes told him he had spoken correctly. "Those are notions created by and for the appeasement of ugly people. Of all your family, you are the only one who is beautiful. Should the others then not try to defend their homeliness? They believe that good as they see it, will be rewarded, and they believe themselves to be good. It follows that since they are good and yet still ugly, beauty must not be good."

Fidelity stared at him, digesting the information thoughtfully. She could not say that she strictly understood it and yet it made her feel less wicked, less like a creature born evil. She felt her distrust of the baron fading in the face of his apparent admiration of her looks. She had never met a group of people who accepted her and admired her as did the Earl of Wyndham and his party.

"Just look at yourself," Pierrepointe was continuing. He placed his hands on her waist and turned her toward the framed mirror atop the dressing table.

Fidelity stared at the elegant reflection in the looking glass. She scarcely recognized herself. She seemed worldlywise, fashionable, and the bright green of her gown was complemented by the charcoal and gray of the baron's attire as he stood behind her. She found her eyes moving away from her own reflection to his and started as their eyes met.

His lips curled into a lazy smile. "We look well together," he hold her. "You are small enough to make me look larger and I am large enough to make you appear more delicate." He waited as though expecting her to speak but she could not. "Divina was right. You would have been a sensation at the Court of Holland. Or anywhere else for that matter."

Fidelity was uncomfortably aware of his near-

ness and of the light pressure of his hands against her
waist. She made a move to step away and heard his
low chuckle.

"So you sense it also, eh?" he asked. "Our little
Parliamentarian has not a heart of ice. That is lesson
number two." With one hand still holding her firmly
at the waist, he used the other to sweep the silvery
curls from the back of her neck and in the mirror she
saw him lower his head as he kissed her.

She gasped slightly as she felt the brush of his
mouth on her skin. It was a fluttering brush so gentle
she could not swear it had happened and yet she felt
an unfamiliar quiver start within her. "No," she
breathed, but she knew there was no conviction in her
voice.

In the silent room the click of the door latch
sounded and, with a jump in her heart, Fidelity was
sure they had been discovered. But it was the countess
who entered the room and secured the door.

"Schuyler," she smiled, not missing the deep
flush on Fidelity's cheeks. "You must take yourself out
of here this instant and let me help Fidelity back into
her own clothes."

Without another word the baron bowed to them
both and picked up his hat. He started for the door
but stopped. "I will show you another Cavalier
custom," he said, turning toward them once again.
Returning to the two women, the baron took the
countess's hand and raised it to his lips. He dropped
her hand and reached for Fidelity's. Once again she
felt the slight shock of contact with him, not so
intense as before but still strangely, wickedly pleasurable. She stared after him as the door closed behind

him. Turning toward the countess, Fidelity found her cousin's wife smiling at her with a curiously knowing look.

# 4

Fidelity lay awake into the night, long after the house was quiet. Even her mother, the hard-working Elspeth who habitually oversaw the nightly securing of the household, had gone to bed.

Now, resigned to her sleeplessness, Fidelity pushed back the rich, burgundy damask bed curtains and walked to the window seat, her white linen gown flowing around her and her pale silver hair pouring down her back and swinging with the motion of her movements.

The night was clear and warm, and the evening air rushed in as she opened the windows. She breathed deeply of the sweetly scented air hoping it would make her drowsy, but neither the scented breezes nor the late hour could force the memory of Schuyler Pierrepointe from her mind.

She remembered him standing behind her in the countess's room; the intensely pleasurable feeling of his firm lips brushing across the sensitive skin of her throat. With her own hands she tried to re-create the gentle yet masterful pressure he'd exerted on her waist but her hands were too small, too weak to duplicate those of the baron.

"Schuyler . . ." she whispered aloud into the

small, curtained window seat alcove.

A sound caught her attention and she looked out of the window.

To her surprise a man had left the stable and walked toward the house. With the brilliant moonlight illuminating the center of the rear courtyard which her window overlooked, she saw the powerful figure of Schuyler Pierrepointe striding toward the house.

He moved with the flowing feline grace so peculiarly his own and Fidelity held her breath as he glanced upward and saw her a floor above him.

He paused and gave a quick glance around, then stepped into the shadows nearest the house. With a few silent movements he had climbed Elspeth Fairfax's rose trellis and appeared at Fidelity's open window.

"Someone will see you!" Fidelity breathed, expecting her father to appear beneath the window with a gun in his hands.

"Who?" Schuyler grinned.

"You'll fall and hurt yourself!"

"Then move away from the window and let me come in."

"I couldn't do that!"

Pierrepointe chuckled at her shocked expression. "Then I suppose I'll have to remain perched upon this rickety trellis." His mocking grin vanished. "How lovely you looked from the courtyard with your hair shining in the moonlight."

"And I don't look lovely from here?"

"What a lively vanity you have for a Puritan," he

smiled. "Yes, you look lovely from here too. Why are you awake so late?"

"I couldn't sleep," she sighed. His face was so near to hers that she could feel his warm breath on her cheek as he spoke.

"And what kept you awake?"

Fidelity knew her blush was betraying her. "You should go now," she told him, embarrassed.

He laughed and there was a trace of triumph in his mirth. "Your innocence is more refreshing than returning to England after so long abroad. Had I known what I was going to find here, I assure you I would have returned much sooner."

"But then my cousin could not have brought you here," she reasoned.

He smiled and shifted his weight on the trellis. "That's true. Well, I must go."

"No!" Fidelity stopped, amazed at her own temerity. "So soon?"

"This trellis is deucedly uncomfortable, my dear. It was definitely not built with midnight trysts in mind."

Fidelity sighed knowing that in the morning they would have to resume the coolly polite demeanor which was necessary in front of her family. "Well," she began, the values of her upbringing in conflict with her desire for him to stay with her. "Why don't you just sit here on the sill?"

"All right." Her decision amused him and he turned on the trellis and sat on the sill of the opened window.

Fidelity pushed wide the other half of the double window to allow him more room and so she wouldn't have to sit behind him on the cushioned seat.

"Where were you returning from?" she asked, her surprise at his sudden appearance now giving way to curiosity as to the reason for his midnight ride.

"I had business in the city," he replied.

"Business?"

"Yes, with a charming old acquaintance of mine."

For an instant Fidelity felt shut out and much too immature in his company. Instinctively she knew his "charming acquaintance" was a woman and she wondered what his "business" with any woman in London at that hour could possibly be. She felt the same intangible emotion she knew when he exchanged glances with Lady Wyndham which bespoke shared memories and experiences of which she could never be a part.

"Why so quiet?" he asked.

Fidelity threw him a smile and inclined her head coquettishly. "Oh, just marveling at the night and the company."

"You're a born flirt, Fidelity Fairfax, and I doubt that you're even aware of it which makes it doubly alluring."

He reached an arm about her and she felt a quiver of fear as he drew her to him. She was pulled into a tight embrace and, through the light linen of her nightdress, she could feel the sharp edges of his coat buttons scratching provocatively against her skin. She was aware of them for only a moment before his mouth came down upon hers.

As he kissed her, restraining himself for fear of frightening her, Schuyler was aware of her hands hesitating for a moment and then sliding through the deep nap of his velvet coat to surround his shoulders. She was not terribly responsive, but he would have been surprised at anything else.

As she received his kiss, Fidelity felt a dizziness at the edges of her consciousness and yet her mind, eager to memorize these new sensations, recorded the most minute details: the feeling of the tickling softness of his moustache as his lips traced the contours of her face, the tantalizing pressure of his hands along her back, even the increasing raspiness of his breathing. When at last he drew away from her she leaned against a sidewall of the window seat and closed her eyes.

"Good night," his voice told her.

"Schuyler," she breathed. "Don't go."

"If I thought you meant that I wouldn't." His hand stroked along her arm making her draw a quick breath. "But you would regret anything more in the morning with your father's harsh eye upon you." He turned and stepped down into the trellis again.

"Good night." She smiled, leaning out the window after him.

Leaning toward her, Schuyler kissed her lightly. "Pleasant dreams," he whispered.

She laughed softly. "As though I could sleep at all."

He let go of the trellis and leaped the last few feet to the courtyard. With a courtly bow he disappeared into the shadows of Fairfax House and, as Fidelity's eyes followed him hungrily, she allowed a shuddering sigh to escape her.

# 5

Fidelity leaned back against the prickly cushion of straw and listened idly to the chirruping of crickets outside the barn. She and Schuyler had begun meeting there, in a secluded and unused stall of her father's stable, and now, as she strained to make out his features in the close darkness of the unlit stable, she allowed a dramatic and exaggerated sigh to escape her.

"I suppose," she began, toying with a piece of straw, "that you'll be leaving soon." The thought had been on her mind since the king's entry into London two days since.

"Yes, I suppose so," Schuyler replied. "I hardly think your father will encourage us to stay a moment longer than necessary."

"I'll be so sorry to see you go. I can't bear the thought of it."

"I can't say that I'll be terribly sorry to be going."

Fidelity jerked herself to a sitting position. "Why Schuyler Pierrepointe! What a horrid thing to say!"

Schuyler smiled. "But it's to your advantage that I leave, my dear. After all, I've waged a battle with temptation that would do credit to Cromwell himself."

A pleased flush rose to Fidelity's cheeks. "Well, I don't ask you to battle temptation."

"No, you didn't, but I knew I had to. How could I have justified leaving you with your reputation in shreds? Your family would have abandoned you. Your life would be ruined."

"You know I don't care about them or what they think." Fidelity protested. "I wouldn't care if I never saw them again." She paused, testing her own temerity, and then plunged on. "As long as I was with you."

"Ah, but that's just it. You couldn't be with me." Sensing the hurt in Fidelity's silence, he continued. "Fidelity, you know I'm not rich." She opened her mouth to protest but he silenced her. "I know, you can say it doesn't matter, but it does. I couldn't provide you with even the barest necessities. For myself, I can get by until I obtain some grants and privileges from the king, but I will not ask you to share the life I'm going to lead until then."

"And after?" she prompted.

"And after, I'm not going to be in the country."

"You're not . . ." She was stunned. She had, in her daydreams, imagined a romantic elopement with Schuyler and a glittering life at Court as the Baroness Pierrepointe. "But why not?"

"I'm going to the New World."

"To America?" Fidelity had heard, through her father's discussion of the merchant interests of many friends, of the growing numbers of Englishmen establishing plantations in America.

"Well, to Barbados actually."

"What part of America is that?"

"It's an island, to the south of the North American continent. It's tropical and I plan to grow many exotic products."

"You're going to be a farmer?" She was disappointed. Having grown up as the daughter of a prosperous farmer she was convinced that there could be no more boring profession in the world.

"If you call a plantation a farm," he smiled.

"Will you be leaving soon?"

"As soon as I can obtain the land grants from the king. I would imagine it will take some time. The king is barely unpacked in Whitehall and is being deluged by ruined Royalists trying to regain their possessions." Schuyler shook his head. "An impoverished monarchy and hordes of followers expecting their rewards. Hardly my idea of a birthday present."

Fidelity knew that the king, Charles II, had ridden into London to regain his throne on May 29, his thirtieth birthday. "Imagine getting a kingdom for one's birthday," she mused aloud. Her eyes were fastened on some faraway vision.

"It was hardly a new acquisition," Schuyler corrected practically. "The kingdom has been his since his father's murder. He has merely come into his own."

"Oh, Schuyler! Be romantic! Don't let's talk about past differences." She pouted for a moment and then regained her wistfulness. "I would so loved to have gone to see the king enter the city. Was it a beautiful procession?"

"Yes, as I have told you many times, it was."

"You are positively dull today, Schuyler Pierre-pointe."

"And you will be glad to see me leave?"

Her face fell. "Oh, no! I won't! Actually, I'm almost sorry to see the king come back because it means you and the earl and countess will be going away."

"Not so very far away. London is very near."

"It might as well be on the other side of the world. Father will never allow me to go into the city."

"Not even to visit your cousins?"

"Especially not to visit my cousins! He is sure I'm well on the way to hell because of them—and you."

The soft neigh of a startled horse brought them to their feet. Fidelity strained her eyes into the darkness for any sign of an intruder, knowing that a witness to their rendezvous could spell disaster, but could see no one.

"I think we'd better go back into the house," Schuyler prompted, and Fidelity, who usually post-poned ending their meetings as long as possible, agreed.

All through the following day Fidelity scanned the faces of those around her for some hint of whether one of them had been the anonymous visitor to the stable the night before. None betrayed any hint of a knowledge of her clandestine meetings. That it would have been her father, she had already rejected. He would have made a scene on the spot; there would have been no waiting, no wondering. Her three brothers she also ruled out; not only would they not have had the caution to sneak into the stable, they would not have had the good sense to keep their knowledge to themselves. That left only her mother and sister. In many ways she hoped it would prove to have been her mother. Elspeth Fairfax had always had a special place in her affections for her elder daughter and Fidelity knew that she would receive only a stern lecture on behavior from her.

The family left the dinner table to scatter to various places in the house and yard in accordance with their own particular interests. Fidelity, ever eager to hear more about life at the court, found herself happily alone with Divina Fairfax.

"Tell me again about the procession of the king and the ball at Whitehall," she urged.

Divina laughed. "You are insatiable on the subject. I vow I've described it to you so many times it scarce seems real to me any longer. I've told you about the procession through the packed streets, the crowds cheering and throwing flowers."

"And the more often I hear about it the less I resent not being allowed to go. Oh, Divina, it's as though I actually had been there!"

"I wish you could have gone," Lady Wyndham said generously. She and her husband had no children of their own and, although it would have made her feel considerably older than her thirty-five years to have a daughter Fidelity's age, this young cousin was the child she would have chosen.

"So do I. I wanted to go but you know Father. We could hear the fireworks and see the light of the bonfires along the Thames but . . ." She shrugged sadly.

"Well, perhaps you can come to visit Henry and me when we are settled in London and I'll take you to visit the Court."

"Will you introduce me to the king?" Fidelity asked eagerly.

The countess laughed. "The king. Ah, yes, I'm sure he would be quite enchanted with you."

"With me?" Fidelity's eyes grew wide. "But he is the king!"

"Rank means nothing to him where ladies are concerned."

"He would never notice me. You said yourself he has eyes for no one but Mrs. Palmer." The countess had told Fidelity of the king's mistress, Barbara Palmer, and described her vivid, red-haired beauty.

"There you're wrong. The king may be mad over Mrs. Palmer but that never keeps his eyes from seeking out other pretty women!"

"Perhaps Mrs. Palmer will divorce her husband and marry the king!" Fidelity speculated. She was surprised by the countess's burst of delighted laughter.

"Fidelity! Not only are divorces almost impossible to come by but the king would not marry Mrs. Palmer if she were scot-free at this very moment!"

"But why not? I thought he loved her."

"And so he does—as a mistress. But the kingdom is poor and the king must marry a princess with an immense dowry to help the country's finances."

"Money!" Fidelity was disappointed. "Why does

everything have to revolve around the question of money?"

"What else revolves around money?" the countess asked, sensing something of a personal nature in Fidelity's tone.

"Schuyler . . ." Fidelity paused and looked around to be sure they would not be overheard. "Schuyler says he cannot take me with him when he leaves here because he hasn't enough money."

"I see," Divina was surprised. "I hadn't realized things were that serious between you and Lord Pierrepointe."

"You sound as though you don't approve." Fidelity scanned her cousin's face.

"I do, my darling, I do. If I sound a little pettish it's only jealousy."

"Jealousy?" Fidelity couldn't imagine why this lovely and sophisticated cousin of hers should be jealous of anything to do with her life.

"Yes. You're so young and innocent. You have a whole life ahead of you and a world of wonderful experiences which, alas, are only fond memories for me."

"You talk as though you were a hundred years old!"

"Well, you know, it sometimes seems that way. When Henry and I followed His Majesty into exile I was only twenty-two, but even twenty-two is an advanced age in a world where the most sought-after women are fifteen or sixteen. And when I was that age I was helping my mother and sisters hold off the Roundhead armies from our estates while my father

and brothers were off fighting for His Majesty's
father, the late king."

Fidelity sat silently, not wishing to disturb Lady
Wyndham's rememberings. "What happened?" she
asked finally.

"My father was killed and my mother lived only
long enough to see my sisters and I placed with
Royalist families leaving to join the exiled Court."

"And then you married the earl?"

"Yes. Even though I didn't have a large dowry
Henry wanted to marry me." The countess's eyes
grew fond in remembrance.

"He wasn't obsessed with money."

Divina patted Fidelity's hand. "He had more of it
than most and lost less of it in the wars."

Fidelity was about to question the countess
further when her mother appeared and hurried her off
to the family's evening devotions.

Fidelity lay in her wide bed half asleep. She
allowed the countess's stories of her husband's
disregard for her poverty and of the king's love for
Barbara Palmer to merge with her longing for a life
with Schuyler Pierrepointe until her musings became
a saga of selfless love and devotion in which she, of
course, was the heroine. She was brought out of her
musings by the squeak of the door hinges as someone
entered her bedchamber.

"Who is it?" she hissed, for the drapes at the
windows were closed and the darkness in the room
was complete.

"It's me," her sister Sarah's voice returned.

"What do you mean?" she demanded impatiently. She had little use for Sarah, and disliked her more than ever because of the way she talked of the earl, countess, and most of all, the Baron Pierrepointe.

Sarah lit a candle which threw huge silhouettes across the walls. They were framed in the posters and tester of the bed.

"I want to talk to you."

Fidelity caught a glimpse of the self-satisfied smile her sister always displayed when she had a piece of particular malicious business to attend to—it was rather like that of the barn cat when he had cornered an especially juicy-looking mouse. "About what?" she asked, bracing herself for battle.

"I know about you and that Cavalier."

"His name is Schuyler," Fidelity informed her sister. It would do no good, of course. To Sarah, Schuyler would always be "that Cavalier."

Sarah dismissed the correction. "I know," she repeated, "about you two. I know that you and he have been meeting in the stable."

"So what?" Fidelity feigned an unconcern she didn't feel.

"So what?" Sarah mocked her crudely. "You know so what! You know what Father would do if he knew about it!"

"Oh, Sarah!" Fidelity forced herself to laugh derisively. "If you weren't so jealous you wouldn't give a moment's thought to this."

"Jealous! I assure you I've nothing to be jealous of!"

"You're jealous because no man has ever even looked at you. You're jealous because Father is going to have to provide a mighty big dowry to buy you a husband."

Sarah's eyes grew hard and glittered with rage and hate. Fidelity knew she had committed a grave mistake in taunting her sister.

"I'll tell Father!" Sarah hissed through gritted teeth. "I'll tell him about the meetings in the stable and how you've become nothing more than a Royalist's whore!"

"That's not true!" Fidelity's words echoed in the still room and for a moment both girls were sure she'd awakened the entire household. When no one came to the door Fidelity continued. "It's not true. Schuyler has never touched me!"

"You don't expect anyone to believe that, do you?" Sarah smiled mirthlessly. "Everyone knows how these Cavaliers are. They won't bother with a woman who's not willing to allow them their way."

"You seem awfully knowledgeable about what these men want, Sarah Fairfax," Fidelity countered recklessly.

"Fine, try to place your sins on others." Sarah pressed her lips together in the prim line Fidelity had seen so often on the sanctimonious matrons of the church.

"Sarah," she said at last. "I swear to you that I've never done anything to be ashamed of."

"Some people are shameless. They see no wrong in whatever they do."

"I have never done anything to bring shame

upon this family," Fidelity amended.

"You admire these guests of Father's too much for any decent person's taste," Sarah preached. "But as far as anything else, see that you change your ways or I swear I'll take this whole story to Father—and I promise he'll believe me." She smiled wickedly as she leaned forward to blow out the candle and the look in her eyes made Fidelity shiver. "I promise he will."

In the darkness, Fidelity stared at the glowing tip of the extinguished candle wick and listened as her sister's hushed footsteps crossed the room. She waited until she heard the door open and close. She lay back in her bed once more and drew the heavy coverlet close under her chin; suddenly, in spite of the warmth of the night, she felt unusually cold.

# 6

Fidelity picked idly at the boiled mutton stew which was rapidly growing cold on the table in front of her. When she heard her father call her name from the other end of the table she knew what he was going to say.

"Fidelity! Eat your food. I'll not have you wasting good food the Lord has seen fit to place in front of you. We're finally rid of the influence of those heathen courtiers, it's time we remembered our rightful ways."

"Yes, sir," she replied with uncharacteristic docility. She began picking at the unappetizing mixture and forced herself to chew a mouthful without a grimace.

"Are you ill?" her mother asked gently. "You seem upset."

"No, Ma'am." She tugged the corners of her mouth into a small smile for her mother's benefit.

"Odd," her father commented with a sly tone to his voice, "that her mood coincided with the departure of our none-too-welcome guests."

Sarah snickered. Fidelity kept her eyes riveted to her food and tried to force a lump of mutton past the lump of fear risen in her throat. She gripped the edge of the table and willed her hands to cease their nervous trembling. Had Sarah taken her pack of lies to their father?

The family was silent, expecting the storm to break at any moment. But Richard Fairfax continued his meal and the awkward moment passed.

Fidelity buried her sobs in her pillow. The house was quiet but for the muffled sounds of some anonymous snoring in another bedroom.

She'd managed to conceal her hurt and depression after the departure of Schuyler and the Wyndhams. She sensed that her father was watching her for signs that she'd done something shameful and she knew Sarah was waiting for any opportunity to spread some of her filthy libels. So far she'd managed very well, until tonight at dinner.

There were guests in the house. They'd arrived for the evening meal.

Thomas Bugby and his wife, Susan, had recently returned from a visit to London and were full of tales of the decadence of the newly returned monarchists. There wasn't a man or woman in the lot, Master Bugby assured them, who had a shred of morals to their name. King Charles II was leading them all straight to hell and they were only too happy to follow. He told them of the plays, masques, and love affairs going nonstop in, out, and around Whitehall Palace. He talked about the painted beauties, led by the king's mistress, Barbara Palmer, who were eager to display their charms, and the men of the Court equally eager to partake of those charms.

The dinner had been an ordeal for Fidelity who imagined Schuyler taking part in the sinful sport of the aristocracy. She tried to appear attentive and properly shocked as her father would have expected but every description of wealthy, bejeweled ladies with Court connections reminded her of Schuyler's need for a rich and well-placed wife.

It made her miserable, or rather more miserable. She sobbed softly but her sorrow enveloped her so completely that she didn't hear the light rustling of leaves on the rose trellis or the tap on her window pane. Only when the window latch was rattled did she jump from her bed and race to the window seat. She threw open the drapes with a smile but quickly recoiled and pulled one of the drapes in front of her. The man clinging to the trellis outside her window was not Schuyler Pierrepointe!

She opened her mouth to scream but the man quickly pulled off the wide-brimmed black hat which had concealed his features. In the moonlight she recognized Schuyler's servant, Robert.

"Oh, Robert!" she cried, opening the window. "You scared the life out of me!"

"Sorry, Ma'am." From inside his shabby coat Robert pulled a small parcel, wrapped and sealed.

Leaving the man to his precarious perch amid the roses, Fidelity sat on the window seat and broke the wax seal.

Scanning the note in the moonlight, Fidelity's heart gave a little leap, Schuyler would come, he promised, in a few days. He'd arrive by night, of course, and she was to meet him in the stable where

they'd met so often while he was a guest of the house.
Wrapped with the note was a little box, covered with
leather. She opened the box and found, on a bed of
crimson satin, a gold pendant with her initials worked
in filigree. It was suspended from a long gold chain
and, after a few fumbles, Fidelity found the clasp and
opened the locket. Inside she found a miniature of
Schuyler, nice although she didn't think it did him
justice, and the date was inscribed on the opposite
side.

She slipped the chain over her head and dropped
the closed locket inside her nightgown. She stared
into the darkness of her room lost in a dreamy reverie
until an impatient sigh returned her attention to the
servant and his dangerous place on the trellis.

"Oh, I'm sorry, Robert. Please tell your master
that I'll be waiting for him."

"Yes, Ma'am." Without waiting for more instructions, Robert started to climb back down the trellis.
He was only too happy to slink back to his horse,
tethered in the shadows, and leave for the more
pleasant attractions of London.

Behind him, in her room, Fidelity left the drapes
open that she might read Schuyler's note once again.
She drew the locket out from its hiding place beneath
her highnecked nightdress and opened it to look at
Schuyler's portrait. He remembered! He was coming!
She returned to her bed and, for want of a better
place, placed the note which had accompanied the gift
in the thick Bible on her bedside table.

Climbing back into bed, Fidelity sighed and
abandoned herself to dreams of Schuyler and herself

and the certainty that they wouldn't always have to meet in secrecy.

Thomas Bugby and his wife took their leave the next morning and the entire family stood in the courtyard to see them off. Fidelity, still too dreamy from the night before to care who came and went, smiled and waved as the coach carrying the Bugbys rounded the turn of the road and rolled out of sight. She started into the house and heard her mother talking to her father.

"God forgive me for selfishness," she said. "But I'd be happy if we had no more guests for a time."

"Or if they arrive in the middle of the night," Sarah whispered into Fidelity's ear.

Fidelity started and stared into her sister's hard, ice-blue eyes. She drew herself up and hissed, "You don't know what you're talking about."

Sarah opened her mouth but was silenced by her mother who called to Fidelity. "Fidelity, I want you to help me. Some of your father's and brother's clothing needs mending and it will improve your sewing skills to help."

With a last glance at her sister, Fidelity turned to follow her mother into the house. "Yes, Ma'am." She was glad to be out of the reach of her sister's remarks but sorry to be sewing as the automatic stitches left her mind free to ponder impending disasters.

It was nearly time for supper when Fidelity cut the final thread on the last shirt she had to mend. Her eyes ached, her hands were stiff, and her fingers were sore from being pricked with needles and pins. She hadn't realized her father and brothers owned so many clothes, let alone had so many to be mended.

When at last her mother released her, she climbed the stairs to her room slowly and turned into the corridor. She was within sight of her door when she saw the heavy wooden door of her room swing open. Swiftly and silently she ducked into the shadows of the landing at the head of the stairs ready to run back down if need be.

Peeking around the corner, she saw Sarah leave her room. She cautiously looked both ways up and down the corridor and then, to Fidelity's dismay, hurried away toward her own room near the far end of the corridor.

After waiting until Sarah was safely in her own room. Fidelity left her hiding place and ran down the corridor. What had Sarah been after? And had she found it? After Sarah's remark of that morning, Fidelity was certain she had seen the messenger of the night before and, with quaking hands, opened the Bible on the bedside table. The note was gone!

Fidelity sat heavily on the edge of her bed. Sarah had the note. Sarah knew! There was no recourse open to Fidelity; she couldn't very well go to her father and demand he make Sarah return a note delivered in secret arranging a clandestine meeting between herself and a Cavalier. There was no question of telling anyone in the house. Sarah held the cards now. Fidelity could do nothing but wait.

The time of anxiety had returned. It was worse now than it had ever been since Schuyler had left her father's house. Worse because now there was proof, tangible evidence of her guilt and that evidence was in the hands of her worst enemy.

There was only one consolation for Fidelity. Sarah had a beau. Not much of a beau to be sure, but Sarah cared for him and he was coming to dinner and perhaps it would keep Sarah's mouth shut at least until after Schuyler's visit.

If only Schuyler was coming to take her away with him! If only she needn't worry about her father or sister. If she could leave and never return—it was what she hoped for and, though it would have scandalized her family, it was what she prayed for.

The day Sarah had stolen the note passed without incident as did the next, and the day arrived when Sarah's beau was coming to visit. That Sarah's beau, gawky and covered with pussy pimples as he was, could arrive and be welcomed into the family group while her love had to come in secret by night was a slight she could not forgive. But for once she thanked heaven for Sarah's beau if only because it took Sarah's mind out of the gutter for a while.

And in fact it seemed to have worked. Sarah's conversation was full of "what shall I wear" and "when Oliver comes."

"Oliver," Fidelity muttered. Born during the Civil War, Sarah's young man had been named for a friend of his family's, Oliver Cromwell, the Lord Protector. Fidelity had once enraged Sarah by declaring that she'd seen a portrait of the by then-dead Cromwell and Sarah's boyfriend had been aptly named, he was every bit as ugly as the Puritan Protector.

"Fidelity!" Sarah called out and, without waiting to be invited in, opened her sister's door and entered her room. She was wearing a modestly cut gown of dark brown with a wide collar of simple lace a touch of which also rounded both cuffs of the long, closely cut sleeves. Her hair was pulled back severely but there was a hint of a blush in her cheeks that made her appear a little less mousy than usual.

"What do you want?" Fidelity snarled. She stood with her hands on her hips as Mrs. Bridger, the waiting woman the girls shared, hooked her deep blue gown up the back. Cut in a style nearly identical to Sarah's gown, Fidelity's dress had lace a trifle wider and a touch frothier than her sister's. The color was more becoming to her eyes, which it nearly matched, and to her hair, which it complemented; its darker tint brought out the silvery highlights in each strand.

"I said," Fidelity repeated with annoyance. "What do you want?"

"You may go, Mrs. Bridger," Sarah told the waiting woman when Fidelity's gown was fastened. She waited until the door closed behind the woman and then turned to her sister with a sneering smile. "I only came to borrow something to wear with my dress."

Fidelity was instantly on guard. "What?"

Sarah's finger found its way between the high lace collar of her sister's dress and her throat and drew out the gold locket. "This."

Fidelity jerked away from her and held the locket protectively in her hand. "How did you know?" she asked, but she knew perfectly well. Sarah had the note and it mentioned the locket. She would have known that Fidelity would never take a chance by leaving the incriminating piece of jewelry hidden anywhere but on her person.

"What do you want, Sarah?" She knew her sister wouldn't actually borrow the necklace. It was too ornate in fashion to be approved of in their household. And it would elicit too many questions. "What is it you really want?"

"I want you to forget about the Cavalier," Sarah hissed. "I want you to begin acting like a responsible member of this family. Do you think Oliver's family would want me for their daughter-in-law if my sister was known to be consorting with a Royalist?"

"Frankly, I don't think they'd say much. There's not many girls who would want your precious Oliver." Fidelity smiled but her triumph was short lived. She saw the hatred in her sister's eyes and knew she couldn't afford to antagonize her. "Sarah," she searched for a way to placate her sister. "Why does it matter to you about Schuyler? What I do doesn't reflect upon you. You heard Father and Thomas Bugby talk about how sometimes children in even the best of families have their heads turned by what's happening in the country right now."

"I don't want you to be one of those children." Sarah insisted. "I don't want it to be known that my sister is off cavorting with Cavaliers and courtiers. I heard what our dear cousin Divina Wyndham said about you. How even the king's head would be turned by your looks. Damn your looks! You're no better than the rest of us! You don't deserve . . ."

Sarah stopped, aware she'd said too much, revealed too much to the one person from whom she should have kept her feelings a secret.

"You're jealous!" Fidelity's tone was incredulous. "That's all this amounts to—jealousy!" She began to laugh, mean, scornful laughter that cut her sister deeper than any of the words they'd ever exchanged in anger. She saw her sister's eyes darken with pain and harden with hatred but the triumph she felt after years of feeling guilty about her beauty and now to find it a source of unreasoning jealousy made her giddy and reckless. It was only after Sarah turned and ran from the room that Fidelity realized the gravity of the way she'd murdered her sister's pride.

Oliver Wickham arrived and was welcomed into the house. The long, glowing table in the dining room was set with the family's best plate and the succulent aromas rising from the kitchen gave promise of the best of Elspeth's kitchen staff's work.

Fidelity arrived with her brothers and stole glances at her sister, but she could tell nothing from her manner. She refused to meet the glances cast in her direction by her sister's beau knowing that he found her far more attractive and that that only added fuel to the fire of her sister's hatred.

She struggled through dinner eating as little as she could without occasioning comment and sat quietly as her parents and Oliver's parents, who had accompanied him, talked of the decaying state of the country and how the only hope of survival for England lay in its up-and-coming merchant class. At last, her father, Mr. Wickham, Oliver, and her eldest brother retired to her father's office for conversations on a more business-oriented level. It was her first opportunity to leave and she seized it eagerly.

Pleading headache, she bade her mother and Mrs. Wickham goodnight and, without a glance at her sister, started up the stairs. It was when she was almost to the top that she heard Sarah excuse herself also.

She hurried up the remaining stairs and to her room, not wishing to be caught up in a conversation of any kind with Sarah. To her surprise Sarah rounded the landing as she was about to shut her door and swept past her without a glance. Fidelity closed her door wondering about her sister's behavior. But then, she shrugged, who could understand Sarah? She was probably planning to absent herself from Oliver's company to make herself appear mysterious and disinterested. Fidelity laughed; she'd better not appear too disinterested or Oliver might realize what a poor bargain he was getting for himself!

She called to Mrs. Bridger to come help her out of her gown and into one of a less somber cut and hue.

The house had at last grown quiet and Fidelity could hear the soft noises of the night creatures outside. She'd opened her window and stationed herself on the window seat straining her ears in hopes of hearing hoofbeats on the road or across the fields. It seemed she'd been sitting there for hours and she'd begun to wonder whether Schuyler was actually coming. Perhaps he wouldn't.

The thought that he might not come made her

want to cry but at the same time she was not sure that
it wouldn't be best for them both if he didn't. She'd
wished earlier that she could send him a warning; tell
him that Sarah knew of their plans. And yet she
wanted desperately to see him, needed to see him. She
even had a small bundle of things packed in case her
fondest wish came true and he asked her to run away
with him.

By the time she'd begun to believe that he was
indeed not going to arrive, she heard the muffled
sounds of a horse in the fields behind the house. Her
heart raced and she held her breath until she saw a
figure dressed in black step from the shadows and
look toward her window. Beneath the black hat,
lying in shining curls on his black-clad shoulders, was
the bright blond hair she remembered so well.

She leaned out the window and gave him a quick
little wave which he acknowledged with an instant
imperceptible nod of his plume-laden hat. He disappeared into the stable leading his horse.

Swiftly Fidelity threw a cloak around her
shoulders fumbling, in her nervous impatience, with
the clasp. She opened her door slowly and sped
noiselessly along the corridor and down the stairs.

The servants, usually the last to retire, were
snoring in their rooms and Fidelity had to move
slowly in the dark to avoid bumping into furniture.
She made her way through the house, through the
family rooms, the dining room, and the entry hall,
and into the less public part, the kitchen and larders.
She had decided to slip out a back way, the door
closest to the stables.

At last she was within sight of her goal and laid a trembling hand on the door latch. It was then that a pair of strong arms encircled her and a hand clamped itself over her mouth.

To her horror, figures emerged from the shadows into the moonlit room. Her father, mother, Sarah, her eldest brother, Nathaniel, and behind them, Oliver Wickham and his parents. She couldn't see the man who held her but she imagined it was one of her father's grooms.

Richard Fairfax's face was hard with disappointment, anger, and shame. "I have nothing to say to you, Fidelity," he said in the cold tone that betrayed his moments of hottest fury. "I can't believe it of a child of mine. I didn't believe it when Sarah told me. I see now that I should have."

Fidelity's gaze shifted to her sister and back again as her father continued.

"I am ashamed that this had to happen at all but especially now, with decent Christian guests in the house. But I assure you, I shall deal with the situation in a fitting manner."

Reaching behind him, Richard brought out the gun he'd fought with during the Civil War. To Fidelity's terror, Mr. Wickham did the same. They opened the door silently and started through the dark courtyard toward the stable where Schuyler waited unaware. From behind the house, several of the stable hands appeared armed with pitchforks and scythes.

Fidelity watched, still held by the groom, still powerless to warn Schuyler. She stared at the stable until the sounds of exaggerated sobbing caught her attention.

Sarah had thrown herself into Oliver's arms and wept, her sobs punctuated with cries of: "I'm so ashamed; oh, Oliver!"

"There's no need for you to be ashamed," Mrs. Wickham assured her. "You did the right thing to bring this matter to your father's attention. And if you hadn't said something this evening, this meeting might well have taken place." She fixed Fidelity with an icy glare.

So that was where Sarah had been going earlier! Fidelity groaned inwardly. If only she'd paid more attention! If only she'd stopped Sarah before she went back downstairs!

A cry from the stable snapped her attention back to the courtyard. Her father and the other men had just disappeared into the stable when the cry rang out and through the open doors of the stable rode Schuyler. His horse vanished into the shadows at the back of the stable and even though some of the hands tried to follow, it was apparent that he was too quick for them.

Fidelity sagged against the groom who held her. She was angry and mortified but her relief foreshadowed any other emotions. Schuyler was safe. Come what may, he had escaped! The groom released her as her father and Mr. Wickham reentered the house.

"He escaped," Richard reported unnecessarily. "With the devil's own help I doubt not."

"I've never seen a man move half so fast as that," said Mr. Wickham with grudging admiration. "But, as you say, Satan helps his own."

"Well, I think we'll all be better off in bed." Richard looked at his errant elder daughter. "I suggest we pray for you, miss," he said with a rancor that made her flinch. "Although, God forgive me, I don't think my heart would be in it tonight. You will be dealt with tomorrow."

Fidelity dropped her eyes and said nothing. She waited to be dismissed when she heard Sarah clear her throat and speak to their father.

"Oh, yes," Richard signaled to the groom who turned her to face him once again. "I'll take the necklace that wretch gave you."

Fidelity's eyes widened and she fixed her sister with a look of such hatred that Sarah recoiled against Oliver. Slowly she returned her gaze to her father. He remained where he was, his arm still outstretched toward her.

"Fidelity," he repeated. "Give it to me!"

She clasped the locket through the thin material of her dress. "No, Father," she begged. "Please!"

His face remained unchanged. "Now!" he demanded in a voice as cold as steel.

A sob caught at her throat and she removed the locket and reluctantly placed it in his hand.

"You may go to your room now," he said.

She turned and started from the room. Behind her she heard him speak to her mother:

"Lock her in and have Mrs. Bridger stay in the room with her."

She was a prisoner, caught in the act, judged, and found guilty. She must wait for her sentencing.

# 7

Fidelity heard her bedroom door swing open but she didn't bother to look up. For eight days she'd been locked in her room. She saw no one except Mrs. Bridger who brought her her meals and water for her wash basin and who slept on a cot in the room every night. She had no reason to believe that anyone else would dare flout her father's orders to visit her.

And she was right. Mrs. Bridger closed the bedroom door behind her, balancing Fidelity's dinner tray on one hip.

"Here's your food, mistress," she said. She tried to be firm and stern with Fidelity as Master Fairfax had ordered, but this child had always been her favorite, the child of her heart, the daughter she and the late Master Bridger had never been blessed with. Her heart softened as she looked at Fidelity's face. It was pale with the strain and tension of the past week.

"I'm not hungry," Fidelity replied listlessly. She walked across the room and huddled on the window seat. Through the window she could see the stable where, on that awful night eight days before, she thought she was about to see the death of Schuyler Pierrepointe.

Mrs. Bridger placed the tray on a table and

moved to where Fidelity sat. She gathered Fidelity's silvery blond hair into her hands and, parting it, began to braid it. It had lost all its usual body and shine; Fidelity's grief and depression, combined with a week of careless neglect, had turned it lusterless and limp.

"You must eat," Mrs. Bridger said with tender gentleness. "At least a little."

Fidelity shrugged and walked to the table where the other woman had left the covered tray. Beneath the cover she found a steaming bowl of soup thick with chunks of meat and vegetables. Sitting down, she picked up a spoon and scooped some of the soup from the bowl into her mouth. The scalding heat startled her and, as she gasped, she began to choke, obliging Mrs. Bridger to pound and shake her vigorously. This continued until the waiting woman realized that Fidelity had ceased her choking and was sobbing; great racking sobs. The older woman gathered her charge into her arms as she had done so many years before after bad dreams and scrapes, and waited for the sobs to recede.

"Oh, Mrs. Bridger," Fidelity whispered at last. "What are they doing down there? What will become of me?"

"There have been meetings with the church council. Your father has told them everything."

"He doesn't know everything." Fidelity wiped her eyes with the back of her hand. "All he knows is what he thinks he saw and the lies Sarah told him. There was never anything shameful between myself and Lord Pierrepointe. Please, please, dear Mrs. Bridger, say you believe me."

Lettice Bridger, a lifelong Puritan with no great love for the Court, either that of the long dead Charles I or the newly restored Charles II, heartily disapproved of the entire Pierrepointe episode and thought it shocking that a daughter of such God-fearing parents would conduct herself in such a way as Fidelity had, looked into the girl's eyes and had to believe her. "Aye, my darling, I believe you. What will happen I couldn't guess, but something's brewing downstairs and to be frank, I don't think it'll be anything pleasant."

The handerkerchief in Fidelity's hands was being wrung to shreds as she stood in her room and allowed Mrs. Bridger to hook up the back of her gown.

Her father's orders had been sent late in the morning. Fidelity was to be bathed and dressed and brought to her father's study at precisely three of the clock that afternoon.

Fidelity's gown was one of her most somber and modest, of a gray linen loosely cut (and even looser as a result of her two weeks of near fasting) with a white linen collar reaching from the base of her throat to her chin. The cuffs of the dress and the cap that hid nearly every strand of her hair were of the same white material.

When at last Mrs. Bridger stepped away from her, Fidelity looked at her questioningly. "Is it almost time?" she asked.

The waiting woman nodded and turned away to hide her emotion.

As the last few moments ticked by, Fidelity crossed the room to the window and stared down into the courtyard. A host of grooms lounged lazily beneath the trees near the stables. They'd come with their masters, the men of the council now meeting downstairs, and now, their masters' horses stabled, they had nothing to do but wait for them to leave. As one of the men glanced at her window and nudged his neighbor, Fidelity moved hastily away. There had, without doubt, been much talk among the servants of those familiar with her situation; no item of gossip was safe from the help for long. She could imagine them calling her a monarchist, a Cavalier's woman, and worse.

A knock at the door caused both women to jump and, when Mrs. Bridger opened the door, Fidelity saw that her mother's waiting woman, Maud, had come to fetch her.

The house seemed unnaturally quiet; and unnaturally large. It had not changed in the two weeks she'd been immured in her room; it had changed little enough in her lifetime, but she'd never been apart from it before and particularly in so confined a space as her own room.

She went slowly down the stairs with Maud on one side and Mrs. Bridger on the other like guards, or keepers, and at the bottom of the stairs she paused for a brief moment before passing on toward her father's study.

The study was dark. The drapes had been drawn for privacy's sake and the candles in two eight-branched candelabra cast flickering shadows across the faces of the men in the room.

Fidelity entered the room cautiously. Her eyes scanned the faces of the men seated along one side of a long wooden table. She stared as she heard the heavy double doors of the room shut behind her, leaving her alone before her judges. She faced them standing on the opposite side of the table. There was no chair provided for her; she was not expected to sit.

Her father was seated in the center of the group of men. Before him on the table lay the note her sister Sarah had stolen from her, the locket Schuyler had given her, and other papers she imagined to be the statements from Sarah, her mother, and probably the Wickhams. Master Wickham was seated next to her father.

"Fidelity."

She forced her eyes to meet the gaze of her father as he spoke her name. There was no warmth in his voice, the two weeks had not softened his heart toward her nor had he forgiven her for what he considered to be her betrayal of her God, her family, and the entire Puritan way of life.

"Fidelity," he said again. "You have shocked and shamed yourself and your family. I was at a loss to know what course I must take and so I have called upon the wisdom of these pious and wise men for their opinions. You have turned against your family and have willingly become involved in an intrigue which is immoral, wicked, and totally without redeemable or forgivable qualities. You have blackened our name and caused irreparable damage to your own reputation by the scandalous nature of your escapades."

Fidelity looked away from him. It sickened her to hear him put such foul connotations on her love for Schuyler. It was a clean love, without shame, without the intimations of rampant lust he suggested.

His voice droned on until she raised her eyes once again. "I did nothing!" she shouted.

"You are not to speak!" her father shouted back.

"There was nothing . . .!" she began again.

"QUIET!" her father roared, slamming his fist onto the tabletop with room-shaking force. "You are not to speak!" He surveyed the others at the table. "This is just another example of her disobedience," he said apologetically, and the others nodded in sympathy.

He began again to a sullen Fidelity. "As I was saying, I turned to these men of the church council to help me decide what is to be done. You must learn your place in life. Your responsibilities to your church and your family as well as to your immortal soul are of the utmost importance. Obviously your mother and I, though we have tried, have not succeeded in instilling the correct values in you. We have discussed the problem and were at a loss for a solution. Now, however, thanks to a generous offer from one of our number, we have found the answer. Master Nichodemus Crichton is the man we must thank."

As the eyes of the council turned toward the end of the table, Fidelity also looked at the object of their attention.

Nichodemus Crichton was an ugly man. Not much taller than Fidelity who cleared five feet by a few scant inches, he was a corpulent and red-faced person whose skin had the look of old pudding ready to become mouldy. His hair, of which there was little on the top of his head and the rest was cut close to his skull, was orange-red, dry and fussy. His eyes, small,

mean, and of a faded blue, were hard to see beneath
the bloated flesh of his face. He had made a great deal
of money during the recent Civil War, much of it as a
result of his clever and subtle use of flattery with the
late Oliver Cromwell, and had retained that money
through the restoration of the monarchy.

Now as Fidelity's eyes met the piggy eyes of
Nichodemus Crichton she perceived a secret smile, a
scantily hidden triumph in the way he accepted the
praise of the others of the council. She had to force
herself to return her attention to her father's voice.

"As you know," her father was saying. "Nichodemus has long been an upright and commendable
member of our faith. He and his late wife, may God
keep her soul, were at the forefront of every drive to
establish the love of the Lord in this land and they
sustained many hardships which contributed to the
regrettable demise of Mistress Crichton at such an
early age. You may be thankful that such a man has
your interest and welfare at heart." The men of the
council turned to murmur their assent and her father
continued. "Nichodemus has generously offered to
take you into his home as his wife. You will be
married to Nichodemus Crichton as soon as possible
and may God have mercy upon his soul!"

Fidelity grasped the edge of the table. She'd
expected to be sent to a school or a home, to be given
strict lessons and rules to obey, but this! To be
married, and to this man! This ugly, loathsome,
repulsive . . . She turned to look at him as the
members of the council watched her. Her eyes alone
were on Crichton's face and, for a moment—a hair's
breadth of time—the pious modesty fell away and his

eyes took on a hard and beady look as they scanned her from head to toe. His face, so unattractive in repose, wore an unmasked look of slathering, unprincipled lust. For her crime of falling in love with Schuyler Pierrepointe—her bright, untarnished, unconsummated love—she was tried, judged guilty, and sentenced to the board and bed of this false-faced, repugnant, and irretrievably evil man.

There was no way her consciousness could absorb the information, no way of soothing her outraged senses. With no hope of being able to respond or even flee from the room, Fidelity took refuge in unconsciousness and slid to the floor in a faint.

The marriage contract had been signed on the evening of Fidelity's learning of her fate. There was a custom, observed among some people of their class, that the groom-to-be had a right to assert his conjugal rights on the night of the contract signing but the custom was not observed among the people of the Fairfaxs' circle, much to Fidelity's relief.

The wedding took place on a rainy morning a few weeks after the signing of the contract. Fidelity had been alarmingly pale and stonily silent. She moved from force of habit, ignoring the congratulations of her family and their friends and the sly looks and smug murmurs of her sister. She was aware of nothing but the clammy touch of Nichodemus Crichton's flesh against her own as he held her hand. Several times she tried to free herself from his grasp but he refused to release her. The sensation of the cool, blubbery flesh pressing itself against her skin was making her nauseous.

Though she was not hungry, she was glad when her mother announced the wedding luncheon. Her husband, though she stubbornly refused to think of him as such, let her go at last in order that he might better help himself to the food.

As soon as the meal was eaten, Fidelity retired to her room to change from her modest wedding gown into a dress and cloak more suited to traveling. Nichodemus announced his intention to leave for his home as soon as possible and it was a journey of several miles. As it was, he said, they would be lucky to reach there before nightfall and the roads swarmed with highwaymen (a result, they all agreed, of the influence of the king and his courtiers).

Elspeth Fairfax and Mrs. Bridger helped Fidelity change. Sarah knew better than to set foot in her sister's room.

"I'm sure you'll grow to respect Master Crichton," Elspeth assured her. She didn't seem to think it incongruous that her new son-in-law was in fact several years older than herself.

"I hate him! And I'll hate him forever!" Fidelity snarled. They were the first words she'd uttered since the ceremony when she'd been forced to repeat her vows. She was sorry of the words when she saw her mother turn away, hiding her face. "Mother," she said gently. Elspeth was a kind woman and Fidelity knew she'd had nothing to do with the marriage. "I'm sorry."

Taking a deep breath, Elspeth turned back to her daughter and forced a little smile into her features. "Try to accept your lot, Fidelity. You'll come to nothing but grief any other way."

Behind her Fidelity heard Mrs. Bridger stifle a sob. She realized she had to leave the room before the three of them collapsed into tears and so, giving each of them a quick hug and kiss, she hurried from the room and toward her fate.

Crichton Manor was an ancient house. It sprawled with uneven roofs and little symmetry in any of its features. It was a pale gray stone which in the moonlight seemed dull and flat. The walls were covered with ivy but half the vines were dead and leafless. It was losing its ivy and it reminded Fidelity of Nichodemus's hair. In fact it was the perfect setting for Nichodemus; it looked like him and he looked like it.

As the carriage rumbled up to the front entrance, Fidelity was only too glad to get out. The ride had been a long one and she'd spent it cooped up alone with her husband and his groping hands. Once or twice he had forced her to allow him to press his blubbery, rubbery lips against hers and she was glad she'd eaten little at luncheon.

The carriage stopped and Nichodemus jumped out as soon as two footmen, one bearing a torch and the other opening the door, arrived. He stood in the flickering torchlight and handed Fidelity into the courtyard. They mounted the steps to the door and entered the house, leaving the footmen and grooms to see to the horses, carriage, and Fidelity's baggage.

Once inside the front hall of Crichton Manor, Fidelity found the interior no improvement over the exterior. Nichodemus Crichton, in his effort to become a respected member of society, had purchased the estate from a ruined Royalist who had given up his attempt to live under Cromwell's regime and was leaving for the Continent and the exiled king's court. The house had been in the man's family for generations and was built when country manors were only beginning to be the fashion rather than fortified castles. There was still a great deal of the fortress in Crichton Manor.

The household staff was lined up in the stone entrance hall. The menservants and womenservants, the kitchen staff, the lowliest maid, all stared at their new mistress as she passed.

Fidelity would have liked to have stopped to meet each and every one, it seemed as good a time-wasting ploy as any, but Nichodemus hurried her past them with a curt, "You can meet them in your own good time."

He did stop before one woman; in Fidelity's opinion the most ill-favored of the whole sad group.

"This is Kate," Nichodemus told her. "She'll be your waiting woman."

The woman was tall and thin with unkempt dark hair and skin pitted fearfully by the pox. She dropped Fidelity a shallow curtsy and smiled but there was no friendliness in her smile which served only to display her broken, stained, and rotting teeth. "How do you do, Ma'am," the woman said. The phrase sounded out of place coming from her and her breath made Fidelity want to turn her face away.

"Get upstairs and see to your mistress's night preparations," Nichodemus told her sharply.

The woman attempted another curtsy and

moved away.

"Are you hungry?" he demanded as he and his new wife moved on through other rooms of the house.

"No," Fidelity answered sharply.

They mounted the staircase and walked along a dark corridor. The floor was stone, scattered over with rugs and here and there a torch was burning in a metal sconce.

"Here is your room," Nichodemus said at last. He left her in front of a door made of wooden planks bound with iron and walked away.

Fidelity entered the room and found the waiting woman scrutinizing her belongings as she slowly unpacked the two trunks Fidelity had brought with her.

"You can leave the rest until tomorrow," Fidelity told the woman. "I just want to wash and change."

"Yes, Ma'am." Kate left the trunks and brought a pitcher, washbasin, and towel to the dressing table.

There was no mirror, Fidelity noticed. An unnecessary vanity, she supposed. The room was furnished in heavy, dark, wooden furniture; a large tester bed stood in one corner, there was a wardrobe, a commode, two tables, and two chairs. The windows, of which there were two, were small and set deeply into the thick walls. The fireplace had been made for function rather than decoration, and the only articles on any of the furniture were the pitcher and basin, a Bible on one of the tables, and her brush and comb which Kate had apparently found in one of her trunks and set out. The walls were gray stone, the hangings on the bed and at the windows and the carpet covering the stone floor were brown. It was a drab setting and it reflected Fidelity's mood.

Kate helped Fidelity out of her dusty traveling garments and, after she'd washed from the basin of water, into her high-necked, long-sleeved, no-nonsense nightgown. It embarrassed Fidelity to dress and undress in front of a stranger, and especially as she felt that this particular stranger was looking her over in preparation for a report to the rest of the staff.

When at last she was ready for the night, Fidelity was only too glad to dismiss the woman and, after blowing out the sole candle she'd lit, she settled into the great bed.

It wasn't long before Fidelity heard a door open. She hadn't closed the drapes and, in the moonlight, she saw Nichodemus enter the room through a door she hadn't noticed as it was partially hidden on the far side of the massive wardrobe.

He was clad in a trailing robe of a material Fidelity couldn't identify in the dim light and he approached her bedside silently on slippers that made no sound across the rug. He stood at her bedside for a long moment before he spoke.

"Did you think I wasn't coming?"

Fidelity clutched the bedcovers tighter around herself and said nothing.

"You're even prettier with your hair undone than with it bound and covered," he said. "But I suppose your Cavalier already told you that."

He sat heavily on the bed and Fidelity moved ever so slightly away.

"Come now, why so shy? You need not pretend with me. I want no false modesty from you." With a jerk he pulled the covers from her grasp and sent them flying to land in a heap that slid off the foot of the bed. Fidelity sidled toward the opposite side of the bed.

"This playacting of yours is getting tiresome," he growled. "I know your story, minx." In one quick movement he wrapped one arm about her waist and with the other he clamped the back of her neck and the base of her skull in a viselike grip. He pulled her to him and kissed with her a ferocity she'd never experienced in the arms of Schuyler Pierrepointe.

With a barely suppressed gag, Fidelity pushed away from him but he pulled her back.

"Enough!" he shouted. "I am your husband and I'll not be denied what you were only too happy to give to your whoring Royalist!" He pulled her tightly against him once again and she knew it would do her no good to resist.

# 8

Fidelity woke up with a start. The room was freezing; the fire had died down and the cold winter air seeped in at the windows.

She dabbed at her forehead with the edge of her quilt. In spite of the cold she was sweating and it took a moment to orient herself. She'd been having a dream—it seemed silly now in the glow of the candle she'd lit—but it had terrified her.

She dreamed she was in hell surrounded by all the fire and the brimstone and tormented souls she'd heard about since childhood. The devil, complete with pitchfork and horns, prodded her and threatened her with torments beyond all imagination. And the devil had Nichodemus Crichton's face.

Reluctantly climbing out of her relatively warm bed, Fidelity touched the stinging cold of the floor with a bare foot. The icy stones sent their cold through the carpet and burned her feet, making them ache as she hopped to the fireplace and tried to prod the fire into life. At last she succeeded in starting a fire but she doubted it would do much good; the cold was piercing and there was little even a fire could do to dispel its searching fingers.

Once back in bed, Fidelity drew the quilts up to her chin. What she would have given to have Schuyler Pierrepointe's warm body to creep close to, but beyond the door adjoining her room and the next was Nichodemus Crichton and she vowed she'd rather freeze than be near him!

Her husband hadn't come near her in nearly a week, she suddenly remembered. Not that she missed him; heaven knew he was just as brutal and insensitive as ever. He cared nothing for her feelings or her needs, he satisfied himself and that was that. Perhaps one day he would merely cease to come to her at all and she would fall into the role of hostess and superintendent of Crichton Manor, a servant working for room and board. And, if she were to be frank, she wouldn't be sorry to see that day arrive.

The worst times, apart from the demands of her husband upon her person, were the public times, the dinners they attended, the church affairs. The members of their congregation, including Fidelity's own family, looked upon her as the local black sheep, the scarlet woman, the horrible example to be held up to wives and daughters. She was stared at, whispered about, and the chief promoter of the church gossip society was Fidelity's own sister—Sarah. Sarah had recently been betrothed to Oliver Wickham and so provided an example of the good daughter, the God- and father-fearing child. People shook their heads and wondered how two such opposite children could spring from the same parents.

Nichodemus, on the other hand, was a paragon. If he was a respected member of the congregation before his marriage to Fidelity, he was a saint after. His sacrifice in taking Fidelity into his home was enough, in the opinion of the church members, to earn him his place in heaven. No other man in their circle would have married her, risked his reputation and immortal soul on the reformation of a young woman who had strayed so far from the path of propriety. No adult in the church could forgive her for turning her back on the teachings of the church and her parents. None of the young men in the church could prevent their eyes from resting on her face or figure or keep thoughts of the gossip they'd heard from their minds. And, as for the young girls of the congregation, Fidelity suspected—though she knew very well that any one of them would have vehemently denied it—they were jealous of her foray into the glamorous world of the nobility and of the romance of a secret love affair with a handsome and dashing Cavalier.

And so when she was at home she longed to be away and when she was in church or visiting, which was as away as she ever got, she longed to be home. It made her life a perpetual round of discontent.

She had no real duties to perform at Crichton Manor when there were no guests in the house. Even then her hostess's duties were limited, for most of their guests came to visit Nichodemus and came in spite of Fidelity. It made for a great deal of free time to be filled.

Fortunately, Nichodmus had a lively interest in horseflesh and the stables of Crichton Manor were well stocked with riding and driving horses. Soon after her arrival at the Manor, Fidelity had taken to riding with a passion. When the weather became colder and the bridle paths were sometimes dangerously icy, she was happy to find a sleigh in an obscure corner of a barn, apparently a relic of the more pleasure-loving former occupants of the Manor.

And, though Fidelity often thought that her husband's chief pleasure in life was plaguing her in any way he could, he didn't seem to mind the hours she spent on horseback or behind a team of horses in the sleigh or a carriage. She went when and where she pleased accompanied by a maid (her own waiting woman, the disagreeable and sly Kate, had complained that horses made her nervous and so was excused), and footmen, with one of the grooms to handle the reins of the sleigh.

One day, when the sun shone coldly on the snow that fell unusually heavily that winter, Fidelity and her maid left the house and walked as quickly as their heavy skirts and voluminous cloaks would allow to the drive where the sleigh and their driver and two footmen-bodyguards were waiting.

"Madam." The young man standing near the sleigh pulled his hat off as she approached. He was newly hired by Nichodemus; she'd never seen him before. But it was his appearance that made her stop and stare.

"Who are you?" she demanded when she'd recovered her composure.

"Jamie Bowyer, Ma'am."

"You're new here?"

"Yes, Ma'am. Master Crichton hired me as a

groom and I was told to handle the horses for your ride."

"I see." Fidelity stared a moment longer. The resemblance was amazing. In build and coloring the young man could have been Schuyler's brother. He had the same blond hair, its lightness bordering on white, and the same green eyes. Realizing that she was drawing curious looks, Fidelity pulled herself from her musings. She allowed the groom to help her maid into the sleigh and then herself. If he lingered with her hand in his for a moment too long she pretended to ignore it but she was overwhelmingly conscious of his presence in the confines of the small sleigh.

The countryside was beautiful but she was too preoccupied to notice. They stopped for a few minutes near a creek that bubbled and flowed between snow-covered banks and Fidelity told him she wanted to get out.

"Just for a moment, Jamie," she said. "I want to stretch my legs and stamp some warmth into my feet."

Handing the reins to one of the mounted footmen, Jamie crossed behind the sleigh and helped her out.

Fidelity started off in the direction of the creek while Jamie helped her maid out of the low convey-ance. As soon as the maid had found her balance on the snowy path, she and Jamie followed. But the maid was soon discouraged by the snow and ice and turned back to engage the footmen in conversation.

"It's so lovely and peaceful here," Fidelity sighed

when Jamie was abreast of her.

"Yes, Ma'am," he answered.

"You needn't be so formal, Jamie," she told him. "I know most masters expect their employees to be silent and respectful but you may speak your mind with me."

"I didn't expect to find you so friendly, Ma'am," he said, his tone only slightly less stilted than before.

"Why? Had you heard that I was an ogre?"

He laughed. "No, I'd heard nothing of you. But I met Master Crichton."

"Ah, yes, Nichodemus can be most disconcerting to say the least. And more so to his help, I expect."

He said nothing and Fidelity understood that he was uncertain of how much he could criticize his master in her presence. She wondered how much gossip he'd heard about her in the short period of his employ in their household. She intended to find out but was aware that they must not spend too much time alone or appear to be talking too familiarly.

"Come," she said, turning away toward the sleigh. "We must be getting back."

Jamie Bowyer seemed to be permanently assigned to be her driver when she rode in a coach or the sleigh and as her companion and bodyguard when she went on horseback. Nichodemus, although he obviously knew that Jamie was young and handsome, didn't realize or didn't care that an admirer was exactly what Fidelity's soul cried out for after the months of ill-treatment she'd received at his hands.

The feeling his admiration evoked in her was especially sharp with the fact of his resemblance to

Schuyler. He was not as well versed in courtly gallantries nor as wise in the ways of the world, and his hair was cropped short rather than falling in the great rolling curls Schuyler had worn, but it was enough.

There was nothing of a physical nature between them. Fidelity's mind was filled with too-recent memories of Nichodemus's brutality to want such a relationship but there was something of the sweetness she'd shared with Schuyler and something of the excitement of a covert romance which, if discovered, could have dire consequences not only for the principals involved, but for all those who may have had knowledge and withheld it.

Fidelity entered the front hall of Crichton Manor and turned toward a window to watch Jamie drive the horses toward the stables behind the house. Her cheeks were flushed red with the chill air and she pressed her nose against the window until she saw the sleigh and its driver disappear around the corner of the house.

"Ma'am?"

Fidelity turned. Her maid, having divested herself of her cloak, waited expectantly to help Fidelity off with hers. When she'd taken the garment, she turned and disappeared toward the kitchen where they would be spread before the fires to dry.

"Kate!" Fidelity called into the silence of the hallway. Her waiting woman, although she never accompanied her on her rides, was usually waiting when she returned. "Kate?!"

The house was silent. No one answered her call. With a shrug, Fidelity started up the stairs hoping there was a warm fire started in her room. She imagined that Kate was somewhere sleeping; the woman took advantage of every opportunity to attend to everything but the duties for which she was employed.

As Fidelity emerged onto the second floor landing and turned down the corridor toward her room, she felt the pins-and-needles of cold flesh exposed to warm air begin in her hands, cheeks, and chin. She chafed her hands and blew into them, using them against her face and throat. Perhaps she would have Kate rub them, and her feet, to warm them. Yes, the more she thought about it, the better that sounded. And she'd lie down for a while, perhaps until dinner.

She opened the door to her room, glad of the roaring fire in the fireplace that had been prepared in anticipation of her return, began unlacing her boots.

And still no Kate. She'd expected to find the woman in her room waiting for her or at least to have her arrive on the run after having been warned of her mistress's return. She pulled off her snow-crusted boots and crossed the room to the fireplace. Standing before it, her hands stretched toward the fire, Fidelity heard sounds coming from the room adjoining hers— Nichodemus's room. A woman laughed. It was a quiet sound, she couldn't be sure she'd actually heard it until it came again.

She walked to the connecting door and listened. She heard a woman's voice, its tone ending in a question, and a man's voice answering. She tried the handle expecting it to be locked against her but to her surprise it gave way and the door opened before her. She caught her breath, surprised by the scene the open door revealed.

Kate, the missing waiting woman, sat amid the tumbled quilts of Nichodemus Crichton's bed pulling her low-heeled work shoes over her dirty feet. Her hair fell in tangled masses about her shoulders and her clothing showed signs of being donned in a hurry. She smiled her black-toothed smile at the other occupant of the room.

Nichodemus, also dressing, faced her a little way from the bed as he tucked the long tails of his linen shirt into his breeches. It was a long moment before they noticed Fidelity standing silently in the doorway.

# 9

There were a few moments of awkward silence before Kate hurried from the room, leaving Fidelity alone with Nichodemus.

"And here is my dear little wife," he said sarcastically. "Can it be you were looking for me? Can it possibly be that you were seeking my company?"

"Don't flatter yourself," Fidelity snapped. "I was in my room and I heard voices." She shook her head "I wondered what it was you paid Kate for since I can never get her to do her duties as a waiting woman."

"Don't try to be snide, it doesn't become you."

"Nothing becomes you; you disgust me!"

Nichodemus threw back his ugly head and laughed unpleasantly. "I disgust you, do I? Well you bore me! Frankly, my dear, I married you because I was tired of the type of woman one finds within the confines of our circle. My sainted first wife was frigid and prudish. When I heard of your situation I thought I'd found the answer. A girl of your background getting involved with a Cavalier under her parents' very noses was an opportunity not to be missed. You've no idea how disappointed I was to find you a virgin." He sighed. "I had such hopes . . . Actually

your parents would have been better off to let you
have your precious Cavalier. To be brutally honest,
your attractions are a bit childish, your cloying
modesty wears on my nerves, and your technique is
all but nonexistent. No doubt your perfect Pierrepointe would have enjoyed you until the novelty had
worn off and then left you."

"Perhaps I might not have been such a disappointment with a teacher who was more than a
rutting pig!"

Crichton laughed again. "You do amuse me at
times. To learn anything well, one first has to have an
aptitude—which, you, unfortunately, do not!"

"And so you amuse yourself with the servants?"

"Can it be that you're jealous? Perhaps I could
convince myself to spend more nights in your bed."

Fidelity grimaced. "Don't bother!" As she turned
and returned to her own room, slamming the
connecting door behind her, she heard Crichton's
loud laughter booming once again.

Fidelity walked slowly up the path that led from
the snow-covered gardens to the terrace which ran
along the back of the house. The house was quiet,
empty of the guests who had descended upon them
for the Christmas and New Year observances. They
were solemn occasions, unlike the gay, frivolous
celebrations that took place at court and in many
homes throughout England. Fidelity was glad to see
the season pass. Receiving guests and returning visits
tired her, the latter in particular because she was not
made to feel welcome in any household she entered.
She was tolerated, as Nichodemus's wife, but it was

made clear that her hosts did not feel she'd made much progress during the months of her marriage.

She tried to push the unpleasant memories from her mind when she heard footsteps on the path behind her. Turning, she saw Jamie Bowyer hurrying up the narrow path.

"Jamie," she smiled. "Good morning."

"Good morning, Ma'am." He bowed the stiff little servant's bow that made Fidelity giggle.

"Jamie, what did we agree about?"

"I'm sorry," he paused as he always did before using her Christian name, "Fidelity."

"What brings you out here?"

"I—uh—I thought you might want to go riding."

Fidelity smiled, knowing she'd sent a message that she'd not be riding for a while. But Jamie's feelings were easily hurt and he was all too aware of the differences in their social position. "Not today I think, Jamie. I don't feel well."

Jamie was instantly concerned. "You're not ill?"

"No, something I ate, most likely." She had reason to believe she might be pregnant although she dreaded the possibility of bearing Nichodemus Crichton's child. Seeing the concern and admiration on Jamie's face, Fidelity couldn't bring herself to tell him of her suspicions. She didn't like to remind him that, although he had the largest part of her affections, her husband had sole claim on her body.

"Are you sure? Perhaps you should see . . ."

Fidelity silenced him by laying a hand on his arm. "Now, Jamie; I'm fine, really."

"All right." He hesitated. Not having had a legitimate reason to speak to her, he was at a loss to know where to take the conversation. "Well, I have to get back to the horses."

"All right, Jamie. Thank you for your concern." Placing her hand once again on his arms, she stood on her toes and kissed his cheek.

His face turned crimson and he moved clumsily away. As he hurried toward the stables, Fidelity smiled and started again for the house. But the path was rough with ice that had melted and refrozen after having had footsteps impressed in it. As Fidelity turned, her foot caught in one of the rough places and, with a cry, she fell on the hard, sharp ice of the path.

In an instant Jamie was beside her. "Fidelity! Are you all right? Let me help you."

Fidelity's hand was bleeding where she'd scraped her palm on the rough ice. Jamie produced a large, coarse handkerchief and tied it around her hand before he picked her up as easily as if she were a child and carried her into the house.

Fidelity paced back and forth across the floor of her room. Jamie had carried her up to her room and turned her over to the care of Kate and a maid. Her clothes had been changed and her hand washed. She felt dizzy and somewhat sick to her stomach. She suspected she'd bruised herself in her fall and fully expected to see ugly purple and black bruises all over her body.

She was leaning against the fireplace when Nichodemus entered the room.

"I see you've recovered."

She didn't bother turning toward him. "I'm well enough, I imagine."

"How kind of our young groom to carry you to your bedroom." His tone was mocking.

"It was kind of him. He didn't have to help me."

"I doubt not he was just waiting to find a reason to make his way into your bedchamber."

Fidelity turned to him, furious. "Jamie isn't like that . . .!"

"Jamie, is it?" Nichodemus's red face was a mask of innocent surprise. "Can it be, madam, that you're up to your old tricks? You seem to have a weakness for pathetically handsome men."

"Your mind is filth ridden, as usual," Fidelity retorted. "And how, pray tell, would you know anything about being even slightly handsome?"

She was rewarded by the deepening of color in Crichton's face and the way the veins bulged in his forehead and massive neck. He made an attempt at nonchalance. "It doesn't matter to me, mistress, what you do so long as you're discreet; but to go from a baron to a stable boy is a bit of a comedown, don't you think?"

Fidelity lifted her chin defiantly. "When my parents forced me into your bed they pushed me as far down as I could go."

With one motion, surprisingly quick in a man of his girth, Nichodemus crossed the small space separating them and, with a vicious blow, knocked her sprawling across the floor where she slammed into the protruding corner of the wardrobe. As she lay there, Fidelity watched her husband stomp from the room, leaving her sprawled across the carpet.

It was later that night when Fidelity found that she was indeed pregnant. It was also that night that her pregnancy came to an abrupt end.

The weather seemed to be warming by the day and the countryside surrounding Crichton Manor gave every indication of an early spring.

Fidelity strolled around the grounds of the house examining bushes and trees, flower beds and borders for signs of the first buds of the new season. Her interest was little more than a way to pass the long hours between the late hour when she rose and the early evening when she retired. Her eighteenth birthday had passed unobserved, for Jamie didn't know about it and Nichodemus didn't care. Life at the Manor was a continuous cycle of boredom. Nothing ever changed; week in and week out, the servants went about their business with dogged regularity, and Fidelity and Nichodemus pursued their own amusements. The chief amusement for Nichodemus was Kate, and Fidelity was all too pleased that this should be so, for while he was engaged in her waiting woman's bed, he was less eager to join her in hers. For Fidelity, amusement was not the right word. She'd felt oddly depressed since the night when she'd lost her child. It was strange, she thought, that she should feel that way since she hadn't been overly anxious to bear a child of Nichodemus Crichton's, but she felt it just the same. Nichodemus had come to her bed only infrequently since then and she'd received him lethargically. Apparently it had been her distaste for him that had spurred on his interest, for the more passive she was in his embrace, the less often he sought her company. He paid little attention to her now but she had the feeling that he paid very close attention to where she went on her rides and who accompanied her.

Jamie treated her like something fragile and precious after her miscarriage. He worried constantly that she might ride too long or over terrain too rough and do herself some harm. He was watchful and concerned and always seemed to be near, even when he was nowhere to be seen.

Early one morning she tried to move a heavy stone bench across a path in the garden so she could climb upon it and peer into a tall, massive stone urn. She had only begun to exert force on the reluctant bench when she noticed Jamie hurrying up the path.

"Fidelity!" he called; her name came easily to his lips by then. "Don't try to move that; it's too heavy."

Fidelity smiled. It was nice to be treated that way. It was nice, after all the months of abuse, to feel special and cherished. She stepped back and watched as Jamie moved the bench to the side of the urn.

"Thank you, Jamie. I could never have done it alone." She smiled as Jamie blushed. He was such a dear young man, so thoughtful and so handsome.

She let him help her onto the bench and allowed him to stand next to her with his arm about her waist to balance her. There was nothing in the urn, she found, except dirt and several years of debris. She waited for Jamie to jump off the bench and then held her arms out for him to swing her to the ground.

Her feet hit the ground but instead of releasing her, Jamie tightened his arms and drew her to him. Fidelity was startled and awkward for a moment but his kiss was so different from her husband's; it was so gentle, so tender. Unfair as it might have been to the unsuspecting Jamie, Fidelity was transported to another place in another time. She was back in the stable of Fairfax House with a man she'd never ceased to love. It was Schuyler Pierrepointe there in the garden of Crichton Manor; it was his lips she kissed and his arms she felt around her.

When Jamie released her she opened her eyes reluctantly and looked at him with a start.

Seeing her so disoriented, Jamie was concerned. He mistook her confusion for dismay.

"I—I'm sorry," he stammered. "I shouldn't have . . ."

"No, it's all right," Fidelity assured him. She felt sad that she'd taken advantage of Jamie to bring Schuyler back to her life for a moment.

Jamie caught her arm and the concern in his voice upset her. "Have I angered you?" he asked.

"No, it's fine, Jamie." Before he could say more she hurried away from him toward the house.

Without pausing, Fidelity rushed into the house past startled housemaids. She ignored the cook who tried to question her about the dinner she was preparing. She didn't stop until she entered her own room and even then she was not alone.

Kate stood folding linen in Fidelity's room. When she saw her mistress enter the room, she turned to her with a sly smile. "I see you've found your young groom has more talents than merely driving horses."

"Shut up!" Fidelity snarled. The woman's relationship with Nichodemus made it impossible for her to dismiss her from the household staff. She had no recourse except to forbid the woman to enter her presence which would curtail the duties she already performed with slovenly disregard. "Get out!"

"Yes, Ma'am!" The woman's triumphant sneer told her that a dismissal was exactly what she wanted. Before she left the room, Kate turned to her once again. "I'm sure," she remarked insolently, "that Nichodemus will be interested in the way you carry on in public with the servants."

Fidelity refused to dignify the woman's impertinence by showing how the remark struck her. No, she comforted herself, Nichodemus wouldn't care what she did. Just the same, she locked her door and drew her drapes, hoping he'd not go to the trouble of confronting her about the display in the gardens.

It was early evening when Fidelity awoke. She'd developed the ability to sleep long and irregular hours as a way to pass the time when all other avenues of entertainment were exhausted. She lay in the cool, dim room wondering why she hadn't been called to dinner when she heard footsteps hurrying down the corridor outside her room and voices in the yard below her window.

It was a moment before she managed to find her shoes and pull a light cloak about her shoulders but in that moment she made out the words "accident" and "barn" among the jumble of voices within the house and from the yard.

The house was nearly empty as she made her way to the door which led to the outbuildings of the Manor. The moment she left the house she saw where everyone had gone. There was a crowd of house servants, grooms, and other assorted people all whispering among themselves and staring toward one

of the barns. As she approached, she noticed the
stares turn on her and the whispers cease. She was just
reaching the barn door when her husband appeared
in the doorway, barring her entrance.

"What is it, Nichodemus?" she asked. "What's
happened?"

"Your young friend, Master Bowyer, has met
with an accident. Apparently your little encounter in
the garden this afternoon made him careless."

To one side, Fidelity saw the smirking face of
Kate but tried to ignore her; all her concern was for
Jamie. She tried to push past the bulky form of her
husband and into the barn. He refused to move.

"Nichodemus please!" she cried. "At least let me
try to help him."

Nichodemus was airly unconcerned. "Don't
bother, my dear. It seems that someone was careless
enough to leave a newly sharpened scythe in an
awkward place and your friend, doubtless still in a
daze with the wonder of your charms, was unlucky
enough to fall over it." Fidelity cried out and resumed
her efforts to push past him but he stood fast. "Stay
where you are, Fidelity," he ordered firmly. "There's
nothing you can do. There's now a considerable
distance between your precious Jamie's head and his
neck."

# 10

In the days following Jamie's death, Fidelity spent the greater part of her time planning her escape. She felt certain that her husband would not always let things go on as they were, one day, perhaps soon, he would decide to kill her. And there would be nothing to stop him. The law was behind him, a man was the master of his wife and had complete jurisdiction over her. He would merely say that she'd been a false and deceiving bitch, call her relatives (particularly her sister, Sarah) and the members of their congregation to bear witness to her many faults and he would be excused for a crime to which, it would be said, she drove him. She was totally within his power, her life or death was subject only to his whim.

As the days became weeks he paid her less and less attention, coming to her only when he'd found some new humiliation to inflict upon her. And Kate treated her with disrespect bordering on a total disregard for the fact that Fidelity was her master's wife and therefore her superior. Fidelity was learning to tolerate the woman's rudeness for Nichodemus merely laughed at her complaints and told her that any time she didn't like her life, she was free to join her dear, departed Jamie.

Fidelity had resumed her habit of taking long rides. She was disappointed, however, when upon rising one morning determined to spend the better part of the day in the saddle, she found the sky overcast and the air heavy with threatening rain clouds. She pouted over her breakfast, alone at the long, polished table of the dining hall, and then Nichodemus happened to pass through the room.

"I love to see you in the morning, Fidelity," he sneered. "You are always so bright and cheerful."

Fidelity pushed her plate away untouched. "I wanted to go riding today," she snarled. "But it's obvious I'm not going to."

"I don't see why you can't."

She looked up at him as surprised by his polite tone of voice as by his interest in her disappointment. "How can I? It's going to rain any minute."

"Take the coach."

"I thought you were taking it." She knew he'd decided to go to London for a few days.

"I'm riding my own horse. I want to be there as soon as possible. I will be taking most of the footmen with me but I'm sure William will be willing to drive you."

Fidelity nodded. "I suppose you'll be taking Kate to London with you?"

"Use your head! How would it look if I arrived in London with my wife's waiting woman but without my wife?"

"It would look like your wife's waiting woman did more than merely wait on your wife!"

Nichodemus smiled in spite of himself. "Mind your tongue!" He leaned over and pecked at her temple in a semblance of a kiss. "I'm leaving now—mind your ways while I'm gone."

Fidelity walked with him out the front door and down to the courtyard where his horse and escort were awaiting him. She watched while he mounted his great black horse and led the group of men away into the distance. With the long afternoon ahead of her, she decided to take his suggestion and sent a lackey to the stable to tell William to ready the coach.

William (Fidelity had never heard of any other name he may have possessed) was the oldest servant at Crichton Manor. He'd served Nichodemus's father and, when Nichodemus bought the Manor after the Civil War, he'd come to oversee the stables. He was old and his age often barred him from the more strenuous excursions such as Nichodemus's trip to London, but he'd never lost his ability with horses and Fidelity felt perfectly safe with him handling the reins.

The great black coach, normally used for visiting and other special occasions, rumbled out of the courtyard with only one passenger—Fidelity. With only William accompanying her, she felt a sense of privacy seldom experienced in her role as mistress of Crichton Manor. The servants were always more than happy to pass on any little bit of gossip they could gather in an overheard argument or a too loud conversation.

But there in the rumbling coach she could be as open with her thoughts, her opinions, her emotions as she cared to be. With an abandon seldom allowed her at home, Fidelity tried to put her feet up on the tufted velvet seat across from her. But the floor of the coach was too wide; her legs wouldn't reach across its broad expanse. Instead she turned and put her slipper-shod feet on the seat she occupied, reclining with her back against the upholstered wall of the coach. The weather, in spite of the gloomy and overcast skies threatening imminent rain, was warm and humid and she unfastened the ribbons at the throat of her cloak and removed the white cap covering her hair. She was tempted to pull out the bodkins securing the knot of hair at the back of her head but the air felt too good against her neck. Instead of undoing her hair, she opened the mother-of-pearl buttons of her high-necked, white-collared gown. After all, she reasoned, who was there to see her? She was alone in the dark coach, its interior made even darker by the sunless day, and William had no way of seeing her from his perch on the top of the coach and no reason to descend until they were back at the manor.

They were driving through a wooded section of the countryside. The close, thick growth made the day even darker and Fidelity could feel the coach picking up speed as William whipped up the horses to hurry them through the eerie area. They emerged once again into open country and she could imagine the old coachman breathing a sigh of relief to be out of the forest.

Black thunderclouds banked across the sky turning the air wet with promised rain and what little daylight there had been was obscured, making it seem like the late evening rather than the height of the afternoon.

The coach stopped and Fidelity leaned out the window to see what the problem might be. William leaned over the side of the coach to speak to her.

"Ma'am?"

"Yes, William?"

"I'm thinkin' we might be better to go back home now." He nodded toward the angry clouds.

"Yes, I think you're right."

Fidelity ducked back inside the coach as William turned the vehicle and started on the journey back.

They were passing through the forest once again when Fidelity heard the sound of voices and hoof-beats on the road. The coach lurched as William used his whip on the horses, urging them on.

"William!" Fidelity cried. "William! What is it?"

"Highwaymen, Ma'am! Keep your head inside!"

The coach bounced off ruts in the road as the horses charged through the forest at a dangerous speed. But it was soon apparent that the four horses drawing the great, heavy coach were no match for those running with only the weight of a man upon their backs. As they closed in on the coach, Fidelity let down the curtains to cover the windows and crouched down on the seat. Her heart pounded as she heard the horses come abreast of the coach and the voices of the highwaymen ordering William to stop the vehicle.

The coach creaked to a jolting stop and Fidelity heard a man's rough voice order the old coachman down from his perch.

"Hold your ground, old man," the voice commanded, "or you won't live to regret it."

Fidelity heard the sound of boots coming closer and closer to the coach and suddenly the dark coach was lit by the dim light coming through the open door. In the doorway stood a man whom Fidelity could see was easily half a foot taller than herself. He had shoulder-length brown hair; not curled like the Royalists, it fell straight down to drape on the shoulders of his coat. He had dark brown eyes with sweeping lashes and a moustache which contrasted with gleaming white teeth as he smiled.

"Well! What do we have here?"

Fidelity blushed. Her hair had shaken loose during the ride and fell in silver waves down her back. Her collar was still open past the base of her throat and her cloak fell in drapes over the side of the seat and onto the floor. As she looked into the man's eyes, she pulled back into the coach. Shifting her eyes away from his, her gaze fell on the hand which held the coach door open. It was tanned to a deep brown and sported an emerald of impressive size and cut, set in a massive gold setting. Its deep green color matched the green of his velvet coat and breeches which, although worn and bare of embroidery, were obviously well made and expensively cut.

"Keep quiet and I'll not have to deal harshly with you. I just want your valuables."

With fumbling fingers, Fidelity slid the pearl earrings Nichodemus had given her from her ears. She untied the ribbons of her pearl necklace and slipped her diamond wedding band from her finger. The highwayman laughed as she dropped them into his hand.

"Very cooperative of you I'm sure," he said examining the items. "Not overly endowed with riches but a good haul nonetheless." He held out her wedding band. "Would you like this back? Don't tell my associates," he nodded toward the other two men who held pistols on William. "I don't expect they'd like to give this bauble up."

"No, no please," Fidelity insisted. "If you're going to take the rest you might as well have that also."

The highwayman laughed. "I was never engaged in an argument with a lady who wanted me to take her jewels! The ring can't mean much."

"I hate looking at it," she muttered.

The highwayman shrugged but over his shoulder Fidelity saw William lunge at him in spite of the other two men. He raised his coach whip to strike but it froze there as a pistol shot rang out and William fell to the ground.

"William!" Fidelity was horrified. There was no doubt that William was dead. The shot had passed through his body and Fidelity saw blood staining the left breast of the old man's coat.

"Foolish old man!" the highwaymen growled.

Fidelity stared at William's body and felt a surge of affectionate grief for the bravery of the old servant.

"Oh poor, poor William!" she cried. "What will Nichodemus think!"

"Nichodemus! You wouldn't be referring to Nichodemus Crichton, would you?"

"Do you know him?"

"I've seen that foul piece of dung on occasion. As a matter of fact, I'd wager you're living under my roof, my fine lady."

"Your roof?"

"My grandfather was the Baron Wilmington, late of Wilmington Manor—now Crichton Manor.

He died, as did my father, in the Civil War. You see before you the younger brother of the present Baron Wilmington, heir to nary a thing. My brother has gone to Virginia as his estates here are now the property of your husband."

With a grand gesture he stepped back and swept his hat, its plumes pathetically bedraggled, from his head and made her a bow reminiscent of those Schuyler and her cousin had demonstrated for her at Fairfax House.

Over his head, Fidelity saw the corpse of William and asked with a shudder. "What are you going to do with me?"

He smiled a lazy, sensuous smile. "I haven't decided."

Suddenly she remembered the plans she'd been making for weeks, the escape routes she painstakingly traced only to discard. "Will you take me to London?"

His face registered surprise. "Eh? What was that?"

"To London, take me to London. I hate my husband, they married me to him as a punishment. Please! My cousin is the Earl of Wyndham—he'd reward you, help you at Court, perhaps. He's a friend of the king!"

"Everyone's a friend of the king who has a claim to lay on the royal estate," he laughed. "But from what I hear the king is no better off than any of the rest of us these days."

They stared at one another for a moment and then the sounds of the other two highwaymen urging him to hurry made him turn. He tossed the jewelry to them. "Here, take these and go on ahead. I've a little business to discuss here."

The other two men didn't wait to be told twice and in a moment Fidelity was alone with the third highwayman—Philip Wilmington he told her his name was—and the corpse of the coachman.

"So your cousin would reward me, eh?" he asked.

"Yes! Yes, he would!"

"How do I know he wouldn't call the constables instead?"

Fidelity shook her head. "If you could deliver me from my husband I would never let him harm you."

"It sounds good." He appeared to be thinking it over but Fidelity was uncomfortably aware of his eyes studying her. "But I think I'd like part of my reward now."

"Here?" She'd not escaped all of her family's Puritan notions which included one which said that sex belonged in the bedroom, beneath the quilts, in the night.

"There's no one around," he smiled. "And the floor of this coach wouldn't be bad if we spread out that cloak of yours."

"I . . . I . . ."

"Unless you want to forget about my taking you to London."

"No!" Fidelity looked at him carefully. He was handsome in a rugged way and God knew that if she could stand Nichodemus's attentions for the past year this would prove no hardship. "All right," she said at last.

He climbed into the coach and helped her spread

her taffeta cloak over the floor. With the curtains down at the windows the coach was dark and Fidelity held her breath as the highwayman's lips touched the exposed base of her throat. His lips and caresses grew more bold and demanding and Fidelity, in spite of her apprehensions, found herself responding with a passion Schuyler Pierrepointe had never been bold enough to elicit and Nichodemus Crichton had never cared to search for. Though she'd tensed herself against an onslaught of the type her husband had accustomed her to, she forgot her surroundings and her circumstances and surrendered herself completely to a man who had robbed her of her jewelry but now gave her feelings of a kind she'd never known existed.

# Part II

---

## London
## 1661

# 11

Fidelity rode pillion behind Philip Wilmington as they entered London. The two highwaymen who had been Philip's accomplices were nowhere to be seen. No doubt, Philip told her, they'd decided the meager jewels of their victim were better divided between two men than among three. As she sat behind her highwayman, her arms about his waist, Fidelity chuckled.

"A private joke?" Philip asked.

"No," she answered. "I was just thinking how shocked my family would be if they knew about this." She chuckled again. "In a coach! During the day! On the floor!"

Philip laughed. "I've been in worse. A coach floor is better than a pallet full of bedbugs with lice biting your arse while the landlord is picking your pockets!"

Fidelity fell silent as they entered the crowded, dirty, stinking, exciting heart of London.

The dingy, narrow streets were swarming with men, women, children, horses, dogs, and rats. Coaches and sedan chairs wove their way slowly through the surging masses with coachmen and chairmen shouting curses at one another and trading insults with pedestrians.

'Prentices hawked their merchandise to pass-ersby on foot as well as those in the stalled vehicles. Dogs and ragged, dirty children fought and tumbled one another into the filthy gutters that served as garbage dumps, open sewers, and public lavatories. Piles of waste, human, animal, and vegetable were alive with rats and maggots.

From the upper stories of the buildings, which overhung the street almost touching overhead, the contents of basins and chamber pots were flung to fall where they would and on whomever was passing under the window at the time.

From her perch on the back of Philip's horse, Fidelity heard the centuries-old cries of the merchants selling their wares. She heard the tattered children, the harassed mothers, swearing 'prentices, and the sweet enticements of the prostitutes who leaned from windows displaying as many of their charms as possible. She saw an amazingly diverse assortment of characters, from the beggars with real or fabricated disfigurements to swaggering fops in satins and laces with diamond buttons, and plumed hats perching on elaborately curled wigs.

As they passed on through the city, Fidelity asked Philip the names of various buildings and the meaning of signs and sayings she heard and saw. There were the churches whose spires dominated the skyline, the huge, awe-inspiring, dreadful Tower of London where the lives of so many had come to an end with the swift stroke of an axe or sword or after prolonged and excruciating tortures. She saw London Bridge, covered with ancient structures, and gaped at the magnificence of Saint Paul's. There were taverns, inns, and alehouses with newly painted signs proclaiming their recent return to business after the long suppressions of the Protectorate.

Fidelity tightened her hold on Philip. She didn't want to be left alone in this sprawling, crowded, frightening city.

They passed a church upon whose front steps a group of men were gathered. Dressed in the somber clothing with which Fidelity was so familiar, they appeared to be taking their leave of one another, for some were mounted and some were preparing to mount. As they passed, Philip called Fidelity's attention to one of them.

"Damn me if I don't see someone you know."

"Who?" Fidelity looked toward the group and then, gasping, turned her face quickly away. One of the men had left the group and started his horse in their direction. It was Nichodemus Crichton! Fidelity turned her head and held her breath. She was glad she had not replaced her white cap for it would have been noticeably out of place on a woman riding pillion with a man dressed as Philip was. Her hooded cloak concealed her gown and hair and she felt her heartbeat race until Philip told her they were well past her husband.

The sight of him reminded her of the last time she'd seen him. That very morning she had still been his wife living under his roof. And now . . . now she was a fugitive, for her flight was a sin against the laws of her church, state, and a lifetime of teachings. She wondered if he knew and then decided that he couldn't. Surely if he'd received word of her disappearance he wouldn't be loitering in London; he would have returned to institute a search for her. And how would he receive the news of the death of faithful old William? She remembered how, after they'd made love, she and Philip had put William's body into the coach and started the horses toward Crichton Manor. Her feelings were mixed as Philip turned his horse past Drury Lane and into the Strand.

The Strand was the main thoroughfare between the heart of London and the king's palace of Whitehall. It ran parellel to the river Thames and, on the land between the two, were the mansions of the privileged.

Built over the course of generations, the houses sat with smug certainty, as though aware of their own importance, of their power to dominate mortals with their impressive facades. They sat behind high walls daring one to cross their boundaries. They sported great names that rang through the history of England, names that were legend even to the sheltered children of those who had no reason to love the great aristocratic heroes of the past. It was in this street that Wyndham House lay.

Wyndham House was not the most impressive mansion in the Strand. It sat, as did the others, behind high stone walls topped with iron spikes. A circular approach passed through gateways guarded with iron, rolled past the front of the house, and back out through another gateway to the street. The mansion itself was a great sprawling hulk without recognizable form or symmetry. Gray walls rose four stories into the air. Windows faced toward the road as well as away, and chimneys dotted the roof. Behind the house an elaborate, though overgrown, garden swept down to the banks of the Thames.

Philip reined in the horse and leaped to the ground at the foot of an ornately railed flight of stone steps which led to the main entrance of the house. He lifted Fidelity from the horse's back and steadied her for a moment. Having straightened her clothing and patted her hair into place, she started up the steps with Philip.

Philip pounded on the heavy wooden doors. They waited in the gathering dusk of evening and then he pounded impatiently once again. At last they heard the rattle of the door handle and one side of the double doors opened to reveal an effeminately handsome young footman in scarlet and buff livery.

"Yes?" The young man looked them up and down, leaving no doubt as to his opinion of such creatures invading the sacred grounds of the aristocracy.

"I want to see Lady Wyndham," Fidelity told him.

"Indeed!" The footman sniffed in distate as he digested the information. "And what is your business here?"

"I am a cousin of the earl." She tried to impress him with an imperious air. "I am Fidelity Fairfax."

"Really!" The man's gaze swept over them both once again. "How amusing! I don't believe you for a moment but the notion is amusing."

"When you are finished being amused," Fidelity told him coldly. "We would appreciate being shown to the countess or the earl."

"I don't really think I can . . . " the footman began, obviously tiring of the game.

From under his coat, Philip pulled a pistol and shoved the muzzle under the man's nose. "You don't really think you can what?" he asked.

Although both Fidelity and Philip knew the gun wasn't loaded, the footman was impressed. "Why I . . . I," the footman stuttered. "I don't see how I can keep you waiting out here any longer."

He swung the door open and stepped back as Fidelity entered the entrance hall followed by Philip who had replaced his pistol beneath his coat. The footman made them a grand bow.

"I shall inform her ladyship of your arrival."

Fidelity and Philip sat in an impressively ornate drawing room where a portrait of Divina Fairfax hung over the mantel of the fireplace. Fidelity allowed the newly respectful footman to take her cloak but Philip refused to relinquish his coat. They sat on a sofa silently, Fidelity tidying her appearance as best she could while Philip ogled a plate of sweetmeats sitting temptingly nearby on a table.

Divina Fairfax entered the room and held out her hands to Fidelity. She looked infinitely more confident and content than the beautiful woman who had so fascinated Fidelity as a guest at Fairfax House.

"Fidelity, darling! This is a most delightful surprise. I had no idea you were coming to London."

"Neither did I," Fidelity admitted, grasping her cousin's hands. "Until very recently."

"We've had little word from your father. We wrote after we'd settled in here and your father's reply was terse and only slightly enlightening. He did mention, however, that you were married—which was a surprise." She looked questioningly in Philip's direction.

"This is Philip Wilmington," Fidelity explained hurriedly. "He brought me to London."

Divina smiled at Philip and held out her hand for a kiss. "You are related to the Baron Wilmington?"

"He is my elder brother," Philip replied. "Although I'm afraid the barony is hardly what it was formerly."

Divina nodded. "That is no unusual state of affairs these days, sir." She noticed the way his eyes strayed to the plate of sweetmeats. "You must be famished if you've only just arrived in London."

"Oh, I'm too excited to eat!" Fidelity protested.

"And you, sir?"

"Well," he strove to appear apathetic and not betray his interest in her offer. "I could make do with a biscuit or a taste of wine," he admitted.

"I'm sure we could do better than that." Going to the door, Divina called and waited until a lackey answered her summons. "Take this gentleman and see that hs is well fed," she ordered. She turned to Philip. "Follow Hoby, Master Wilmington, and he will see to your needs."

When they were alone, Divina turned to Fidelity. "And so you are related to the Baron Wilmington now."

"No, I'm not."

The countess was confused. "But your father told us you had married; and you said the young man with you had brought you to London."

"Yes, he brought me to London, but he is not my husband."

Divina crossed the room and drew Fidelity down next to her on the sofa. "I think we have a great deal to discuss."

Spurred on by the presence of a sympathetic listener, Fidelity recounted the experiences that had brought her to Wyndham House that evening. She told her cousin of the circumstances of her marriage to Nichodemus Crichton. Divina nodded and urged her to continue her narrative. Fidelity told her about Crichton Manor, about Kate and the death of Jamie Bowyer. At last she arrived at the present day and told Divina of her coachride, the highwaymen, the death of old William, and even of her part of Philip's reward on the floor of the coach. As an afterthought she mentioned seeing Nichodemus in London on her way to her cousin's house.

"God's body!" Divina exclaimed, using one of the king's favorite oaths. "You've had a busy year, Fidelity!"

"Yes," Fidelity admitted. "But I could stay no longer under my husband's roof. I hated him so."

"And with reason!" Divina smiled slyly. "You were lucky Philip Wilmington happened along when he did. Frankly, I think that beneath his threadbare garments there lies a most handsome man. One could find a worse price to pay for passage to London than lying with him, I'd vow."

In spite of herself, Fidelity had to agree. "I was shocked at myself for my lack of hesitation, but . . ."

"No, no, no," Divina cooed. "If you're going to be in London associating with courtiers your first lesson is that handsome and virile young men are not such a plentiful commodity that one should take them for granted."

Fidelity paused. She'd wondered several times during her journey to London whether her cousin would be willing to take her in when she had neither money nor even clothing to call her own. "Divina, when you say I'll be associating with courtiers . . ."

The countess held up her hand. "I noticed that you had no luggage, and the story you've just told me explains it. You are going to live with us from now on, Fidelity. I want no argument. If your family can do naught but abuse you, they do not deserve to have you among them. His lordship and I have been most fortunate. We have lost little, practically nothing compared to others; we have plenty to share with you."

"Thank you! Oh, Divina! Thank you!" Fidelity threw herself into the powdered and scented, satin and lace embrace of her cousin.

"You're more than welcome, my dear. As I said the first time I saw you, you're the daughter Henry and I were never blessed with. We love you dearly. You can't imagine how upset we were when we heard you'd been forced into a marriage. And Schuyler! He felt completely to blame for what happened—he told us about the episode in your father's stables . . . "

"Schuyler!" Fidelity sighed. "I wished to see him so often, you have no idea! If I hadn't had the memories of Schuyler," she paused. "I would have gone mad! Oh, Divina, where is he? Is he still in London?" She hesitated before asking the last question. "Is he married?"

The countess laughed. "Yes, he's still in London, and no, he's not married."

"Where is he?"

A deep masculine voice came from the doorway. "He's right here."

Fidelity whirled. Lounging in the doorway, resplendent in a deep blue velvet suit with a lace cravat of snowy white, and holding a hat, spilling over with blue and white plumes, which he tapped against his high riding boots, stood Schuyler Pierrepointe.

"Schuyler," Fidelity whispered. He was more handsome than she remembered and it made her more conscious than ever of her own dishelved appearance. Her hand shot to her loose and flowing hair and the other hand smoothed her dress.

Schuyler laughed and held out his arms. "Come on, sweetheart. You've never looked prettier in your life."

Joyfully, Fidelity ran across the width of the room and flung herself into his arms. He lifted her off her feet so her face was level with his own. "Welcome to London," he said softly and, without waiting for an answer, pressed his mouth to hers.

Fidelity, who had been so innocent and inexperienced when last they'd met, returned his kiss eagerly, surprised at the depth of her feelings for this man who'd become a sort of foggy memory, half remembrance and half dream.

There in the doorway of the drawing room at Wyndham House they renewed their feelings for one another with several deep, passionate kisses and so involved in each other were they that when Philip Wilmington returned from his meal neither saw him stop and stare in surprise at the sight which greeted him. And neither saw him clap his hat with its bedraggled plumes upon his head and leave the house, disappearing into the London night without his promised reward.

# 12

Fidelity sighed contentedly as she watched Schuyler dress. She was lying in the wide four-poster she'd shared with him since her arrival in London nearly two months before.

"Schuyler," she sighed. "Do you have to leave?"

"Yes," he answered, tucking his cream linen shirt into his breeches. "It's very important that I get to Whitehall early. The best time to get a few words with His Majesty is during his morning stroll."

Fidelity pulled herself to a sitting position. "Does that mean you're still planning to leave England?"

He sat on the edge of the bed while he tied his cravat. "Yes, I am still planning to leave. My plans, however, seem to have hit a snag."

"What's that?" she asked, hoping it would be something that would keep him with her a little longer.

"I find I may only be able to get the land from the king. I still need the money to cultivate the land."

"What will you do?"

"Find a rich old woman who wants a young husband in her bed." He chuckled but there was an edge of bitterness. He saw the look on Fidelity's face and the way her chin began to quiver. "Oh, Fidelity. I thought you'd grown up enough to understand. My success hinges on having the money to invest in cultivating whatever land His Majesty grants me."

"But Schuyler . . . !"

He stood. "There cannot be discussion in this matter," he told her firmly. "I told you a year ago that my plans were made. I have worked too hard to give up now."

"But Schuyler . . . !"

"No, Fidelity. Now I must be going." He walked to the door and opened it. Before he left the room he turned to her. She was still sulking in bed. "If you'd prefer," he said coolly, "I shall speak to Lady Wyndham about having my belongings moved to another room." Without waiting for her reply he left, closing the door forcefully behind him.

Schuyler was as good as his word. When Fidelity returned to their room after a particularly exhausting session of fittings for her new wardrobe, she found the cupboards and chests bare of Schuyler's personal belongings. He'd had everything of his not only moved from the room but, as she was to learn, to a small apartment at Whitehall he'd been invited to occupy in his new capacity as a Gentleman of the Bedchamber in the household of King Charles II.

Fidelity didn't have much time to feel sorry for herself over the departure of Schuyler from Wyndham House. Her days were filled with fittings for gowns, cloaks, shoes, and even the most intimate articles of her personal apparel. She was taught to walk, speak, and ply a fan. French lessons, dancing lessons, and lessons to teach her the accepted way of speaking her native English (her country accent, so said her tutor, would mark her out as a fool) were included as were a rudimentary tuition in music and history. She was to go to Court the end of May, the twenty-ninth to be exact. The occasion was the king's birthday as well as the anniversary of his entry into London upon his restoration, and Divina had decided that a new and beautiful young girl would be an especially apt addition to the festivities.

That occasion, however, would not be the first opportunity for Fidelity to see the king. Her cousins had promised she would be able to see the king's procession the day before his coronation.

April twenty-second dawned a beautiful sunny day and huge crowds lined the route of the king from the Tower of London to Whitehall Palace.

The procession wove its way along the flower-strewn streets. The militia fought in vain to keep the crowds back as they tried to touch the king or at least the shimmering trappings of his horse. Scaffolds, specially constructed for the throngs, groaned beneath their weight. As the king passed beneath the triumphal arches, surrounded by his courtiers, ministers, guards, pensioners, footmen, and pages, he acknowledged the cheers of his subjects and smiled at the pretty women in windows and balconies along his route.

Charles Stuart was by nature a sardonic man, amused by the ironies of life. He was amused by the thought that many of the people gathered to watch the splendid, colorful, glittering procession had

gathered eleven years before outside the Banqueting
House at Whitehall and cheered just as vociferously
when the axe fell ending the life and reign of Charles I,
his father.

They were a fickle people, he mused, all the
while nodding and smiling. They'd been glad enough
of the first Charles's execution, anxious to honor
Oliver Cromwell, and now they were deliriously
happy to watch the silver- and gold-studded, gem
encrusted procession of Charles II in preparation for
his coronation.

Fidelity stood on the roof of Wyndham House
with Divina Fairfax. The day was warm and bright
and to protect their skin and shade their eyes they
wore wide-brimmed Cavalier's hats piled with plumes
that waved in the spring breezes blowing up from the
river behind them.

In the distance, across the wide lawn and on the
other side of the wall, they could see the throngs
crowding the street and the sun glinting from the
men, horses, and coaches in the procession.

Fidelity watched as the procession passed on
toward Whitehall and listened as Divina pointed out
the blond Duke of York—James, brother of the
king—the Lord Mayor of London, the Lord Great
Chamberlain of England, the Lord High Constable,
the Earl Marshall, and numerous Gentlemen Pensioners, Yeomen of the Guard, and Sergeants-at-Arms. In
vain did they attempt to pick out the Earl of
Wyndham and Schuyler Pierrepointe although, to
Divina's amusement, Fidelity professed not to care if
she saw the latter or not. At last, with a great roar that

marked his progress along the streets, Charles II came
into view.

Fidelity stared at the glitteringly attired man on
his equally glitteringly outfitted horse. He was a most
impressive man, she decided. His horsemanship was
superb and his above average height—more than six
feet tall—was evident even on horseback and from a
distance. Although she was too far away to see his
features clearly, and as his face was shaded by his
plumed, diamond-buckled hat, she saw the beautifully shining, jet black hair falling into great natural
curls over his shoulders and back. He nodded to the
crowds as the shouts rang out and as he passed
Wyndham House he looked toward the two women
in courtly dress framed against the blue April sky.

Fidelity, without hesitation, pulled her plumed
hat from her head and, with her hip-length silvery
hair whipping about her, waved the hat at the passing
king.

To her surprise, the tall, swarthy man on the
magnificent horse plucked his own hat from his head
and held it as he nodded to her. Even from her distant
vantage point, Fidelity could see his lips part beneath
his black moustache as he smiled. Then, replacing his
hat, he rode on, leaving Fidelity to turn to Divina
excitedly.

"He saw me!" she exclaimed. "The king noticed
me!"

Divina smiled, wishing she were eighteen and so
naively lovely. "Yes, he noticed you," she answered.
"Could you have doubted that he would?" She
laughed at Fidelity's surprise. "Do you know what

will happen now? The first opportunity he has, His Majesty will demand to know the identity of the lovely woman he saw on my roof."

Fidelity was amazed. "You mean he will remember?"

The countess laughed wryly. "Our king remembers a beautiful woman long after he forgets everything else."

Fidelity stared into the distance, trying to see the king as he progressed on toward Whitehall. She was uninterested in the rest of the procession, and she was suddenly disappointed that on the morrow, the day of the king's coronation, there would be no place for her in the galleries of Westminster Abbey where the gorgeous spectacle of the coronation would take place.

# 13

Fidelity stood in the center of her large, airy bedchamber at Wyndham House. She was being readied for the king's birthday ball at Whitehall Palace. She'd been bathed in perfumed water, her hair was carefully washed and polished with silk to add luster, and she'd sat in silent fascination as her cousin's maid applied a light dusting of powder, rouge, and eye shadow. Unaccustomed to wearing cosmetics, it made her feel wickedly sophisticated to be what her father would have called a painted harlot.

She stood in her chemise and petticoats, balancing on one foot and then the other as a maid rolled her silk stockings up and fastened her silken garters. She stepped carefully into her high-heeled, square-toed shoes and surveyed herself in the mirror with such goggle-eyed admiration that the maids helping to dress her broke into laughter.

Divina, already dressed in mulberry satin and black lace, entered the room to oversee the final preparations of her young cousin's ensemble.

"How beautiful you look, my darling," she said.

Fidelity laughed, "I'm not even dressed yet!"

"I assure you that you are beautiful." The countess sat carefully on a stool, draping her gown to avoid wrinkling it. As she watched the maids lower Fidelity's gown over her head, she felt a fierce pang of envy. How wonderful to be eighteen and so lovely when such exciting years appeared to be before them. She herself was thirty-six. True, she was beautiful, but it was a more mature beauty and it was not much appreciated by the wits of the Court who fervently voiced the opinion that a woman was on the downhill slide when she reached twenty-two. Her own peak of youth and beauty had occurred during the violent years of the Civil War when there was no leisurely, colorful Court, no opportunities for a young girl to flirt and tease.

She sighed, it would do her no good to try to regain those lost years, but she could not help envying her cousin whose opportunities seemed so much brighter.

"Be careful, don't smudge the dress!" she cautioned the maids. She watched closely as the gown was smoothed and its folds settled.

Fidelity's dress was of sapphire satin which exactly matched her eyes. Over the sweeping skirt which was gathered at the waist, and the fitted, pointed bodice, was a delicate covering of silver lace. The sleeves, full from the shoulder and ending at the elbow, were slashed to reveal a silver brocade undersleeve. Her shoes were of silver brocade with sapphire buckles and on the dressing table lay a silver lace fan. A silver ribbon was tied around the base of her throat above the deep, rounded neckline of the gown. Suspended from the ribbon was a sapphire pendant lent her by the countess. Her hair was left loose and flowing down her back except for the locks at her temples and the top of her head which were drawn back and tied with a sapphire satin ribbon. On each wrist was clasped a sapphire bracelet and sapphire drops glistened at her ears.

The countess's eyes swept over her, taking special note that she looked fresh and natural. She wanted Fidelity to appear as young as possible in direct contrast to the overpainted women of the Court. She stood as Fidelity picked up her fan.

"Ready?" she asked.

"No!" Fidelity breathed. "I'm so nervous!"

"Nonsense!" Divina stood still as a cloak of mulberry taffeta was draped over her shoulders. "Come now, we must be going."

With encouragement from the maids, Fidelity left her room and started for the coach that would take her to the palace.

The Strand was full of sound as coaches rumbled toward Whitehall where the ball in honor of the king's birthday was being held in the Banqueting House. From the window of the coach, after they'd made the turn at Charing Cross into King Street wherein lay the palace, Fidelity could see torches lighting the way for exquisitely dressed men and women to alight from their coaches and ascend the steps leading to the entrance of the grand Banqueting House.

"I wonder how the king can feel, having to dine and be merry in that building," Divina said as the palace loomed before them.

The earl brushed a speck of dust from his sleeve. "Royalty, my dear, even for all of its privileges must occasionally make the best of unpleasant situations."

"What do you mean?" Fidelity asked.

The countess pointed at the magnificent Banqueting House, its windows ablaze with light. "From a window in that very building the king's dear, dear father stepped out onto the scaffold to be executed."

Fidelity said nothing. Although not quite six years old at the time of the first King Charles's execution, she remembered that it had been a day of great rejoicing in her father's house. And now she was going to a ball in honor of another king—the son of the king her father had called a tyrant.

The countess read her thoughts. "You won't be the only former Parliamentarian there tonight, my dear," she laughed. "There will be the daughter of another of your father's cousins. Do you know Mary Fairfax?"

"Mary Fairfax!" Fidelity exclaimed. "Indeed I do! Her father, Sir Thomas Fairfax, was commander-in-chief of Cromwell's Parliamentarian armies. My father's regard for him was exceeded only by his regard for Cromwell himself."

"Be that as it may, Mary Fairfax will be there tonight as Mary Villiers. She is married to George Villiers, second Duke of Buckingham."

The earl laughed. "He is cousin to Barbara Palmer, the king's mistress. Royal mistresses run in their family."

"That's true," the countess agreed. "The present duke's father, the first duke, achieved his title through the bed of the king's grandfather, James I."

Fidelity stared from one to the other dumbfounded. Seeing her shock, they laughed and the countess patted her hand.

"How innocent you are of the decadence of the privileged. Nevertheless, at Court some practices are a matter of fact."

"Tell me why," Fidelity began, "the Duke of Buckingham wanted to marry Mary Fairfax. Did he fall in love with her?"

"Hardly," the earl replied. "Cromwell granted Buckingham's estates to Fairfax and, as Mary is her father's only heir, they will devolve upon her. As her husband, Buckingham will regain his estates. Soon probably, as her father is said to be very ill in his exile on the continent."

Fidelity opened her mouth to ask another question but the coach swayed to a halt. They had arrived.

As they entered the building, their cloaks were taken from them and they proceeded toward a set of double doors flanked by footmen in brilliantly colored royal livery.

The countess turned to Fidelity: "We'll go in first. After we've gone, you give your name to the men at the door. And don't worry!"

"But . . . but," Fidelity stuttered. She'd been nervous enough about coming at all, but to go in alone!

She watched as the earl gave their names to the lackey at the door. The lackey bowed and opened the doors for them. From where she stood, Fidelity could see the room bathed in light from hundreds of candles. She heard her cousins' names announced over the dull hum of conversation and music.

"The Earl of Wyndham! The Countess of Wyndham!"

The doors closed them from view as they began their walk to the other end of the long room where the king awaited his guests on his throne.

Fidelity hesitated but then she saw another couple entering the foyer and she knew she must hurry. The earl had told her that he would wait near the throne to present her and if others were presented before her there would have to be a lengthy explanation of their relationship to remind the king.

She moved toward the doors and was about to give the lackey her name when a voice whispered from behind her:

"Would you like company on your walk?"

She turned and found Schuyler Pierrepointe smiling down at her. "Oh, Schuyler! Yes, please, please come with me!"

Together they approached the doors and Schuyler gave their names. The gilded double doors swung open and, as Fidelity stepped through the doorway into the brilliantly lit room, she heard their names called out:

"The Baron Pierrepointe! Madame Fidelity Fairfax!"

"Madame," Fidelity remembered, was a courtesy title used for untitled ladies, married or not. With her hand resting on Schuyler's arm, Fidelity stepped into the room.

The Banqueting House, built by the great architect Inigo Jones for King James I, with its magnificent ceiling commemorating that king and painted by Rubens, was a riot of color as the mob of courtiers in their silks, satins, taffetas, and moires of every hue, gossiped and laughed, their jewels sparkling in the candlelight. The huge paintings on the ceiling seemed endowed with life as the flickerings of the candles made them seem to move.

But there was only one man who caught Fidelity's attention once she'd seen him. At the far end of the room, beneath a canopy of scarlet and silver, sitting on a silver throne, in a suit of black slashed with cloth-of-gold, sat Charles II—the king.

As Fidelity approached, she was scarcely aware of the uproar her appearance had caused. The ladies and gentlemen of the Court were a fairly small group of people who, because one was either born into the aristocracy or not, were unused to newcomers among their ranks. And such a beautiful young girl! The gentlemen were interested, the ladies enraged. It was the Court of a bachelor king who as yet showed no inclination to take a wife, and who was much affected by pretty women. They resented another entry into the royal sweepstakes.

But Fidelity's eyes were held by the tall, slender man with the flowing black curls and the wide black eyes. As she neared, she saw his white teeth flash beneath his black moustache as he smiled at her. She didn't notice the fabulously beautiful red-haired woman standing near the throne fix her with a murderous glare. More than any other woman at

Court, Barbara Palmer—the king's mistress—hated seeing a pretty girl presented to her royal lover.

As they reached the throne, Fidelity and Schuyler knelt and kissed the long, slender, deeply tanned hand of the king. His fingers were covered with rings set with emeralds, diamonds, and rubies of immense size. As they rose, the king rose from his throne, drawing Fidelity, whose hand he still held, to her feet. Shyly she looked up at the man who looked down on her from the twelve inches in height by which he towered over her. His long-lashed, black eyes held hers and she couldn't look away even when she heard her cousin, the earl, step up to them.

"If it please Your Majesty, I'd like to present my cousin, Fidelity Fairfax, who has come to live with my wife and me."

"It does please me indeed, my lord," the king drawled in his deep voice. "You are far more lovely at close range than you are from the top of Wyndham House, my dear."

Fidelity's mouth dropped open. "You remembered!" she exclaimed.

"I have a long memory for beauty," he said smiling. "Much to the dismay of my ministers who would rather I attended their lessons on policy as carefully." He raised Fidelity's hand and kissed it. He nodded to Schuyler. It was a dismissal and another couple were approaching to be presented, but Fidelity had to be drawn back into the crowd by her cousin.

"It seems our little Parliamentarian is struck with royalty," Schuyler smiled.

"Oh, shush," Fidelity hissed. She wished he

didn't have such a taste for political humor.

"I see," he persisted. "Now that you've met the king, you've no more use for your poor Schuyler."

"Schuyler!" Fidelity pleaded. She was aware of courtiers nearby straining to overhear them and she didn't want them to hear Schuyler making fun of her.

As the evening progressed, Fidelity found herself the center of much attention. Young gentlemen in satins and laces with the newest fashion in long, curled periwigs argued over her attentions and squabbled over who would eat supper with her. When the dancing began she was at no loss for partners and was glad for a slow coranto which was mostly walking and posturing, and for dances with her cousin and Schuyler with whom she didn't feel frightened of making a mistake in etiquette.

Between two dances she stood fanning herself languidly, resisting the impulse to flutter the fan violently to dispel the hot, stuffy air of the room. She saw a man making his way toward her as she stood flanked by the earl and countess. He was a large man, florid of face and gaudily dressed in chartreuse satin trimmed with gold lace. His hair, for it looked undeniably natural, was of a golden blond and curled haphazardly over his shoulders. He approached them and, bowing grandly to her as she curtsied, was presented as George Villiers, Duke of Buckingham. She stared at the tall blond man realizing that this was the husband of her cousin, Mary Fairfax, son of James I's favorite, and the cousin of the king's mistress— Barbara Palmer. Although he was only a few years older than the king—they had been playmates in the nursery—the duke's legendary perversions and vices were rapidly taking their toll and showed in the coarsening of his face and the slightly demented malice in his gaze. He took Fidelity's hand and kissed it and then held it imprisoned within his own. Subtly, Fidelity tried to draw her hand out of his grasp but the duke held firm. All the while he spoke to her his eyes swept over her in a way that made her want to pull away and run; he seemed to plumb the very depths of her soul with a look and he watched her as a butcher might look at a prize cut of meat.

When the king moved toward them, Madame Palmer on his arm, Fidelity was glad to be rescued from her captor.

Fidelity curtsied to the king and once again found herself staring enraptured into the depths of his black eyes. But she wasn't so mesmerized that she missed seeing Barbara Palmer tighten her grasp on the king's arm; her long, clawlike nails curled, digging into the sumptuous material of the king's sleeve, and Fidelity had the fleeting notion that the woman would have as easily raked them across her face. Nor did she miss the quick glance the king threw Buckingham. The duke responded to the king's unspoken command by taking his cousin's arm and pulling her away from the king.

"Come, Babs," he told Mrs. Palmer. "Come dance with me."

"No, George!" the exquisite paramour protested. But the king lifted her hand from his arm and placed it on Buckingham's arm. Rebellion flared in Barbara's violet eyes but she allowed herself to be pulled onto the dance floor.

"Would you like to dance?" the king asked Fidelity in his low, surprisingly soft voice.

"If you like, Your Majesty," she answered. She was tired and her feet ached but if the king wanted to dance with her she certainly would not refuse.

"No, I think on second thought, perhaps not." He seemed to have read her thoughts and Fidelity remembered that Divina had told her about this man's love of women and his uncanny understanding of their feelings. "How do you find the Court?" he asked when he'd led her to a window through which a cool breeze reached them from outside.

"It's beautiful! And so exciting!"

The king smiled and Fidelity recognized the same amused smile she saw in the faces of her cousins and Schuyler—the smile of the sophisticated courtier at the wonder of the newcomer. She felt a deep blush rising into her cheeks.

"I've embarrassed you," the king said in a kind voice. "It's just that we're not used to anyone who is honest enough to admit to being impressed by anything. We all strive to be more bored and boring than anyone else."

"You could never be boring!" Fidelity exclaimed, and then, remembering to whom she was speaking, blushed hotly once again.

The king's rich laughter drew attention to them as they stood apart from the crowds, near the window. "How charming you are, my dear," he smiled. "We must see that you are at Court more often. I enjoy your conversation immensely."

Fidelity curtsied and, when she rose, she saw Barbara Palmer pull away from her cousin the moment the music ended and rush to the king's side. He held out an arm to each of them and walked back toward the ever-moving crowd of people where Fidelity saw her cousins in conversation with the Duke of York—the king's brother—and his wife the former Anne Hyde, daughter of the king's Lord Chancellor. Their marriage the year before had been a great scandal as the Duke of York was his brother's heir and Anne was a commoner and the populace had no great love for her father.

Fidelity curtsied as she was presented to the Duke of York. He was blond and blue-eyed and not nearly, she decided, as attractive as his brother. His duchess was a plain, dumpy woman who had recently lost the child that had caused her hurried marriage. She smiled as Fidelity was presented and her look was gentle and a little wistful. Fidelity decided it would be easy to be friends with the unhappy duchess.

The king and Mistress Palmer, and the Duke and Duchess of York took their leave of the Wyndhams and Fidelity and moved away into the milling crowd. But before they were lost from view in the mob, Barbara Palmer turned her head and fixed Fidelity with such a vicious glare that Henry Fairfax burst out laughing in spite of himself.

Divina joined his laughter. "Why, you're a sensation!" she told Fidelity. "Your first night at court and you've managed to put the king's mistress's nose out of joint!"

But dirty looks from an irate mistress couldn't dampen Fidelity's spirits and so involved in the wonders of the ball was she that she didn't even notice that Schuyler was busy in a secluded corner paying outrageous compliments to the overaged, over-painted, overblown, but enormously wealthy Dowager Baroness Anna Melford.

# 14

Fidelity was soon the fashion at the Court. The king admired her and made no secret of it. Because the king admired her, the gentlemen of the Court admired her; and because the king and the gentlemen admired her the ladies made her their chief topic of malicious gossip. She and her cousins became the most sought-after guests for parties and suppers because it was said that the best way of assuring that the king would appear was to assure him that Fidelity Fairfax would also attend. The Court was splitting into factions by the day. One, composed of those who had attached themselves to Barbara Palmer's rising star, hated Fidelity with a passion and strove to invent new lies about her, hoping to turn the king from her. The other group, which saw Fidelity as the woman who would oust Barbara, squelched the rumors started by their rivals and praised Fidelity's modesty, beauty, simplicity, and unaffected manner. No virtue was too good for her to possess and no fault could possibly be found in her character. Among the latter partisans was the Duke of Buckingham, not because he cared about Fidelity but because he liked to annoy his cousin, Barbara. He had formed an unofficial committee whose professed aim was to replace

Barbara Palmer in the king's bed. Their candidate to fill that vacancy was Fidelity. For Buckingham it was a proposition with no possibility of loss. If the king were to fall out of love with his cousin by blood, Barbara, and then fall in love with his cousin by marriage, Fidelity, he would still be closely related to the most powerful woman at Court.

The Earl and Countess of Wyndham were by no means adverse to their cousin's rising importance at Whitehall. They were in demand as never before and new opportunities arose for them in the form of friendships in quarters to which they'd previously had limited access. Ministers and members of the king's closest circle were interested in guarding their positions at Court and that included courting the likeliest prospect for the king's next mistress and her family. And so, when the earl and countess sent out invitations to a ball at Wyndham House, those who received the invitations gladly accepted and those who didn't found it hard to conceal their disappointment.

Wyndham House was lit from without with flaming torches along the wall and circular drive and, within, crystal chandeliers and silver candelabra shimmered in the light of new candles. The floors were polished to a rich gloss and, at the windows, new drapes were bright in color and glittering with golden and silver embroidery. The servants complained of the stiffness of their new livery and the cooks in the cavernous kitchens complained of the enormous amount of food they were expected to prepare.

Divina hurried through the house checking on everything, followed closely by her steward whose job it should have been. Henry surveyed the supply of wine to be sure he had enough. Fidelity wandered around the house nervously, knowing that the party was largely being held as a result of her living with the earl and countess and she was worried that she would prove a disappointment in her capacity as assistant hostess and chief attraction.

She was dressed in a gown of magenta moire and the subtle changes in the material with the changes of light delighted her. Her accessories were of pearl, a single strand at her throat, a triple strand around one wrist, and drops at her ears. Her hair was left hanging loose as it was obvious that the king found it attractive. Part of it was pulled back into a small chignon at the back of her head and tied with a ribbon of magenta moire with long strands hanging to mingle with the rest of her hair.

At last the guests began to arrive, some by the front entrance and some, who lived near the river, by the water gate at the end of the garden where their stately barges were moored on the Thames. The guests began to mill about the house awaiting the arrival of the king, and the two court factions gossiped as Fidelity moved among them. Barbara's friends said that she was insipid and mealy-mouthed, and Fidelity's allies praised her beauty and poise.

The king's gilded barge slid into its moorings on the river and King Charles dressed in pale blue satin and gold and Barbara Palmer in bright lavender entered the house amid the bows and curtsies of the assembled lords and ladies.

Lady Wyndham accepted the king's compliments on her home and appearance and Barbara Palmer accepted Lord Wyndham's arm as he escorted her into the beautifully decorated dining hall. Tactfully, Lady Wyndham excused herself on the pretext of having to check on the kitchens so the king could speak to Fidelity. Following their hostess's example, the guest moved into the dining hall and stood behind their chairs to await the king.

"You look particularly lovely tonight," the king told Fidelity when they were alone.

Fidelity giggled. "I'm afraid, Your Majesty. I must differ. I look no more lovely tonight than I ever do."

"Ah, but you are not seeing yourself through my eyes," the king countered.

Fidelity giggled again. "If it pleases Your Majesty for me to look particularly lovely, then I am happy to oblige you."

"Thank you, my dear." Offering her his arm, the king escorted her into the dining hall where she was seated to his immediate left while a glowering Barbara sat on his right.

Soft music filtered from a drawing room where several of the older guests sat and conversed. From another room livelier music was played for dancing and in still another room several tables were set up for the gambling which was a passion of the Court.

It was at one of the latter that Madame Palmer was to be found. Gambling was her special addiction and, as the king paid all her debts, she had no need to worry about whether she won or lost. Her debts were enormous but while she was sitting with a pack of cards or a pair of dice in her hand, the king was free to pursue his own pleasures.

It was while Barbara was playing that the king asked Fidelity to accompany him on a walk in the sprawling gardens behind Wyndham House.

At the back entrance of the house there were flaming torches flanking the door. For the rest of the garden, the bright light of a full moon had to suffice. Fidelity and the king walked slowly along a path in the garden. From shady bowers which hid discreetly placed benches, the whisperings and murmurings of trysting lovers could be heard. As they progressed toward the river, Fidelity's hand clasped in the hand of the king, the atmosphere was almost unbearably romantic. They reached the end of the path and stood near a massive weeping willow that swayed with the breezes from the river. The Thames, on the other side of the garden wall, slapped at its banks and the barges moored there bumped on the waves.

In the shade of the willow, Fidelity heard the soft breathing of the king beside her. She cast about for something witty to say to break the overtly suggestive feeling evoked by the sounds and smells of the night. The fragrance of the garden, the sound of the water, the soft music filtering from the house, and the bright moonlight flickering through the branches of the willow, created a spell of enchanting romance that made Fidelity dreamily aware of the tall, darkly handsome man beside her.

While she was still trying to think of something to say, she felt the king's arm steal around her waist. She allowed her hand to slide up the soft, slick material of his satin sleeve. She made only a token protest as he drew her into his arms, and stood on her toes, stretching up to allow his lips to meet hers as he bent his head toward her.

Of the men she'd kissed in her life, Schuyler Pierrepointe, Nichodemus Crichton, Jamie Bowyer, Philip Wilmington, and now the king, there had been no two alike. She'd thought to find no man's kiss more exciting than Schuyler's for he held her heart in his grasp and she was passionately and romantically in love with him. But the king's kiss was different, subtly more experienced and exotic than Schuyler's. With Schuyler she had felt a wave of romance, a tender passion; with Philip there was the wicked excitment of a forbidden affair. With Nichodemus and Jamie there had been no sexual excitment; Nichodemus was a duty, Jamie a pleasant diversion. But this, this was something different. The king was an expert in lovemaking. Gossip had it, and the king never bothered to deny, that he'd made his first foray into the pleasures of love when fifteen years of age and with the nurse of his childhood—a woman of an age with his mother. During the years of his exile his chief pleasure and favorite means of taking his mind off his troubles had been the pursuit and conquering of exquisite women. His son, Jemmy, a delightfully handsome boy of twelve, already lived at Court. He was the illegitimate son of the king and his first long-term mistress, Lucy Walter, born while the king lived at the Dutch Court in 1649.

And now, in the secluded gardens of Wyndham House, Fidelity felt her will slipping away with each of the king's languid, probing kisses and the soft caresses of his long brown hands on her shoulders and body. At last he released her for a moment and, with a raggedly indrawn breath, she moved away as he would have drawn her into his arms once again.

"Your Majesty, please," she breathed. She looked up at him and found him looking at her with an intensity she had never seen even in her most intimate moments with Schuyler. His eyes, if it were possible, seemed darker, the black pupils dilated until they hid the walnut-colored irises. His lips were parted and a sudden breeze from the river ruffled his long hair into elegant disarray around his shoulders and face. Fidelity swallowed and trembled as the breeze swirled about, chilling her as it struck the light sheen of perspiration on her face and shoulders.

"Fidelity," the king said softly and, stepping toward her, kissed her cheek and forehead.

"No, please," she repeated, stepping away. She was trembling visibly but the cold had nothing to do with it.

The king was not offended. He was a patient hunter and liked to track his prey, preferring the fought-for victory to the too easy, too willing victim. He sighed expansively. "You're right," he said in slightly mocking tones. "I should have expected as much. You're so beautiful and even in the dark I'm an ugly fellow."

Fidelity, not used to the king's sardonic sense of humor, was alarmed. He was a kind man and so very appealing to her. "You're not ugly," she assured him.

"Oh, but I am," he told her ruefully. "My own mother was ashamed of me."

"Oh, no! It's not possible!"

She looked so concerned that he laughed in his

low, velvety tone. "Indeed she was," he told her. "But I fear it is something different that causes you to pull away from me."

"I . . ." She hesitated. The king was so cynical in his opinions of the world and especially, for all his prowess, in his opinions of love. She was loath to tell him of her love for Schuyler but she felt she must if he was to understand why she'd pulled out of his embrace. "I am in love with someone—" she began.

"The handsome Baron Pierrepointe if I'm any judge," King Charles replied.

Fidelity was dumbfounded. "Is that obvious?"

"Not to most, perhaps. But I make it a point to notice the romantic attachments of all the pretty women to whom I am so powerfully attracted."

He offered Fidelity his arm and they started back toward the rear of the house in which the dancing and gossiping and gambling would continue until the sky over London was showing the first rays of morning.

As they entered the house, Fidelity asked a passing footman where the Baron Pierrepointe could be found. To her surprise, he directed her to the room in which the dowagers and elderly lords sat quietly discussing the morals, or lack of same, of the younger members of the Court. As Fidelity stepped into the room several people nodded to her. She smiled in return but the smile froze as she spied Schuyler deep in conversation, on a small, cozy, upholstered window seat, with the Baroness Melford.

When she didn't disappear into or step out of the room, the king stuck his head through the doorway and saw what it was that had caused the reaction in her. Gently he drew her from the room and they stepped into a deserted anteroom where he waited for her to regain her composure.

"I don't know what to say," she began, struggling against the constriction in her throat that threatened to bring choking sobs with it. "I just . . . "

"It's nothing against you or the feeling he has for you," the king told her gently.

"But why? She is not young, or beautiful!"

"But she is very, very wealthy. When her husband died, his estate, which he miraculously kept intact throughout the war, went to his son. His country home, his town home, his title, two-thirds of his money. But the one third of his money that by law went to Lady Melford, his widow, was still enough to make her the richest woman in England. I've just granted Pierrepointe twenty-five hundred acres in the New World upon which he will grow the crops of his choice. It's an immense undertaking that will require a huge amount of money. Pity him, my dear, he is bartering the only possession he owns—his young and extremely handsome self—to buy a future he could not otherwise afford."

"But it's so cold, so calculating," Fidelity objected.

"It's also the accepted way of doing business. When I myself come to marry, and Providence knows my ministers are badgering me to do just that, I will sell my only possessions, the crown of England and the promise of English sea power for a dowry large enough to help make England at least reasonably solvent."

"But I thought you and Madame Palmer . . . "

"Yes, well, unfortunately Madame Palmer thinks

so too and there'll be hell to pay when she finds out the truth. As lovely as Barbara is she is not only married but nearly as poverty-stricken as I am myself."

He took her hand and led her out of the anteroom and back to the crowded salons where the ball went on. Taking her to her cousin's side, the king nodded to the Countess of Wyndham and sent a page to tell Barbara Palmer of his intention to leave for Whitehall. Leaving his mistress to hurry down to the mooring accompanied by the earl, the king walked back through the garden flanked by Fidelity and Divina.

"A most enjoyable evening, madame," he told Divina, kissing her hand as she curtsied.

"As for you," he told Fidelity. "We see far too little of you at Whitehall. I think that should be remedied." He kissed her hand as well but lingered noticeably longer than he had with Divina. "Would you like to spend more time at the palace?"

"Very much, Your Majesty," she told him.

"Good." His eyes told her he was genuinely pleased.

Barbara Palmer arrived at a hurried pace and, taking her abrupt leave of Fidelity and her cousins, stepped aboard the king's barge for the return trip to Whitehall.

Schuyler Pierrepointe and the Dowager Baroness Melford were married soon after the ball at Wyndham House. As Schuyler had already secured his grant of land from the king, there was nothing to keep them in England and they sailed for Barbados within a few days of their marriage.

Fidelity lay in bed. It was not her bed at Wyndham House but a magnificent four-poster liberally embellished with beaten silver. The hangings and tester were of a purple and silver brocade as were the drapes at her windows. The bed, and Fidelity, were in the bedchamber of the Wyndham's new apartment at Whitehall Palace. Though the apartment was given to the earl and countess, it was understood that it was primarily a way to have Fidelity at Court—and near the king. The bed in which she lay, far too expensive a decoration for even the earl's budget, had been a gift from the king. A welcoming gift to Fidelity; and there were many at court who were betting on how long it would be before he was sharing it with her. The marriage and departure of Schuyler seemed to the courtiers to prove their theories. It was well known that the Wyndham's young cousin was infatuated with the Baron Pierrepointe and now that he was gone there were none to stand in the king's way.

But if the king was optimistic and cheered by the departure of Baron Pierrepointe and his new baroness, Fidelity was not. For days she'd been morose, even the splendid rooms she'd moved into did nothing to cheer her.

The apartment was off the Stone Gallery, the main artery of Whitehall. The king's own private apartments lay off the corridor as well as his council rooms. The favorite phrase of the Court which preceded almost every choice piece of gossip was "It runs through the gallery . . . " On the opposite side of the apartment, Fidelity's windows overlooked the king's Privy Garden, the chief attraction of which was a sun dial whose perfection was famous throughout Europe.

Fidelity, in the opinion of most at Whitehall, was to be envied. The king was deeply infatuated with her, they said, and if she refused him for a while longer he would almost certainly be in love with her. She was the most serious threat to Barbara Palmer's eminence yet to appear at the palace. But could she take the prize in the contest? If her present behavior was an example, they doubted she could. To have the king ready to lay his heart at your feet and spend your time sighing over a mere baron! Unthinkable and yet her behavior seemed to intrigue the king. He sent several times a day to inquire after her health and once each day saw that she had a beautiful bouquet of fresh flowers from his garden delivered to her rooms. Each time she answered through a page and each time she refused to accept his invitations to leave her rooms and join him. As the days passed and the king continued to sue for her attentions, the ladies of Whitehall began to believe that Fidelity had not been so mistaken in her strategy. Had she, they asked one another, found the way to keep the king dangling? It seemed so. But, if they only knew, Fidelity was not locked behind her handsome doors planning her assault on Barbara's position as chief mistress. She was as depressed as she acted and as reluctant to get on with her life as it seemed. But then none of the courtiers would have believed it; one didn't admit to being depressed at Whitehall, it might displease the king and lead to a dismissal to the country. Surely

Fidelity didn't want that! Had they but known, Fidelity couldn't have cared less if she stayed at Court or retired to Wyndham House forever.

# 15

Barbara Palmer was frightened. She'd been the king's mistress for a year and a half and no one in that entire time had taken the king's attention away from her as Fidelity Fairfax was doing. Suppose he left her? She'd met him when she and her husband, Roger, had gone to him in exile at The Hague to take him a gift of much-needed gold. It was there that she'd fallen in love with him and had become his mistress. Roger had threatened, coaxed, and finally vowed never to have anything to do with her. She hadn't cared at the time—she had visions of a crown. If only the kind would marry her! To be Queen of England was worth whatever scandal there might be over her divorcing Roger. But the king showed no inclination to marry her. He was content with their present relationship—or at least he had been until the Wyndhams had brought their country cousin to Court.

The king was more infatuated than she'd ever seen him. Even in her own case there'd been an immense physical attraction from the time they'd first met. He was a physical being, delighting in the gratification of his senses, and she was as physical in her drives, but there hadn't been the feeling he seemed to have for Fidelity. He sighed over her, talked of her incessantly even in Barbara's company, and would have catered to her every whim had she been willing to let him.

If he was like this now, Barbara reflected, how would he be if she surrendered? If only she would indicate her willingness to surrender. Charles would gratify her every wish. What was her price? Barbara sensed that the girl was not innocent of the possibilities open to her as the king's mistress. And even if she were, her cousin the countess would have been more than happy to illuminate the situation for her. Suppose she asked, as the price of his entry into her bed, that Barbara be banished from the Court. It was a reasonable request. A new mistress would not be expected to enjoy the presence of the woman she was replacing. Where would that leave Barbara?

Barbara stared into her mirror. She was twenty, at the height of her beauty, although dangerously near the age when women were supposed to be past their prime. Fidelity was eighteen. Did those two years make so much difference? But it was more than age. Fidelity was beautiful; not more beautiful than Barbara but their beauty was of completely different types. Barbara's beauty was flamboyant, it struck one with an almost physical force. Fidelity was subtly beautiful, her looks made people stare, look away, and be drawn back to stare again. It was also the type of beauty that would last. It didn't depend on youth to be radiant. But it wasn't just beauty that attracted the king to Fidelity. If that were all it took there was an overabundance of beautiful women at Court.

It was more than that. The king was attracted to Fidelity's lack of guile and the fact that she didn't seem to understand that she had the potential to be the most powerful and important woman in England.

Barbara brooded. Perhaps she should have held out against the king instead of allowing him into her bed; indeed even urging him into her bed. But it wasn't her way to deny herself the pleasures she craved. She'd always been that way from the first time she'd taken a man into her bed. She couldn't be something she wasn't. And now she had reason to believe that she was with child by the king. What would she do if he turned her out? He might support the child; in fact he probably would, but what would her position be? Pensioned off at twenty; of no use to anyone. There must be something she could do. She wouldn't give up without a fight.

She put her mind to her problem with a passion. And she came up with an idea. Radical, perhaps, but only just possible. The king was a demanding and experienced lover; perhaps Fidelity was forbidding the king her bed not out of modesty but out of a dislike for lovemaking. For all his cynical good humor Barbara knew he was vulnerable and especially so where women were concerned. If Fidelity were delivered to his bed and showed that he disgusted and even repulsed her, he certainly wouldn't want her at Court for long!

A new piece of news ran through the gallery. Barbara Palmer had been seen knocking at the door of the still-sequestered Fidelity Fairfax.

Even Divina who answered Barbara's knock was so surprised by the visit that she could not conceal her shock. With no reasonable excuse to keep Barbara out, she stepped back and allowed the king's mistress to enter the apartment.

Fidelity sat in the drawing room in an elegant wing chair upholstered in blue and buff velvet. Dressed in a buff silk dressing gown, she seemed a part of the furniture. She thumbed through a book that she'd found in the apartment and looked up in surprise as the flame-haired Barbara entered the room.

"Mistress Palmer?" she said in a dubious tone.

"Good day to you, Mistress Fairfax," Barbara replied.

"Please sit down." Behind her guest, Fidelity saw her cousin trying to decide if she should leave her alone with her visitor. With a reassuring smile, Fidelity signaled Divina to leave them alone and the countess disappeared into one of the other rooms.

"Thank you," Barbara flashed Fidelity her most dazzling smile. As Fidelity tossed her book aside, her visitor surveyed her carefully.

Through the thin silk dressing gown, Fidelity's figure was plainly visible. She was elegantly slender although her body was femininely rounded. She seemed delicate, fragile, and beside her Barbara's more buxom and voluptuous charms seemed almost vulgarly obvious. Noticing that Fidelity had fixed her with a look of impatient curiosity, Barbara was prompted into conversation:

"What a lovely apartment you have," she remarked looking around the room that she knew had been decorated expressly for Fidelity at Charles's expense.

"You're very kind, Mistress Palmer," Fidelity answered.

"Barbara," she corrected.

"Barbara. Your rooms overlook the Privy Garden also, don't they?"

Barbara seethed. Her own rooms did indeed overlook the Privy Garden, but from its other side. That she, the king's mistress, should have rooms on the far side of the palace while this upstart's rooms were on the Stone Gallery was galling. "Yes," she answered, fighting to hide her irritation. "They do overlook the garden."

"How nice it is in the evenings. May I offer you some refreshment, Mis—er—Barbara?"

"Yes. I do feel a bit dry."

Fidelity started to rise from her chair. "Don't bother yourself," Barbara protested. "Why not call your woman?"

Fidelity returned with a glass of wine for her guest. "I have no waiting woman as yet. I imagine my cousin could spare me one of hers, though."

"Why, I've an idea," Barbara exclaimed taking the wine from Fidelity. "My own woman, Mattie, has a sister she's been badgering me to take into my household. Perhaps you'd like to engage her. My Mattie is an honest woman and a hard worker. Shall I send her sister to you?"

"If you like. I'd be happy to speak to her."

Barbara's fingers tightened around the stem of her wineglass. The girl was so cool, so self-possessed. Perhaps she felt she had no reason to fear her guest. But no, if she began thinking that way she'd weaken and lose faith in herself. "You really shouldn't hide yourself this way, Mistress Fairfax," she said sweetly.

"Fidelity," Fidelity corrected.

"Fidelity. It's so lovely outside, it seems a crime to stay in one's room. I'm sure His Majesty is most concerned about you."

Fidelity smiled, "Yes, His Majesty has been so sweet and generous. He sends me notes—and flowers." She nodded toward the bouquet of freshly cut blossoms in a crystal vase on the table.

Barbara longed to break the vase over Fidelity's silver-blond head. Instead she smiled and admired the flowers. "It was most intriguing about the Baron Pierrepointe's sudden marriage, wasn't it? I vow, it was the talk of the gallery . . . I'm sorry, have I said something? Oh!" Barbara pressed her hand to her mouth in mock surprise. "I'd forgotten that you and Lord Pierrepointe were involved with one another."

Fidelity recovered her calm and smiled. With an airy wave of one hand she dismissed the subject. "One must make the marriage which will benefit one most, mustn't one? Lord Pierrepointe needed Lady Melford's money to finance his enterprises in the New World." She remembered the king's words at Wyndham House. "Why, it's not so unusual. I suspect the king will one day find a woman whose dowry will help the country's finances." She saw Barbara's eyes harden and pressed her point home. "And one whose blood is royal enough to give the country children worthy of their heritage."

Barbara's hand was trembling and she sat the wine-glass down so its convulsive movement could be hidden in the folds of her skirt. "I expect that's true," she murmured.

If the courtiers in the Stone Gallery were surprised to see Barbara visiting Fidelity's rooms, they were even more surprised to see Barbara and Fidelity walking arm-in-arm up and down the gallery. Barbara, red-haired in white satin, and Fidelity, silver-haired in crimson silk, strolled the length of the gallery talking in whispers while Barbara pointed out various members of the Court and regaled Fidelity with tales of their many and varied habits and vices.

They were passing languidly down the gallery when, upon reaching the velvet drapes which hung in the entry to the king's private apartments, Barbara veered suddenly and pulled Fidelity through the doorway with no protest from the halberd-armed guards who flanked the draped entrance.

They passed council chambers and withdrawing rooms which were only slightly less crowded than the gallery itself. No one tried to stop them although many eyes followed them and many tongues began to wag. Without any hesitation, Barbara pushed open a closed, guarded door and pulled Fidelity into the king's bedchamber.

The king's bedchamber was more modestly furnished than many of the private apartments of his courtiers. Thick carpets covered the floor and two massive fireplaces yawned in the walls. Table and chairs stood in front of the fireplaces and near the wide windows that afforded one a magnificent view of the Thames as it ran behind the palace.

But the main feature of the chamber was the royal bed. Huge and massively built, it was covered in silver and hung with richly embroidered drapes. At the four corners of the tester groups of ostrich plumes, set in gold, nodded with the air currents.

Fidelity stroked the luxurious material of the drapes as she knelt on the window seat looking at the river. Barbara crossed the room and pounded on yet another door that led from the room. After a moment's silence, footsteps could be heard and the door opened.

"Barbara!" King Charles's head appeared around the edge of the slightly opened door. "Did I send for you?"

"No," Barbara admitted. "But I've brought a visitor to see you."

The king looked around the door and Fidelity smiled. He grinned at her and opened the door to enter the room. As he did so, a half dozen scampering spaniels rushed into the room.

Fidelity scooped up one of the dogs and it licked her face delightedly. Barbara, having become used to the dogs and their less attractive habits, pushed one away from her skirts with a gentle but firm shove of her foot.

The king, Fidelity, and Barbara sat near the windows, Fidelity still held the little dog on her lap while she answered the king's questions on her reasons for remaining so long in her apartment.

"I hope you are not disappointed in the Court," he said.

"No, not at all," she answered. "I didn't feel well."

He nodded and she knew he understood her meaning. "I hope you are over your discomfort."

"Thank you, Sire," she smiled. "I'm much better now."

"If you'll excuse me," Barbara told them, getting up. "The afternoon sun through these windows is giving me an intolerable headache." She drew the thick drapes across the windows shutting out all the light except a little at the far end of the windows. The room was dim now and Barbara returned to her chair, apparently pleased with herself. "That's much better, isn't it?" she asked, although not asking for or expecting an answer.

The conversation continued until Barbara ostentatiously placed a hand against her forehead. "God's blood, Your Majesty!" she moaned. "I fear the bright sunlight has already done its work upon me. I vow I must ask permission to return to my rooms."

"Very well," Charles agreed. He kissed Barbara's hand as she curtsied and watched as she walked to the door and left the room. He turned his attention to Fidelity and the conversation trailed off into an awkward silence.

Fidelity could feel the king's eyes boring into her and was conscious of his eyes at the white flesh of her bosom where her crimson gown with its white lace-trimmed neckline and her skin met. She raised her eyes and studied him as intently as he was studying her.

He had been in his private office when Barbara called him. He was writing letters and was dressed simply in breeches and a thin linen shirt. The diamond buckles on his shoes were his only jewels and his cravat was untied and hanging down on either side of his neck. The buttons of his shirt were undone at the throat and his shirt was open to reveal the thickly matted black hair on his chest. To Fidelity he looked much less intimidating than he had on the night of the ball at Wyndham House, and much more attractive.

After a few moments of tense silence he laughed softly, "Oddsfish!" he said. "Barbara must indeed love me! Enough at least to attempt to play the pimp!"

"I beg your pardon?"

"Do you think she actually had a headache?" His eyes were amused.

"Why I . . . no, I suppose not."

"No, not at all. I expect she thinks to get you into my bed hoping I will tire of you after I've had you."

"And do you think you would?" she asked mischievously.

"Never!" He paused. "I don't suppose . . ."

Fidelity glanced at the huge bed so prominent in the room. She lowered her eyes and concentrated on the silky ears of the spaniel she was stroking.

The king sighed. "I didn't think so." He stood and tied his cravat. From another chair in the room he picked up his velvet jacket and slipped into it. From a table he got his plumed hat and clapped it onto his head. Returning to Fidelity's side, he held out his arm. "I think if we stay any longer, gossip will have us lovers."

They left the chamber and, crossing the Stone Gallery, walked out into the sunshine of the Privy Garden. Fidelity held the king's arm and they laughed at the antics of the spaniels that had followed them from the king's apartment. Pausing by his prized sun dial, the king checked his watch and explained the workings of the dial to Fidelity.

As they walked in the garden, they were watched and by no one as closely as by Barbara Palmer who stood in her apartment window. She realized that her plan had failed and was disappointed but not discouraged. If one thing didn't work, she would try another. If Fidelity wanted a fight she'd get one and she'd rue the day she dared try to oust Barbara Palmer!

# 16

Fidelity walked along a gallery of the Royal Exchange, the mall whose shop-lined galleries sold everything the lady or gentleman of fashion could want. But it was more than a storehouse of merchandise, it was the meeting place of the fashionable world and the busiest place in London—excepting Whitehall Palace itself—for exchanging gossip, and making assignations.

As she walked, followed by Divina and her new waiting woman—Peg, sister of Barbara Palmer's woman whom she had recently hired—Fidelity heard a wave of comment rise in her wake. After more than two months at Court she had not ceased to be a source of speculation. Nor would she unless the King suddenly lost interest in her and that was unlikely, said the wits of Whitehall, unless she either refused his advances or gave in to them.

Nodding to the left and right, the black plumes of her beige, cavalier-style hat swaying, she acknowledged greetings from courtiers she knew and others who wished to have those about them think they knew her. It didn't matter to Fidelity; gossip would follow any woman on whom the king cast a covetous eye. The best course of action was to ignore it, for the best way to confirm rumor was to deny it too vehemently.

Leaving the Royal Exchange, Fidelity steered a course toward the street where her coach waited. Many of those in her way stepped hurriedly aside as she passed but stood closely enough to get a good look at the woman who had become the talk of not only the palace but those of the upper class in London whose chief occupation it was to ape the nobility.

Once away from the worst of the crowd, Fidelity slowed her pace and waited for Divina and Peg, who carried her purchases, to catch up with her. As she stood beneath the many-columned portico of the Exchange, Fidelity noticed a man who stood with his back to her in conversation with a pair of merchants. Hat in hand, the man's head was revealed and, although bald on top, what hair he had was closely cropped and red, not the deep flame-red of Barbara Palmer, but a bright orange-red which reminded her of Nichodemus Crichton. With a gasping intake of breath Fidelity turned her head away as the man swung toward her. It was her husband! Without waiting any longer for her cousin and servant, Fidelity pushed through the crowd and, startling a footman who hadn't seen her coming, made a running leap into her coach. She ventured a peek from the coach window but the crowd had closed around Nichodemus and she couldn't find him again. At that moment Divina and Peg arrived and, barely waiting for them to seat themselves, Fidelity pounded on the coach wall ordering the driver to take them back toward Whitehall at the opposite end of London.

"Fidelity!" Divina exclaimed as she saw how her cousin was trembling. "What is the matter with you?"

"Nichodemus!" Fidelity whispered. "I saw Nichodemus!" She pulled her hat from her head and leaned back against the tufted velvet of the coach seat.

"Nichodemus!" Divina's eyes mirrored the shock in Fidelity's voice. "Where?"

"Outside the Exchange," Fidelity told her. "He turned toward me, I was so frightened lest he see me!"

Peg looked curiously from one to the other. She'd never heard of Nichodemus; indeed Fidelity had only begun to take her into her confidence concerning the most insignificant of her feelings. But if she was waiting for enlightenment she received none.

"Do you think he saw you?" Divina continued.

Fidelity shook her head. "No, I lowered my face and my hat concealed my identity. I can only hope no one pointed me out to him and that gossip doesn't reach his ears."

The ride through London was a slow one on the best of days. Traffic was thick and delays frequent and in Fidelity's scarlet-lined, gold-trimmed, black coach with its six black horses and scarlet and gold liveried footmen and driver, all a gift from the king, conversation was at a minimum. Nothing Divina could say could drive the memories of the horrendous year she'd spent as the wife of Nichodemus Crichton from her mind. She relived the days, the nights, and the constant terrors and disgusts and they all contributed to the fear of being returned to him that was growing in her mind. If she were returned to his house, and by law he could force her to return, his vengeance would be terrible and lingering.

The grand coach turned through the gates of Wyndham House where Fidelity was to leave her cousin. A footman leaped off the back of the vehicle and, opening the door, handed the countess to the ground.

"It seems Henry hasn't returned from the city as yet," she said, looking for her husband's coach. "He said he was going to pay a visit to his goldsmith." She glanced at the pile of packages in the arms of a lackey who had come from the house to meet her. "I hope he gets enough gold to pay for all this." She smiled gaily at Fidelity but her humor was lost on her cousin.

"I'm sorry, Divina," Fidelity apologized. "Good-bye."

"Good-bye," the countess said as the door closed and the footman climbed up onto the back of the coach. "Try not to worry."

She waved as the coach rumbled out of the courtyard and into the Strand, turning in the direction of Whitehall, but Fidelity didn't look back and didn't return her farewell.

The Stone Gallery was crowded as Fidelity made her way toward her apartment followed by Peg and a footman who carried her purchases. The gallery was always crowded for, like the Royal Exchange, it was not open exclusively to the nobility but to anyone decently dressed and reasonably presentable. As they had at the Exchange, the crowds parted as they became aware of her identity, but Fidelity did not acknowledge their greetings as she passed; she did not even hear them, she was too preoccupied.

When at last she entered her apartment, Fidelity passed through her salons, reception rooms, and anterooms, going directly to her bedchamber. She allowed herself to be undressed and pulled on a dressing gown of forest green silk and matching mules. Plopping into a chair, she brooded as the shadows created by the sun's lowering toward the roofs of the palace entered her bedchamber's windows which, like the others in her apartment, overlooked the Privy Garden.

"Madame?" Peg stuck her head through the doorway.

Fidelity looked toward her disinterestedly.

"Will you be wanting to bathe before you dress?"

"Dress for what?"

"His Majesty is engaged to dine with you tonight."

"Oh! Dear God!" She jumped out of the chair and crossed the room to a massive wardrobe. She pulled a pink taffeta gown from the cabinet and held it out to the waiting woman. "I'll wear this; get the shoes, stockings, petticoats, chemise, and pearls I wear with it from the other cabinets. And for God's sake, tell someone to start heating some water!"

For the next hour the pace was frantic in the apartment allotted to Fidelity. She was bathed in a little tub set on the richly colored Perisan carpet of her bedchamber. She sat on the edge of her bed as her stockings were rolled up and garters of pink lace fastened at her knees. Her shoes were of pink brocade with buckles trimmed in pink pearls. Her petticoats were a froth of snowy white lace and her chemise was of a light pink which showed where the sleeves of her dark pink gown were slashed, and also at the neckline. The bodice of her gown was trimmed with pink pearls which matched the strand round her neck and those dangling from her ears. Her hair, left loose in the way for which she had become renowned, was curled at the ends and had two long curls at the sides of her face which were called "heart-breakers" and a sprinkling of tiny curls across her forehead called "favorites." Her face, due to the pink cast her dress lent her skin, was painted so lightly as to be unaffected and natural.

In her largest reception room a table had been set near the windows to afford a view of the moonlit garden, and a single candelabrum burned on a discreetly placed table. Silver plate and crystal glimmered on the table, and the room, hung in buff and blue and furnished with furniture of the latest French styles, was surely the most elegant Fidelity had ever seen.

"It is beautiful, isn't it?" Fidelity asked Peg who stood near her watching the lackeys readying the accessories for the meal.

"Oh yes, Ma'am!" Peg agreed. She'd been anxious to join the household of Madame Palmer and had begged her sister, Mattie, to find her a place. But when Mattie told her about Fidelity and her need for a woman, she'd been even more excited. Mattie had so often boasted of her importance as the waiting woman of the king's mistress that she'd been eager to join Fidelity's household, hoping that one day she would be the waiting woman of the woman who'd ousted Mattie's precious Madame Palmer from her high-and-mighty position. "His Majesty will have no eyes for the room though, once he sees you!"

"Now, Peg," Fidelity cautioned. The woman, not really any older than herself, was even more vociferous than the Duke of Buckingham when it came to prodding her in the direction of the king's bed.

As the clock on the black marble mantel of the fireplace in Fidelity's salon was chiming ten a lackey flung open the door and announced, "The King!"

Charles, dressed in royal blue satin and white lace, entered the room. The high red heels of his shoes, a recent import from the Court of his cousin, Louis XIV of France, were muffled by the carpet in the salon.

Fidelity sank into a deep curtsy and rose to welcome the king. "I hope you have brought a healthy appetite with you, Your Majesty," she said.

"Upon what did we agree the last time I supped with you, Mistress Fairfax?" he asked feigning severity which was betrayed by the twinkle in his dark eyes.

Fidelity remembered. "Charles," she said with a smile.

The king nodded. "Formally is quite all right for the public portions of our day but I would prefer to dispense with it in private. And in so pleasant a company." He kissed her hand and led her to the table near the windows.

As the moonlight illuminated the Privy Gardens, Fidelity and the king dined on roasted pigeons, rabbits, roasted chine of beef, marrow-bone pie, and anchovies. After the meal the table was taken away and Fidelity and the king sat on a walnut daybed with cushions of striped blue and white velvet. Fidelity leaned against the bolster at one end and the king sat near her feet, one hand caressing her ankle and the pink silk stocking encasing it.

"You seem preoccupied, my dear," he said after Fidelity sent for a decanter of Rhenish and goblets.

"I'm sorry," Fidelity said with a sigh. "Something happened today that reminded me of my—my family."

"I've always intended to ask you about your family. I've been given to understand that you're a member of the Puritan branch of the Fairfax family."

Fidelity blushed. She knew the king had no reason to enjoy the company of his family's enemies. "I'm sorry, Your Majesty, I . . ."

"No, do not apologize." He held up one long-fingered, brown-skinned, gem-encrusted hand. "I was merely getting my facts into perspective. It seems odd to me that your family would allow you to live with the Earl and Countess of Wyndham. Most people of their persuasion have little use for me or my Court."

"Your Majesty," she began. "Charles. I . . . that . . . they do not know I am here."

The king's black eyes widened. "Can it be you've run away from your parents?"

"No, that is what reminded me of my past. In the city today I saw the person I ran away from . . . my husband—Nichodemus Crichton."

Behind them, though they hadn't heard it, Peg had entered the room with a silver tray upon which sat the wine and glasses. Now she started and sat the tray and its contents down with a clatter.

"Just leave it, Peg," Fidelity told the girl. They were silent until they were again alone.

"Your husband!" The king chuckled. "God's body, Fidelity, you are full of surprises!" His full laughter rang out in the quiet room. "I confess I'd like to hear the entire story."

Hesitantly at first, then like one who sees an opportunity to find a much-needed release, Fidelity poured out her story to the king. Licentious he might be, a womanizer and carouser, but there were none who would accuse the king of betraying a confidence, and he listened to Fidelity's story patiently. His lean, dark face mirrored his distaste when Fidelity told of the circumstances of her marriage and of the treatment she received at the hands of her husband. He grimaced as she told him of Jamie Bowyer's death and her husband's part in it. But when she got to the part about her flight to London, she stopped.

"What's wrong?" he asked after she'd been silent for several moments.

"I don't know how to tell Your Majesty about this and still retain your affection and respect for me."

The king laughed again. "My dear, you have not the ability to have done some of the things I and many of my closest friends have done. There is nothing short of treason which could change my feelings for you."

At last she told him about the coach ride and Philip Wilmington, her highwayman. When she'd finished he laughed again.

"He's a lucky man," he said. "I would it had been me who found you and rescued you from your fiendish husband. Then perhaps I'd have collected his sweet reward."

The look in his eyes made Fidelity turn away. She rose from the daybed and, walking to the table where Peg had left the wine, poured a serving for herself and the king.

"I think you're trying to lead me from my objective, Mistress Fairfax, or should I say Mistress Critchton?"

"Fairfax, please!" Fidelity corrected. "I don't even like to think about Nichodemus! When I saw him today . . ." She shuddered and sat on the daybed once again.

"Let's not concern ourselves with it," the king suggested. "Shall I play you my newest tune?"

"Oh yes, please!"

Setting his wine aside, Charles rose and picked up a guitar which stood against the wall in the corner. Returning to Fidelity, he sat on the edge of the daybed as she lay propped against the padding of the bolster, her legs stretched out on the cushions.

After he tuned the instrument, which Fidelity had bought because it was the fashion to play the guitar, the king began a slow intricate melody. His low, bass voice accompanied by the guitar sang a song of love unrequited and the breaking of a heart.

Fidelity listened, her eyes closed in the darkened room. The only light source, the candelabrum across the room, was dim, its candles guttering out. The song was sad but exquisitely romantic and the king's voice softened in the silent room.

It was some time before Fidelity realized the king had stopped singing and had leaned the guitar against a table. He bent over Fidelity whose head lay back against the cushions of the bolster. Gently he kissed her throat and was rewarded by a low moan of pleasure. The song, the cool fragrant air from the garden, and the dark room lit only by the filtering moonlight had robbed Fidelity of her ability to refuse him and she opened her eyes to see his face poised above hers.

"Charles," she whispered and felt his arms around her as he kissed her passionately.

As Fidelity stared into the eyes of the king, she was startled by the sudden opening of a door and the light of two many-branched candelabras as Peg entered the room.

"Ma'am, I noticed the candles were going out when I brought in the wine . . . oh!"

Blushing, Fidelity pushed past the king and stood shakily. She opened her mouth to speak but Peg had already put the candelabra on a table and run from the room.

"Fidelity," the king's voice was husky as he reached for her from the daybed.

"I . . ." She turned from him and went to the windows. She stood fingering the drapes and heard the king sigh as he stood.

He came to her and wrapped his arms around her. "We can blow out the candles," he whispered.

She shook her head. It seemed silly even to her and she couldn't have explained it to the king but the shock of seeing Nichodemus had reminded her of so many things which lay so near the surface of her mind. Most of all, it reminded her of her family's teachings and of the physical side of her marriage.

She saw Nichodemus's face and heard him when he'd
mocked her and told her he'd lain with her waiting
woman, Kate, because as a woman she'd failed
miserably. How then could she dare make love with
the king, the most famous lover in the kingdom,
renowned throughout Europe? He'd find out that she
was all surface attraction and turn from her.

"I think I should be going," he said.

Fidelity walked with him to the door and
curtsied deeply. Rising, she held her face for him to
kiss but instead he took her hand and lifted it to his
lips. In a moment he was gone and the door closed
behind him.

From her bedchamber Fidelity could hear the
clock in the salon chiming four. The sun would soon
be rising to signal a new day and she'd been unable to
sleep for even a moment. She lay sprawled across her
bed atop the satin counterpane. She deeply regretted
her actions of the evening and yet she understood
them. It was the conflicting emotions of regret and
understanding that were at war within her, prevent-
ing her sleep.

She climbed from her bed and walked to her
windows to open one, hoping the fresh air would lull
her to sleep. Her fully cut lawn nightdress swirled
about her legs and the long bell-shaped sleeves
brushed her hands. As she pushed open a window she
saw a figure walking on one of the paths crisscrossing
the garden. She squinted into the darkness, for the
moon had disappeared, and recognized the tall, lean
figure of the king. He paused about halfway across
the garden and turned toward the other side of the
palace. Another figure stood framed in a window of a
dimly lit room. While Fidelity watched, the king

doffed his hat and waved it to the figure across the garden and the other person, obviously a woman from her silhouette, leaned from the window and waved back to him. Barbara Palmer! Fidelity backed away from her own window as the king again turned toward her and resumed his walk to the garden door which would lead him to his own apartments.

He had gone to Barbara Palmer! She could have kept him with her tonight but she had sent him away and he had sought satisfaction in the arms of her rival!

Fidelity was surprised at the wave of jealousy that washed over her. She'd come to depend on the king for her peace of mind and she couldn't deny that he stirred her senses. She hadn't realized she coveted him so strongly. She'd given herself so completely to Schuyler that she'd thought her feelings for the king were merely a substitute for her lover. But perhaps not. Could she replace Schuyler with the king? Schuyler, although he'd explained his reasons, had rejected her. But the king . . . the king would also reject Barbara Palmer someday when he married. Or would he? While it was fashionable for married men to keep mistresses, the mistresses of mere men were considered whores whereas the mistresses of kings were great ladies, feared and courted. If she couldn't have Schuyler perhaps she could have the king. Perhaps . . . She climbed back into bed, this time beneath the coverlets, but still sleep eluded her. Her thoughts this time, however, were not of regrets and betrayal, but of a future about which she must very soon make important decisions.

# 17

As the summer wore on, Barbara Palmer began to relax. Fidelity was showing no signs that her defenses were weakening before the king's attacks. So long as the situation remained that way Fidelity had no chance of gaining enough power at Court to have her sent away. And so long as Fidelity refused the king entry into her bed he would continue to seek out Barbara for his pleasure, and with Charles it was the woman who held sway over his senses that had the most power at Court.

But that was not to say that Barbara had dismissed the danger of Fidelity surrendering to the king. That was why she cultivated Fidelity's friendship, making herself the girl's best friend and trying to become her confidante. That was also why she continued formulating plans for ridding herself of the threat to her position.

Fidelity walked in Saint James Park with the Duke of Buckingham. She loathed the man, reminding her as he did of a dandified Nichodemus Crichton. His vices were long since legendary and although he possessed the intelligence and skill to become a valuable part of the king's government, he spent the greater part of his time and energy pursuing new ways of amusing his jaded senses. He'd given up his schemes for making Fidelity his puppet and thereby ruling the king through her but it amused him to annoy his cousin, Barbara, and so he continued to court Fidelity's favor and to urge her to supplant Madame Palmer.

Fidelity waved at a group of courtiers who had paused beneath a large shade tree and they returned her greeting. She passed alongside the canal the king had had dug by the soldiers out of work after the war's end. He'd had it stocked with miscellaneous water fowl and their antics amused her. She was eager to get away from Buckingham but was unsure of how to do it. And so she was glad to see Barbara hurrying toward her along the walk.

"Fidelity," she smiled. "I give you good day."

"Good day to you, Barbara," Fidelity returned. "Our cousin here has just been enumerating the many reasons why I should become the king's mistress."

Barbara shot the duke a murderous glare. "Someday, George, I shall slit your throat with pleasure."

"And someday, Barbara," the duke smiled, unperturbed by his cousin's threat, "I shall see you sent packing."

"I'll see you in hell first!"

Buckingham shrugged his satin-clad shoulders. "We'll see one another there one day at any rate." Turning to Fidelity he bowed gracefully, "Your servant, madame."

Fidelity curtsied. "Your servant, Your Grace." She waited a moment until he was out of earshot and began to laugh. "I swear, Barbara," she said. "Our cousin is not the most loyal relative I've ever seen."

"No, George amuses himself seeing how much trouble he can conjure up. He hatches plots like a chicken hatches eggs!"

As they walked, Barbara recounted a story she'd heard of the king and several of the younger, wilder Gentlemen of the Bedchamber going incognito into London to visit Madame's Bennet's, a fashionable whorehouse in Whetstone Park. When the bill was presented, however, the king found his companions had deserted him and he barely escaped a beating at the hands of Madame Bennet's bouncers before the proprietress herself recognized her royal guest and extended him credit for the evening's pleasures.

When she'd finished her story, Fidelity laughed. "I doubt not Madame Bennet would like to impersonate the ladies of the Court on occasion."

"Why?" Barbara demanded. "She is in the company of the gentlemen of the Court as much as we and she gets paid for it."

"It would be fun, I suppose, to go unrecognized among the people. The king is always so besieged by petitioners wherever he goes."

"Would you like to find out if it's fun?"

Fidelity looked at Barbara curiously as they stopped to sit beneath a shade tree on a stone bench. "What do you mean?"

"I mean we could go into the city and have a supper at a tavern. Not downstairs, of course, but perhaps in a private room."

"I don't know." Fidelity hesitated. She'd lived, since her arrival, in the comparative protection of Wyndham House and then in the guarded security of

Whitehall and she admitted that the sprawling, brawing city of London frightened her.

"Why not?" Barbara wheedled. "It will be a pleasant evening. We'll leave from Whitehall, go in a coach into the city, and come right back to the palace."

Fidelity allowed herself to be persuaded and they sat formulating their plans.

The King's Arms Tavern (and Barbara confessed she'd chosen it for sentimental reasons since she'd spent many a pleasant evening in the king's arms) lay in Philpot Lane not far from the immense and forbidding Tower of London. It was rapidly becoming dark when a black coach without identifying arms or any recognizable sign of ownership drew up before the tavern and two women stepped out. The footmen, dressed in plain black livery, were sent away and the women entered the tavern.

The taproom was crowded and as Fidelity and Barbara entered murmurs began running along the tables where men sat drinking, some holding buxom and flamboyantly painted women on their laps. There was no way the men could have identified the king's mistress and the talk of Whitehall; both women were enveloped in voluminous satin cloaks of nondescript design and color and hoods of the same material covered their hair. Their faces were covered from forehead to chin with black vizard masks which revealed only the eyes. But, covered as they were, their appearance still evoked comment; it was only a moment before the host, seeing them through the haze of the dimly lit room, hurried over and bowed awkwardly.

"Haply I could help your ladyships?" he asked. Like the men in the room, he didn't know the identity of his guests, but he recognized the tilt of a chin and the posture of confidence that marked the quality.

"I sent to reserve your best private room," Barbara told him.

"Oh, Yes! Yes!" Along with the reservation, Barbara had sent a generous deposit, with the promise of more. "Follow me."

The man turned and started toward the back of the room where a staircase led to the private dining rooms on the second floor. Barbara followed, herding Fidelity before her. Once a large man with oily black hair caught Barbara by the wrist but she gave him such a quick, smart rap on the arm with her fan that he pulled his hand away without protest.

As they mounted the stairs, Fidelity heard the speculative murmurs start again in the taproom. That they would be the topic of discussion for the evening she had no doubt.

The room to which the host ushered them was large and surprisingly fashionable after the damp, ill-lit taproom. Its floor was covered with a worn but obviously well-made carpet and the paneled walls were dark and softly gleaming in the light of the already lit candelabra placed on the table and on a cabinet against the wall. When she'd given the man her orders concerning dinner and the door was closed behind them, Barbara removed her cloak and mask and gestured for Fidelity to do the same.

"We can put these in the wardrobe," she told Fidelity, taking the cloaks to a large armoire against the wall. "But keep your mask for when the host comes back with dinner."

Closing the armoire, she sat on a brocade upholstered loveseat near a window and patted the seat beside her. "Come, we can talk."

Fidelity sat next to Barbara and smiled. "I confess I thought it would be more difficult than this."

"Coming to London for supper?"

Fidelity nodded.

"Nonsense, many people do it. If one brings the proper protection there's no reason why one can't go anywhere in the city, whenever one wants."

It wasn't long before the host and a young boy were back with trays of steaming food. As the places were set on the table, Fidelity realized that Barbara had ordered all her favorite foods. She felt a rush of gratitude for the red-haired woman who had no reason to like her.

When Fidelity had finished the last of her custard, Barbara called in the host and waited while the dishes were cleared away. When they were again alone, she sat down at the table and motioned for Fidelity to join her.

"I hope the dinner was to your satisfaction," she said with a sweet smile on her lips.

"Yes, it was wonderful! I fear I've stuffed myself."

"I'm glad you enjoyed it. You may have to do without food like this for a while."

Fidelity was puzzled. "Why? What do you mean?"

The sweet smile vanished and a look of angry resentment replaced it. "You have been nothing but a plague to me since the moment you arrived at Court. I'm sick of you and your airs. I'm sick of the way you keep the king dangling by denying him what you've no doubt given every man you've ever met!"

Fidelity stood and walked around the table. "Barbara, what are you talking about?"

"More of your innocent airs, Mistress Fairfax?"

"Barbara! I thought you were my friend."

"Oh, yes! You think everyone wants to be your friend. Well, they don't! And that was your mistake. Your fatal mistake. I've wanted nothing but to get rid of you since I first set eyes on you. I hate the sight of you, the thought of you!"

Fidelity sank into a chair and put her hand to her head. "I never suspected. You never gave a hint that . . ."

"That I hated you?" Barbara's smile was cruel. "No, I never gave a hint. But I waited. I waited to find a way and at last it was you yourself who provided me with a means." She waited for Fidelity to say something and when she didn't, continued:

"You act as though you stepped from a storybook, whole and pure like an angel. Saint Fidelity, the last of the holy vestals! Well, that's so much drivel and you know it! I've found your past, your secret, and I know how to use what I've found. I've gotten my revenge, Fidelity Fairfax. Or should I say Fidelity Crichton?"

The look of shocked terror on Fidelity's face was pure bliss for Barbara and she walked toward a door which connected the room in which they stood with another. Rapping sharply on the door, Barbara called "Come in!" to the occupant of the adjoining room and stepped back to watch Fidelity's reaction as the door swung inward.

The door opened with agonizing slowness and Fidelity rose and began backing toward the hall door. She knew what she was going to see, she knew what was there. And yet, when her fears were confirmed, the shock nearly drove her to her knees.

The door was fully opened at last and Barbara, grinning delightedly, watched Fidelity's face as Nichodemus Crichton entered the room.

# 18

"Nichodemus," Fidelity whispered. She longed to turn and run but the sight of him froze her to the spot where she stood.

"Good evening, my dear wife," he sneered. Turning to Barbara he bowed and kissed her hand.

"How . . . how?" Fidelity stuttered.

"Not very articulate, is she?" Barbara asked.

"Never was," Nichodemus replied.

"I assume you want to know how I found out about your marriage. It was simple. I suggested that you hire Peg as your waiting woman and of course you did. Because I was being such a good friend." Barbara's laugh was mockingly cruel. "Peg was sure that you were going to replace me in the king's bed and everytime the king visited you she would run to Mattie and recount the entire evening moment by moment. And so, when she heard you telling Charles about running away from your husband, naturally she thought it made you a romantic adventuress and she had to include the story in her narrative. You slit your own throat."

"What are you going to do?" Fidelity asked. She saw the evil smile on both their faces and panicked.

"If you harm me the king will punish you."

"Yes, yes," Barbara agreed impatiently. "Peg told Mattie how the king promised to protect you. Charles can be so gallant; when it's convenient. You'll find his good intentions quickly fade when it means exerting himself."

Fidelity looked at Nichodemus who had moved perceptibly nearer. "I won't go back to you!" she shouted. "I won't be your wife again!"

"I wouldn't have you back if you crawled on your knees," he snarled. "You were nothing but aggravation from the day I married you."

"Then why did you bother?"

He came closer and, closing one meaty red hand around her arm, jerked her to him. "Because you were beautiful and I wanted something in my bed besides a cold-fleshed, emotionless, callous-kneed Puritan, which my first wife was. I wanted you." He leaned closer to her and when his face was level with hers she spat, hitting him squarely beneath his left eye. With a roar of outrage he jerked away and slapped her across the face.

Fidelity heard Barbara gasp as she stumbled away from Nichodemus but he was after her and slapped her again. In his tiny eyes Fidelity saw the same light she'd seen there the day of Jamie Bowyer's death. She knew he meant to kill her and she scrambled desperately to move away from his grasp. But she saw him reach beneath his doublet and pull out a wickedly gleaming dagger and her fear found vent in a high-pitched, hysterical moan.

It was Barbara who pulled him away from her.

"Stop it, stop it, you fool!" she screamed. "We want her alive, we need her alive!" She pounded her fists against his wide back and finally succeeded in pulling him back and convincing him to give her the knife.

Fidelity slid down the wall and sat, panting with terror, on the worn pile of the rug. "Barbara," she whispered. "Barbara, I don't want to die."

"I didn't plan anything so drastic," Barbara replied, obviously a little shaken herself. In spite of herself she could well understand why Fidelity had run away from this man and thanked heaven for her own husband, the meek, retiring, complaisant Roger Palmer. "As I said before, I only want to be rid of you."

"Someone will find me. The king will search for me."

Barbara laughed; she had regained a little of her previous composure. "Don't flatter yourself," she smirked. "There is a kingdom full of women who would sell their souls to step into your shoes; women who won't be so niggardly with their favors as you were. It won't be long before you are a dim and infrequent memory."

"But someone will look for me. Divina and Henry, at least."

"No doubt they will miss you. They've never been so important at Court as they have since Charles has been running after you."

Fidelity huddled against the wall. She saw Nichodemus cross the room to a cabinet and, opening a drawer, pull out a sheet of paper, an inkhorn, and a quill. He laid them on the table and growled at her to come to the table.

"I don't want to," she said, feeling more brave since Barbara had relieved him of the dagger.

"I said come over here!"

"No!"

She watched him warily as he approached her and, grabbing her hand, pulled her to her feet. "Are you going to slap me again?" she said defiantly. "Go ahead, it won't be the first time."

He looked at her for a moment and his ugly face broke into an even uglier smile. "No," he told her, his voice sly, "I'm not going to hit you. I don't want to mar your looks. As a matter of fact, I find myself as attracted by your spirit as I was the first time I saw you. No, I don't want to hit you. I've been wondering whether your experience with men has improved your technique since the last time I shared your bed. Perhaps we could find out." He pulled her against him and buried his face in her hair.

"No! No!" Looking across the room, Fidelity saw a malicious smile touch Barbara's lips. "I'll do what you want," she told him.

Nichodemus released her and she walked to the table and sat down near the writing supplies.

As Barbara dictated and Nichodemus stood over her threateningly, Fidelity wrote a letter to her cousins. She told them she'd decided to go home, decided to return to her parents in the hopes that they would forgive her. No mention was made of Nichodemus because, Barbara said, there was no reason to arouse undue suspicions. At the end of the letter, Fidelity entreated her cousins to express her apologies

to the king and request that he not try to correspond
with her in any way. When she finished the letter she
signed it and Nichodemus whisked it out of her reach
lest she try to append some message of her own or
destroy the letter.

"You don't really think they'll believe that, do
you?" she asked.

"Does it matter?" Barbara sneered. "If your
cousins tried to contact you, would your parents
cooperate even if you actually were back with them?"

Fidelity's look told Barbara she was right. "When
they find I've left all my belongings they'll know I
didn't just pack up and leave."

"If you were to really go back to your parents
would you take all your Court finery with you?
Would you appear in church in your ball gowns and
jewels?"

With a sinking feeling, Fidelity realized that
Barbara had been thorough in her plans. She racked
her memory to find something which could save her.
"Peg!" she said at last. "Peg will tell!"

Nichodemus walked to the door through which
he entered the room and gestured for Fidelity to
follow him. Reluctantly she rose from the table and
walked to the door. When she'd reached his side he
pushed open the door and shoved her inside.

The room was dark and the force of his push
propelled her across the floor. Her foot struck
something soft and she tripped, grazing her hands on
the rough boards of the floor. She scrambled to her
feet as Nichodemus entered the room with a candelabrum. The room was dimly lit with the flickering light

of the candles and, on the floor between them, Fidelity saw a bundle covered in a grimy cloth that looked as though it may have once been a velvet coverlet. Setting the candelabrum on the floor, Nichodemus pulled back a corner of the material and looked up at Fidelity as she recoiled.

Peg lay beneath the coverlet. Her eyes were closed but above them, at her hairline, was a deep gash clotted with blood that matted her hair into a gooey mass.

"Is she dead?" Fidelity asked, fighting the nausea that threatened to overcome her.

"What do you think?" her husband smirked. He dropped the coverlet back over the girl and it settled, being already saturated, over the wound.

Fidelity stumbled back into the dining room, tears blurring her vision. She sat heavily on the loveseat and clasped one hand over her mouth. She used the back of the other hand to wipe away her tears. Her nose was running and, too frightened and sickened to worry about proprieties, she wiped her nose on the white lawn sleeve of her chemise. In her fear she didn't notice Nichodemus produce a small bottle from his pocket.

Barbara sat beside her and wiped her face with a handkerchief. "Come, come, you mustn't snivel."

"Leave me alone," Fidelity muttered.

"That's the spirit!" Barbara exclaimed and Fidelity knew she was being mocked.

"Let's get this business done!" Nichodemus snarled. "It's getting late. We have a schedule to meet. He won't wait forever!"

"He's paid to wait until we're ready!" Barbara snapped.

"Who are you talking about?" Fidelity demanded.

"You'll find out, soon enough."

Nichodemus sat down beside Fidelity on the loveseat after Barbara had risen and moved away. In his hand he held a small green bottle, about the length of his hand. It was none too clean and inside sloshed a murky liquid in which particles of something floated.

"What's that?" Fidelity asked.

"Full of questions, aren't we?" her husband growled. "Keep your questions to yourself, I'm sick of hearing them."

Fidelity looked at Barbara but the look of triumph on her face told Fidelity that there was no possibility of her changing her mind now. She was too near her goal to turn back.

Nichodemus pulled a mouldly cork out of the bottle's neck and threw it away. He wiped the mouth and neck of the bottle with one hand and held it out to Fidelity. "Drink it!" he commanded.

She lifted a hand to strike it away but the expression in his eyes halted her. She remembered Peg lying beneath the coverlet in the next room with her blood oozing from the gaping gruesome gash in her head. "Nichodemus, please!" she begged. It made her sick to plead with him knowing even as she did so that he saw her as a threat to his reputation even as she was a threat to Barbara's position.

"Drink it!"

She reached out and took the bottle from him. Its

surface was gritty and the thought of putting it to her mouth repelled her. "What is it?" she repeated.

"Drink it or I will pour it down your throat myself."

"Is it poison?" she asked. "Will I die from this?"

"You will die if you don't drink it!" Nichodemus shouted. He had little enough patience under the best of circumstances; under these conditions his patience was long gone and his nerves were dangerously frayed.

Slowly she raised the bottle and felt its mouth against her own. Small bits of the mouldy cork still adhered to its surface and, as Fidelity tilted the bottle, she felt them with the tip of her tongue. The liquid ran into her mouth and its foul taste caused her to choke. She spilled a little on her gown and Nichodemus steadied the bottle as she coughed. When she'd recovered he pushed the bottle toward her face again and she drank the rest of the fluid.

"Is it gone?" Barbara asked.

Nichodemus examined the bottle and bobbed his head. "Yes, every drop."

Fidelity gagged and swallowed trying to erase the bitter taste from her mouth. She waited for the cramps and agonizing pains she'd heard accompanied poison but all she felt was a growing sense of dizziness and the way the room seemed to be growing hotter. She felt a sheen of perspiration cover her face and shoulders and stood. Taking a few steps she gasped and threw out a hand grasping for something with which to steady herself. She started to fall but was swept up into Nichodemus's arms. He carried her back to the loveseat and lay her down with surprising gentleness. She felt herself being lifted once again and her cloak was wrapped around her. Through blurred eyes, Fidelity saw Barbara pull her cloak around her shoulders and clap on her vizard mask.

Nichodemus pulled her hood over her face and tied it as Barbara admitted four men to the room. As she gave them directions, Nichodemus pulled a wide-brimmed hat low over his face and shrugged into a cloak, turning up the collar to obscure those features the hat did not. He turned and followed Barbara out of the room and, as she hurried away to the coach she and Fidelity had come in and which was waiting for her in the street, he stopped and watched as two of the men brought the coverlet-covered form of Peg from the adjoining chamber while the other two plucked Fidelity from the loveseat.

It was done, there was no reason for him to stay. Without waiting to see the men and their limp cargoes leave, Nichodemus walked quickly toward the street where his horse was saddled and waiting.

# Part III

---

## The Voyage
## 1661

# 19

Fidelity opened her eyes slowly. Her head ached, throbbing dully, and her stomach was queasy and felt sore. Placing a hand on her stomach she felt, with alarm, that her ribs stood out sharply beneath her skin. She held a hand up in front of her eyes and was shocked at its appearance. Her skin was so pale as to appear nearly translucent and seemed merely a thin covering over the bones of her fingers. As her eyes became more accustomed to her surroundings she realized that she was lying in a bed apparently built into a corner, for two of its walls were paneled in dark wood and the other two were drapes from floor to ceiling.

Listening for a moment, trying to determine whether there might be someone waiting for her on the other side of the drapes, she decided she must be alone and reached a cautious hand out to draw back the hangings.

Slowly she slid to the edge of the bed and dropped her feet over the side. She pushed back the drapes and looked around the room. It was a large room; the walls were the same dark paneling she'd seen when she awoke. The bed on which she sat was indeed built into a corner and the other furnishings of the room were a table with two chairs, some cabinets, a secretary with several shelves and others items of furniture, all expensive-looking and apparently well crafted.

Across the room, one entire wall was taken up with banks of windows divided by a door. Drapes of a bright green trimmed with silver covered the windows and, Fidelity noticed, they matched the drapes on the bed. The floor was covered with a thick, deep-piled carpet of the same green into which a pattern of silver was woven.

Holding on to the post at the free corner of the bed, Fidelity stood. She realized, for the first time, that she was dressed in her chemise and looked around for her gown but it was nowhere to be seen. She rubbed her hand over the front of her chemise and found it stained and stiffened in places. How had she gotten so dirty? How long had she been here in this garment?

She walked slowly across the room toward the windows and tried the door between them. It was locked. She moved to one side and drew back the drapes from the window. Gripping the window jamb she trembled as she stared from the window and saw nothing but water. She was at sea! The strange unsteadiness she'd felt was not caused by her illness but by the motion of a ship!

"Oh, dear Lord!" she moaned. So this was what Barbara meant when she said she wanted to be rid of her. But where was she? Where was she going? She stared from the windows trying to see some hint of land. Perhaps they'd only just left England; but no, there was nothing that could possibly be land. She leaned against the side of the window. How was she going to escape, where would she go?

She tried the door again but it was definitely locked—not that it would do her any good if it had been open. It led nowhere except to a gallery, an open balcony running across the stern of the ship. It could take her nowhere except into the ocean.

Behind her she heard the rattle of a door latch. She turned. There were three other doors in the room; where they led and who might have the keys to them she had no way of knowing.

Stumbling slightly because of the motion of the ship, Fidelity hurried back to the bed and crawled in. She jerked the drapes back together and drew the covers back up to her chin. She heard the door open and footsteps enter the room as she fought to compose her face. The footsteps neared the bed and she turned toward the wall and waited trying to control the trembling her fear had started within her.

She closed her eyes just as the drapes around the bed were pulled back. She tried to breathe evenly but gasped in surprise when a man's voice said:

"Fidelity, I know you're not asleep. I heard you moving around the cabin."

She turned over reluctantly, knowing that her captor had found her out and obviously knew who she was. When she was sitting up she forced her eyes to meet those of the gaoler and when she did she nearly screamed. "Philip!"

Philip Wilmington smiled as he fastened back the drapes of the bed. When he'd finished he made her a little bow and said, "Give you good day, madame."

"What are you doing here?"

He sat on the edge of the bed. "I am, and I use the term loosely, the captain. You are aboard the *Virginian*, my ship."

"Your ship? You're the captain? But Philip, I didn't know you were a sailor."

He shrugged. "I did a little sailing during the king's exile. There weren't many Royalists who didn't since it was the only way to get out of the country."

"Then how did you . . ."

"Get to be the captain?" he supplied. "Right after I left you at Wyndham House I decided I'd had enough of England and the life of a highwayman. I went to America. Do you remember my telling you that my brother lived in Virginia?"

She nodded. "The Baron Wilmington."

"Yes. He and some other gentlemen have formed a partnership wherein they transport crops from America and bring back goods it's difficult to obtain there. As for me—one needn't be the best candidate when one's brother is the main contributor in a company. He wanted me to have gainful employment and so here I am."

"And you're able to keep everything under control?"

"The crew's experienced and my first mate is fully qualified to sail the ship but doesn't want the responsibilities of a captaincy."

"Oh, Philip! I'm so glad to see you!"

"Are you?"

Blushing, Fidelity knew that he hadn't forgotten what happened at Wyndham House. "You should have stayed that night."

"And intrude on your reunion? How did your

gentleman friend let you get into this predicament?"

"He married, for money, and went to Barbados."

"And left you . . ."

"Yes."

"How did you fall back into your husband's clutches?"

Fidelity told him of the Court, the king, and Barbara Palmer's betrayal of her to Nichodemus. "And when they took me from that room," she concluded, "they were bringing me to you."

He smiled. "I was approached by an agent of your husband's about taking an unnamed woman to America where I was to leave her; when I heard the name Nichodemus Crichton mentioned it wasn't hard to figure the identity of the woman."

Fidelity nodded and grabbed as her chemise slid from her thin shoulder. Pulling the garment up she gave him a rueful smile. "It seems to be too big now."

"You're much thinner than you were when they brought you aboard. You've lost so much weight. I don't know what it was they gave you but you've been very ill."

"For how long?"

"Almost two weeks. I've spooned what I could down your throat but it wasn't enough to do more than barely keep you from starving."

"Thank you, Philip, I appreciate . . ."

She was interrupted as a knock sounded on the door by which Philip had entered. Rising, he crossed the room and opened the door just enough to speak to someone outside.

From where she sat on the bed, Fidelity couldn't hear what was said but she recognized the deep tones

of a man's voice. Apparently it was a member of
Philip's crew. After a moment, Philip closed the door
and returned to her.

"I have to leave for a while. I'll be back."

Fidelity nodded. It was hard to realize that he
was the captain of the ship but as such he had to
attend to duties. He leaned over to kiss her but she
pulled away.

"Philip," she cautioned. "I must stink like a
dungeon."

He laughed. "I won't flatter you but believe me,
on a ship you can get much ripe worse. Sailors are not as
concerned with their appearance as are courtiers."

"Oh," she contradicted. "I've smelled a few fairly
ripe courtiers in my time."

They laughed and she leaned toward him so he
could kiss her.

After he'd left, she lay back in the bed and found
herself feeling as happy as she could under the
circumstances. Philip was a good man, he would take
care of her.

"Philip," she asked after he'd come back with a
bowl of stew for her supper. "Can't I have a bath?"

"I don't know," he replied. "The only fresh water
on the ship is in casks down in the hold. It's drinking
water and there'd be hell to pay if the men found out
you were in here dipping your bottom in water they
could be drinking."

"But Philip, I don't use so much water. Perhaps
not a bath, just enough to wash a little."

"I'll see what I can do."

He took her tray out when she'd finished and it

was a little while later when he returned.

He walked to another door and gestured for her to follow him. "Step into his room for a moment. I'll call you."

Stepping into the room, Fidelity found it to be much like her own but dreadfully cluttered. The clothes discarded over the furniture were all items of masculine attire and she assumed it was Philip's cabin. It adjoined her own.

She hadn't been waiting long when he called her back. As she walked into the room she found a cask and a large basin in the room.

"I had the men bring it up from the hold. You can use some of this to wash in, I'll have a rain barrel put on deck so perhaps we can catch some water for you to use."

"Why did I have to go into the other cabin?"

"I didn't want the men to see you in that," he pointed at her thin chemise.

"It's so dirty too, as dirty as I am. I don't suppose they sent any of my clothes with me."

"No, they didn't. I can get you one of my shirts if you want something else to put on. It's clean at least."

"Thank you. That would be fine." As he started for the connecting door between their cabins, she called to him. "And Philip?" He stopped and turned back to her. "Do you have a hairbrush and some soap?"

When he'd brought her the items she'd asked for and left the room, Fidelity pulled her chemise over her head and threw it on the floor. She poured several dippers full of the water into the basin and stepped into it. It was cool and it felt so good that she took her time lathering her skin and rinsing it again and again. Finally she knelt in the basin and washed her hair. When she'd finished, she reached for the towel Philip had given her and dried her skin and rubbed the water from her hair. When she'd wrapped her hair in the towel she pulled on the shirt Philip had given her. It fell below her knees and she had to roll the sleeves, which flapped past her hands, to an acceptable length.

When a knock sounded on the door she started. "Who is it?" she asked.

"Who do you think?"

"Oh, come in."

Philip entered the room and smiled at her. "I never appreciated that shirt until now."

Fidelity giggled. "How is it, Captain, that your cabin just happens to adjoin mine?"

"Because they're both part of the same suite," he replied. "These are the cabins my brother and his wife use when they travel."

"Then it's not really the captain's cabin?"

"No, that's upstairs just below the poop deck. My first mate is using it. I only use it when my brother is using these rooms."

"What should I do with the water?"

"The water?"

She pointed at the basin full of dirty water she'd washed in.

"I'll take care of it." He walked to the door between the banks of windows and unlocked it. Returning for the basin, he picked it up and took it to the door and out onto the gallery on the stern. Fidelity followed him and stood in the doorway as he poured the contents into the thrashing water behind the ship.

"Can I come out here, Philip?"

"Not dressed like that!" he pointed upward and there was another gallery above them. "It wouldn't take much to lean over that railing. I wouldn't want to lose one of my men because he leaned out too far trying to see you." He stepped back into the room and closed the door, locked it, and handed her the key. "Come with me, I'll show you where you can look at the ocean." He took her across the room to the third floor. It was unlocked and, stepping through, she found herself in a kind of sunporch. Enclosed and roofed, it hung on the side of the ship.

"And no one can come in here except me?" she asked.

"No. There's another like it off the other cabin on the other side of the ship. It's a convenience for stormy weather."

In the distance she saw another ship under full sail. "Who's that?" she asked, pointing.

"That's the reason we're here. It's a merchant-man, and there's another on the opposite side of us. They're loaded with goods bound for Virginia."

"And is this ship loaded with goods?"

"No, loaded with cannon. We're an armed escort to guard against privateers."

"And your brother's cabins are on this ship? I'd think he'd want to be with his merchandise on one of the other ships."

"If you were sailing and were attacked by privateers, which ship would you want to be on?"

Fidelity laughed. "The one with the most cannon aboard," she admitted.

"You're learning quickly."

Excusing himself, Philip left to return to his men and the running of his ship. As he left, Fidelity sighed and returned to her cabin from the observation room. Perhaps this had been a blessing in disguise, she mused to herself.

# 20

With the brief knock that had come to signal his entry, Philip stepped into Fidelity's cabin. He saw her immediately as she lay propped up on her pillows reading a book she'd found in the glass-fronted cabinet in the room.

"Philip!" She smiled. "Are you through for the day?" The sunset streaked the sky over the endless ocean surrounding them in spectacular shades of pink and purple.

"Yes," he answered as he rolled his long, full sleeves past his elbows. "Barring any major disasters." He dropped his hat onto the table and stopped to pull off his boots. In his stockinged feet, he padded across the room and sat on the edge of her bed.

Fidelity closed her book and rubbed the back of her neck. "It's getting too dark to read."

"Would you like me a light a lantern?" he asked.

"If you like," she shrugged. "But I'm not going to read any more tonight either way."

"Then I'll let you sit here in the dark."

Fidelity smiled and then remembered what she'd wanted to ask him. "Philip," she began. "When I was at the tavern in London the night I . . ."

"The night you were brought to me," he supplied.

"Yes. There was another woman there; my waiting woman, Peg. She was a young girl; Barbara Palmer placed her in my employ to gather information. The last time I saw her she was grievously injured. I thought that perhaps . . ."

He nodded, a serious look on his face. A flare of hope caught within Fidelity but his look smothered it.

"It was part of the arrangement," he told her. "I was to dispose of her body."

She felt tears sting her eyes and flow onto her cheeks. "Her body?"

"She was dead when you were brought on board. From the way I understood the arrangements, they always meant for her to die."

"What did you do with her?"

"A few days out of port we gave her a burial; a Christian burial such as any one of my crew would have if he should die at sea."

"You threw her into the ocean?"

"Fidelity . . ."

"Oh Philip, Philip, it's my fault. If I hadn't hired her she would be alive." She hid her face in her hands and grief and guilt overwhelmed her. "I killed her as much as if I struck her down with my own hands."

"No, Fidelity. It was a senseless death that you had nothing to do with. She did nothing serious enough to cost her her life. It was that Palmer bitch and Crichton . . ."

"But it was because of me that she became involved with them . . ."

She pulled the covers away and began to get off the bed to pace the room. Philip caught her and held her against him, encouraging her to give vent to her grief.

"I should never have gone to London," she sobbed. "I should have stayed . . ."

"With Nichodemus?" he asked. "Then perhaps it would have been you whose body slid over the rail into the sea. Or it could have been you whose neck was sliced through with a scythe."

"Two people," she said, remembering Jamie Bowyer and his innocent love for her which cost him his life. "Two people have died because of me."

"Two people have died because of Nichodemus," Philip corrected. "The man is mad. You can't rationalize the actions of a madman. For myself, I can think of one thing to thank him for."

She pulled away and stared at him, incredulous. "What could you possibly thank him for?"

He smiled gently. "If you had been a contented lady of the manor you'd never have been riding through the forest that day, a prime target for highwaymen."

Fidelity smiled. "I think, Philip, that we would have met somewhere, at some point in our lives."

"Perhaps," he conceded. "Perhaps."

Wrapping her arms around him, Fidelity allowed herself to be comforted and relaxed as he rocked her to and fro as he might have a child. She leaned her cheek against the rough linen of his shirt, her head cushioned by the thickness of his ruffled cravat.

It was pitch dark in the cabin when Fidelity awoke. She was tucked beneath the coverlet which was pulled up to her chin. Apparently she'd fallen asleep and Philip had lifted her into bed and tucked her in.

She lay in bed feeling the gentle motion of the ship moving along on the calm seas they'd experienced thus far on their voyage. The ship creaked and groaned and occasionally she could hear noises from the decks above, below, and on the same level as her own cabin. As she lay, images entered her mind but she couldn't deal with the conflict of emotions that accompanied them. The relief she felt at her own escape clashed with the guilt she felt over the death of Peg, who'd never been other then cooperative, loyal, and ready to be a friend.

She thought about the people in her life, her family to whom she'd never been other than a trial and an embarrassment—true, her mother had loved her but if she could have changed her daughter to please her husband she wouldn't have hesitated. Nichodemus—well—enough said, he'd never loved her, only lusted after her and when she'd failed to please him, he'd come to hate her. Her cousins had cared but she suspected they cared more because she could advance their popularity at Court. The king had cared for her, but who could say what might have happened if she'd become his mistress? Perhaps when he'd tired of her . . . And Schuyler, Schuyler was a sore spot that ached within her. She wished she could hate him, she felt she should despise him, but she could not. If he'd walked through the door this moment . . .

She shook her head trying to exorcise the thoughts of Schuyler. Schuyler had betrayed her, had valued money higher than her love for him. She mustn't think of him. Philip—she'd think of Philip. But so long as she remained there in her cabin, awake in the night, she would think of Schuyler.

Resolutely, she pushed back the coverlet and slid to the edge of the bed. Standing, her feet struck the soft carpet and her chemise, which she alternated with her only other garment, Philip's shirt, swirled around her calves and the sleeves fell into place around her arms. The neck was still loose and the ribbons which trimmed it at the neck, elbows, and hem were a little worse for the washings it had received. But it was clean and, at any rate, it was all she'd salvaged of the ensemble she'd been wearing at the tavern her last night in London. Her gown, Philip had assured her, was hopeless as were her stockings.

She walked silently to the door connecting her cabin and Philip's. The door latch gave easily beneath her hand and the door opened. She entered Philip's cabin and closed the door behind her.

Philip's cabin was much lighter than her own. The drapes at his windows were open and she could see the sea lit by a bright moon in a cloudless sky. The light, reflected from the water, lit the room and she picked her way around clothing and equipment Philip had left lying on the floor.

He lay in bed, the drapes of which were also fastened back. His deep brown hair lay spread around his head on the pillow as he slept on his back. One arm was thrown straight out away from his body and the other lay across his stomach. His hand was relaxed, draping down his side and the other was hidden beneath the edge of a pillow. His mouth was faintly smiling.

Fidelity knelt beside the bed and, with one careful finger, lifted a strand of the richly brown hair from where it lay across his forehead and let it fall onto the pillow.

"Philip," she whispered.

He came awake instantly and with one swift movement drew his hand from beneath the pillow. Fidelity, startled so that she fell back onto the carpet, found herself with a gleaming cutlass pointed at her nose.

"I surrender!" she exclaimed.

"Fidelity!" He laughed nervously. "I could have slit your throat!"

"I'm glad you didn't!"

She pulled herself to her feet as he put the cutlass aside. "Do you sleep with that sword every night?" she asked.

"It's not a sword," he corrected. "It's a cutlass."

"Well, that's a kind of sword."

"All right," he conceded.

She sat on the edge of his bed smugly as though his concession was a major victory.

"Is something wrong?" he asked.

"No," she replied. "Not really. I woke up and began thinking."

"You should never think at night. It's deucedly

hard to get back to sleep when you've been thinking of weighty matters."

"So I discovered." She hesitated for a moment feeling suddenly shy and awkward. She stood suddenly and started for the door. "Good night," she said.

"Good night," Philip said, trying to hide his amusement.

"I'll see you tomorrow," she said.

"Yes, I'll see you tomorrow."

She inched a few steps closer to the door. "I hope I can sleep now."

"Yes, I'm sure you will be able to sleep."

"Pleasant dreams, Philip."

He chuckled. "Pleasant dreams, Fidelity."

She backed toward the door and collapsed as she tripped over his boots lying on the floor. As she thudded to the floor she blushed furiously while Philip's laughter filled the room. Scrambling to her feet she stumbled toward the door and fumbled with the latch that had given so easily before. "Oh, Philip," she groaned as he laughed the harder. She turned back to him and saw him wiping his eyes. She picked up one of his boots and threw it at him but luckily her aim was as bad as her coordination and it missed by a wide margin.

"Fidelity."

She looked up from her hands in which she'd hidden her face.

He held out his hand to her. "Come on."

"Really, sir! Does your impudence know no bounds?" She assumed the injured dignity of a Court lady when confronted with an indecent proposal.

"Your airs make a scant impression, wench," he answered in his best threatening-sailor voice, "when you're standing in my bedchamber in the middle of the night with the moonlight shining through your shift."

She laughed and stepped, more carefully this time, back to his bedside.

He slid over in the bed and lifted the blankets so she could slide beneath.

"Sir!" she cried in mock alarm as he did so, "Have you no modesty?"

He laughed, lifting the covers farther from his naked body. "None whatsoever!"

She slid into the bed and lay still as he tucked the blanket around her. He propped himself on one elbow and draped his other arm over her.

"You know, Philip," she mused, stroking his arm with her hand. "This is the second time you've rescued me."

"My pleasure, milady," he smiled.

"I'm serious," she chided.

"So am I. I assure you when I met you in the forest in England it was nought but a pleasure for me."

"And me," she admitted.

He lifted his arm and stroked his fingers through her hair which shone silver in the moonlit cabin. Lifting a strand he let it slide through his fingers and drop.

"Oh, Philip," Fidelity sighed. She placed her hands on his sides; his hard, tanned flesh was surprisingly soft. Sliding her hands up his sides to his shoulderblades, she pulled him toward her and arched toward him, meeting him halfway in a tender, probing kiss that left her breathless.

Catching hold of the hem of her chemise, Philip lifted her and drew it over her head. As he lowered her to the bed once more he dropped the garment to the floor.

His sun-tanned body was warm against her own and she trembled in anticipation as he pulled her to him. His broad chest with its thick mat of brown hair crushed her breasts as they strained toward one another and their arms and legs intertwined.

Surrounded by the ocean that rocked the ship with its gently relentless motion, Fidelity was able to forget her past and the doubts and guilts that plagued her. She had found her contentment in the arms of a man who had been paid to be her captor and had become, for the second time, her deliverance.

# 21

Fidelity sat wrapped in a quilt as her chemise and Philip's shirt hung in the cupolaed observation room off her cabin. She'd washed them both and they were taking their own time to dry. She sighed as Philip entered the room.

"What?" he teased. "The sun's up, milady, and you still abed?"

"Your pardon, my lord," she replied sarcastically. "But it seems my wardrobe is slow a-drying this morning." She brushed a stray strand of hair over her shoulder. "Don't you have another shirt I can use? I really need another, two items of clothing just won't do!"

He laughed. "The eternal complaint of women." She shot him a look of exasperation and he stifled his amusement. "I'll see what I can do, sweetheart. Perhaps I can work something out." He leaned over to kiss her but she turned her face haughtily away. "Ah! I see how it is. I'll see what I can do and if I succeed, then . . ."

"Then I'll see what I can do!" she supplied.

He laughed again and bowed to her. "I'll try my best, milady, for I've a mind to spend a pleasant night in your company."

Fidelity sat before Philip's shaving mirror and brushed her hair. Her chemise had dried before Philip's shirt so it was in that garment that she was clad. She tossed the brush onto the table and pulled her hair on top of her head. She wished she had the supply of combs, bodkins, ribbons, and cosmetics that had been hers at Whitehall.

Through the open door connecting Philip's cabin, where she now sat, and her own cabin, she heard his familiar knock at her cabin door. "Coming!" she shouted and ran into the adjoining room.

She opened the door and stepped back in surprise as Philip entered the room bearing a large, ornately painted wooden chest.

"Why, Philip! Whatever in the world is that?"

"You'll see if you'll be so kind as to close the door." Fidelity closed the cabin door and hurried to Philip's side as he deposited the box on the table and unfastened the clasp. Carefully he lifted the top from the box and set it aside. She gasped as she caught sight of a pile of satin, pearl gray and pink.

With a flourish, Philip pulled from the chest a cloak of pearl gray satin lined with satin of a delicate pink. Draping it over a chair, he pulled out a gown of the gray satin with a deeply pointed bodice, a full skirt, and sleeves slashed to show the undersleeves. The slashes of the sleeves and the one down the front of the bodice were fastened at intervals with pearl clasps. Laying the gown aside before Fidelity's bemused eyes, he pulled out a pink brocade underskirt, a pink satin chemise, and a petticoat of frothy pink lace.

"Oh, Philip!" Fidelity sighed. "Wherever did you . . ."

"We're not finished yet," he told her. Reaching into the depths of the roundtopped chest he pulled out a square of satin wrapped around several pairs of pink silk stockings. There were also pink garters with pearl buckles and gray slippers tied with pink ribbons, as well as elbow-length gloves of gray. "Well," he said, sweeping the box from the table. "I said I'd see what I could do."

"You're a wizard! A sorcerer!"

"No, a captain," he corrected.

Fidelity ran her hands over the exquisitely fashioned garments, deeply creased from their long weeks in the box.

"Where did they come from?" she asked.

"From London," Philip replied, teasingly.

Once again Fidelity shot him the look he had become accustomed to when she was exasperated by his constant teasing.

"Actually," he began, sitting on the bed, "it's part of my sister-in-law's new wardrobe. She ordered it from a London dressmaker the last time she was there and I was instructed to collect it this trip. I had this brought over from one of the other ships where it's all stored."

"Will she be angry?"

"No." Philip shook his head. "She's a very generous woman and one ensemble out of her entire wardrobe won't make a great deal of difference."

With Philip acting as lady's maid, Fidelity pulled her old chemise over her head and waited as he dropped the softly luxurious pink satin chemise over her head. Over that he slipped the pink lace petticoat and then the underskirt of pink brocade which would show beneath the lifted skirt of the gray gown. But before she could don the gown itself, she remembered her shoes and stockings and, sitting on the edge of the bed, fumbled with the full skirts to draw on her stockings.

"Here, sweetheart," Philip offered. "Let me do that." He went down on one knee beside the bed and, holding first one foot on his knee and then the other, rolled on her pink silk stockings, fastening them at the knee with the lacy garters with their pearl buckles. He slipped one of the gray slippers onto her feet but it was at least a size too large.

"Oh," Fidelity pouted. "They don't fit."

"Never fear," Philip smiled. From a pocket he drew a large linen handkerchief and, tearing it in two, stuffed half into the toe of each shoe. Slipping the shoes again onto her feet, there were more nearly her size and, with the ribbons securely tied, would give her no more trouble.

Excitedly, Fidelity stood and held her arms above her head so that Philip could lower the gray satin over her. Once in place, she adjusted the neckline to show the beribboned edge of the satin chemise, pulled the sleeves of the undergarment down to show through the slashes of the sleeves, and arranged the slash down the front of the gown's bodice. Lastly she drew on the long gray gloves.

When Philip had finished fastening the back of the gown she found that it was a surprisingly close fit. The bodice, cut to fit the wearer tightly, was perhaps a shade too loose for fashion but then Philip had told her that his sister-in-law was not so slender as she. Nevertheless, after weeks in her worn chemise and Philip's shirt, she would have gone into ecstasies over a gown not half so lovely.

"What do you think?" she asked, turning slowly for him.

"You'd do justice to Whitehall itself, m'dear," he said with a bow.

Fidelity picked up the hooded cloak that completed the ensemble. With a swirl, she pulled it around herself and fastened it at the throat. "Well, my Lord Wilmington, do you think I may be allowed outside on the gallery now?"

"I can do better than that, Mistress Fairfax. What would you say to a stroll on the deck?"

Fidelity's eyes widened. "On the deck? Oh, yes!"

They left the cabin and, for the first time, Fidelity saw more of the ship than her cabin and Philip's. They went up a staircase and emerged onto the quarterdeck of the ship. Fidelity saw the merchantmen under escort, one on each side of the *Virginian*. She also saw crewmen nudge one another and point in her direction. She had apparently been a topic of conversation among the crew.

A tall man, dressed in dark blue from head to foot, approached them and made her a deep bow.

"Fidelity," Philip said, "may I present the first mate of the *Virginian*, James Macrae."

"Master Macrae," Fidelity nodded.

The first mate bowed again. "Madame. I am pleased to see you up and about. We all frankly thought you'd follow the other lady over the side."

Fidelity smiled. There was no use grieving for Peg; it would do no good and this man had no way of knowing that Peg was anything to her. "There were days, sir, when I thought so myself."

With another bow, the first mate returned to his duties. He was older than Philip and had about him an air of confidence that left no doubt of his abilities. She wondered why such a man would reject the captaincy of a vessel and be satisfied to be second-in-command.

During the course of her stay on the deck, it seemed that a constant flow of crewmen found excuses to ask their captain questions. Philip, the corners of his mouth twitching amusedly, would solemnly present them all and they made their bows with differing degrees of awkwardness. After one crewman, a particularly rough-looking character with a matted beard and skin turned a permanently sun-burned red beneath a thick coating of dirt, took it upon himself to kiss her hand, the others followed his lead and the men who'd merely bowed to her racked their brains to find another excuse to approach them in order that they might do the same. Fidelity was polite and offered her hand willingly, not showing the amusement she found in seeing them scrub their hands on their grimy shirts before they took hers, and their exaggerated politeness, sprinkling their compliments with "miladys" and "yer ladyships."

They were interrupted when, with a shout, the crew discovered another ship in the distance.

It was a smaller ship than the *Virginian*, perhaps a third smaller or more. It was traveling alone and Philip studied it carefully.

"It's a fluyt," he said at last.

"It's a what?" Fidelity shaded her eyes and stared at the approaching vessel which was approximately the same size as the merchantmen escorted by Philip's ship.

"A fluyt, a Dutch merchantman—and traveling without protection."

Philip began shouting orders and, after a barrage of commands passed between the *Virginian* and the two merchantmen flanking her, the *Virginian* began to pull away and steer toward the Dutch ship.

"Get back to your cabin," he ordered her.

"What's going to happen? What are you going to do?" she demanded.

He didn't take his eyes from the other ship when a crewman ran up to him and handed him a bandolier with a brace of pistols and his cutlass.

"Philip!" Fidelity cried. "Don't . . ."

He turned to her for a moment. "Get down to your cabin or I'll have you carried there!"

The crewman who'd brought Philip his weapons smiled. "I'll volunteer for that duty, Cap'n."

Fidelity turned and fled back down the stairs to her cabin where she bolted the door and threw off her cloak. She crossed the room toward the cupboard observation room but grabbed at a chair for support as a deafening blast of cannon fire made the ship tremble. Reaching the glassed-in room which hung on the side of the ship, she saw the prey, the fluyt, coming nearer, unable to match the superior speed of the *Virginian*. The ships closed in on one another but the fluyt made no attempt to return the volley of cannon fire Philip had directed at it. It was meant as a warning for the ships were only now coming to within range of one another.

But still the fluyt made no attempt at self-defense. In fact, as she watched, a dozen or more men emerged from the deck and the rigging and stood silently as the *Virginian* approached. The ships were lashed together and men from the *Virginian* swarmed over onto the Dutch ship.

From below decks, the crewmen emerged carrying chests, crates, boxes, and barrels which were handed into waiting hands on their own ship. A group of the crewmen brandishing pistols and cutlasses held the fluyt's crewmen at bay while their ship was methodically unloaded. When there was nothing of value left on the ship the ropes lashing the two together were cut and the *Virginian* pulled away, its decks loaded with booty and its crew boisterous in their victory.

The crew of the Dutch ship went back about their duties with a resigned air and soon the gulf between the victor and its victim widened.

The *Virginian* swung around and made its way back to the merchantmen awaiting it and the Dutch ship was lost to Fidelity's view.

There was generally rejoicing on the *Virginian*

that night. Among the treasures taken were barrels of liquor bound for New Amsterdam and the crew took these as their share of the loot. But in her cabin, Fidelity found herself facing an obviously annoyed Philip.

"But Philip," she argued. "They didn't attack us."

"They didn't dare," he argued back. "They hadn't the firepower or the crew. Those fluyts can sail with a crew of fifteen, there are one hundred and fifty men aboard this ship, we outnumbered them ten to one. And greedy bastards that they are, they're so anxious to carry cargo they never have enough cannon to protect themselves."

"They were merely merchants."

"They were Dutchmen. The Dutch are our enemies. I should have sunk them."

"The Stadholder of Holland is our own king's nephew."

"And the King of France is our own king's cousin but I wouldn't mind sending a score of Frenchmen to the bottom."

"You're a pirate."

"I am an agent for my brother. He is a merchant. Why do you think we are along on this voyage? Not to keep those other two ships from being lonely, I assure you."

"I don't want to discuss it anymore."

Philip nodded. "Good. Neither do I. And I suppose since it's stolen merchandise, you won't be wanting this?" From his pocket he pulled a packet which he dropped into Fidelity's lap as she sat in a chair.

She opened the packet and inside found a fabulous set of sapphires set in gold. A necklace, earrings, two bracelets, and a ring made up the set and Fidelity suspected Philip had chosen them knowing she couldn't resist and, by accepting, it would make her out a hypocrite. She handed them back to him. "Thank you sir," she said softly, "but they don't match my gown."

"Thank you, sir," Philip mocked, "but they don't match my gown." He tossed them onto the table. "Then throw them overboard for all I care." He made her a stiffly formal bow. "Your servant, madame." Without waiting for a reply he strode through the door connecting their cabins and, for the first time since they'd spent their first night together aboard the ship, the door was closed, separating their rooms.

Fidelity was torn between going to him and trying to reconcile their differences or going to bed and hoping all would be forgotten by the next day. She decided to go to bed.

Wrapping the sapphires in their packet, she tucked them away in a drawer of a chest which contained her old smock which she would now use to sleep in, and Philip's shirt. She laid the smock on the bed and reached back to unfasten the hooks which ran down the back of her gown. But they were intricately fashioned with material over-lapping them and the gown was made with the lady who had the help of a lady's maid in mind. She could have slipped it over her head, for the neckline was large enough, except that fastened, the tight waist was too small to pull over her breasts and shoulders. There was no help for it, either she was going to have to sleep in her new gown or she was going to have to ask Philip for help.

Meekly, she knocked at the door between the cabins.

"What is it?" Philip asked gruffly.

"May I come in?"

She heard footsteps approaching the door and it opened to reveal Philip in his shirtsleeves, a journal in his hand. He waited expectantly, one eyebrow raised.

"I need your help," she said quietly.

"With what?"

Exasperatedly, she stamped her foot. "I can't get out of this damned dress!"

Philip stared at her for a moment and then threw back his head and laughed uproariously.

"I fail to find the humor," she told him icily. But she turned her back and waited impatiently while he opened the tiny hooks at the back of her gown. She was embarrassed and angry, though more with herself for needing his help than with him for laughing at her. When he'd finished opening the hooks she turned and, with a curt "thank you," shut the connecting door in his face. The action afforded her a small share of satisfaction until she heard him laughing again as he recrossed his cabin to return to his journal.

She was still angry when she climbed into bed and jerked the quilts up to her chin. It didn't help her mood when she heard Philip, whose bed shared a common wall with her own, humming merrily while he prepared for sleep. Somehow, she felt, he'd succeeded in winning a battle of wills, a battle in which she was sure he must have held an unfair advantage. It was a long time before she managed to relax into sleep.

# 22

The ship rocked and the rain ran in thick rivulets down the panes of the windows in Fidelity's cabin. It had been two days since the rain had started and the damp seemed to creep into her very bones.

She lay on her bed giving less than complete attention to a book she'd begun several days before. The darkness of evening, not so very much darker than the overcast skies of the past two days, would soon make reading difficult. Not that it particularly mattered, she'd read a number of pages but if someone had asked she wouldn't have been able to tell them what the pages contained.

With a sigh she rose from the bed and crossed her room to replace the book in the secretary against the wall. As she closed the glass door of the secretary, she heard the door in Philip's cabin close and footsteps thud, muffled in the carpet.

"Philip?" she called as she went to the open door between their cabins. She was wearing her old chemise. She rarely wore the gray satin gown; only when she was going up on deck. She wanted to save it for the day when she had to face Philip's relatives. If they were going to have an uninvited house guest, she could at least be a presentable one. And she wouldn't want Philip's sister-in-law seeing that she'd ruined one of the gowns from her new London wardrobe.

Philip was pulling off his rainsoaked clothing and tossing it into a soggy pile.

"Philip!" Fidelity cried. "Those wet things are going to ruin the rug!"

"Uh huh," he grunted. Wearily, he pulled back the coverlet and slid beneath it.

"You're soaking!" Concern was plain in her every expression and gesture. She got a towel and, kneeling on the bed, rubbed his dripping hair. She pulled back the coverlet and toweled his skin where droplets still clung. At last she pulled up the coverlet and tucked it beneath his chin. She ran a hand across his forehead and was startled by the heat emanating from it.

"Philip, are you ill?"

"No," he managed a wan smile. "Just tired."

"I'll leave you then." She slid off the bed and hesitated. "Will you call me if you're ill in the night."

"Yes, I will."

"Promise now, if you're ill you will call."

"Yes, Fidelity, I promise."

"All right, if you're sure."

"Uh huh."

"Philip . . ."

"Fidelity!"

"Good night, Philip." Leaving the room, she closed the connecting door to be sure she wouldn't wake him with any noises she might make. She'd wanted to talk to Philip about his family and what she would do when they met but she couldn't keep him from his sleep. After all, he was the captain and he needed his sleep more than she needed to hear about what might happen at some point in the future.

The rain stayed with them doggedly, refusing to allow them out of its clutches. Fidelity stayed in her cabin pacing restlessly or sitting and staring out at the rain. She spent hours sitting in the observation room sometimes reading, sometimes pondering the turns her life had taken since she'd been at Fairfax House the stormy night that Henry and Divina Fairfax had arrived, bringing with them Schuyler Pierrepointe.

And she thought about Schuyler. Was he happy with his wife? Was he finding her money worth the life of a handsome young husband trading his desirable company for the money to buy a dream?

She thought about it more dispassionately than she thought she ever could. In London, when she first heard about Schuyler's marriage, she had been outraged, her pride was shattered. Now she could understand his action. Had Barbara Palmer's action been any less an act of self-preservation? How would she herself react if her most precious goals and values were threatened?

And Schuyler himself, how did she feel about him? As she stared out at the rain and the tossing sea surrounding the ship, she thought about Schuyler. Her love for him had been idealistic. Schuyler had been the perfect man; the perfect example of gallant young manhood. Now the image was tarnished but the man remained. In spite of her hurt she often wondered what she would do if he reentered her life. If he wanted her once more. There was more to be considered than old wounds; there was Philip.

When she'd spent hours debating her feelings for Schuyler and the door opened and Philip entered the room, she often felt a blush rise to her cheeks as though she'd been caught in some shameful act. She owed everything to Philip; she owed him her very life. What would have become of her if she'd been delivered to some other man that night; some ship's captain who cared only for the money Barbara and Nichodemus had given him. They had obviously made no provision for her well-being after she was aboard the ship or after she'd reached her destination. A less honorable man might not have cared if she lived to reach her destination. He might have put her overboard with Peg. He might not have even cared if she was alive or dead. She stared out at the cold, gray sea. Imagine being put into that water alive!

She shuddered and rubbed the goose flesh that had risen on her arms. She heard the door of her cabin open and was content to turn from the morbid thoughts of the past minutes to the more pleasing prospect of Philip's company.

Sitting in a chair before the banks of windows which overlooked the stern gallery, Fidelity gestured hopefully to another chair which faced hers. She'd been lonely for the last few days, Philip had had so little time for her. He sank into the chair and breathed a sigh of fatigue.

"You're not getting enough sleep," she told him.

"No one is," he shrugged. "Perhaps if this damned weather would clear."

"How long before we reach Virginia?"

He shrugged again. "Three days, or five, depending on the weather. If it clears and we get a good wind we could make up some of the time we've lost."

"How are your brother and sister-in-law going to react to having me there?" The question had been on her mind a great deal as they got closer and closer to their destination.

"They won't mind. They will be happy of your companionship for my niece."

"They have a daughter?"

"And a son. The daughter is seventeen, her name is Henrietta. The son is fourteen, his name is Charles. As you can tell, they were named for the late king and his queen."

"What is Henrietta like?"

"Plain, a little insipid. She's rather unhappily married."

"Seventeen and unhappily married?"

Philip smiled. "How old were you when you married Crichton?"

Fidelity blushed. "Seventeen."

"Her husband is a young man named John Hingham, his parents own a plantation just upriver from Edmund's."

"Edmund?"

"My brother. My sister-in-law is named Anne." He seemed to be warming to the subject. "Edmund is thirty-five, nearly five years older than myself. Anne is almost the same age."

"They married very young."

"Yes, they married during the war. It wasn't prudent to wait in those uncertain years."

"But you didn't marry."

"I wasn't in any one place long enough to find someone, and the life I led wasn't exactly one you'd ask a woman to share."

"Are you sure your family will have room for me?"

He laughed. "You've been listening to too many stories of how savage the country is and how primitive. Edmund and Anne have a fine home called Wilmington Hall. It sits on nearly two thousand acres of choice land and you'd be hard put to find a more serene and modern home anywhere in England."

"Then they don't mind having guests?"

"It's a rare day when there isn't someone visiting. The families visit one another often traveling up and down the river. And of course Henrietta's in-laws come frequently."

The tone in his voice changed as he spoke of his niece's in-laws. "Why do I get the impression that you're less than fond of John Hingham?" Fidelity asked.

"He's not the sort of man I'd imagined Henrietta would marry. At least not the sort I thought Edmund would permit her to marry. He is rather handsome in a foppish sort of way, the type you see at Whitehall paying more attention to the cut of his clothes and the curl of his wig than anything else. I suspect it's his looks that attracted Henrietta. He's going to inherit his father's plantation someday and he seems content to wait for it, doing nothing in the meanwhile. That's why he convinced Henrietta that they should live with my brother. If they'd moved to his father's home he would have been put to work. This way he plays the guest and spends his days at leisure."

"I think I met him at Court," Fidelity laughed.

Philip nodded. "His sort at any rate. You'll get to

judge for yourself if this cursed rain ever lifts."

But the rain didn't lift. The ship, although making slower progress than they might have under ideal circumstances, moved relentlessly toward land and the closer they got, the more nervous Fidelity became.

She found herself awake in the night unable to dismiss the feelings of doubt she was experiencing. She lay beside Philip as he slept the deep slumber of the exhausted, but she herself was unable to sleep. Afraid of disturbing his rest, she often rose and went to her own cabin where she could toss and turn or get up and pace as she pleased.

After four days the rain stopped. The morning dawned bright and breezy and as Philip dressed, Fidelity could hear him humming a little song. Well, he, for one, was happy to see the good weather return. She felt a pang of guilt that she'd wished for more rain. She thought of the crew who had to work in the foul weather and sleep in the damp clothes they worked in. But, though it might be selfish of her, she begrudged the ship every mile it sailed taking them closer to Virginia and Wilmington Hall.

Philip entered the room, dressed and ready for his day. He looked brighter and more cheerful than he had for nearly a week.

"Well, sweetheart," he said brightly. "Today is going to be a busy day for both of us!"

"Really? Why is that?"

"If this weather and this wind hold, we should reach Virginia by nightfall!"

"Oh, how exciting."

He noticed the lack of enthusiasm in her voice and looked at her with a little smile. "You're not still worried are you? I told you there was nothing to worry about." He hugged her and kissed the top of her head. "They'll love you, I promise."

With another kiss he left the room to go up on deck. But if he thought Fidelity was much reassured by his words, he was mistaken.

With the air of a condemned man ready to make his last public appearance on a gallows, Fidelity went about getting ready for an encounter with Philip's relations. She filled the basin she'd used for bathing and washed her skin and hair. She sat by the open windows of the stern and brushed her hair as it dried in the morning sunshine. Oh, how she wished she had cosmetics or even a few bodkins. But then perhaps they would feel more compassion for her if she looked like she needed their help.

Perhaps she should go ashore in her old chemise. Then she would appeal to their sense of pity, and no doubt to Edmund Wilmington's other senses too. The thought made her laugh. That was surely no way to incur Anne Wilmington's hospitality!

She opened the wardrobe and looked at the gray satin gown and its accessories which hung there. How would Anne Wilmington's sense of hospitality hold up when she saw a perfect stranger parading down the gangway in one of her new gowns? She felt the flutters of nervousness start in her stomach again. It would do her no good to worry, she told herself sternly. She resolved to push all thoughts of impending disaster from her mind. No, it wouldn't work. As

soon as she pushed all her old worries from her mind,
new ones rushed in to take their place.

Gathering any courage she could muster, Fidelity
began to dress and found herself fumbling with the
buckles of her garters and the ribbons of her shoes.
And the hooks of her gown were hopeless. Just as she
couldn't get out of it the first night she'd worn it, she
couldn't get into it without Philip's help. She sat
carefully on a chair waiting for him to come in so she
could solicit his aid.

The sun was lowering toward the horizon and
turning into a huge orange disc when Philip called for
Fidelity to join him on deck. He'd come to her cabin
once, earlier in the day, and hooked her dress. After
he'd gone she'd folded her chemise, old and worn as it
was, and put it into the large chest the gray gown had
been in. Also in the chest, folded in her extra pairs of
stockings, were the sapphires Philip had given her. All
her belongings barely covered the bottom of the big
wooden box but at least she didn't feel totally empty
handed.

She walked out onto the quarterdeck of the ship
and felt the breeze pull at her skirts and whip past her
face. Her hair was carefully tucked beneath the hood
of her cloak to avoid its being tangled.

"Fidelity!" Philip called to her from behind; he
stood on the poop deck at the very back of the ship.

She climbed the short staircase to the upper deck
and joined him near the rail.

"Look!" He raised his arm and pointed off
toward the horizon.

The sun, nearly beneath the horizon, silhouetted

the land now in sight. After almost two months at sea, they were fast approaching their destination.

The crew was jubilant, Philip was excited, and Fidelity was terrified. But whatever their mood, there was no mistaking the fact that they were home.

# Part IV

---

## Virginia
## 1661

# 23

Wilmington Hall stood on a wide promontory jutting out into the York River not far upriver from the Chesapeake Bay.

The *Virginian* lay moored with the two merchantmen at the hall's private docks.

It was dark when they docked but the light of a hundred torches lit the night as men swarmed over the ships. Philip went to supervise the unloading and from where she stood, Fidelity saw another man join him.

Fidelity knew it must be Philip's brother, Edmund, Baron Wilmington. They were of a height and nearly identical in coloring and build. There was a subtle difference which made Philip handsome while his brother was distinguished, but they were both very attractive men.

She studied the baron carefully until she saw Philip gesture in her direction and his brother turned to look at her. She busied herself watching the ships being unloaded and only turned back when she heard their booted feet climbing the stairs to the poop deck.

"Fidelity," Philip said, "may I present my brother, the baron Wilmington. Edmund, this is Fidelity Fairfax."

The baron bowed gracefully as Fidelity curtsied. "Welcome to Wilmington Hall, Mistress Fairfax. Philip tells me your journey was a dramatic one—you must be very tired. Permit me to escort you to the house where you will be able to refresh yourself."

Fidelity looked at Philip. "Shouldn't I wait?"

Philip shook his head. "I'll be here most of the night. You'd be better off to go with Edmund and I'll see you tomorrow."

"All right," she conceded. "Good night, Philip."

"I'll escort the lady, sir," another voice said behind her.

Fidelity looked around and found herself faced with a vision straight from the Stone Gallery of Whitehall.

John Hingham, husband of Edmund Wilmington's daughter Henrietta, stood on the poop deck of the *Virginian*. He was dressed in a suit of orchid satin with a profusion of lavender and violet loops of ribbon draped at his elbows, knees, and waist contrasting with the startling whiteness of the lace ruffles at his throat and wrists. His hat, of violet felt, had lavender and orchid plumes and his cloak, thrown about his shoulders to ward off the chill of the November night, was of purple velvet lined with lavender satin. His hair, partially concealed beneath his hat, fell past his shoulders in a cascade of curls. Fidelity couldn't tell if they were his or an elaborate periwig, but he was, in all, an incongruous sight among the sensibly, even plainly dressed men swarming over the ships.

When they were introduced the young man, who looked to be twenty-one or two, made Fidelity a bow that would have done credit to the Duke of Buckingham himself.

"Thank you, John," the baron told him in response to his offer. "I'll take my own guest to the house if you don't mind. You stay here and try to make yourself useful"—his eyes took in John's costume with the withering glance—"somehow," he finished.

Taking the arm he offered, Fidelity accompanied the baron off the ship and stumbled as they started up the path from the river.

"Oh!" she said, surprised. "I'm sorry."

"Not at all, my dear," he said. "Not at all. Weren't you awkward when you were first a passenger aboard ship?"

"Yes, I was," she admitted.

"If it was an adjustment to get used to the motion, it follows that there will be an adjustment to the lack of motion."

"Yes, I suppose . . . " she began but was interrupted by a figure running toward them on the ill-lit path.

"Charles!" Edmund snapped.

The figure skidded to a halt on the gravel of the path. Standing near him, Fidelity could see that he was a young man of fourteen or fifteen. This was Philip's nephew, Charles.

"Yes, sir," the young man said.

"Walk, do not run. The ships will be there when you arrive."

"But Uncle Philip . . . " the young man began.

Will also be there when you arrive. Say hello to our guest; this is Mistress Fairfax, a friend of your

Uncle Philip's."

Fidelity curtsied as the young man bowed to her. "Pleased to meet you, Ma'am," he said.

"Pleased to meet you, sir."

The amenities observed, Charles bowed to his father and walked sedately past them toward the docks. He wasn't far from them, however, when he again broke into a run and disappeared along the tree-lined path.

"He's a very handsome boy," Fidelity told the baron.

"We're very proud of him," the baron admitted. "Which leads me to my apology."

"Apology?"

"My wife is not here. A lady at a plantation up the river has been taken ill. As she is a great friend of my wife's, Lady Wilmington has gone there to help with her household until the lady is well again. I am sorry she is not here to welcome you as I am sure she would like to be."

"Please do not apologize. An unexpected and uninvited guest is no reason to take any trouble with accommodations."

"Any guest of my brother's is a guest of mine. I will send someone upriver in the morning to bring my wife home."

The trees which lined the path fell away as they entered a clearing in the middle of which stood Wilmington Hall.

In the light of the torches around its base, Fidelity could see that the house was large and impressive. All her preconceived notions of the primitive accommodations she would find in America were swept away.

Wilmington Hall was two stories high and only slightly longer then it was wide. The roof was steep and ringed with tall dormers. Four massive, ornate chimneys projected from the roof and the entrance sported a handsome white portico a single story in height. The white pillars and window shutters contrasted attractively with the dark brick of the walls.

As they approached, the front door was opened by a lackey dressed in deep blue. He bowed to Fidelity and the baron as they entered the foyer of the house. It was lit by a single, large, many-branched candelabrum which stood on a table opposite the lower flight of the grand staircase, and the light of the candles gleamed off the highly polished walnut paneling of the hall. Three other doors led from the foyer aside from the one through which they'd just entered the house. One of these doors opened allowing Fidelity a glimpse of a handsome parlor hung in green and lit by a crystal chandelier. Through the doorway, a young woman appeared—Henrietta, Philip's niece, dressed in yellow satin.

Henrietta stopped in the doorway, surprised by the appearance of Fidelity on her father's arm.

"Henrietta," the baron said as the girl entered the hall. "This is a guest of your Uncle Philip's. Mistress Fidelity Fairfax, this is my daughter, Henrietta Hingham. You met her husband on the ship."

"Ah, yes," Fidelity smiled. "Your servant, Mistress Hingham."

"I want you to show our guest to her room," Edmund directed. "Put her in the blue bedroom, I think."

"The blue?" Henrietta's eyes grew wide.

"Henrietta," her father said sternly.

Henrietta dipped a little curtsy. "Yes, Father."

Fidelity curtsied to the baron and, with a bow, he left them going back out the door which was again opened by the lackey who had appeared at precisely the correct moment.

"Sedley," Henrietta said. The lackey turned and waited silently for instructions.

"Go down to the ship and fetch Mistress Fairfax's baggage. And that of my uncle also."

"Go down to the ship, madame?" the lackey was shocked.

"Well, send someone then." As the man disappeared, Henrietta shook her head. "Heaven forbid a house servant should do the work of a yard servant."

"I saw a great many servants working on the ship," Fidelity observed as a young girl in a drab green linen dress took her cloak at Henrietta's bidding.

"Those were only the dockmen. There are also the slaves who work on the tobacco."

"Slaves?"

"Yes, you know—blackamoors from Africa."

"Really?" Fidelity was amazed. She'd seen only one blackamoor in her life and that was a dwarf in the household of the wife of the French Ambassador to the Court of England. He'd been a great curiosity wherever he went. "How many slaves do you have?"

"Counting the dockmen who aren't really slaves, they are indentured servants, there are a few over two hundred."

"Two hundred!" Fidelity followed Henrietta

across the hall and up the staircase, her hand sliding up the ornately carved banister. "It takes so many slaves to process tobacco?"

"Oh, yes," Henrietta assured her. "And my father is considering buying more."

"God's fish!" Fidelity exclaimed. "I would never have imagined it! My father had only a dozen servants to help run the farm."

"Your father is a farmer?"

"Yes." Fidelity stepped onto the landing behind Henrietta and started down a long hall which ran straight to the other end of the house where a tall, roundtopped window admitted light from the torches outside. The hall was lit by candelabra set at intervals up and down its entire length. They started along the corridor passing several doors. Henrietta pointed to one as they went by.

"My husband and I have rooms through that door. I wish we had our own home but I suppose that must wait."

They reached a door near the end of the hall and, opening it, went into a room hung in pale blue.

Fidelity stood in the room and looked about her. The room was large and its two tall windows faced the front lawn of the house. Through the windows she could see the flickering torchlight shining around and through the branches of the trees between the house and the docks. She turned back toward the center of the rooms as Henrietta lit a candelabrum on a table near the bed. She lit two more candles in pewter candlesticks on the mantel and another candle near the windows. The blue of the walls was enhanced by the white of the ceiling and the fireplace which was across the room from the bed. The drapes and the hangings on the wide, high tester bed were of blue and white brocade. The carpet was a dark blue into which was woven a pattern of light blue and white. Three doors, also painted white, shone brightly in the blue walls. One they had entered through; Henrietta opened another to reveal a generously sized closet. The third she opened with a little giggle. Through the open door, Fidelity could see a room hung in light green.

"Whose room is that?"

"Can't you guess?" Henrietta smiled. "It's my Uncle Philip's!"

"That's why you were surprised when your father wanted you to take me to this room?"

Henrietta nodded, giggling again.

The hall door opened and a maid entered. Taking a bedwarmer from the fireplace, she left the room and returned with it full of glowing coals from elsewhere in the house. With these she easily kindled a fire in the fireplace of Fidelity's room which soon began to lose its chill.

"Elly," Henrietta addressed the maid. "Bring our guest some warm water and towels." She turned to Fidelity. "Are you hungry? I could have something brought from the kitchen."

"No, thank you. I don't feel hungry at all."

With a wave, Henrietta dismissed the maid and then moved around the room. She showed Fidelity the desk with its supply of stationery, quills, and ink. She showed her the various drawers of a large chest and the extra quilts and sheets in a chest at the foot of the bed.

A knock sounded at the door and a lackey entered with the painted wooden box Fidelity's gray gown had been in. He placed it on the chest at the foot of the bed and, with a bow to the ladies, left the room.

"Where is the rest?" Henrietta asked.

Fidelity shrugged. "That's all there is."

Henrietta walked to the chest and opened the box atop it. Folded at the bottom were Fidelity's old chemise and Philip's shirt.

"I left England rather unexpectedly," Fidelity explained. "I didn't have time to pack."

Henrietta was burning with questions but something in Fidelity's posture told her she was straining their newly born friendship with her curiosity. Suddenly she snapped her fingers. "I have something that will be just perfect!" She left the room and Fidelity heard her footsteps moving away down the hall. There was the sound of a door slamming and then the footsteps returned.

Henrietta reentered the room, a streak of bright crimson cloth in her hands, and behind her the maid arrived with an urn of water and towels over her arm. Depositing them on a chest of drawers, she filled the bedwarmer from the hearth and, moving to the bed, drew back the coverlet and sheet and swept the bedwarmer across the bottom sheet. She went about her duties doggedly while Fidelity wondered what Henrietta was holding and Henrietta was bursting to show her. At last she was finished and Henrietta dismissed her with a wave.

Alone together, Henrietta brought Fidelity's attention to the garment she'd brought back from her rooms down the hall. It was a nightgown of crimson silk trimmed with wide ruffles of cream lace.

"Oh, Henrietta, it's beautiful!" Fidelity exclaimed.

"I'm glad you like it," Henrietta told her. "I want you to take it."

"Oh, no," Fidelity protested. "I couldn't! This gown I'm wearing belongs to your mother. Philip got it for me from her new wardrobe."

Henrietta bit back the questions that information aroused in her. "Nevertheless," she insisted. "You take this. It will look much better with your hair than it ever did with mine!"

Fidelity had to agree. Henrietta, although the same height and of similar build as herself, had hair of a dull brown that was neither golden or auburn. In the candlelight it had no highlights whatsoever and the bright red of the nightdress would only make it seem more dull.

Gratefully, she accepted the garment and saw the light shining in Henrietta's eyes. It seemed to her that the young woman was eager for a female friend and needed to be accepted.

After drawing the drapes at the window, Henrietta helped Fidelity out of her gown, petticoats, and chemise and hung them in the closet while Fidelity stored her shoes in a cabinet and her stockings and garters in a drawer of the chest. Taking the shirt she'd gotten from Philip and her old chemise from the wooden box, she hid them quickly in a drawer before Henrietta could closely examine them. She put the rest of the stockings in the drawer with the pair she'd been wearing and tucked her garters and the packet of sapphire jewelry in with her old garments.

Henrietta helped her as she slipped the feather-light silk nightdress over her head and it fell to her feet. Cut fully, it swished around her feet as she walked and the sleeves brushed her hands.

"It's beautiful," she told Henrietta. Stepping to a cheval glass in the corner of the room, she fluffed out her hair and watched as it lay against the red silk covering her back. The contrast was striking; she had to admit that Henrietta had been right.

Henrietta left the room again and returned with a gold hairbrush and comb. Fidelity ran the comb through her hair, pulling it over her shoulders, and then threw it back to cascade down her back once again. Henrietta took the comb from her and began to run it through Fidelity's hair.

"I envy you so," she sighed.

"Why ever would you?"

"Because you're beautiful." She saw Fidelity begin to protest but shook her head. "No, you know it's true. My father tells me I'm pretty and John does too but I know I'm really not. I see the way John looks at other women and then at me and I know he's comparing me to them."

"But he's your husband."

Henrietta shrugged. Changing the subject with a smile she asked, "You've come from England?" Fidelity nodded. "Will you tell me about it? I was only a child when my parents went to Holland after my father learned of the sale of his estates. He realized there was little point in going back to England. There were so many other poor courtiers."

"Your father's created all this in only two years?" With a wave, Fidelity encompassed the plantation.

"Not entirely. He bought the plantation from another man. But he's enlarged it considerably and he's also very successful as an entrepreneur."

"I see. He's . . . " Fidelity stifled a yawn and Henrietta jumped to her feet.

"I'm sorry! I'm keeping you from sleeping!"

Fidelity assured her she wasn't but she was not completely sorry to bid Henrietta good night. She'd never had close women friends and she found it hard to be as openly friendly as Henrietta obviously wanted her to be.

Pouring water from the urn into a basin, Fidelity washed. She dried her face and hands on one of the soft towels, pausing to stifle another yawn. There was a knock on her door and the maid who'd brought the water entered the room and took the wash water away, curtsying as she left.

Alone, Fidelity blew out all the candles in the room and stood for a moment in the glow of the fire in the fireplace. She went to the window and looked again at the torchlight from the docks. Philip was there. He must be tired. She looked around the room she'd been allotted and felt a rush of gratitude for the man who'd brought her across the ocean to the safety of this house.

Letting the drapes fall together, she crossed the room and slipped between the warmed sheets which were lightly scented with lavender. It was only a few moments before she fell into a deep, restful sleep.

# 24

"Philip," Fidelity said as she sat on the edge of his bed. "What did you tell your brother about me?"

He smiled and reached out to take her hand. "I told him you are the cousin of the Earl and Countess of Wyndham and you went to Court where the king was greatly attracted to you. I told him that the king's mistress conspired with some others to have you abducted to America and that I happened to be the one they contacted about transporting you. It's all true, isn't it?"

Fidelity nodded. "Yes, it's true. Not a word about Nichodemus?"

"Would you want me to tell them about him?"

"No!"

She smiled at Philip, feeling that the dangers of England and Nichodemus were far behind her. She was in Wilmington Hall nearly half the world away from London and the intrigues of the Court.

Philip's room was furnished much like her own but with those personal touches that spell the difference between one's room and a guest room. The morning sun lit the windows behind the green velvet drapes but as they were very thick the room was only dimly lit. As Fidelity's room was painted and hung in shades of blue and white, Philip's was in shades of green and cream.

"I am so very grateful to you, Philip," she began.

Philip shook his head and placed his fingers over her lips. "There's no need."

Fidelity kissed his fingers and, leaning over, kissed him softly. As his arms went about her, they heard pounding on Fidelity's hall door.

"Fidelity! Fidelity?" Henrietta's voice could be heard through the open door which connected Fidelity's and Philip's rooms.

"It's Henrietta," Fidelity sighed.

"What do you think of her?"

"She's really very nice and eager to be friends," Fidelity told him as the knocking continued. "But she has a horrid sense of timing!" She kissed him again and stood. "I suppose I'd better let her in."

Returning to her own room, Fidelity closed the connecting door and opened the hall door to admit Henrietta.

She stepped aside in surprise as Henrietta, followed by two maids, entered the room. Their arms were loaded with gowns of every color and description. Linens, velvets, satins, and silks spilled from their arms as they draped them on the bed. Two lackeys followed with boxes which they set on the chest at the foot of the bed. Henrietta waved them all out of the room and the door closed leaving her and Fidelity alone.

"Henrietta!" Fidelity exclaimed. "What is all

this?"

"Gowns, of course. And I want you to have them all."

"I couldn't possibly . . ."

Henrietta waved a hand, dismissing her protestations. "Nonsense. I have so many gowns. I've never even worn these. You see, there's only one mantuamaker in this whole area and when she comes to Wilmington Hall I order everything in sight because I'm afraid I won't have enough gowns to last until she comes back. And I order the wrong colors. With my coloring, I should only wear pastels. These bright colors make me fade terribly. But with your coloring, they will look marvelous!"

She began pulling the gowns from the bed and holding them up for Fidelity's inspection. Bright pinks, deep blues, forest greens, dark violets, vivid apricots, they were all beautifully fashioned and exquisitely made and, as she displayed each gown, she opened a little box from the chest near the bed and showed Fidelity the accessories that went with the gown. Shoes (which, to Fidelity's delight, fit her exactly), gloves, fans, a large fur muff which went with a black velvet, fur-lined, hooded cloak, and with a flourish Henrietta opened a large lacquered box to display an array of cosmetics, combs, bodkins, and ribbons. From the corner of the last box, Henrietta produced another, smaller box of silver. Inside Fidelity found a collection of tiny black taffeta patches like the ones worn by the ladies of the Court.

"I could never get enough nerve to wear them," Henrietta confessed sheepishly.

Fidelity laughed. "I'll wear them if you will."

"I will then!" Henrietta agreed. "I'm so glad you've come!"

They sorted through the pile of gowns happily, trying them on and laughing. Fidelity was holding a gown of sapphire blue in front of herself in the mirror, thinking how lovely Philip's sapphires would be with it, while Henrietta went in search of the accessories that went with it. She was wearing a chemise of delicate cream lace and blue high-heeled shoes with cream silk stockings. As she stood before the mirror she heard the tiny squeak of the hall door opening and, thinking it was Henrietta returning, asked: "Did you find what you were looking for?"

"So it seems," a masculine voice replied.

Fidelity spun around holding the gown before her for cover rather than for effect. She found John Hingham standing just inside the doorway. He wore a suit of sea green velvet trimmed with gold embroidery. "What do you want?" she demanded.

"What I don't expect you're willing to give me," he told her insolently. "Actually I'm looking for my wife."

"She went to your rooms to . . . " She was cut off by Henrietta's arrival.

"Why, John," Henrietta said, seeming not surprised to find him there. "Were you looking for me?"

"Yes," he answered coolly. "I've been instructed to tell you that your mother will be returning shortly. And also that your breakfast has been waiting downstairs for some time."

"Very well, as soon as Fidelity is dressed we will

be down."

"She looks very tempting just the way she is."
His coldly blue eyes swept over Fidelity once more.

Henrietta giggled. "Oh, John! How naughty you
are!" She pushed him playfully from the room and
turned back to Fidelity. "He always tries to make me
jealous!" She giggled again. "You mustn't let John
upset you."

"No, I won't," Fidelity assured her, but the look
she had seen in John's eyes was not the look of a
harmless prankster. Could Henrietta really be so
blind to her husband's lechery?

Fidelity dressed in a pretty linen gown of apricot
trimmed with lace. Leaving her room, she went with
Henrietta downstairs and to the dining room for their
morning meal.

Ann, the Baroness Wilmington, stepped off the
barge on which she'd returned to Wilmington Hall
and smiled as she saw her family there on the dock
waiting for her.

She was a handsome woman, not much taller
than Fidelity or Henrietta but with a plumpish figure
and rosy cheeks. Her coloring was similar to Henrietta's and, in fact, she looked like an older, more buxom
version of her daughter.

"Welcome home, my dear." The baron stepped
forward and slipped his arm affectionately around his
wife's waist. "Philip is home as you see. And he has
brought with him a lovely guest."

The baron brought his wife to where Fidelity
stood and said: "My dear, this is Mistress Fidelity

Fairfax. She is a cousin of Henry and Divina Fairfax. Fidelity, this is the Baroness Wilmington."

Fidelity curtsied and returned Anne Wilmington's warm smile as the baroness said: "Ah! The Earl and Countess of Wyndham! And how are your cousins?"

"Very well, your ladyship. Frequenting the Court."

"How exciting! You must tell me all the newest gossip."

"I'd like that, very much."

"So would I, but don't tell Edmund." She leaned closer and whispered, loudly enough for her husband beside her to hear, "Edmund doesn't know I like gossip."

The baron laughed and they started for the house. Fidelity noticed, as they went, that the baroness had been most happy to see her daughter and son and was quite pleasant in her welcome of Philip, but dismissed her son-in-law with a curt, "Hello, John." Obviously, Master Hingham was not the most popular inhabitant of Wilmington Hall and she wondered what it was, apart from his apparent lack of inclination for work and dandified appearance, that caused it.

Wearing a plumed hat to protect her face from the bright afternoon sun, and a velvet cloak to ward off the chilling November breezes, Fidelity walked through the gardens at the back of Wilmington Hall with Philip who had volunteered to take her on a tour of the plantation.

"Philip," she said when they were past the wrought-iron garden gates and well away from the house. "Why don't your brother and sister-in-law like Henrietta's husband?"

"Do you find him a particularly likeable man?"

"No," she admitted, remembering the scene in her room that morning, "but there seems to be more than mere dislike of his laziness and attitude. They seem, at times, to positively loathe him."

Philip waved his hand in acknowledgement of a greeting from a huge black man he identified as Joshua—a slave who'd shown an amazing aptitude for the exotic plants of the garden and who now regarded it as his private domain. "Soon after Henrietta and John were married last year, there was a scandal concerning the daughter of an indentured servant on his father's plantation. It seems John had attacked the girl, forced himself upon her. She found she was pregnant and drowned herself. Her father, in his grief, tried to kill John and was himself killed— John shot him. Of course, since the attacker had been a servant and John was the son of the master of the plantation, no charges were brought against him. Few questions were asked in fact. Henrietta knows nothing of this, or of the rumors that John's frequent business trips to neighboring plantations are really assignations with the wives and daughters of the planters. There have also been rumors of his interest in the young slave women but, that I know of, those are nothing more than rumors."

"I see." Fidelity shuddered. She felt sorry for Henrietta and suddenly thought she'd been fortunate in that Nichodemus had had only one mistress, her waiting woman. Apparently John had the same capacity for violence that Nichodemus had had but at least Henrietta was protected, living as she did with her parents. She resolved to stay as far away from Master Hingham as possible.

They left the garden and moved toward the long, open sheds where the tobacco was hung and processed. Beyond the sheds, the slave quarters, and the many outbuildings belonging to Wilmington Hall, lay the broad, open fields where the Hall's crop of food and tobacco was grown.

"So much land," Fidelity marveled.

"It's necessary," Philip told her. "Growing tobacco wears out the soil in a few years. The fields must be left to lie fallow to regain their nutrients."

Across the wide field Philip saw a white man mounted on horseback and waved to him. "Excuse me for a moment," he told Fidelity. "I want to talk to the overseer."

Leaving her there on the path Philip strode away toward the man on the horse.

Fidelity stood alone, the Hall and its gardens far behind her, the Hall's dependencies to her right and left, the wide fields as far as she could see before her.

To one side, between the buildings and the field, a small wooded area was left growing wildly. As she turned toward it she saw John Hingham at the wood's edge astride a tall chestnut stallion. He sat there motionless, staring at her. Fidelity stood still, rooted to the spot, terrified that he would come toward her. She looked for Philip and saw him, as if on cue, start back toward her after finishing his conversation with the overseer. When she turned back toward the woods, John was gone. He had disappeared and, although Fidelity knew he must have gone into the woods, it seemed ominous that his coming and going had been so silent and stealthy.

# 25

Fidelity celebrated her nineteenth birthday at Wilmington Hall not many weeks after the celebration of the New Year. It was celebrated with as much ceremony and joy as if she'd been a member of the family rather than a guest.

A many-course dinner was served in the Hall's beautifully paneled and crystal chandeliered dining hall with gold plate and crystal glittering richly in the candlelight. After the dinner, they retired to the baron's library where, to Fidelity's surprise, gifts awaited her spread over a thick-legged library table.

"You needn't have," she whispered, overwhelmed by the generosity of her hosts. "You really shouldn't . . ."

"Nonsense!" Henrietta laughed. "Open them!"

Her gifts, with the exception of an exquisite fan of inlaid ebony and black point de Venise lace, were jewelry. Pearls, emeralds, and a strand of diamonds with matching eardrops, left Fidelity gasping. She'd never contemplated owning so many wonderful gems.

She felt tears sting her eyes. "I don't know what to say," she told them.

Philip leaned over and kissed her cheek. "There's no need to say anything, sweetheart."

At last she gave up trying to find words and, with Philip, bade them all good night and went up to her room.

Philip left her at her door. "I have to go down to the docks. I'll be back shortly."

Without bothering to call a maid, for her bodice fastened down the front and she could manage it herself, Fidelity slipped out of her clothes and into the cool softness of a lawn nightdress. She lit a single candle and sank into the comfort of an armchair near her windows. It felt so good to be among people who cared for her and who liked her, who were happy to accept her without reservations or ulterior motives. She leaned her head against the back of the chair and closed her eyes. She would relax until Philip returned.

But a knock sounded at the door and she looked up, perplexed. Was the knock at her hall door or the door connecting her room and Philip's? It couldn't be at Philip's door because she recognized his knock and what she'd just heard wasn't it.

"Yes?" She opened the door a crack imagining it to be the maid asking if she required anything before she retired for the night. As she peeked into the hall she was pushed roughly aside by John Hingham as he forced his way into the room.

"Get out of here!" Fidelity hissed. "I'll call Henrietta or the baron!"

He regarded her insolently. "Call whomever you please! Henrietta and the baroness are downstairs at the other end of the house and the baron and my dear wife's Uncle Philip are down at the docks." He clapped one hand on her throat, his fingers and thumb pressing slightly at the points just beneath her ear lobes. "And if you make a sound I'll press harder and harder. Will you be quiet?"

Fidelity nodded. He released his grasp and she pushed past him and ran for Philip's room. She misjudged his reflexes, however, and he grabbed her as she passed, knocking her to the floor and landing with a heavy thud on top of her.

Trapped, Fidelity strained her muscles trying to force her way away from him but the futility of her efforts only amused him. Her struggles seemed to increase his passion and her fists glanced off his body, having no effect.

"Don't waste your energy," he smirked.

"No! Let me go! Philip!"

John laughed. "I told you, I saw him going down to the docks."

"But you didn't see me return."

John froze and, looking up, saw Philip stride through the door from his room. A pistol was grasped threateningly in his hand.

His nephew clambered awkwardly to his feet and stood gazing into the barrel of Philip's pistol as Fidelity picked herself off the floor and, rearranging her nightdress, stepped behind Philip.

"If you so much as look at her again I'll kill you," Philip growled. "You're a bastard and a blackguard and I've not exposed you only because of Henrietta's misplaced love. But I won't stand by while you force yourself where you're not wanted. Now get out!"

John started for the door but stopped when he heard his wife's voice calling him from the head of the stairs. He turned back toward them.

"Go out through my room," Philip told him. "Tell her you were discussing something with me." The other man started for the door. "This is the last time I will lie for you, Hingham!" Philip called after him.

The door closed behind John and Fidelity buried her face in the linen ruffles of Philip's cravat.

"Do you want to be alone tonight?" Philip asked.

Fidelity shook her head. "No! No! That's the last thing I want tonight!"

Fidelity lay in the crook of Philip's arm. The fire had died in the fireplace but it made little difference. Spring was arriving in Virginia and the chill of the winter was giving way to the gentle warmth of the southern spring.

"Fidelity?" Philip moved almost imperceptibly.

"Hmmm?"

"Fidelity?"

"I'm awake."

"I'm leaving at the end of the month."

"That's nice, Philip." She sighed contentedly, and then sat up in the darkness. "You're doing what?"

"I'm leaving at the end of the month."

She stared at him through the shadows. "Leaving? Why? To go where?"

"Now, now." He drew her back into the warmth of his arms. "I'm leaving for Barbados. My brother recently purchased a plantation there and I have to see that it's under competent management."

"Can I go with you?"

"No. The area can be dangerous; it's rife with privateers; English, French, and Spanish. It will be better if you stay here."

"But Philip, if you'll be in danger I want to be with you!"

"An admirable attitude, I grant you, but I'll feel better knowing you're safe."

"But Philip . . . !" She sat up again.

He laid a gentle finger across her lips. "Now, hush. I'll hurry back knowing I'll find you here waiting for me."

"How long will you be gone?"

Philip hesitated, knowing his answer would provoke a storm of protest from her. "However long it takes to get the plantation under trustworthy and competent management."

"You are avoiding the question, Philip. How long?"

"At least two months."

"Two months!" Fidelity was dumbfounded. "Two months! I don't want to stay here alone for two months!"

"You'll hardly be alone."

"You know what I mean."

"Yes, I do. But I work for my brother and I must attend to my business. Please, Fidelity, don't make this any harder than it already is."

Fidelity bit back the protests that raced to her lips. If Philip was going to leave, he mustn't leave with sour feelings between them. She lay back down beside him and allowed him to gather her into his arms, but long after his breathing had settled into the deep, rhythmic patterns of sleep, she lay awake staring miserably into the room's darkness. It was nearly time for Philip to be up and attending to his day's work when she fell into a restless and troubled sleep.

The days passed all too quickly, bringing nearer the day when Philip would sail away from Wilmington Hall. Fidelity stalked the budding gardens as she had a year before at Crichton Manor.

"Fidelity?" Henrietta called to her from beyond the wrought-iron gates separating the house and the gardens.

"I'm here, Henrietta," Fidelity replied. She waited on the garden path while Henrietta hurried toward her.

"Why have you been so sad of late?" Henrietta asked when they'd settled onto a bench beneath a spreading oak tree.

"You know that Philip is leaving for Barbados soon."

"Ah, yes. I should have realized." Henrietta patted Fidelity's hand. "Times like these are when I understand how lucky I am in John. He has no desire to go to sea and travel to faraway and exotic places."

He has no desire to do anything except pursue other women! Fidelity thought, but she didn't say so.

"Philip's life is the sea now," she told Henrietta. "And it's a better life than he had when we met."

"What do you mean?"

Fidelity hesitated. Philip had told his brother he'd met her when she'd been brought aboard his ship. No doubt Henrietta had also heard the story—most probably from the baron himself.

"We . . . that is, Philip and I . . . well, we met before I was taken aboard his ship. We met in England a year ago. It was a brief meeting, it hardly counts at all. And Philip was having a difficult time as many Royalists were."

Henrietta seemed to accept the explanation and Fidelity was grateful she didn't ask the exact circumstances of her meeting with Philip.

"The time will pass quickly enough." Henrietta assured her. "We have to prepare for the ball at Staunton House; that will take your mind off Philip!"

Fidelity smiled, but wasn't greatly comforted.

Fidelity stood in the warm March sunshine watching the *Virginian* being readied to sail. She fought to keep her composure; she didn't want Philip's parting memory of her to be one of tears and sobbing. When the ship was ready and the crew aboard, Philip took Fidelity's hand and led her off the dock and away from the group of spectators which included the Wilmington family and several of the baron's business partners and their families.

He led her onto the lawn of Wilmington Hall where they were shaded from curious eyes by the trees and thick hedges. He pushed back the hood of her taffeta cloak and kissed her softly. But Fidelity wrapped her arms about his neck and clung to him, refusing to release him.

"Oh, Philip! Philip! Take me with you!" she begged. Sobs caught in her throat. "Please!"

Philip hugged her to him but his voice was firm. "You know I can't, Fidelity. Even if I wanted to."

She pulled away from him. "Then you don't want to?"

"I didn't mean that. It's just . . . no, by God, it's true. I don't want to take you where you might fall into the hands of some buccaneers. You don't know what they do to women."

"I don't care, Philip! I know you'll protect me."

"Fidelity, please. Don't make this any more difficult than it is. My first responsibility is to my crew and my ship. I must protect my brother's property."

"And that's more important than I am?"

"Right now, yes! Fidelity, I want you safe so I can concentrate on my work."

"Well then, Master Wilmington," she said, knowing it wasn't the right time or place to say it but unable to stop herself, "perhaps you'd rather I found someone else to protect me so you could concentrate on your work!"

If she expected Philip to be alarmed or jealous she was cruelly mistaken. He threw back his head and laughed. "If you think you can find anyone, sweetheart, go ahead! Much as I love this land, I've no illusions about the lack of suitable company one comes across. Perhaps you've a mind to a rich old plantation owner. Or is it John Hingham you fancy?"

"Oh!" Fidelity was exasperated and, turning,

marched back toward the docks. But Philip was faster and he caught her before she'd passed the shield of trees and moved into the line of sight of the company on the ship and dock.

"Kiss me, Fidelity," he said. "And smile once again before I have to leave."

She allowed him to embrace her and held her face up toward his for a kiss but the parting, which should have been bittersweet and romantically sad, was marred for her by her own foolish pride.

She stood on the dock as the ship slid away and down the river to the Chesapeake Bay. She waved and tried to smile but in the end only stood on the end of the dock and watched helplessly as Philip sailed out of view.

# 26

Fidelity stood on the dock long after everyone else had returned to the house. She didn't hear the footsteps approaching and so jumped in surprise when Henrietta slipped an arm about her waist.

"Come back to the house," Henrietta coaxed. "My mother's dressmaker has arrived. We must have final fittings on our gowns for the ball at Staunton House."

"All right," Fidelity agreed. Philip and his ship were gone from view, there was no reason to stand there staring after him.

They sat in the Baroness Wilmington's sitting room waiting while the baroness was fitting into her new gown. A maid brought them each a serving of coffee—fashionable and expensive—which Fidelity privately hated. She sipped at it trying hard not to make a sour face.

"Tell me about the Court," Henrietta demanded suddenly.

"Whatever made you think of that?"

"Oh, Father mentioned the king to Mother, and I heard her say she envied you as you had frequented the Court and become a favorite of the king."

"Well, the Court is exciting but not very genteel.

287

One would think that courtiers would be polite and strive to be a fine example to the common people, but the only example they make is on how to be the best man in the nation at whoring, drinking, cursing, and dissipating one's resources!"

Henrietta nodded. "It's not so different now than it was when the king was in exile in Holland."

"You were there, weren't you?"

Henrietta shrugged. "Some of the time. Father lived there but Mother, Charles, and I lived some of the time with the Queen Mother in France."

"Was that exciting?"

"No! The queen was very poor and in mourning for her husband, the first King Charles. We lived as pensioners of the King of France, Louis XIV."

"Then you weren't well acquainted with King Charles?"

"I was presented, of course. My mother and I lived in Holland when we first went there, and then we were there occasionally until we sailed for Virginia, but I can't say I was acquainted with him. And he wouldn't have noticed me at any rate. He was madly in love with Lucy Walter."

"Jemmy's mother?"

"Yes, she had a babe named Jemmy. How did you know?"

"He came to live at Court after the king's restoration. He's a beautiful boy."

"Lucy was a beautiful woman. It's a pity she died so shortly before the king regained his kingdom. But tell me about the Court now; tell me about King Charles."

"I will if you'll tell me about France and King

Louis."

Henrietta agreed and Fidelity recounted the details of the ball at the Banqueting House when she'd first been presented to the king, the ball at Wyndham House, her apartment at Whitehall, and the jealousy of Barbara Palmer. She stopped when she reached the night Barbara and Nichodemus lured her to the tavern and carefully avoided any mention of Schuyler Pierrepointe. When she'd finished, Fidelity told Henrietta: "Now it's your turn, tell me about France."

In her turn, Henrietta told Fidelity about the Court of France as she remembered it. She'd left before King Louis's marriage to the Infanta of Spain and so the Court she remembered was the Court ruled by the Queen Mother of France, Anne of Austria, and Cardinal Mazarin who was rumored, Henrietta whispered, to be the queen's lover or even her husband. She told her of balls at the Louvre and the widowed English queen's spartan and chilly apartment at Saint Germain.

"But what about the king, himself?" Fidelity asked.

Henrietta shrugged. "I never knew him; we were beneath his notice. He's very vain; of course he's been king since he was five years old and his mother worships him and tells him he's a god incarnate and such things. I suppose it's only natural he should be vain and concerned only with himself. He is very handsome, which only adds to his vanity. He's not so tall as King Charles, he's really not much taller than you or I. He's lighter in coloring than King Charles; his hair is light brown and his eyes are gray."

"I think I'd prefer King Charles. He's much nicer

than King Louis sounds."

Henrietta agreed. "Are all the ladies at the Court in England beautiful?"

"Well, at least a good portion of them."

"But not many so beautiful as you, I warrant." John stood in the doorway. Bowing as they looked at him, he vanished into the hallway.

"Pooh!" Henrietta snorted. "He always flatters other women to make me jealous."

Fidelity looked at Henrietta, trying to understand her love for the foppish John Hingham with his illumureful habits and oly behavior.

Their discussion was cut off by the baroness who emerged from her bedchamber in her dressing gown. She sent Fidelity and Henrietta into the chamber for their fittings.

Fidelity stood in the center of the baroness's bedchamber in her ball gown. It was of white satin covered with gold lace onto which were sewn tiny gold spangles that glittered when she moved. Her gloves, fan, shoes, and stockings were of gold and her hair was to be worn coiled high and threaded through with golden ribbons. She had a necklace, earrings, and bracelets of gold set with topaz which completed the ensemble.

"Oh, Fidelity!" Henrietta breathed, when they were dressed. "How wonderful you look!"

"You look beautiful, Henrietta."

Henrietta stared at their reflections, side by side in the mirror, and sighed. "But you are so lovely. No one will notice me after you arrive."

"Nonsense, everyone will be staring at you from the moment you enter the room."

They giggled and Henrietta squealed. "I can't wait until the ball. I simply can't wait!

Fidelity, Henrietta, John, young Charles, and the baron and baroness stepped off the dock at Staunton House leaving the barge on which they'd ridden up the river and followed a liveried manservant up a terraced path toward the great house. It was not so very different from Wilmington Hall in its basic design but it was less ornate and had a long wing which extended away from the rear making it a T-shape.

Rather than entering the house, they were ushered around one side from where they could see the gardens and several groups of ladies, gentlemen, and children of varying ages. They moved toward those people and Fidelity noticed the maids who had accompanied them being shown into the house. They carried the ball gowns and accessories of the baroness, Henrietta, and Fidelity for it was still afternoon and they wouldn't don their evening finery until after dinner.

When they'd passed through the gateway in the garden wall, a gentleman and lady left the people they'd been talking to and came toward them, arms outstretched.

The man looked slightly older than the baron, perhaps in his early to middle forties while his wife looked several years younger. They were introduced to Fidelity as George Staunton and his wife Mary. Neither was exceptionally handsome nor particularly unattractive; they had no characteristics which would make them noticeable in a crowd. As they turned to lead the way back to the other guests, George Staunton told the baron:

"By the way, Wilmington, have you heard? I've sold Yorkby."

"You don't say!" exclaimed the baron. "I thought that plantation was to be a wedding gift for Melintha when she married."

"I'd dare say she'd rather have the money! And no doubt she'll marry a man with his own holdings. The man I've sold the place to is interested in joining our partnership. You'll meet him later, he hasn't arrived just yet."

"Business," Mary Staunton sighed to the baroness. "Always business! Come, we'll join the other ladies. Melintha! Henrietta's here!"

From the center of a group of young women, Melintha Staunton appeared. She was Henrietta's age, having just turned eighteen, and was truly her parents' daughter, having their nondescript coloring and looks. She was dressed in a gown of beige silk which neither enhanced her looks, as Fidelity's bright green dress enhanced her silvery blondness, nor detracted from them as did Henrietta's gown of dull brown. She was neither beautiful nor homely, but she had a giggly sort of personality that was childishly engaging.

"Henrietta!" she said after making her curtsy to the baroness. "Where is that devilishly handsome husband of yours?"

Henrietta giggled as she always did when John was mentioned. "Probably bragging to some of the other gentlemen."

"Bragging about what?" Melintha teased and

they both burst into a gale of giggles that seemed utterly ridiculous to Fidelity.

Henrietta introduced Fidelity to Melintha who seemed just ever so slightly annoyed that a girl of such obvious beauty should intrude while she was trying to be the belle of the ball. Several of the younger men, including Melintha's twenty-two year old brother James, and some of the older men could already be seen glancing Fidelity's way and speculating among themselves. When Fidelity saw some of them approach John Hingham she imagined with chagrin the stories he would probably tell them.

Melintha took Henrietta and Fidelity to join the group of girls she'd left when she came to greet them, and Fidelity was accepted among them with a kind of grudging admiration of her looks and curiosity about how she came to be with the Wilmingtons.

Dinner had been served and eaten and afterward, while the gentlemen retired to the library for more business discussions and the older ladies to the parlor to rest before changing into their ball gowns, the daughters and younger wives retired to the upstairs bedroom of Melintha Staunton to rest and gossip while waiting to be dressed and summoned to the ballroom.

"Who did your father sell Yorby to?" a young woman named Susan asked Melintha.

Melintha shrugged her shoulders. "I don't know. I don't worry myself about business. I just hope he's handsome and his wife is ugly!"

The girls giggled. "Henrietta," one of them called across the room. "You know that husband of yours is going to get his face slapped one day. I declare! He volunteered to help me down a steep bank near the river and made a little too bold with those hands of his!"

The other young women looked mildly shocked though not particularly surprised but Henrietta only giggled.

"You shouldn't mind John," she told them. "He only tries to make me jealous."

The room was still for a moment and then there was a flurry of new subjects introduced. Fidelity sensed that she was not the only woman in the room who'd had occasion to fight off the advances of John Hingham.

After a while Henrietta became tired of their conversation and she suddenly said:

"You know Fidelity lived for a while at Whitehall!" Encouraged by the attention her statement received, she continued: "The king was in love with her!"

Fidelity was besieged with questions and, as she was being dressed for the ball and stood wearing only her chemise and petticoats, she could hardly leave the room to escape them. Instead, she answered their questions tactfully, if somewhat incompletely, and was much relieved when the summons came for them to join their parents, siblings, and husbands in the ballroom downstairs.

Fidelity descended the stairs flanked by Melintha Staunton, eager now to play hostess to such an exciting and worldly guest, and Henrietta, proud that she'd brought the object of such admiration to the ball.

The ballroom of Staunton House was located in, and in fact took up, the entire rear wing of the house. Lit by chandeliers and sconces, their candles blazing, it was a beautiful room with softly hued walls of pale pink and a white ceiling. The windows, which ran up both sides of the long room, had tall white shutters, and an impressive white marble fireplace was centered in each of the long side walls. The floor was polished parquet of an attractive design and its darkness reflected the gleam of the candlelight above.

Fidelity stood back allowing the other girls to enter the ballroom after Melintha. Soft music wafted from the room over a hum of conversation and it was so pleasant in the little hallway that connected the ballroom with the main hall of the house that she was reluctant to leave it for the round of socializing in the ballroom. She opened her golden fan and languidly moved it, forcing a little breeze to sweep across her face. From the corner of her eye she caught sight of her own reflection in a pair of tall glass doors and admired the way the gold spangles on her gown and her golden jewelry caught the light. Then, realizing how vain she would look to someone who happened to see her, she blushed and entered the ballroom just as Melintha approached her father and mother who stood with another man whose back was to Fidelity. She heard the master of Staunton House tell his daughter:

"Melintha, may I present the new master of Yorby, the Baron Schuyler Pierrepointe. My lord, my daughter Melintha."

The tall blond man in the suit of midnight blue

turned and bowed over Melintha's hand while she, blushing, curtsied. The group of girls who'd accompanied Melintha downstairs murmured with admiration and no one noticed Fidelity, who stood near them, blanch until she and the white satin beneath the gold lace of her gown were almost of a color.

# 27

Fidelity edged her way to the end of the ballroom opposite the spot where Schuyler Pierrepointe stood with George Staunton, being introduced to the other gentlemen with whom he would be doing business. Across the brightly lit room, Fidelity saw Mary Staunton presenting Anna, the Baroness Pierrepointe, to the older women who sat near the open windows close to one of the unused fireplaces.

Marriage had not improved Anna Pierrepointe. She had aged in the year since her sudden marriage, and she could scarcely afford to age. Fidelity felt her heart harden at the sight of the older woman who'd had the money to pay for Schuyler's dreams and therefore buy his life. The baroness, looking like an overgrown citrus fruit in orange satin with her cheeks painted with vivid red spots and her hair chalkily black with dye, accepted the introductions to the Stauntons' guests and tittered when they complimented her on her young and handsome husband. Fidelity turned away from the people in the room and stared out at the gardens through an open window. She was startled by a masculine voice:

"Mistress Fairfax?"

She found Melintha's brother, James, standing before her.

"May I have the honor of this dance?" he asked.

He was not unhandsome, nor was he as colorless as his parents and his sister. He was only a few inches taller than she and his hair, moustache, and eyes were all the same light brown which were not made more vivid by his suit of tan satin trimmed with white lace.

Fidelity hesitated but she couldn't see a polite way of refusing him. "Of course, sir," she smiled at last, and allowed him to lead her onto the floor.

The musicians struck up a gentle tune and Fidelity and James moved around the floor, their movements echoed by the other dancers. Fidelity looked carefully at James's cravat trying to avoid meeting anyone else's eyes but as they passed very close to another couple, she heard Melintha's voice cry:

"James! Fidelity! Have you met Lord Pierre-pointe, the new owner of Yorkby?"

James smiled and made Schuyler a little bow while they danced. Fidelity, realizing she could no longer avoid the inevitable, raised her eyes and met the surprised green eyes of Schuyler.

"My lord," she murmured. "Forgive me if I don't curtsy."

"Quite all right, madame," he said in the same velvety soft voice she remembered so well.

"Madame?" Melintha giggled, unused to the Court use of the term for married and unmarried ladies. "Oh, Fidelity Fairfax is not married, my lord. She's a guest of Lord Wilmington, or rather of Lord

Wilmington's brother, Philip."

"Pardon me, Mistress Fairfax," the baron corrected. "I hope we'll have an opportunity to—get acquainted."

As the dance separated them, Fidelity heard Melintha's high-pitched giggle and wondered what Schuyler had said. At the first opportunity, the moment the music ended, Fidelity smiled a dismissal to James Staunton and retreated to a window seat in a far corner of the huge room. She sat quietly hoping no one would notice her there and invite her to rejoin the throng of dancers; but her hopes died an early death.

"Fidelity," Schuyler's voice was close behind her.

"Schuyler, please. Go dance with Melintha or your wife."

"I want to dance with you."

Sighing, she walked out onto the floor again and reluctantly allowed him to lead her into a merry and quick folk dance which she'd danced at Whitehall with the king. When that dance was finished she started away from him but he refused to let her go and the next dance, to her chagrin, was a slow, sensuously rhythmed, sweeping dance which required the partners to move in gentle synchronization.

"What are you doing in Virginia?" she asked over the music of the dance.

"I could ask you the same," he replied.

She turned her face away and refused to say a word.

"Very well," he agreed, "I'll tell you. I sold my lands in Barbados because Anna hated living in the islands. The tropical heat and lack of society, you know."

"So you're still jumping to your wife's tune?" Fidelity said sarcastically.

"And you're still jealous of my marriage?" he returned with her exact tone of sarcasm.

"Jealous!" she cried, a little too loudly.

"Shhh!" he hissed. "You're drawing attention."

She ignored him and he said, "Now you tell me why you're in Virginia."

"Only if you promise not to tell anyone." He nodded and she continued: "The king was attracted to me. Barbara Palmer was afraid I'd replace her and she found out about Nichodemus. She contacted him and they conspired together to be rid of me. They lured me into London and drugged me, then put me onto Philip Wilmington's ship. I don't think they cared if I made it to Virginia or not."

"And this Philip Wilmington simply offered to take you to his brother's home?"

"Well, no," she admitted. She didn't want to tell him that Philip had been the highwayman who'd brought her to London. "Philip and I had met before in London and it was fortunate that Barbara and Nichodemus happened to set me aboard his ship."

"Fortunate indeed!" he agreed with his usual mockery. "How lucky that you have such a wide circle of admirers. Tell me, Fidelity, how far have you come from that innocent girl your father tried to kill me to protect?"

The music ended and Fidelity ignored his mockery with a haughty lift of her chin. Dropping him the barest semblance of a curtsy, she turned and walked away, returning to the window seat she'd occupied when he'd asked her to dance.

She sat fanning herself, not so much to cool her skin, for there was a lovely breeze coming though the tall window, but to work off the anger, frustration, and confusion she felt.

"Wine, Mistress Fairfax?" Schuyler was back.

Fidelity looked at him askance, her eyebrows raised. "You're being indiscreet, my lord," she said softly as he sat beside her. She took the goblet of wine and held it with both hands to still their trembling.

"I'm the envy of every man in the room because of your attention. Smile at me, Fidelity, I don't want to argue."

"Schuyler, don't. I have a life of my own now. And so have you. We have responsibilities."

"Responsibilities? I work for the money my wife gives me. I invest it and work to make it increase."

"I have responsibilities then, even if you haven't. I owe Philip a great deal. I literally owe him my life. He loves me, Schuyler. I know he does."

"Do you love him?"

"I care for him."

"Where is he?"

"He went to Barbados. His brother had bought a plantation there and . . . " She stopped as Schuyler began to laugh. "Your plantation? The baron bought your plantation?"

"As far as I know, mine was the only plantation sold recently. So your new lover's brother has made it possible for your old lover to come back to you."

"Schuyler . . . " she pleaded.

"You said you cared for Wilmington, you didn't say you loved him. Is there someone else you love? Do you love me?"

Fidelity breathed deeply of the cool evening air and refused to look at him. "Have a care, Lord Pierrepointe," she said. "You'll scandalize your new associates if someone hears you."

He laughed. "Anger them, more likely, for taking the most beautiful woman in the room for myself and monopolizing her time."

"Perhaps we shouldn't stay here." She started to rise but he stopped her with a hand on her arm.

"Let's go into the gardens," he whispered.

"Schuyler, you're incorrigible!" She giggled in spite of herself and glanced past his head. Her giggle died and her smile faded as her eyes met the angry glare of Anna Pierrepointe.

The baroness stood, ostensibly listening to one of the other ladies, but her rage was obvious in that the rest of her face was as red as her rouged cheeks and her mouth was set in a tight, thin, line.

"I think your wife wishes she were back in Barbados!" she told him.

He glanced over at her and gave her a quick, happy flip of his hand. "She won't stay angry long. Not with me at any rate; I know how to allay her fury."

"How?"

He waggled his eyebrows comically and she giggled. Suddenly he took his glass of wine and hers and placed them on the floor. "Shall we dance?" he asked, airily offering her his arm.

They sailed past the baroness and Schuyler threw her a polite smile. "Enjoying yourself, my pet?" he asked. "Ladies." He nodded to the ladies to whom she was talking.

The music had started and they waited a moment to catch the rhythm of the dance.

"Your wife will strangle you in your sleep!" Fidelity whispered, as they danced.

"Never!" he answered. "She's mad about me!"

When the dance ended, the Baroness Pierrepointe lost no time in reclaiming her husband. For the rest of the evening, Schuyler was a prisoner of his wife. When he danced he danced with her and none of the young women dared face her wrath in order to capture her husband's attentions.

Fidelity, freed from the exclusivity of the baron's company, was the belle of the latter part of the ball. By the time the sleepy guests went to their assigned bedchamers, it was early morning and she'd danced with nearly all the men at the ball.

The same young women who'd shared Melintha's room while they rested, shared it for the remainder of the night. None of the guests would return home until the middle of the following day and assigning bedrooms to married couples or families was impossible due to lack of space. Most of the older couples did have rooms of their own but the younger men and women, married or unmarried, were assigned to rooms dormitory-style, several men to a room and several women to another.

"Oh, Fidelity!" Henrietta squealed when they were being helped out of their gowns. "How ever did you manage to capture the attention of that delicious Baron Pierrepointe?"

"Yes," Melintha agreed spitefully. "However did you manage?"

Fidelity sighed. "I must confess something. Tonight was not the first time I'd met Lord Pierrepointe. We were acquainted in London. He is a great and old friend of my cousin, Lord Wyndham."

"I knew it!" the girl named Susan cried. "I knew he knew her! Didn't I tell you?"

Fidelity was grateful when they were dressed for bed and the candles blown out. She was sharing a bed with Henrietta and Melintha and she edged toward the bedside close to a slightly opened window. The window faced the front lawn of the plantation and she could see the river when she tucked back the edge of the drape.

She breathed deeply of the cool air tinged with moisture. Schuyler's arrival was the last thing she needed when she was already unsure of her emotions. She damned the fluttering in her stomach that started when she saw him and the trembling that brought goose flesh to her arms when he was near. She felt ashamed when she thought of how badly she wanted to touch him and have him touch her as he had at Wyndham House in London.

"Fidelity?" Henrietta whispered in the darkness.

"What is it?" she replied.

"Will you introduce me to Lord Pierrepointe?"

"Ask Melintha to do it," Fidelity snapped. "He's her father's guest."

"He'll be spending a lot of time at Wilmington

Hall."

"Why?"

"He's going to join the partnership of the planters on the river. He'll probably be there very often."

"Oh, Henrietta! Go to sleep."

"He'll be there when Uncle Philip gets back."

Fidelity turned over and hissed at Henrietta: "What is that supposed to mean? Are you accusing me of something?"

They were quiet for a moment, afraid they'd awakened Melintha who slept on the opposite side of Henrietta. Then Henrietta, who looked as though she was going to cry, whispered, "I was only teasing, Fidelity!"

"I'm sorry, Henrietta. I'm so tired, please forgive me! I didn't mean to snap at you."

"All right. Good night, Fidelity."

"Goodnight, Henrietta."

"Fidelity?"

"Yes?"

"You know, I suppose I should feel wicked about admitting it, but I wish I could have had a room with John tonight."

"Henrietta! You wicked thing!" Fidelity teased.

Henrietta giggled and they settled down to sleep. But Fidelity couldn't sleep, she understood Henrietta's feelings only too well and the thought of Schuyler under the same roof in the night, much as she cared for Philip, disturbed her.

Sleep eluded her long even after Henrietta was deep in slumber. Carefully, so as not to awaken anyone, Fidelity slipped from beneath the covers and sat framed in the purple-draped posters of the bed. She pulled back the window drapes and gazed at the carefully manicured lawns of Staunton House.

Below, on the moonlit lawn, something moved and Fidelity strained her eyes to make it out. The shape in the shadows split into two shapes and moved out into the moonlight. Fidelity drew a breath and glanced at the sleeping Henrietta, assuring herself that she was not awake to witness the scene on the lawn. For there, illuminated by the soft moonlight and partially shielded from the house by shrubbery, strained together in a tight embrace and engrossed in a passionate kiss, were Charlotte Burdett, the young and attractive wife of the elderly Peter Burdett— master of Spring Grove, another river plantation— and John Hingham about whom Henrietta was no doubt dreaming at that moment.

Fidelity let the drape fall at the window. And she'd expected America to be savage and primitive! Apparently the settlers had brought their intriguing natures right along with their family heirlooms and native traditions!

# 28

Soon after the ball at Staunton House, Schuyler
Pierrepointe officially entered the business partnership of the planters along the river. As the Baron
Wilmington was the senior member of the partnership, much of the business was transacted at
Wilmington Hall. Schuyler found a great many
reasons to come down the river, not all of them,
Fidelity suspected, strictly business. He came to
transact many dealings he could easily have sent
messages for or waited until more pressing matters
brought his fellow partners together.

Since it was obvious that he and Fidelity were
acquainted—word had spread quickly after the
ball—no one was surprised when he stopped to pay
his respects to her on his way to or from the meetings
with the baron.

For her part, and to Henrietta's confused conster-
nation, Fidelity strove to avoid Schuyler, often fleeing
to her room or hiding in the now-blossoming
gardens.

"Fidelity!" Henrietta cried one day as they
watched Schuyler walk toward his barge after a
meeting with the baron. "Why don't you go and talk
to him? He obviously came to see you—he didn't stay

307

with my father for more than a few minutes."

"You don't understand," Fidelity told her, turning away from the window. "There's so much you don't understand."

"Then tell me! We're friends, aren't we?"

"Yes, we're friends. Oh, Henrietta, I just can't bring all that up again. All I can tell you is that Schuyler and I were—involved—in England. There were a great many difficulties for both of us that resulted from our involvement and I don't want to begin all that again."

"But he's so gorgeous! Most of the women I know would give everything they own to be involved with him."

"Even more gorgeous than John?" Fidelity teased.

"Fidelity! You're changing the subject!"

"Schuyler is a married man," Fidelity reminded her. "And I am here as a guest of your uncle. Now how would it look if I began carrying on with a married man while your Uncle Philip is away?"

"Anyone who saw Lord Pierrepointe would certainly understand!"

Fidelity thought of the night Philip brought her to Wyndham House in London and, seeing her kissing Schuyler, had fled into the London night. She shook her head. "I don't think Philip would understand."

Fidelity walked among the blooming beds of the gardens. It was the beginning of May and although she desperately wished Philip would return she knew he wasn't due back for at least a week or two. Hearing footsteps approaching along the paved path, Fidelity stepped quickly under a curved trellis thickly over-grown with vines. It was Schuyler, she knew, for she'd seen his barge moored at the docks. She sat, holding her breath, on a bench which was one of two that faced one another beneath the vines. But it was too late. Without hesitation he approached the trellis and ducked his head through the foliage.

"Give you good afternoon, Madame Crichton . . . er . . . pardon me, Mistress Fairfax."

"You needn't remind me of my past, my lord," Fidelity told him without looking at him. "I'm well aware of my status as a married woman. I wonder if you could say the same."

"Heigh ho!" he laughed as he sat opposite her on the other little bench. "We are in a haughty mood, are we not?"

"Pray tell me, my lord," she asked, looking at him coolly. "Who runs your plantation since you're never there?"

"I have a very competent overseer."

"A pity your overseer doesn't have as competent a master. Aren't you afraid you'll be shot one day because your overseer will fail to recognize you and shoot you as an intruder?"

Schuyler laughed and brushed his finger over his white-blond moustache. "Your wit and your tongue are both honed to a wondrous sharpness today!"

"What do you want, Schuyler?" she asked impatiently.

"Only to be admitted to your presence. To bask in your sweetness and charm."

"Any time you're through, I'm still waiting for

an answer."

In a swift, fluid motion he moved from the bench opposite her to the same one she occupied but her quick movement away from him prevented his putting an arm about her shoulders. "I want to see you, Fidelity. I want to be with you."

"There's no point in our seeing one another," she told him. "Philip will be home soon."

"Philip, Philip," Schuyler sighed. "He brought you to Virginia, his family allowed you to live with them. Does that mean they own you? Does that mean you can't see old friends?"

"Old friends, perhaps. Old lovers are another matter. And since you were so kind as to remind me of my husband, may I remind you once again that you are a married man?"

Schuyler waved a dismissing hand. "Your husband, may hell take his foul soul, means nothing to me. Why can't you take the same attitude about my wife?"

"In the first place, my husband is half a world away, in the second place, I didn't marry Nichodemus voluntarily and I didn't sleep with him voluntarily."

He smiled slyly. "And what about Philip?"

"I will not discuss Philip with you," she snapped.

Schuyler wrapped one satin-clad arm about her shoulders. "Fidelity, what games you play. I know you still love me, your eyes betray you. Look at me." Slipping a finger beneath her chin he tilted her face toward his and she gazed into the green depths of his eyes. "You owe the Wilmingtons nothing. What they gave they gave of their own free will. Kiss me, Fidelity, like you did in London."

He kissed her, pulling her closely and enfolding her tightly in his arms. Fidelity felt her reluctance and resolutions slip through her fingers like the silken strands of Schuyler's blond hair as she slipped her arms around his shoulders. She pulled away when their lips parted and pushed against his shoulders when he would have embraced her once again.

"No, Schuyler! No, please!" She struggled as he became more insistent. "Schuyler!"

" 'Scuse me, Ma'am?" Joshua, Baron Wilmington's blackamoor gardener, stood in the arch of the trellis, a wicked-looking, three-pronged pitchfork in his hand. "You needin' help?"

"Thank you, Joshua." Fidelity took advantage of Schuyler's surprise to slip away and squeeze past Joshua and out of the trellis bower. "I'm fine."

Joshua shrugged and moved away toward another part of the gardens. Fidelity, still trembling from Schuyler's kiss and the violence of her own reaction, hurried away out of the gardens and into the house. Schuyler, she imagined, would leave the gardens and return to his barge and his plantation but she didn't look to see him go.

Fidelity descended the stairs, a book in her hand. She planned to read it in the warm spring sunshine, not in the gardens where she'd had far too many unpleasant encounters, but in the apple orchard where the trees were a festival of pink and white blossoms.

As she reached the hall at the bottom of the staircase, Fidelity heard voices just without the front door of the house. Deciding to wait rather than present the imminent arrivals with her retreating back, she stood in the foyer as the door opened and the Baron Wilmington entered with the elderly Peter Burdett.

"Fidelity!" The baron smile. "How pretty you look today."

"Thank you, my lord," Fidelity replied, curtsying.

"Let me add my compliments, Mistress Fairfax," Peter Burdett said as he leaned heavily on the walking stick which was not only a fashionable accessory to him

"You're very kind, Master Burdett," Fidelity smiled.

She felt a little sorry for Peter Burdett. He was old, nearly three score and five, and life in the colonies was hard enough for a man half his age. He doted on his twenty-two-year-old wife Charlotte who had, so the gossip said, been an heiress in England whose guardians had made a tidy profit bargaining her desirability against Peter Burdett's attraction. But then, she reasoned, he should have expected other men to be attracted to her and her to be attracted to other men.

Leaving the two men who were going to the baron's study for more of their interminable business discussions, Fidelity slipped out a side entrance and walked toward the orchard.

The day was fine and Fidelity crossed the wide side lawn of the hall, walking languidly along a brick-lined path bordered with plants that would blossom later in the summer. As she passed near a stone bench, one of several which, alternating with great stone urns, formed the boundary separating the side yard from the orchard, she heard a voice hailing her.

"Fidelity! Fidelity!" It was Henrietta.

"Hello, Henrietta." Fidelity tried to hide her disappointment; it seemed she'd never get to read her book. She was curious, though, for it was not Henrietta's custom to seek solitude. "What brings you out to the farthest reaches of the yard?"

"I wanted to be alone to think." Henrietta giggled. It was also not her custom to spend a great deal of time in thought. "Fidelity, can you keep a secret?"

"Of course."

"Sit down." She patted the bench she occupied.

With a suppressed sigh, Fidelity sat next to Henrietta and waited for her news.

"You must keep this a secret, no one knows except Mother; not even John knows."

Fidelity was becoming impatient. "I can keep a secret, Henrietta," she said firmly.

"Well, then," Henrietta leaned close, as though they were in a crowded room rather than alone surrounded by expanses of empty yard. "I'm with child!"

Fidelity hesitated, thinking not about Henrietta but about the father of the child she carried. "That's fine news," she said at last. "Congratulations."

"Oh, Fidelity!" Henrietta gushed. "You have no idea what it is to be carrying a child!"

Fidelity looked away. Little did Henrietta know, little could she have suspected that Fidelity had known, if only briefly, the feeling of having a child within the warm confines of her body. But Henrietta's case, she had to admit, was different. She loved her husband, however much of a scoundrel John Hingham was. Fidelity had not loved the father of her child, the despicable Nichodemus Crichton, and did not mourn its loss quite as much as she might have the child of a man she loved. She cast around for something to say but was saved the trouble when a young black boy used by the baron and baroness as a page came running up the path and told Henrietta her mother wished her to go back to the house.

Fidelity bade Henrietta a good afternoon and, hopefully freed at last from social amenities, resumed her trek to the orchard and her book.

But it seemed there was no retreat on the great plantation where she could have the peace and solitude she craved. She sat beneath a white-blossomed apple tree and opened her book, a romance newly received from England for the private collection of the Baroness Wilmington. The story absorbed her so completely that she didn't even hear the thuds of John Hingham's booted feet as he entered the orchard and approached the tree beneath which she sat.

"Give you good day, Mistress Fidelity," he said, twining a gauntleted finger in her hair.

"Leave me alone, John Hingham," she snapped. "Go to the house and find your wife. Pardon me if I betray a confidence but she happens to be carrying your child. It's time to mend your ways."

He shrugged off her news and laughed unpleasantly. "Ah! A sermon on behavior, and with such a lovely preacher!"

Roughly he pulled her to him and kissed her with

none of the gentleness of Philip or the sensuous
sensitivity of Schuyler. She pushed him away with
distaste.

"Keep your hands off me!" she snarled.

Her persisted in his attentions and she flung her
book into his face. He flinched as it hit him in the nose
and eye.

"Bitch!" he growled. "You're more trouble than
you'd be worth! Keep your questionable chastity,
then; I know a woman who won't be so miserly with
her favors!"

"Go to her then!" Fidelity shouted. She'd scrambled to her feet and stood warily at a careful distance.
"But I can't imagine that any woman except a
lovestruck girl like your wife would welcome your
attentions willingly!"

Without another word he turned and strode out
of the orchard. Fidelity, one hand pressed to her
breast which heaved with emotion, watched until she
saw him pounding out through the rear gates of the
plantation yard on his immense chestnut stallion. He
left by the little used narrow drive and disappeared
past the orchard and up the wooded lane.

Fidelity sighed. It was obvious that she was not
now going to be able to concentrate on her reading.
She might as well return to the house; perhaps Lady
Wilmington would need her help for some project.
She dreaded hearing Henrietta giggle and coo about
her pregnancy, particularly when she'd just seen
Henrietta's "perfect" husband gallop out of the yard
en route to a rendezvous with his married mistress.

Steeling herself for Henrietta's giddiness, Fidelity
walked out of the orchard and back to the front of the

house. Just as she approached the front door it opened and the baron and Peter Burdett, their business finished, were leaving the house and moving toward Master Burdett's barge moored on the river.

"Master Burdett," Fidelity smiled, curtsying once again.

"We meet again, Mistress Fidelity." The old gentleman who was barely of a height with her, smiled. He leaned on his gold-headed walking stick and pressed the other gnarled hand to his side.

For a moment, Fidelity thought he must have been having an attack of some sort but then she realized, watching him walk slowly toward the river, that it was a habit for him to place his hand there. His hand, rather than resting merely on his green-and-gold-brocade-covered side, rested on the butt of an ornately fashioned pistol.

After watching the two men until they disappeared around a bend in the walk, Fidelity turned and entered the house.

# 29

John Hingham was dead. Poplar Hill, the plantation of his parents, was draped in black crepe inside
and out and in its largest reception room his body lay
in state in a black-swathed mourning bed.

From the neighboring plantations the relatives
and friends of the Hinghams came and were provided, upon their arrival, with mourning accessories
including black nightclothes, black toilet accessories,
and mourning gloves and scarves.

While any member of the Hingham family was
present, the tone of conversation was polite and
sympathetic but the moment two or more of the
guests were alone together the true details of John
Hingham's death were discussed with relish.

It had been decided by Thomas Hingham—
John's father—and the Baron Wilmington, that John's
death would be announced as an accidental shooting
which had occurred while he was cleaning his pistol.
It was not explained how he managed to shoot
himself accidentally in the back.

Of the three hundred people, family, friends, and
slaves gathered at the plantation, perhaps only two
people did not at least suspect the truth about John's
death. Those two were Henrietta, who was treated

with great care because of her pregnancy and because the unborn child within her was now the heir of Poplar Hill, and John's mother, Elizabeth Hingham, who was perpetually ailing and it was thought that the truth would be too great a shock for her system to bear.

But gossip spread like wildfire among the families and slaves of the river plantations and by the night of the funeral the two women for whom the story had been concocted were the only ones who believed it.

The rumors were confirmed by the many people who knew about John's liaison with Charlotte Burdett as they quickly pointed out the noticeable absence of that lady and her husband.

John Hingham had died the same day he'd accosted Fidelity in the orchard of Wilmington Hall.

Peter Burdett, whom Fidelity had seen leaving the Hall not long after she'd watched John ride away from the plantation, had gone home by way of the river. Upon his arrival he strode straight to his wife's bedchamber, as was his habit, and throwing open the door, found his wife and John Hingham engaged in making passionate love.

It was said, and the story came from the house servants who'd dared follow their master to his wife's room, that he'd seemed to turn to stone in that moment. With no trace of emotion he'd drawn the ornate pistol Fidelity had seen him fondling and, while his wife screamed and clutched lavender-scented sheets over her nakedness, had shot Hingham in the back as he tried to scramble for cover.

Then, gossip went on to say, Peter Burdett had

ordered two of his strongest field hands to hold Charlotte while a third whipped her with a carriage whip until her white skin broke and her blood dripped to the floor to mingle in the pile of the carpet with that of her lover whose body was fast growing cold on the floor near her.

While this punishment was being meted out Peter Burdett had sat, displaying no visible emotion, in a brocaded armchair with his reloaded pistol cradled in his hand.

Fidelity had learned of John's death as she was helping Lady Wilmington sort through some family heirloom baby clothes intended for Henrietta's child. They'd rushed to the head of the stairs after hearing hoofbeats pound into the yard and the baron's shocked exclamation upon hearing the news.

Stunned, he'd mounted the stairs and broken the news, leaving it to them to tell Henrietta who slept, blissfully unaware, in the bed she would share no more with her philandering husband.

John's body was placed in his coffin which was covered with a black velvet pall and, after a cold meal was eaten by the mourners, the procession started out from the mansion to the lonely hill where lay the Hingham family cemetery.

The night, for the funeral took place at night as did all funerals of the planters and their families, was cold and windy and black, billowy clouds obscured the moon and threatened a downpour. The chilling wind made the torches, carried by slaves, flicker.

The procession wound its way out of the house, across the lawn, and up the hill toward the yawning grave where they formed a three-quarter circle around the coffin.

First in the procession came the immediate family, John's father and mother supporting between them Henrietta whose black veil, which she would wear from that day forward unless she remarried, covered her head completely and trailed to the ground. She sobbed continuously and dabbed at her face with a bedraggled black handkerchief.

Behind them came the close relatives of whom there were few. The Wilmingtons were included in this group and Fidelity was with them.

Then came the other planters and their families. After them, in the rear of the procession, came the plantation overseer, his associates, and the slaves in the order of their duties, house servants first and then down to the field hands.

Fidelity stood with the Wilmingtons—the baron, baroness, and young Charles—amid the crowd of black-clad mourners. The drone of the service was punctuated by the mournful sobs of Henrietta and her mother-in-law as they clung to one another. At a distance stood the slaves of Poplar Hill most of whom had known John Hingham from the cradle. Most were not sorry to see him die; he had been a cruel child and harassed and victimized his father's slaves. When he grew older, although this aspect of his character was discussed only in whispers, he had no qualms about forcing one or another of the young female slaves into his bed.

The funeral service was over and the mourners started away from the grave and moved en masse toward the crepe-draped mansion where they would stay for the rest of the night before returning to their own homes.

"Fidelity." The deep, masculine voice seemed borne on the chilling night breezes.

Fidelity looked over her shoulder and saw Schuyler, his blondness—like hers—startling in contrast to his black clothing, standing behind her in the flickering torchlight. His wife was already moving away toward the house, her comforting arm around the grieving figure of Elizabeth Hingham.

"Really, Schuyler," Fidelity said indignantly, "this is hardly the time or the place for a tête à tête!"

"Pah!" he snorted. "Don't be a hypocrite! You hated that miserable bastard as much as anyone, perhaps more since, if he'd had his way, it would have been your bed he'd been in rather then Charlotte Burdett's"

"Then what do you want?" She was aware, as they stood near the grave and heard the first thuds of falling earth being shoveled onto the lowered coffin, that the mourners were nearing the cemetery gate and more than one curious glance was being directed at them as they lingered behind.

"I need to talk to you."

"Here?"

He lowered his voice and drew her a little away from the slaves who busily filled John's grave. He didn't want their conversation to be repeated throughout the slave quarters the next day. "Have you been in the gardens here?"

"Yes, I walked there this afternoon with Melintha Staunton."

"Then you know where the lawn temple is?" He waited for her to nod. "Good. Meet me there at three, everyone will be asleep."

"Three in the morning?"

"Of course, three in the morning! Will you come to me there?"

"I'll try," she promised.

Fidelity lay awake long after Melintha Staunton, with whom she was sharing a room, was asleep. She had allowed herself to be undressed and then dressed in her nightdress which, like all the other nightclothes worn in that mourning household that night, was black. She climbed into the black-hung bed while the black window drapes were drawn.

Melintha, always interested in scandal and gossip, had lain beside Fidelity in the dark, and prompted:

"Did you hear the rumors about John Hingham?"

"Yes," Fidelity answered truthfully.

"Were they true?"

"How should I know?"

"Well!" Melintha was indignant at Fidelity's uncooperativeness. "You live with the Wilmingtons, you should know what is happening there!"

"John Hingham was not in the habit of confiding in me," Fidelity said coolly. "And I won't spread gossip about Henrietta's husband. There are plenty of others who would be only too happy to trade scandals with you."

"Aren't you the high-principled young lady! Don't think I didn't notice you scheming with Lord Pierrepointe in the cemetery, and it's not the first time." With a violent motion Melintha turned away from Fidelity in the black-draped bed and sulked until she fell asleep.

Fidelity, however, did not fall asleep. She had decided not to go to the lawn temple to meet Schuyler, but she heard the clock on the mantel chime midnight, then one, then two. With each chime her resolve weakened and, as she lay beside the sleeping Melintha, she found herself alternately eager and anxious as the hour of their meeting approached.

She pictured Schuyler awaiting her in the lawn temple, savored his disappointment if she didn't appear, but recognized her own longing to see him. Why? she demanded of herself. She had Philip who loved her and would protect her with his life if necessary and yet she longed to see Schuyler who had never caused her anything but grief. Their pleasure in each other had been the pleasure of the senses and yet she needed him.

In the darkness she heard the mantel clock chime three and, after a moment's hesitation, slid silently and carefully out of the high bed. She froze for a moment at the bedside to be sure she had not awakened Melintha with her movements. Melintha didn't stir nor did the even breathing of her slumber change its pace. Satisfied, Fidelity crept to the armoire and drew out a black silk cloak. She stuck her feet into a pair of black mules and, slipping the rustling cloak about her shoulders, pulled the hood over her disheveled hair and tied it beneath her chin.

Pausing again and wondering what she'd tell Melintha were she to awaken at that moment, she sighed her relief as Melintha continued her slumber. Tiptoeing to the door she opened it as quietly as she could and slipped into the long, cold, third floor hallway.

The hallway was deserted, as she'd hoped. She walked quickly down the hallway, her steps muffled in the deep pile of the carpet.

Reaching the stairway she paused but there wasn't a sound to be heard in the house. She went down the dark stairs carefully, her cloak and nightgown gathered into one hand and the other sliding cautiously down the handrail. At the bottom she paused, standing in the center of the second floor hallway, before starting down the wide staircase leading to the reception hall below.

From the reception hall, Fidelity went to a side entrance of the mansion and slipped out into the cool air of the night.

She paused for a moment inside the lattice-enclosed porch of the side entrance and released the breath it seemed she'd held since leaving her bed. For a moment she debated returning but she'd come so far already, taken so many risks, that it would be a mockery of her efforts to return to her room without finishing what she'd begun. Taking a deep breath, she opened the door of the porch and stepped down the three steps and onto the side lawn of the mansion.

Before her lay the high, wide garden gates of the formal gardens of Poplar Hill and beyond them, hidden from sight by a terraced hill, was the lawn temple.

Inside the lawn temple, hopefully, Schuyler was awaiting her.

# 30

Fidelity slipped between the ornately wrought iron gates of the garden. The air was, if anything, even colder and more damp than it had been during John's funeral and the billowy black clouds had gathered to obscure the night sky, hiding the stars and moon. She shivered. There were occasional reports of people being attacked by runaway slaves or Indians who could still be a threat in the area. She quickened her step as a twig snapped somewhere in the darkness and prayed that the foot that snapped it belonged to some little animal straying from the forests.

She strained her eyes into the night, eagerly awaiting a glimpse of the lawn temple. Where was it? Had she gotten confused and gone in the wrong direction? She was not particularly familiar with the Poplar Hill gardens, having walked there only briefly during the previous afternoon. She wondered if she should turn back to the house before she was hopelessly lost.

A flash of lightning illuminated the gardens momentarily and it was enough to show her the white lawn temple not far ahead.

She breathed a sigh of relief and hurried toward

it. The lightning had turned the white temple pink as it lit the gardens but, when the brief flash subsided, she could see it standing gray against a background of trees.

The lawn temple was a structure simple in design but elegant in its simplicity. It consisted of a circle of columns supporting a high-domed roof and sheltering a pair of white-painted, wrought iron loveseats.

As she approached, she saw Schuyler awaiting her on one of those loveseats. He stood as she neared and left the circle of columns to meet her.

"I thought you weren't coming," he said as he took her hand and led her into the little temple.

"I said I'd try. I had to be sure Melintha was asleep before I could leave."

"But you thought about not coming at all, didn't you?"

Fidelity lowered her eyes; he had always been able to fathom her thoughts. "Yes," she admitted. "I did consider it."

She shivered as a gust of wind struck her as it blew through the temple. She was sorry she'd come out into the gardens dressed in her thin silk nightdress and taffeta cloak. Schuyler was wearing the suit of black satin he'd worn to the funeral and, over it, a cloak of black velvet. She envied him its warmth.

She waited impatiently for him to speak and allowed him to sit closer than she might have under different circumstances.

"You're shivering," he said at last.

"Well it's cold!" she snapped.

"You should have gotten dressed before leaving

to come out here," he said and, seeing her about to speak, continued: "I know, you didn't want to wake Melintha Staunton. I do confess that I get a distinct pleasure at seeing you in such charming déshabillé."

"Schuyler!" she said threateningly.

"I'm sorry, my dear." He spread his cloak around her and she was drawn against him.

Ordinarily she would have moved away for she was painfully aware of his effect upon her but the warmth of his cloak and his body was like heaven and she couldn't force herself to pull away from him.

"Are you going to tell me why we're here?" she prompted when he said no more.

He was silent and she looked up at him wondering at his silence. When she'd turned her face up toward his, he looked down and in an instant she felt the warmth of his lips against the cold flesh of her temple.

"Oh, Schuyler, no," she groaned wearily. He was so warm, and she felt protected and cared for in the warm circle of his arms. Feebly she pushed his face away and felt his lips moving against her fingers. She started to stand.

"All right," he conceded. "Sit down. You'll catch your death if you don't stay with me."

"Are you going to tell me why I'm out here catching my death?"

"I saw you there in the cemetery today and I wanted to tell you how I cared for you. I know it hurt you when I married . . . "

"Rather impious thoughts when you're supposed to be praying for the repose of John Hingham's soul."

Schuyler laughed shortly and tossed his head making the black plumes on his black hat shake. "John Hingham's soul can repose in hell for all I care; it probably already is. May Satan light a fire under him for me."

"Schuyler!"

He laughed again with more humor. "Come now, my dear. You've been away from Fairfax House for how long? A year? A year and a half? Don't let your Puritan upbringing resurface at this late date."

"So the only reason I'm here at this godforsaken hour in this weather is to hear you protest that you always cared even though you married another woman?" Her tone was sarcastic.

"I couldn't marry you, you were already married."

"And poor," she supplied. "Frankly, Schuyler, we've been through this so many times that it fails to interest me any longer. If you'll excuse me." She pushed away from him once again, but then paused. "Does this have anything to do with the fact that Philip is due back in a week or so?"

"In a way," he admitted.

"We've been through this before also." She tried to be firm and sound stern and forbidding but she was again shivering and longed to slip back into the warmth of his arms. She fought her impulses and continued: "I will absolutely not see you after Philip returns except on such occasions as when our meeting one another is unavoidable. I will not deceive Philip while I am a guest at Wilmington Hall living on his and his brother's hospitality." She waited for him to reply and when he did not, prompted: "Well?"

He smiled. "You're beautiful in black, you should wear it more often."

"Schuyler!" Fidelity was exasperated. "You're impossible! You're . . . " She jumped as a bolt of lightning struck nearby in the forest and a rolling boom of thunder echoed against the mansion of Poplar Hill.

"Fidelity," Schuyler took advantage of her startledness to say, "I think it might be better if you didn't live at Wilmington Hall any longer. Would that make a difference in the situation?"

"What are you proposing?"

"You could come live at Yorkby. Then you wouldn't feel obligated to Philip Wilmington."

She wrapped her cloak more tightly around herself. "I doubt if your wife would appreciate my presence on the plantation she's paying you to . . . "

"Now, now," Schuyler stopped her. "We aren't going to discuss my financial arrangement. As for my wife, I can deal with that situation."

Fidelity's eyes grew wide. "But . . . but a divorce is all but impossible to obtain, even in England! Unless your wife can prove you impotent!" She smiled with wicked malice.

"Would you like to find out if she has grounds for that charge?" he asked insolently.

"We're getting off the subject," she replied hurriedly. "Could your wife be persuaded to return to England? She has children there, doesn't she, from her first marriage?"

Schuyler shook his head. "She'll never leave, not

while I'm here. She has too much invested in me."

"Then what exactly is it you're proposing?"

"There's a cottage at Yorkby; it is well away from the main house at the far end of the gardens and up a little path at the edge of the forest. It's quite beautiful, one story in height but rather like a miniature mansion. There are dependencies, servant quarters, a brick kitchen, stables, and so on . . . " He saw her open her mouth to speak but continued: "You really could live there most comfortably. I would, of course, provide you with everything you'd need; a staff of servants, a coach, horses, a barge . . . whatever you want." He paused and drew his cloak collar higher as the rain began to fall and, although they were protected from the worst of it by the roof of the temple, gusts of it struck them borne on the wind. "No one," he continued at last, "would be permitted to disturb you."

Fidelity was silent for a moment as she drew the hood of her cloak forward and hunched her back against the rain that rapidly soaked her thin cloak and nightdress. "And you would come to visit occasionally, I take it?"

"Well of course. Isn't that the purpose?"

"How dare you!" In her anger she forgot about the rain and the cold. "How dare you propose that I leave Wilmington Hall to become your hidden mistress!"

"After all," he replied, standing. "It wouldn't be the first time you've been my mistress."

Fidelity stood, buffeted by the wind and rain. His quick cynicism coming so soon after his protestations of affection surprised her. Not that it should have, he'd always been quick to ridicule when one of his whims was refused. She suddenly saw herself and her presence in their situation as ludicrous and turned away from him.

Silently she left the lawn temple and stumbled into the rain and wind, retracing the steps which had brought her to him earlier. She hadn't gotten far when she felt his hand close on her arm through the soaked material of her garments and she nearly slipped on the wet grass as he pulled her to a halt and spun her toward him.

She struggled violently while the rain pelted them both. "Let me go!" she screamed over the thunder. "Let me go!"

"You love me! I know you do, you can't lie to me!" Schuyler shouted. He pulled her to him and held her fast. "Tell me that you love me."

"I hate you!" Fidelity hissed. She looked up at him and her hood fell back allowing the rain to soak her damp hair. "I hate you more than anyone in the world!"

With one hand holding the back of her head in a viselike grip, he tipped her face up and kissed her while the rain poured over them.

When at last he released her, she slumped against him crying, her tears unidentifiable among the rivulets of rain.

"Admit it," Schuyler demanded. "Admit that you love me and not Wilmington."

"Why?" Fidelity whined. "Why are you doing this to me? You have everything you wanted, why can't you leave me alone?"

"I have to know! Tell me, now!"

She stood, defeated, with her face against the wet velvet of his cloak. Concession would mean more than admitting the truth to him, it would mean admitting it to herself. At last she raised her eyes and looked at his face above hers.

If she'd hoped to see a glimmer of pity in his eyes she was mistaken. If she'd hoped to be allowed to escape with her pride intact she was disappointed. She knew he would not release her without her admission and if she refused she might well find herself in this same position when dawn broke over the river. She swallowed a gulp of the wet, chilled night air and said:

"Yes . . . yes . . . I love you. I've never loved anyone except you, and may God damn you for it!"

She pushed away from him and turned once again, resuming her stumbling flight across the garden toward the mansion. She didn't know if he was behind her but she could hear, over the rumble of the thunder which had moved into the distance taking with it the worst of the storm and leaving behind only a gentle, cool rain, the triumphant laughter of the man she hated with a passion only equaled by the love she bore for him.

It seemed, as she ran, that the gardens had begun to spin and she could hardly keep her footing as she was seized with a violent trembling. The cold which up until then had been merely uncomfortable was unbearable, but very shortly it began to alternate with short periods of steaming heat. She felt a strong desire to rest but pushed onward toward the gates and the house beyond.

Once she fell when coming upon a stone path cut deeply into the lawn across which she ran and, putting her hands out to catch herself as she fell, she felt the sharp sting of tiny pebbles scraping her palms and knees.

At last, when it seemed she'd never see the mansion again, she reached the iron gates and wrestled them open enough to pass between. She climbed the three steps to the lattice-enclosed side entrance and opened the door. It seemed heavier than it had when she'd left the house just over an hour before. She passed through the entrance-way and into the main hall of the house. At the foot of the curving staircase she stopped. The staircase loomed before her and her room was two floors and four flights up. She sat heavily on the bottom step and leaned her head against the intricately fashioned newel post.

"Ma'am?" A woman's voice sounded beside her.

Fidelity opened her eyes and saw a young girl standing there. In her hand she carried a black nightdress of some sort of woolen fabric.

"What? Who are you?" Fidelity mumbled. She couldn't remember having ever seen the girl before.

"My name's Rose, Ma'am. My master said I was going to work for you now. He sent me to help you change your clothes and get back to bed."

"Your master? Who's your master?"

"Why," the girl seemed astonished. "My Lord Pierrepointe, of course!"

Fidelity studied the girl. She was about her own

age, short and stout, with a head of golden curls.
Fidelity felt she should send the girl back to Schuyler.
She was dimly annoyed that he'd been so sure of
success as to engage a maidservant for her, but for the
moment the nightdress the girl held looked so dry,
and warm! And going to bed sounded so good, even
going to a bed already occupied by Melintha Staunton!

She allowed the girl to help her up and take her
to a parlor where she was stripped of her cloak and
nightdress and rubbed dry with a towel Rose
produced from the folds of the woolen gown. She
held her arms up as Rose slipped the thick gown over
her head and waited while the girl took her soaking
garments away. She knew not where they were being
taken and she couldn't have cared less. When Rose
returned, she helped her new mistress up the four long
flights of stairs and tucked her into bed beside the
softly snoring Melintha Staunton.

"Where shall I sleep, Ma'am?" Rose whispered.

"Hmmm?" Fidelity asked. She felt long waves of
fatigue washing over her even though she couldn't
seem to get warm.

"Where shall I sleep?"

"Is there a trundle under this bed?"

Rose looked. "No, Ma'am."

"There's a sofa." Fidelity waved in the direction
of the brocaded sofa near the window. "Can you
sleep there?"

"Oh, yes, Ma'am!" Rose smiled.

"Take a quilt out of the chest if you want."
Fidelity was hardly aware of what she was saying.

"Yes, Ma'am! Thank you, Ma'am! I'm going to enjoy working for you more than I did my Lady Pierrepointe. There's a foul old toad for you! Pardon me for talking about the quality, Ma'am, but if she's the quality then I'm . . . " She stopped, realizing that Fidelity had dropped off to sleep.

With a smile, she took a quilt from the chest at the foot of the bed and crossed the room to the sofa. She was going to enjoy her new job, she was sure! Of course, she was going to miss Lord Pierrepointe. She sighed, what a handsome man he was! She'd never slept with a gentleman of quality before she went to work for Lady Pierrepointe. But now, so the gossip at Yorkby ran, he was going to set this girl up as his mistress in the cottage. Rose envied her. But as her maidservant she'd be there when he came to visit and perhaps there'd be times when her new mistress would be indisposed. She didn't look like the overly healthy type. Rose lay down on the sofa and smiled. Yes, she was going to enjoy her new position as maidservant to Mistress Fidelity Fairfax!

# 31

Fidelity awoke slowly, emerging from her slumber like one who dives deep into a pool and then feels as if she will never reach the surface. Her eyes seemed filmed by a gauzy haze and the weight of several thick comforters over her still-feverish body made her feel unbearably hot and steamy.

Though the drapes were closed, she saw the glow of bright sunlight through them and, hearing someone moving in the room, struggled to say: "What time is it?"

A hazy shape bent over her and an unfamiliar feminine voice said, "Mistress? Can you hear me?"

"I . . . I," Fidelity muttered, her head felt heavy and swaddled in wool. "Who is it?"

"Well, it's me, Rose," the shape said. "Your maid."

"Rose," Fidelity tried to remember.

"Wait," the shape said, moving away. "I'll go get . . . " The name of the person she was going to get was drowned out by the opening and closing of the door.

"Rose," Fidelity repeated, struggling to stay awake. "Rose." Dimly, though her head was begin-

ning to ache from the effort, she remembered a girl
named Rose. The maidservant Schuyler had sent to
her at the Hinghams' house. Was she still at Poplar
Hill? She squinted at her surroundings which, although blurred, she could see were not the black
mourning of the room which she'd occupied at Poplar
Hill. She must be home, at Wilmington Hall. But
Rose was here; Schuyler had sent her. Schuyler. She
remembered the stormy night in the lawn temple.
Was it last night? How long had she been ill, for ill she
must be. No one felt as badly as she did unless they
had been very ill. She lost her train of thought as sleep
began to overtake her once again.

　　She was sinking into a sleep bordering on
unconsciousness when she heard the door opening
and footsteps crossing the floor. Rose had returned
and she saw her bending over the bed once more.

　　"Rose?" she whispered.

　　"She's still awake, sir," Rose said.

　　Fidelity heard more footsteps and another, larger
shape bent over her on the opposite side of the bed
from the shape which identified itself as Rose. She felt
a large, rough hand sweep itself across her brow. It
was cool on her fevered skin and she closed her eyes
and sighed as it moved, taking with it some of the
salty perspiration that sheened her forehead. The
hand moved again brushing aside a strand of hair that
was sticking to the side of her face. It was such a
gentle hand, such a loving hand. She sighed again and
the shape came nearer and a low-pitched, masculine
voice whispered her name. She smiled, a weak ghost
of a smile, and remembered the night in the lawn

temple when she'd heard Schuyler whispering her name. Her dry, fever-cracked lips parted and she ignored the pain of her throat to whisper:

"Schuyler, oh, Schuyler."

The shape moved upward blurring even more and she gave up the fight against the sleep dragging at her eyes and drifted away.

Philip Wilmington, still wearing the clothing in which he'd just stepped off his newly docked ship, stood by the bedside and gazed down at the sleeping Fidelity. Schuyler! That bastard who'd come between them in London had come between them once more. He lifted his eyes and looked at Rose. She'd run down to the docks to fetch Lady Wilmington who was telling him about Fidelity's illness. When he'd heard she was awake he hadn't bothered to ask about this girl he'd never seen before.

"She thought you were Lord Pierrepointe!" Rose giggled thinking that although this man was quite handsome she much preferred the blond good looks of her former master.

Philip was taken aback. If Fidelity had told this girl about Schuyler, he thought, she must have cared about him all along.

"You know about Lord Pierrepointe?" he asked Rose.

She giggled again. "Of course I know about him! I used to be his wife's maidservant, until he sent me to Mistress Fidelity. I suppose, though, that since she's shortly going to live with him I still work for him."

"What do you mean, she's going to live with him?"

"At Yorkby, his plantation." Rose clapped a hand over her mouth. "I don't think I'm supposed to tell you that. It's supposed to be a secret from his wife, but I don't think she'd be in the dark for long with her husband's mistress just at the other end of the gardens." She looked at Fidelity fondly and sighed. "He's mad about her! Arrangin' secret meetings; that's how she got sick!"

Philip sank into a chair and Rose, warmed to her subject and happy to have a willing audience, continued:

"It was at Master Hingham's funeral, at Poplar Hill. They met in the little temple in the gardens in the dead of night! It began to rain and she, in just her silk nightdress and a cloak, got soaked. It's no wonder she caught her death of cold! Lord Pierrepointe sent me down to help her into bed." She stopped, seeing the look on Philip's face. "Have I said something wrong, Sir?"

Philip didn't answer. He rose from the chair and, without another glance at Fidelity, left the room.

"Well!" Rose said to herself, thinking he was annoyed at her gossiping. "You asked!"

It was the middle of the morning, two days later, that Fidelity climbed out of her bed for the first time in nearly two weeks. She stood in a large basin while Rose helped her bathe and sat while her hair was dried and rubbed to a glossy sheen with a piece of silk. It was while she was being dressed that she noticed the toll her illness had taken.

"My dress doesn't fit!" she exclaimed as Rose tied

the laces of her powder blue silk gown with its dark blue trimmings. "But it's new and it fit so well!"

"You've gotten mighty spindly since you've been sick," Rose agreed.

"Do I look terribly ugly?" she asked her maid fearfully.

"Lord, Ma'am! I would I looked half so good as you do! Let me tie these laces a bit tighter."

"Why hasn't Henrietta been in to see me?"

Rose applied her teeth to the knot she'd tied and, when she had it undone, answered: "Why, she never came back from Poplar Hill! Mistress Hingham, the older one, convinced her to stay so they could worship the memory of the young Master Hingham together."

"I see. Well, I hope she doesn't spend the rest of her life wasting her sorrow on him. I suppose that sounds awfully irreverent but I can't mourn the likes of John Hingham!"

When she was ready to leave her room, Rose accompanied her down the stairs. The air seemed fresh and clean after the stifling air of her sickroom and she hoped Lady Wilmington would send some of the servants up to give the room a good airing before she had to return to it.

"It still feels a little warm to me," she told Rose as they descended the first flight of stairs. "Would you go back to my room and get a fan?"

While her maidservant started back up the stairs, Fidelity waited for her on the landing. She could see the main hallway below and, as she stood there, a door opened and a gentleman she didn't know stepped out of the drawing room.

Looking up, the man saw her and immediately started up the stairs. He was a short man, and rather plump, with rough, pitted skin that bespoke a bad bout with the smallpox. He wore a suit of crimson satin with very wide breeches reaching to his knees and a short doublet which did not reach to the waist of his breeches. In between the breeches and doublet one could see a great deal of his shirt of spotless white linen. The ends of his cravat and the ruffles of his sleeves were decorated with deep flounces of white lace and his doublet and breeches were decorated further with loops of crimson and white ribbons.

"Mademoiselle! Mademoiselle!" he cried. "You should not be walking about! I was just suggesting to Madame la Baronne Wilmington that you should be bled to allow the ill humors to leave your body!"

"Bled?" Fidelity asked, staring at the gentleman. She'd heard nothing of a Frenchman in the area.

*"Mais oui!"* he insisted. "I am qualified . . . " He fumbled in the front pocket of his breeches then pulled out his hand and stuck his finger into his mouth with a muffled oath. Reaching gingerly into the pocket once again, he pulled out a lancet and showed it to her.

Seeing the little double-edged knife, Fidelity stepped back a step or two. "Thank you, monsieur," she said without taking her eyes from the lancet. "But I am quite well now."

"But the humors," he insisted. "If they are not allowed to escape . . . "

"Gaston, leave her and her humors alone!"

Fidelity looked past the man and saw a woman standing just outside the same drawing room from which the man had emerged. She too was unmistakably French.

"But, Aurore," the man reasoned. "She may become ill once again."

"She looks perfectly fine to me! Come down, mademoiselle, before Gaston tries to force his lancet upon you!"

Rose, who'd just returned from Fidelity's room with a blue fan, gasped at the sight of the oddly dressed man holding the wicked-looking surgical instrument and followed her mistress down the stairs quickly, pressing herself far against the balustrade as she passed him. She joined Fidelity and the Frenchwoman in the hall just as the baroness Wilmington stepped to the door of the drawing room.

"Why, Fidelity!" she exclaimed. "How nice to see you up and about! I knew you were better but I had no idea you were so well recovered. Please, may I present the Marquis and Marquise de Saint-Quentin?" She gestured at the man on the stairs and the lady who'd saved Fidelity from the lancet. "Madame, monsieur, this is Fidelity Fairfax, a guest of my husband's brother Philip, although she seems more like one of the family."

Fidelity curtsied to the marquise, who was a short, plump woman not so different in looks from her husband, although her skin was not pitted as was his. She turned to curtsy to the marquis but he seized her hand and kissed it so suddenly that she forgot to make the gesture.

"Come into the drawing room," the baroness invited. "Fidelity has a lot to catch up on."

Gaston, the Marquis de Saint-Quentin, excused himself saying he wanted to find the baron and bowed to his wife and hostess. Then, turning to Fidelity, said: *"Mademoiselle Fidélité, vous etes tres belle et trés charmante."*

*"Merci, Monsieur le Marquis,"* Fidelity replied. She hoped he would not press her because she hadn't gotten much farther in her French lessons in London.

He didn't. With another kiss on the hand he turned and left the house.

"I didn't know you spoke French," Lady Wilmington said when he was gone.

"I'm afraid you've just heard most of my French," she confessed. The ladies laughed and Fidelity said to the marquise, "How long have you been in Virginia, Madame la Marquise?"

The Marquise de Saint-Quentin arranged a fold of her russet silk gown which accented her rather high coloring. "Only for two days," she said. "We came from Martinique with Monsieur Wilmington. We are going to go to England on his next trip there. I have a sister who married an Englishman when King Charles was in exile. After we visit her we will return to France."

"Ah, I see." Fidelity started. "You came with Monsieur Wilmington?" She looked at the baroness. "Philip is back?"

"Yes," the baroness replied. "He was up to see you as soon as he returned but I believe you were still too ill to recognize him."

"Where is he now?"

"At the docks. He and Edmund are supervising some repairs on the ships."

Fidelity stood. She dropped a hasty curtsy to the other two ladies and said: "I must go down to the docks. Will you excuse me?"

"Of course," they said together, and the baroness added, "You'd better wear a cloak. It wouldn't do you good to catch a chill so soon after your illness."

"No!" the marquise agreed, laughing. "If you were to fall ill again we would have to post a guard to keep Gaston and his lancet away from you!"

Stepping into the hall, Fidelity found Rose talking to one of the baron's footmen. "Rose," she called. "Will you get me a cloak? The dark blue satin, I think."

"Yes, Ma'am." Obediently Rose started up the stairs once again and the footman went back about his duties.

When Rose returned, Fidelity could hardly bear to wait while the cloak was draped over her shoulders and tied beneath her chin. It did not have a hood and her hair, which she'd left hanging loosely with only a dark blue ribbon in it, hung over the deep blue fabric in a silver cascade.

"Will you be wantin' me to come with you?" Rose asked.

"Yes, if you like," Fidelity agreed.

"Then I'll have to get a cloak for myself."

"Then get one!" She hadn't meant to snap at the girl but she was impatient with the delay. It seemed to take much longer for Rose to fetch her own cloak than it had to get Fidelity's, but at last she returned and they stepped out of the house and started down the path toward the docks.

The river glittered in the sunshine of the early afternoon and the scene at the docks reminded Fidelity of her own arrival at Wilmington Hall. The three ships, Philip's own *Virginian* and the two merchantmen, were swarming with activity and she searched the busy men with her eyes trying to find Philip among them.

At last she found him. Standing on the dock between two ships, he was talking to Edmund Wilmington and the Marquis de Saint-Quentin. She stood still and stared at him, finding him more ruggedly handsome than she remembered even though she had thought of him often in the two months he'd been gone. She started forward intending to go to him regardless of the presence of his brother and the marquis but stopped when she heard her name being called from just beyond the barrier of trees that divided the dock area from the lawn of the Hall. She turned just as a great bay galloped into view and, handling him expertly, Schuyler Pierrepointe.

He reined the horse to a halt near her and leaped to the ground. "Welcome back to the world!" he said. "It grieved me to think that I'd been the cause of your illness."

"I can't talk to you, Schuyler," she said impatiently. "I have to talk to Philip."

"Yes, I'd heard he'd returned," Schuyler said idly. "I rode over to meet him since, as an employee of the partnership he is, in a way, working for me." He smiled at Rose and chucked her under the chin.

Fidelity frowned at her maidservant as the girl blushed and giggled. "I'm sure he'll be overjoyed at the prospect," she said sarcastically.

"Pierrpointe! Come over and meet my brother!" the Baron Wilmington called.

"Well," Schuyler told Fidelity. "We'll soon find out how overjoyed he is!"

Taking her hand with a deceptively tight grip, he forced Fidelity to either accompany him to Philip's side or make a scene trying to escape from him. She chose to go and they walked together toward the three men on the dock.

Fidelity looked at Philip pleadingly but, except for a brief moment, he refused to return her look. Instead he fixed Schuyler with a cold glare.

"Fidelity," Edmund Wilmington said. "I'm glad to see that you are well enough to be out of doors. We were quite worried about her for several days, you know." This was addressed to Philip. "It's a pity you weren't here during the worst of her illness."

Philip continued to stare at Schuyler. "I'm sure," he replied, "that she was in very competent hands during my absence."

Edmund missed the significance of the remark and Schuyler did not deign to answer the verbal accusation thrown at him. But the marquis, with his single-mindedness, said: "She would have recovered sooner had she been bled!"

"Yes, I'm sure," Edmund said politely to his guest. He turned back to Philip. "Lord Pierrepointe has purchased Yorkby plantation from George Staunton. He has also become a partner in our little company."

"I see," Philip said, never once removing his gaze from Schuyler's face. "I hope you won't regret it."

"I'm sure I won't," Schuyler replied with arrogant self-assurance. "I've already had some most unexpected, and very pleasant, dividends as a result of my association with Wilmington Hall."

The two men eyed one another silently and it was Edmund who said at last:

"Come, Lord Pierrepointe, Monsieur de Saint-Quentin, why don't we go up to the house and let Philip get back to his work."

"Yes," Philip agreed. "I have a great deal to do although I don't suppose you know much about ships." His remark was directed at Schuyler and the mandatory "my lord" was noticeably missing.

"No, I admit that I don't," Schuyler replied. "But then one doesn't have to know a great deal when one has employees who can do the work for you."

Fidelity saw Philip's nostrils flare angrily and she was not sorry when Edmund began to walk toward the house urging Schuyler and the marquis to come along. She lagged behind but was caught in the tight circle of Schuyler's arm as he pulled her along with him.

"You shouldn't stay near the river too long your first day outside," he said. "The breezes are too moist and you are apt to be chilled."

"But . . . but," she sputtered, trying to resist.

"He's absolutely right," Edmund agreed.

"But I wanted to . . . " Fidelity started to protest.

"No, no, no!" the marquis corrected. "If you become chilled you will suffer a relapse and have to be bled!"

"But I wanted to talk to Philip!" she finished. They were nearing the trees and she turned her head to look over her shoulder at the ships.

Philip stood where they'd left him on the dock and he watched as they moved away from him toward the house. But as Fidelity resisted the grip of Schuyler's arm enough to look back at him, he turned and leaped onto the ship and disappeared into the swarming crowds of men.

"You may want to talk to him," Schuyler said softly into her ear, "but it doesn't appear he wants to talk to you. If you want my opinion, my dear, I would say something has vexed your privateering lover."

"Oh, Schuyler!" she snapped as she broke away from him and hurried to catch up with the baron and marquis who had gone ahead of them. "Shut up!"

Schuyler shrugged as they moved through the barrier of trees and onto the lawns of Wilmington Hall. He winked at Rose who giggled again and laughed aloud knowing that, although they couldn't be seen from the ships, both Rose's giggle and his laughter would be heard by Philip aboard the ship. Would Philip be able to tell that the delighted giggle was Rose's and not Fidelity's? Schuyler didn't think so. Would Philip think Fidelity had giggled at some amusing story or lover's gesture? Schuyler was sure of it.

# 32

Wilmington Hall was dark, its inhabitants having retired for the night with two notable exceptions: Philip Wilmington who had not yet returned from wherever he'd gone that afternoon, and Fidelity who lay awake waiting for Philip to return.

Rose slept in Fidelity's room on a trundle bed and she, unlike her mistress, was undistrubed by anything. She lay on her back with her mouth open making ungodly noises.

Down the hall, in the rooms once occupied by Henrietta and John Hingham, the Saint-Quentins were sleeping and at the far end of the long hallway, the Baron and Baroness Wilmington had also long since fallen asleep.

But Fidelity could not find peaceful rest in slumber. She tossed and turned and at last resigned herself to lying awake listening enviously to her maid's snores and mumbles.

She heard the clock strike one. Perhaps Philip was not coming home at all. Perhaps he'd decided to remain wherever he was for the night and then return in the morning. Resignedly she rolled onto her side and pulled her quilts up to her chin. Lying awake all night wouldn't do any good if Philip wasn't coming home.

She sat up in the darkness and listened. Had she heard footsteps mounting the stairs? Straining her ears, she heard the sound of booted feet walking down the hallway. The steps passed her door and stopped at Philip's. He had come home! She started to get out of bed and then stopped. What if he went straight to bed? And if he didn't, how was she to approach him to talk about Schuyler? She lay back down. Perhaps it would be better to speak to him in the morning. He was probably tired now and would not welcome her presence.

She lay silently and watched as a light glowed beneath the door between her room and Philip's and then saw the light go out. Philip would, no doubt, have little trouble getting to sleep. She turned away from the wall the two rooms shared and closed her eyes, but the clock had struck three before she finally found refuge in sleep.

Fidelity awoke with a start after Rose dropped a porcelain wash basin she was carrying and it smashed into a thousand pieces on the floor.

"Oh, Ma'am!" Rose wailed. "I didn't mean to drop it, I swear I didn't!"

"No, I don't suppose you did," Fidelity mumbled, rubbing the last clinging vestiges of sleep from her eyes. She watched as Rose began gingerly picking up the broken basin, placing the smaller pieces into the larger. The mantel clock began to chime the hour and, as had become her habit, she counted the clear bell tones as they rang the hour. One . . . two . . . three . . . four . . . five . . . six . . . seven . . . . eight .

. . nine . . . ten. Ten! Fidelity hopped out of bed and ran to the window. Jerking the heavy drapes aside, she saw the yard and the docks swarming with the activity of a normal day.

"Good Lord, Rose!" she cried, "you should never have let me sleep so long!"

"You didn't say anything about gettin' you up," Rose reasoned from her place on the floor. "And you were sleeping so soundly."

Fidelity drew a dressing gown over her night-dress and crossed the room, stepping carefully around the shards of broken porcelain on the floor, to the connecting door between her room and Philip's. Although she would have been surprised to find him still there at this late hour, she knocked and then, receiving no response, opened the door. The room was empty, Philip had gone.

"Damn!" she cried to the empty room.

"What is it, Ma'am?" Rose asked. She dumped the broken pieces of the basin into the pitcher that had been part of the set. The rest of the set would have to be taken out and replaced now that the basin was gone. Lady Wilmington would undoubtedly give them to one of the servants. Rose stepped to the door where Fidelity was still framed. She peeked into the adjoining room.

"Who's room is this?" she asked. "I thought this was another closet or something."

"This is Philip Wilmington's room." Fidelity replied, snappishly. "I wanted to speak to him before he left this morning for the docks. Now I suppose he'll be too busy. I'll have to wait until this evening."

"So this is Master Wilmington's room," Rose

mused disapprovingly. "I don't think my Lord Pierrepointe would like this."

Fidelity slammed the door. "I don't care what your Lord Pierrepointe likes or dislikes," she growled. "Your Lord Pierrepointe can go take the plague for all I care."

Rose stepped back, shocked. "That will have to change," she said authoritatively, "after we move to Yorkby."

"We are not moving to Yorkby!"

"But Master Schuyler told me . . ."

"Master Schuyler! My Lord Pierrepointe! That's all you can say! I don't know what Schuyler told you but I told him that night at Poplar Hill that I would not be his mistress and I would not live in the cottage on his plantation! Get me some clothes, I can't stay in here all day!"

Sullenly, for she'd lived for the day when they would go back to live at Yorkby, Rose went about her duties as Fidelity's maid. At last, while she was hooking up the back of Fidelity's pale green gown, she said: "You were anxious enough to see Master Schuyler while you were sick! You even called Master Wilmington 'Schuyler' when he came to see how you were."

Fidelity whirled about to face her maid. "I did what?"

Rose nodded with self-satisfaction. "That's right, he came in and bent over you when you first came awake and you called him 'Schuyler'. 'Schuyler, oh, Schuyler,' that's what you said. Like you were seeing a dream come to life."

Fidelity blanched. "And what did Philip do?"

"He got sort of white in the face, like you're doing right now. He asked me who I was and I told him. I told him how Master Schuyler sent me to take care of you after you met him in the garden at the Hinghams'. And I told him how we were going to move back to Yorkby so you could be Master Schuyler's mistress."

"You told him that!" Fidelity was trembling so that she had to sit down.

Rose shrugged. "Well, I thought it was true at the time. How was I to know that you'd turned poor Master Schuyler down?"

Fidelity stood and started across the room. "I have to talk to Philip! I have to explain . . ."

Rose shook her head. "Poor, poor Master Schuyler . . ."

"If you care so much about poor Master Schuyler," Fidelity snapped as she passed the girl. "Why don't you go back to Yorkby and sleep with him?"

Rose lifted her chin. It was a sore spot with her that Schuyler had been willing to go to such lengths to provide for Fidelity when she herself would have been happy to continue in the post of his occasional mistress. "It wouldn't be the first time," she said proudly.

Fidelity paused and looked at the girl seeing, in Rose's blind caring for Schuyler, a portrait of herself. It would be useless, she knew, to try to make Rose see that there was no hope of ever having a place in Schuyler's heart. His heart belonged to whomever had enough money to buy it. But Rose wouldn't believe her anymore than she would have believed her parents' warnings about him. Without another word she left the room and hurried down the hall to look for Philip.

She hurried past the rooms of the Saint-Quentins just as the door swung open and the marquis stepped into the hallway. *"Mademoiselle Fidélité,"* he said, giving her name the French pronunciation. "You are looking pale, you are ill?"

"No, monsieur," Fidelity assured him hastily.

The marquis was a little overly anxious to practice medicine to suit her. She didn't doubt for a moment that somewhere in the pockets of those wide-legged breeches he wore, that she'd learned were called "Rhinegraves" and were all the rage in France, was his trusty lancet ready to do its work on any willing vein it could find.

"Monsieur," she asked. "Have you seen Philip Wilmington this morning?"

"Philippe?" he repeated. "No, I have not seen him. Is he missing?"

"No, I wanted to speak with him but slept too late this morning. Please excuse me." She dropped him a hasty curtsy and, without waiting for his bow, stepped swiftly away and down the stairs.

As she left the Hall she stopped and wondered where Philip was most likely to be. In the fields? On the docks? Perhaps he was inside the house speaking with Edmund or one of the other partners in the business. Ahead, on the path that ran from the front of the house to the river, she saw Charles Wilmington apparently returning from the docks.

"Charles!" she called, hoping to catch his attention before he decided to run off to some other part of the plantation. He stopped and she hurried toward him.

"Give you good day, Fidelity," Philip's nephew said with a smile. He made her a bow that she suspected he'd copied from the elaborate style of the Marquis de Saint-Quentin.

"Good day, Charles," she replied. She wasn't surprised that he addressed her by her first name. They'd long ago agreed that she was not his uncle's wife so he couldn't call her "Aunt" and was too close to his own age to be called "Ma'am". "Have you seen your Uncle Philip this morning?"

"Only for a moment before he left."

Fidelity was crestfallen. "Left?"

"He rode over to Poplar Hill to see Henrietta. He hadn't seen her since he returned and with John dead and all, he thought he should pay a visit."

"I see. Did he say when he'd be back?"

Charles shook his head. "No. He might have decided to ride on to the Staunton's or to check on Spring Grove."

"Spring Grove: He has business with Peter Burdett?"

"Peter Burdett's not there anymore. He and Charlotte took ship for England very shortly after he shot . . . I mean after John died." Charles blushed, he'd been told not to speak of Peter Burdett's part in his brother-in-law's death. "They're going to sell Spring Grove," he continued quickly. "The overseer and the house steward are running the place right now. Father promised he'd send Uncle Philip over to check on things now and again."

"I see." Fidelity saw Charles glance in the

direction of a slave who was leading some horses toward the river. He was obviously anxious to join the man and so she said: "Thank you, Charles. I won't keep you any longer."

Charles swept her a grand bow and, with a giggle, Fidelity dropped him an elaborately formal curtsy. Then, abandoning formality, Charles took off at a run toward the horses and the river.

Night had again fallen over Wilmington Hall after what had seemed, to Fidelity, an interminable day. She'd picked at dinner provoking concerned comments from Anne Wilmington and Aurore de Saint-Quentin and speculative glances from Gaston de Saint-Quentin. As soon as she decently could, Fidelity excused herself and went upstairs to her room.

She sat in an armchair before the windows as the last streaks of the sunset faded. She heard the door of her room being opened but recognized the clomping footsteps as Rose's and so did not turn around.

"Ma'am?" Rose said quietly after several long minutes of silence.

"Yes?" Fidelity replied, still refusing to turn from the window.

"I'm sorry about what I told Master Philip."

Fidelity turned at last. "I know you thought it was the truth, Rose," she said. "And you didn't intentionally lie. Still, even if it had been the truth you had no business telling anyone else about it."

"Yes, Ma'am," Rose agreed softly. She looked as though she would cry. "If you want me to, I'll pack my things and be out of the house in the morning."

Although she said nothing, Fidelity doubted that Schuyler would receive Rose back into his service. She did not doubt that the girl had been placed with her to try to convince her to accept Schuyler's offer and if she returned now having failed, Schuyler would probably turn her out. "That won't be necessary, Rose," she said. "If you'd like to stay, you're welcome to."

"Thank you, Ma'am," Rose sniffed. "I'll tell Master Philip the truth if you want me to. I'll tell him that I was mistaken when I told him about you and Master Schuyler."

Fidelity shook her head and turned back to the windows. "No, I'll have to do that myself. And I will, if he ever returns!"

She sat before the windows until the darkness outside was so complete that she couldn't have seen a ship under full sail if it sailed right up to the front door. When she turned, Rose had lit candles on the mantel and on the table next to the bed. She had pulled her trundle out from beneath Fidelity's bed and turned back the covers on both beds.

"Would you like me to help you change your clothes?" she asked as Fidelity rose from her chair.

"Yes," Fidelity agreed. "And when you've finished you can go on to bed. You needn't keep me company."

She stood while Rose helped her out of her gown and into her nightdress and dressing gown. Then she sat while Rose picked up a gold and ivory brush, which Philip had brought her from Martinique, and began to stroke it though Fidelity's hair.

"Such lovely hair," Rose sighed. Her own head

was covered with tight little curls that caused her no end of chagrin.

Fidelity said nothing, preferring to sit quietly and be comforted by the long, slow, gentle strokes of the brush through her hair. When Rose had finished it would hang around Fidelity like a silvery veil, for Rose kept it washed and brushed and polished with silk.

"That's enough, Rose," she said at last. "You may go to bed now if you wish."

"Yes, Ma'am." Obediently, Rose stepped out of her plain brown gown and climbed into bed in her shift.

"Give you good night, Ma'am," she said.

"Good night, Rose," Fidelity replied. She walked to the mantel and blew out the candles there, leaving only a single one on the table by her bed burning.

As was her habit, Rose fell asleep in a few moments and Fidelity ruefully looked forward to a repetition of the night before.

The mantel clock struck half past eleven when Fidelity heard Philip walk past her door to his own. She held her breath hoping he might see the light of her candle shining beneath the door and come to her. But he didn't. She heard him open and close the closet door, open the window, slam drawers, and, finally, drag out the chair from his desk. Apparently he did not intend to go directly to bed.

Waiting to find courage that didn't present itself, Fidelity finally, as the clock on the mantel chimed midnight, drew her dressing gown around her and, walking around the trundle bed containing the snoring Rose, crossed the room to the door separating her room from Philip's.

Her hand touched the handle but then, on impulse, she raised her hand and knocked lightly.

There was a moment's silence when she thought he might choose to ignore her but at last she heard him say: "Come in."

The door handle gave beneath her hand and she opened the door. Philip sat at his desk, a quill in his right hand and his left hand resting on a ledger open before him. He was dressed in his breeches and bell-sleeved linen shirt. His discarded cravat lay in a small pile on the desk and his boots were on the floor near his stockinged feet. As he looked up he tipped back his head to force a lock of his dark hair to fall back over his shoulder where it lay after having fallen forward while he was writing.

"May I come in?" Fidelity asked timidly.

"Of course," he replied. His tone, she noticed, was that of a courteous friend rather than an enamoured lover.

She crossed the room and sat near him, perching tentatively on the edge of a chair. She took a deep breath while he put down his pen and closed his ledger and at last she said:

"Rose told me what happened when you came to see me while I was sick." She paused but Philip waited silently, his face carefully betraying nothing, and she continued: "It's true I went to meet Schuyler the night of John's funeral. It's also true that he asked me to go live in the little cottage by Yorkby. But I refused! I told him I wouldn't go, I wouldn't be his mistress! Rose found me that night; I was already chilled and numb—I couldn't even think clearly. Schuyler had told her she was going to be my maid when I moved to Yorkby and I was too tired and ill to talk about it that night. By the next morning I was so sick, so fevered. No one corrected her thinking. So by the time you came she still thought I was going to Yorkby. And as for me calling you Schuyler . . . well . . . I associated Rose with Schuyler and I thought I was still at Poplar Hill, and you were all blurry . . ." She stopped, wishing he would say something and, when he didn't, leaned forward and caught his hand in her two. "Please, Philip, please say you believe me! I'm telling you the truth!" She stopped breathlessly and waited for Philip to reply.

At last he said: "I believe you. But I also believe that you still love Pierrepointe."

Fidelity lowered her eyes and felt a blush rise into her cheeks. "I admit that, Philip, but you have to understand. When I met Schuyler I was so young, so naive. He seemed like someone out of a dream, all velvet and lace and plumes. And so handsome! And when he began to pay attention to me I could hardly believe it! I fell in love with him. I know now what kind of man he is—selfish and self-centered—but there's still that image of him in my mind. He stood in the hall of Fairfax House and it was as if everything glamorous and sophisticated had just swept into my life." She sighed. "I don't like the man, but I still love the image."

Philip nodded. "I suppose that might pass in time. Perhaps by the time I return from England."

"England?" Fidelity sat back in her chair. "When are you going to England?"

"In a few weeks. I have some goods to deliver

and some to buy. And I have to take the Marquis and Marquise de Saint-Quentin to London."

"Take me with you!" she begged. "Please!"

Philip shook his head. "Do you know what's waiting for you in England? Nichodemus Crichton and Barbara Palmer. You know Nichodemus could have you severely punished as an adulteress."

"But you'll be there to protect me this time."

He smiled, but refused to change his mind. "I'd feel that you only wanted to go so you could run away from this situation with Schuyler." She started to speak but he went on: "My absence will give you time to set your feelings in order. Until you can come to me with no other man in your mind or your heart, we can't be completely happy. You've never told me that you love me which is admirable honesty and I'm thankful for it, but the day you can look me straight in the face and say 'Philip, I love you' is the day I'll know you've finally exorcised all your feelings for Pierrepointe."

Fidelity was silent and, when he stood and offered her his arm saying, "Now, sweetheart, I'll escort you back to your room," there was nothing more to be said on the subject.

Taking his arm, she walked back to the door which she'd entered through only a few minutes before. Philip opened it and she stepped through. She turned back toward him hoping he would relent and at least kiss her good night but, with a polite nod, he closed the door firmly in her face.

# 33

The Baron and Baroness of Wilmington, their son Charles, Philip, Fidelity, and the Marquis and Marquise de Saint-Quentin sat at the heavy, polished, plate-laden dining table of Wilmington Hall. Dinner was nearly finished and the talk centered primarily on trifles to keep it away from what Anne Wilmington called "that interminable business."

"I think," Aurore de Saint-Quentin said, "it is marvelous of Monsieur Pierrepointe to hold a ball in our honor. Don't you think so, Gaston?"

"Yes, yes indeed.," the marquis agreed. "Although I hope it will not cause any problems with our voyage to England. It is a pity he has chosen the night before our departure to hold the ball."

"It will pose no great problems," Edmund assured them. "We will have to return very early in the morning, however. If Yorkby were closer I would suggest we return the same night, after the ball is over but of course, being so far . . ." He shrugged to illustrate the impracticability of such a suggestion.

"Do I have to attend?" Charles asked his father. "Mightn't I stay behind and help Uncle Philip with the ships?"

"I imagine you'd be more of a hindrance than a help."

"I could use Charles's help," Philip told his brother. He smiled at Charles who shot him a look of gratitude.

"Very well, then," Edmund agreed. "You may stay here."

"What are you planning to wear?" Aurore asked Fidelity. There was no reply and she repeated her question.

"I beg your pardon?" Fidelity said, looking up from her dessert.

"I asked what you were planning to wear to the ball at Yorkby?" the marquise said again.

"I don't know, madame," Fidelity replied. "I was thinking that perhaps I'd stay at home."

"Stay home?" the marquis cried. "But I was planning to claim every dance with you!"

"Surely you're not serious!" Anne Wilmington exclaimed. "Why everyone would be disappointed if you failed to attend!"

"Oh yes!" Aurore added. "Gaston and I have become so fond of you. You must attend the ball if only for us. We will miss you when we leave."

Fidelity looked across the table at Philip but if she expected him to support her she was mistaken. He smiled at her lazily.

"They're right, sweetheart," he said softly. "It would do you good to put on a beautiful gown and go be the belle of the ball."

"You see," Edmund laughed. "Even Philip wants you to go. I'm afraid you have no choice!"

"No," Fidelity admitted. "It would appear that I don't."

When dinner was finally over and the Saint-Quentins and Anne and Edmund Wilmington had gone for an early evening stroll in the gardens, Fidelity asked Charles if he knew where Philip was.

"I believe he's in the library, Fidelity," Charles replied. "Father has given me a new horse, would you like to see him?"

She smiled. "Thank you, Charles. Perhaps tomorrow. I'd like to talk to your Uncle Philip just now."

Charles left and Fidelity went to the library. Not bothering to knock, she pushed open one of the heavy double doors and found Philip sitting behind Edmund's desk, a book open before him. The motion of the opening door caused the candles of the candelabrum on the desk to flicker, and he looked up.

"Do you mind if I come in?" she asked from the doorway.

"Not at all," he shrugged. "Is there something I can do for you, or did you come to find a book to read?"

She looked around the darkly paneled room with its lining of floor-to-ceiling bookshelves. They were full, each book having been brought from England on one trip or another, carefully wrapped to protect the rich leather bindings.

"I came to talk to you," she told him.

Philip closed the book he was reading and, standing, took it to a bookcase near the black marble fireplace and slipped it into the space it had come out of. Returning to the desk, he sat again in the chair and she sat on the edge of the desk near him.

"Why did you support everyone else when I said I didn't want to go to Yorkby?"

He shrugged. "I thought there was no reason for you not to go. Unless you're afraid of going."

"I'm not afraid of going. There's nothing there to frighten me. And I will go. I'll go and you'll see that there's nothing, and no one, there that means anything to me."

"I'm afraid I won't see anything of the kind. Weren't you listening at dinner? I'm not going to Yorkby. We have to sail the day after. I have to be ready as soon as the Saint-Quentins are back from Yorkby and settled on the ship."

"Then what is the point of my going? If I'm going to the damn ball to prove something to you, how am I going to do that if you're not there?" She was becoming angry and Philip's complete calm didn't improve her mood.

"You don't have to prove anything to me," he told her. "You only have to make your choices. I'm leaving the day after the ball, and you'll have six months to decide while I'm away. You should, however, not refuse to see Pierrepointe, at least socially, so you can have a basis for your decision."

"Philip, damn you! How many times do I have to tell you . . .!" She was interrupted by a knock on the library door.

Rising, she went to stand near the fireplace with her back to the door in order to have a moment to compose her features and calm her angry breathing.

"Come in," Philip called.

One side of the double doors opened and Rose leaned into the room. "Beggin' your pardon, Master Philip," she said. "But her ladyship and Madame de Saint-Quentin want to see Mistress Fidelity about her gown."

Fidelity turned. "I'll be right there, Rose." The maidservant left the room and she looked back to Philip. "I want to discuss this further."

Philip leaned back in his chair. "What's the point? You know how I feel about you, but I want you to be happy and the only way for you to do that is to be with the man you really love. All you must do is decide who that man is."

Fidelity said nothing. She felt somehow guilty that Philip's love for her could be so straightforward and selfless while her own emotions were not in the least as clearly defined. She left the room without meeting his gaze.

Wilmington Hall was immersed in preparations for two events—the ball at Yorkby, and the departure of Philip and the Saint-Quentins for England.

Lady Wilmington's dressmakers had come as soon as plans for the ball had been announced, and had brought with them their latest collection of little dolls dressed in the latest fashions. From these collections, the ladies would make their choices and the dressmakers would then make full-sized replicas of the gowns and accessories.

Fidelity's gown, she'd decided, was to be black satin covered over entirely with a delicate webbing of gold lace. Her gloves, fan, and shoes would be black and her stockings would be of black silk with gold embroidery.

"Why black?" Rose asked as she looked at the sketch the dressmaker had given Fidelity.

"Why not black?" Fidelity shrugged.

"Black is a sad color. Master Schuyler likes . . ." Rose flushed and stopped as she saw the look Fidelity threw her. "Of course, you look pretty in any color," she finished quickly.

For Fidelity, the nights were the worst. Nights which, she thought, she should be spending with Philip. Time lost when she should have been storing up memories to keep her for the long months when he'd be gone. But he didn't come to her, didn't give her any sign that, should she go to him, she would be welcome. She was afraid to go to him uninvited; afraid that he would send her back to her room. She lay awake for hours hearing Rose's snores and watching as the light from Philip's room shone beneath her door and then went out. Time seemed to drag and yet somehow the day of the ball at Yorkby arrived much too quickly bringing with it the day after, when Philip would sail away from her for six long months.

It was nearly midday when they went down to the river. Edmund and Anne Wilmington, Aurore and Gaston de Saint-Quentin, and Fidelity, dressed in the clothes they would wear for dinner at Yorkby, were followed by servants carrying the newly finished evening clothing into which they would change for the ball. Philip and Charles came away from the loading of the *Virginian* and the merchantmen to bid them farewell.

They stepped onto the Wilmington's barge which would take them upriver to Yorkby. As the other two ladies made themselves comfortable and the gentlemen directed the situating of the servants and their clothing. Fidelity lagged behind to speak to Phillip.

"Are you sure you can't leave the ships for a few hours?" she pleaded once more.

"No, I've already explained . . ."

"Yes, yes, you've already explained that you have to supervise the ships," Fidelity supplied. "But I don't think that's the entire truth. Why don't I stay behind, I really don't . . ."

"No," it was Philip's turn to interrupt. "You go and enjoy yourself, sweethart. I'd be too busy to spend any time with you even if you stayed home."

She hesitated and he looked at her questioningly. Finally she blurted: "Well, aren't you even going to kiss me good-bye?"

He looked suspicious. "Do you really want me to, or do you want a basis for comparison?"

She flushed. "I didn't deserve that, Philip."

"No, I'm sorry." Leaning over, he kissed her quickly on the cheek. "Good-bye, Fidelity."

She paused a moment longer but he turned to say something to his brother and she knew there was no more to be said between them. She allowed Charles to hand her aboard the barge.

As the barge moved away from the dock and

was propelled up the river by the baron's oarsmen, Fidelity glanced over her shoulder for one more look at Philip but he had disappeared, apparently having gone immediately back to his duties aboard his ships. He had not waited to see them go and she knew that, should she decide to leave him for Schuyler, he would not wait to see her go either.

The great stone mansion of Yorkby stood, as did most of the great homes of the planters along the 'Yuk, facing the river that represented a large part of its livelihood. It was built in an L-shape, solid and plain, and rose two stories before being capped by a low-hipped roof.

As the party from Wilmington Hall was escorted to the mansion, they were met by Lady Pierrepointe.

With a feeling of anger directed at herself, Fidelity fought down a flash of the resentment she'd felt against the woman since she first learned that Schuyler had sold himself to her.

"Lady Wilmington, Lord Wilmington!" the hostess, whose plump figure was encased in silk of a bright yellow-green, exclaimed. She smiled at the Saint-Quentins and swept them the same wobbly curtsy Fidelity had seen her make to the king in London. "Madame, monsieur, my house is honored to receive you." Aware that she could not slight the fifth member of the party whom she remembered all too well from London, she gave Fidelity a curt nod. "Good day, Mistress Fairfax," she said as her eyes swept Fidelity from head to foot and back again.

Fidelity, refusing to curtsy to the woman,

returned her nod and said, "Good day, madame."

Lady Pierrepointe seemed a little annoyed with Fidelity's lack of respect but her eyes widened as she saw Rose standing a little behind Fidelity.

"Rose," she said in surprise. "What are you doing here? Schuyler told me he'd sent you to help an old friend of . . ." Her eyes ran from Fidelity to Rose and back again and, with a haughty lift of her chin and a slight flush staining her cheeks, she directed her attention to her guests of honor.

"Please come in," she invited. "Please, I'm sure you'd like to meet the other guests before we . . ."

As the Baroness Pierrepointe pattled on, Fidelity and Rose exchanged a glance. Rose screwed her face into an exact replica of the baroness's and Fidelity giggled in spite of herself. Ahead of them, escorting the Saint-Quentins, Lady Pierrepointe knew she was being mocked and threw them both a scathing look over one plump shoulder.

# 34

Fidelity entered the ballroom as inconspicuously as she could. She had lagged behind as long as possible and only convinced herself to go when she did by telling herself that to wait any longer would only serve to draw even more attention to herself.

The ballroom and formal dining room of Yorkby were located in the back-reaching wing of the L-shaped house. The dining room, where they'd eaten a splendid dinner, was at the far end of the wing and was nearly thirty feet square, exquisitely paneled in walnut, and lit with chandeliers of a beauty and excellence of craftsmanship Fidelity hadn't seen since leaving England. The ballroom, into which she now stepped, was similar in design to that at Staunton House but the paneling, which was the same dark, gleaming walnut she'd seen in the dining room, was much more beautiful and the entire atmosphere was one of more courtly beauty and refined elegance.

As Fidelity moved among the guests of the Pierrepointes, she heard hums of conversation following her. It was, she supposed, because she stood out so startlingly among the brightly colored gowns and suits of the ladies and gentlemen in her gown of black satin with its covering of delicate gold lace. Her

shoes, the toes of which peeked out as she lifted her
skirts to step over a dropped fan, were black; the fan
in her hand and the ribbons which were threaded
through her hair were black. She heard the conversations but didn't pay any attention. She didn't care
what people said. She'd wanted to wear black to this
ball. She hadn't felt like dressing in a brightly colored
and gaily decorated gown and so she hadn't.

She walked toward one of several groups of gilt
chairs where anyone who didn't wish to dance could
sit and converse. She intended to sit far enough away
from the whirling, graceful dancers that perhaps she
could go unnoticed and be left alone. But, as she was
nearly halfway down the length of the room and the
guests were pairing off for another dance, a figure in
magenta satin and silver lace stepped in front of her.

The Marquis de Saint-Quentin bowed gracefully
and asked: "May I have the honor of this dance,
Mademoiselle Fidélité?"

"Well, I," Fidelity began, but there was no way
she could think of to turn him down gracefully and so
finished: "I would be happy to dance with you,
Monsieur le Marquis."

She took his arm and walked with him out onto
the polished wooden dance floor. She held her eyes on
him as the music began but soon noticed another
couple standing nearby also waiting the start of the
dance. She looked over toward them. Melintha
Staunton was dressed in a gown of palest blue satin
with flounces of white lace and ribbons of blue and
white. Her partner smiled as Fidelity looked once,
then again, and her mouth opened into an "O" of
surprise and indignation.

Schuyler Pierrepointe was Melintha's dance partner. He'd changed his costume since dinner when he'd appeared in a suit of deep forest green over buff silk. Now he stood near Fidelity in a suit of black velvet over gold satin with wide flounces of golden lace at the wrists and throat.

Fidelity continued to stare at him, repressing anger to fly into a rage which would have only drawn more attention to the similarity of their clothing and its distinctive difference from that of everyone else. The dance began and she was grateful when the marquis led her away from Schuyler and Melintha. They were hidden from view by a multitude of dancers but their absence from her line of sight did little to allay the seething anger boiling within her. When the dance ended she bade the marquis a hasty adieu and returned to the chair she'd been about to take when he'd invited her to dance.

Snapping open her fan she swished it back and forth more to allay her anger than create a breeze.

"Ma'am?" a voice hissed in her ear.

She looked around and saw Rose standing near her.

"Hello, Rose," she said sarcastically. "Have you seen your dear Master Schuyler's latest means of tormenting me?"

"Yes, Ma'am," Rose admitted. "I saw him in the hall earlier, just after he'd changed into the black suit."

"Why didn't you warn me?" Fidelity demanded.

"Well, Lord, Ma'am! It's up to him what he wants to wear. Just as it was up to you what you wanted to wear."

"Don't you dare defend that man to me!"

Rose adopted her good servant demeanor and dropped her eyes. "Yes, Ma'am. Would you like a glass of wine? You look a bit flushed."

Fidelity sighed. "Yes, get me one, please."

Rose curtsied and left her side, returning a few moments later with a crystal goblet of wine.

"Sit down, Rose," she invited.

"Oh, no, Ma'am!" Rose shook her head. "Lady Pierrepointe doesn't ever allow her servants to sit with the guests.

"Well, you're not her servant, you're my servant! And if Lady Pierrepointe wants to complain about it, she'd best complain to me!"

Rose sat beside Fidelity and watched as her mistress sipped politely at her wine. When it was nearly gone she offered to get her another, but Fidelity declined.

They watched as the dancers performed the stately, dignified dances of the Court and the merry, rigorous folk dances of the countryside but Fidelity looked away as she felt her head begin to swim.

"What is it, Ma'am?" Rose asked worriedly as she saw Fidelity grimace and place a hand on her forehead.

"It's nothing, just the heat of the wine," Fidelity answered. "Perhaps something I ate at dinner."

"Would you like to go outside for a moment? I know the gardens, there are some benches just outside where we could sit until you feel better."

"Yes, perhaps that would be nice," Fidelity agreed. Some fresh air would do her good and so would absenting herself from the hall.

Outside the ballroom were several flowerbeds set out in intricate patterns with benches here and there to allow one to enjoy the sight and scent of the blossoms. Fidelity followed Rose to one of these and they sat, side by side, for several long minutes but even the cool, moist night air did nothing for her increasing dizziness.

She told Rose who said: "Perhaps you should go up to your room and lie down."

"Do you think I should?"

Rose shrugged. "Why not? If you're not feeling well, you should lie down and I didn't think you were really anxious to stay at the ball."

"All right." Fidelity stood but, as the gardens seemed to tilt and whirl like the dancers at the ball, sat on the bench once again.

"Stay there," Rose commanded. "I'll get a lackey to help you."

Fidelity sat on the bench, eyes closed tightly, and waited until Rose returned with a tall, large man in the red and gray livery worn by the Pierrepointe servants.

"Come on," Rose said gently. "Sam here'll help you."

Fidelity stood again and once again began to weave slightly. Sam, who looked as though he'd be more at home on one of Philip's ships than in satin livery, swept her into his arms and she gratefully leaned her head against his shoulder and closed her eyes.

Even the slight swaying motion of his walk as he carried her made her feel giddy and lightheaded and so, with her eyes tightly shut, she didn't see that Sam was carrying her away from the house toward the far end of the gardens and a miniature mansion whose white walls and thick white columns glistened in the moonlight.

Sam stood Fidelity on the floor and, for the first time since he'd picked her up, she opened her eyes. She found herself in a bedchamber with walls of a delicate green and hangings of green damask. She held onto a post of a fine poster bed, and although she didn't feel well enough to scrutinize the furnishings of the room in great detail, she sensed that this room was far more tastefully, and expensively, furnished than the room she'd been assigned upon her arrival.

"Whose room is this, Rose?" she asked. "This isn't my room."

"This is a room you won't have to share," Rose told her. "You can have this room all to yourself."

The explanation seemed plausible to Fidelity who was in no condition to argue and she held onto the bedpost while Rose removed her gown and accessories and hung them in the armoire to prevent their being wrinkled. When she returned from storing Fidelity's clothes, she helped her mistress, clad in her chemise, into the high softness of the bed.

Fidelity had no idea how long she'd slept when she awoke. It could have been hours or only moments. Through the open window she heard the music of the ball and smelled the lush fragrance of the gardens and, in the light of a candle which stood on a table across the room, she saw a large bouquet of flowers decorating the ornately carved, marble mantelpiece.

She closed her eyes and sighed contentedly as she heard the door open and Rose reenter the room.

"Oh, Rose," she sighed. "I'm feeling so much better. Would you mind fanning me a little?"

She felt the bed give as Rose sat down and a gentle little breeze began to play around her face.

"Ahhh," she said, her head lying far back on the pillows, "that's so nice. Could you find me a glass of water?"

The fanning stopped and the bed moved as Rose stood. Fidelity heard her footsteps recrossing the floor and leaving the room. It was only a moment when the opening and closing of the door signaled her return. Languidly enjoying the comfort of being pampered, Fidelity held out her hand and felt a cold glass being pressed into it.

"You're awfully quiet tonight, Rose," she said lifting the glass toward her lips. She opened her eyes and looked into the depths of a crystal glass filled with sweet, cool water. Then, looking over the rim of the glass, choked and gasped as she saw that it was not Rose who stood next to the bed, but the black-and-gold-clad figure of Schuyler Pierrepointe.

"Schuyler!" Startled, Fidelity dropped the glass and it rolled across the bed spilling its contents over the coverlet. In a convulsive movement, she threw the coverlet away from her body and jumped from the bed. Running to the door, she flung it open and fled from the room but, instead of finding herself in the upstairs hall of Yorkby mansion, she found herself standing in a salon she'd never seen before.

The salon was painted in a soft yellow and the draperies, rugs, and upholstery of the sofa and chairs

were in patterns of yellows, blues, and greens and
depicted flowers and ferns. A chandelier as beautiful
as those she'd admired in the dining room hung over
the center of the room but none of its many candles
were lit. The room was lit softly by a three-branched
silver candelabrum on the mantelpiece and the drapes
covering four tall windows were discreetly drawn.

She ran across the beautiful room and tried to
open the door but it was locked, and before she could
discover how to work the mechanism of the lock, she
heard Schuyler's voice coming from behind her.

"Do you like it?" he asked. "Isn't it every bit as
beautiful as I told you it was?"

She stood with her back pressed against the
door. "You tricked me!" she accused. "You and Rose
together! There was something in the wine, wasn't
there?"

He smiled. "Of course. You're really quite
trusting, which is a charming trait."

"Let me out of here!"

"Where do you want to go?"

"Back to the house! Back to the ball! I'll tell your
wife what you have in mind! I'll tell everyone!"

"Of course you can go," he said calmly. "But
don't you think you'll be a bit conspicuous dressed as
you are?"

She realized she was still clad only in her
diaphanous chemise. Crossing her arms over her
breasts, she turned away from him and leaned against
the door. "Why are you doing this?" she asked,
shivering. "Why do you torment me when you have
everything you want?"

He came up behind her and she felt his fingers

unwinding the ribbons and pulling out the bodkins that held her hair atop her head. She felt its sudden weight as he let it cascade down her back and heard him say:

"Do I torment you?"

"I hate you!"

He laughed softly. "Hate is an emotion as passionate as love."

He turned her around and held her tightly. As she looked up into the green depths of his eyes, her arms relaxed and she followed as he led her across the room to the sofa near the windows.

She allowed herself to be lowered to the silky brocade of the sofa making no protest against Schuyler's searching lips or his fingers which gently but firmly worked at the delicate ribbons of her chemise.

It wasn't that she loved him; she'd realized that their love was a doomed love. There would always be something or someone standing between them. It was only that Philip had left her alone for so long, left her alone when her very soul cried out to be held and caressed. It was only that there, in the beautiful little cottage with the night air sweetened by the perfume of the gardens and the music from the ball reaching them on the cool, moist breezes; on that particular night at that particular moment, she wanted Schuyler more than she'd ever wanted anything else in the world.

Schuyler stood in his shoes, stockings, breeches, and gold satin shirt, tying his cravat and adjusted its lace ends. Fidelity stood before him, her back turned, and waited for him to hook the back of her gown. When he'd finished, she picked up a brush from a table in the bedchamber and began stroking it through her hair.

"I'll never get it fixed the way Rose had it," she sighed. She returned to the armoire for her gloves and fan.

"It's prettiest hanging loose that way," Schuyler smiled as he returned from the salon where he'd gone to get his coat. As he shrugged into it, and pulled the lace ruffles of his shirtsleeves out to show at the ends of the coat sleeves, he asked: "What do you think of the cottage?"

"It's very beautiful," Fidelity admitted as she pulled on her gloves.

"When will you come to live here?"

"I won't."

He sighed as she saw him appear behind her in the mirror. Silently he appraised his appearance and ran the brush she'd finished with through his own long blond curls.

"What other choice do you have?" he said at last. "Will you marry Philip? Do you think no one will know about your husband in England? I'll know, of course, but I could be persuaded to be silent."

"How?"

"Provided Philip doesn't mind his wife taking a lover."

"He'd never agree to that even if I would, which I wouldn't!"

"He might agree, rather than have every man, woman, and child on this river know you for an adulteress, and a bigamist. Once the information was made public, no respectable home on the river would open its doors to you. Baron Wilmington might just have to find another captain for his ships and where would Philip be then?"

Fidelity stared at his reflection in the mirror. "You wouldn't really destroy Philip that way?"

"I'm a bad loser, my dear."

"I hate you!"

"So you've said before. That's what makes you fascinating. I hate docile, clinging women. But I can always depend upon you for at least a token resistance. Once I can get past that resistance, though, there are times when you love me!" He looked at his watch and gave his clothing a last check. "Come, are you finished dressing? It's time we returned to the ball."

"So your wife won't miss you? You talk of mistresses," Fidelity turned as he moved away from the mirror, "but you're nothing but a whore yourself!"

Schuyler was unperturbed. "That may be so. That's where you and I are alike, but I'm rather more successful at it than you—I have Yorkby, money, power, position. All you have is one room in someone else's house. Come now, our guests, or rather my guests of honor, will think I've deserted them! They're leaving tomorrow, aren't they, with Philip?"

Fidelity looked away from him. "I don't believe you'll tell anyone about me," she said stubbornly.

He appeared again behind her in the mirror. "Promise me you'll come to me as soon as Philip's ships are clear of the bay. Promise me or I swear I'll denounce you in that ballroom this very night!"

"I don't believe you!"

"Oh no?" He disappeared from the mirror and strode out of the bedroom, through the salon, and out through a little entrance hall into the gardens. His steps took him purposefully toward the ballroom.

Fidelity stood in the bedroom and heard him leave the cottage but at last her courage failed and she ran after him. Catching up with him she held him by the arm.

"Please, Schuyler! Don't tell anyone," she pleaded. "Phillp would be ruined. His ships and his work for Edmund are his life! If you took that away he would have nothing!"

"Then promise me you'll come as soon as he is gone. Promise you'll come to the cottage."

Defeated, Fidelity lowered her head. "I promise," she whispered. "I promise."

# 35

Fidelity stepped off the Wilmington's barge the moment it was secured at the docks of Wilmington Hall. Running toward the swarms of men who worked readying the ships for departure, she stopped Philip's first mate.

"Master Macrae," she said, a restraining hand on the rough material of the man's sleeve. "Do you know where Philip is?"

"The captain went up to the Hall to fetch some of his papers and books."

Without waiting for Rose or any of the other members of the party just now leaving the barge, Fidelity hurried up the walk to the house and ran up the stairs. She met Philip in the upstairs hall, his arms full of books.

"Philip!" she cried. She threw herself against him without a care for his books and papers.

"Did you enjoy yourself at the ball?" he asked.

She blushed and stepped back. Could he somehow have found out about her and Schuyler and the cottage? No, she decided, it was impossible.

"It was dreadful! I wish I hadn't gone!" That, at least, was the truth. "Oh, Philip, why don't you come and sit down for a moment?"

He shook his head. "I can't. We have to leave. As soon as Madame and Monsieur de Saint-Quentin get to the house they will have to supervise the loading of their baggage and then we'll be off."

"But Philip . . ."

"No, we've been through all this more times than I care to remember." He balanced his books in one arm and put the other around her waist. Drawing her to him he kissed her deeply and with more feeling than she'd had from him in months. When she clung to him he gently but firmly pushed her away. "We'll say good-bye right now, Fidelity. I've a great deal to do and to be brutally honest I will not tolerate you weeping and getting in the way on the ship. I think it would be best if you stayed here until we left."

"Stayed here? Not even be present when you leave?"

"You can see part of the river from your windows, or use mine if the view is better. But I've said all I can say and you know how I feel about all this. Good-bye, Fidelity. I must go, these books are getting deucedly heavy!"

He turned and, as she stood in the hall behind him, walked away without another glance.

"Philip!" she wailed when he started down the stairs.

He didn't reply but, just before his head disappeared below the floor of the hallway, he gave her a look that told her he would brook no disobedience.

She whirled and ran to her room, reaching the window in time to see him striding down the walk toward the dock with his armload of books. She pressed her face against the soft fabric of the drapes. "Philip, oh, Philip," she whimpered. "I've made my choice! I've reached my decision!"

Philip disappeared through the bank of trees and Fidelity left the window and threw herself across the bed.

She didn't look up as Rose entered the room with her gown from the ball of the night before. "Ma'am," the maid said before she saw her mistress lying dejectedly across the bed. "All Lady Wilmington's maids have been asked to help Madame de Saint-Quentin pack for her voyage and Lady Wilmington asked if I would mind helping." When she heard no response, she looked around the door of the closet where she was storing the black and gold gown. Seeing her mistress she cried, "Ma'am, what is it? Are you ill?"

Fidelity lifted herself onto one elbow. "No, I'm not ill. What was that you said about Madame de Saint-Quentin?"

Philip stood on the deck of the *Virginian* watching the baggage of his passengers being loaded. It wouldn't be long, he told himself, before they could leave. He watched as a group of chattering maidservants came on board loaded down with boxes and chests. It was a brisk, cool day and the cloaks and hoods they wore against the wind whipped about them, sending more than one of them crashing to the deck. Over their heads, he saw a lone horseman approaching and muttered a curse as he recognized the resplendently clad figure of Schuyler Pierre-pointe.

"What does that bastard want?" he muttered aloud.

A sailor, working near him, looked as Schuyler brought his horse to a halt and jumped to the ground. "Maybe he wants to book passage, Captain."

Philip laughed softly. "I wouldn't take him farther than halfway. Then he could swim the rest of the way to England!"

With a resigned sigh, Philip went to meet Schuyler who was boarding the ship. "What can I do for you, Pierrepointe?" he asked. He steadfastly refused to address Schuyler by his title and something told Schuyler not to insist.

Schuyler shrugged. "I thought I'd come and inspect your work, Wilmington. After all, a good employer must needs know how his investment is being used."

"Inspect anything you wish," Philip said. He moved away as Lady Wilmington and Madame de Saint-Quentin came aboard the ship with a bevy of maidservants.

"Good morning, ladies," Schuyler smiled. Bowing over the marquise's hand, he said, "I hope you enjoyed the ball, madame."

"Oh, indeed, indeed, monsieur," she answered. "Gaston and I are most grateful to you for your kindness."

"It was my pleasure, I assure you," he replied. "Lady Wilmington, I hope you and Lord Wilmington had an equally pleasant time?"

"Oh, indeed we did," the baroness replied.

Schuyler looked at Philip. "I already know that Mistress Fidelity enjoyed herself."

Philip ignored the barb and helped the marquise direct her maids to the cabin she and the marquis would be sharing.

"You know, Monsieur Wilmington," the marquise laughed. "Every time I travel it seems my baggage somehow multiplies. It seems that I have more and more to pack and load than I had before."

"A lovely lady requires lovely clothing," Philip told her gallantly and the marquise giggled. She stepped through a door and onto a staircase that would take her and her maids below to the cabin. As he stepped back, Philip bumped into a maid in a cloak of blood red and knocked a heavy box out of her hands.

"I'm sorry," he apologized. He picked up the box and found it indeed very heavy. "Toby!" he shouted. One of his sailors answered his call. "Take this box downstairs for the lady."

The sailor took the box and the maid, her eyes downcast and her lowered head completely concealed by the wide, forward-falling hood of her cloak, dropped him a little curtsy and hurriedly followed the sailor with the box she'd been carrying.

"Wilmington." Schuyler was again at his side.

"If you have any questions," Philip snapped, "you can ask them of my brother. I have work to be done, unlike some of my so-called betters."

"Does that work include bidding a fond farewell to a lady we both know?"

"That's none of your business."

"On the contrary. I know when she left Yorkby this morning, and I know how long it takes for a barge to get here from there. You can't have spent much time saying your good-byes. Didn't you wish to, or had she already given the news to you?"

"What news?" Philip asked suspiciously.

"Why, that she's realized how much more I can offer her than you can."

"I don't know what you're talking about and what's more, I don't care to know." Philip turned his back on Schuyler and left the ship to walk up the long dock toward the shore.

Schuyler followed him. "She's leaving you, you know. Oh, I'm sure she didn't tell you, not wishing to spoil your leavetaking, but she's agreed to come and live at Yorkby as my mistress."

"I don't believe you!" Philip growled.

"Don't you? After all, I can give her everything. Not marriage, of course, but then you can't give her that either. Be sensible, man. You should have known that, when it came to a choice, she'd choose me. Better the mistress of a rich man than the whore of a poor one, eh?"

Philip's movement was so swift that it caught Schuyler completely unaware. He was still smiling when Philip's fist came into contact with his jaw snapping his head back and sending him splashing into the river next to the dock. Without a glance, Philip strode back down the dock and, amid cheers from the men of his ships, boarded the *Virginian* and gave orders that anyone not embarking should leave the ship.

Lady Wilmington and Lord Wilmington, who had been below bidding the marquis and marquise farewell emerged onto the deck in time to see some of the baron's slaves pulling Schuyler from the water.

"Lord Pierrepointe!" Lady Wilmington cried.

"Pierrepointe! What happened?" the baron called.

But Schuyler ignored them all and, soaked to the skin, his satin suit dripping, his blond curls in sopping bunches, and his boots squishing, remounted his horse and rode away.

"Philip, what happened?" the baron asked.

"Well, Edmund," Philip shrugged. "It would appear he fell into the river."

Edmund regarded his brother suspiciously but decided it wasn't the time for accusations or reprisals.

"Have a good voyage," he told Philip. "And may you return safely."

The baroness echoed his sentiments and, with the maidservants who'd helped settle the marquise into her cabin, left the ship to stand on the shore as the ships left the dock.

Philip waved good-bye to his brother, sister-in-law, and nephew. Charles had begged for days, but his father refused him permission to sail on this trip. As the ship moved away toward the Chesapeake Bay, Philip looked toward Wilmington Hall and, just in case she were there, watching, waved toward the windows of Fidelity's room.

The *Virginian* and her two merchantmen companions had cleared the bay and were well away from

the shoreline when Philip left the deck for his cabin. It
was evening and the great lanterns on the stern of the
ship had been lit. Wearily, he went down the stairs
leaving the Saint-Quentins who stood up on the deck
watching the shore of Virginia disappear from view.
He paused as he passed the door of the cabin Fidelity
had used when he'd brought her from England; the
cabin which now belonged to the Saint-Quentins.

He thought about Schuyler Pierrepointe. Had he
been lying? Was Fidelity even now packing to leave
Wilmington Hall? He shook the thoughts from his
mind and opened the door of his cabin.

"What the hell?" he said as he saw boxes and
chests littering the floor. The bed curtains were drawn
and, as he squinted into the darkened room, he saw a
figure standing near the windows. It was the maidservant into whom he'd bumped on deck. The one in the
red cloak.

"What are you doing here?" he asked. "Don't
you know we'll have to turn the ship around and take
you back? Do you know how much that will cost the
baron?"

The figure turned and drew back the window
drapes admitting the last rays of the setting sun and
the light of the stern lanterns.

Philip's eyes widened. "Fidelity!"

Fidelity put a finger to her lips. "Shhh," she
cautioned. Walking to the curtained bed she drew
back the hangings to reveal a slumbering Rose.

"Rose, too?"

Fidelity shrugged. "I had to bring her. She was
afraid of what Schuyler would do to her when he

found I had gone. And I promised to present her to the king when we get to London."

Dropping the bed hangings back into place, Fidelity led Philip across the room and out onto the gallery which ran across the stern of the ship.

"But Pierrepointe told me you promised . . ."

"I did," Fidelity said quickly. "I promised to become his mistress because he threatened to ruin you by exposing my past. I only promised so that he would not tell anyone about Nichodemus." She looked at him shyly. "Do you mind terribly that I stowed away?"

"Not if this is where you truly want to be."

She nodded. "There is nowhere else I'd rather be. I don't want to stay anywhere without you, Philip." She smiled. "Of course, since the Saint-Quentins have my cabin, Rose and I will have to stay with you."

"Rose?" he asked plaintively as one of her loud snores erupted from within the cabin.

Fidelity giggled. "Philip, there's something I want you to know. Last night, at Yorkby, I realized that any love I may have had for Schuyler is dead. It died a slow and agonizing death, but it's gone at last. I love you, Philip, and no one else."

From far above them a voice called to Philip. It was Master Macrae and he requested the captain's presence on deck. Fidelity sighed and Philip shrugged. With an all-too-brief kiss he left her and returned through the darkened cabin to the staircase that would take him to the deck and his duties.

Fidelity stood on the gallery. The shoreline was hidden now. Any last glimpse she might have had was concealed by the darkness. Below, the ship's wake churned blackly as the wind in the sails carried her away from Schuyler and the intrigues of Virginia. She'd return some day, she had no doubt of it, but what she'd do then was not something she'd worry about now.

Ahead lay England. Nichodemus would still be there, and Barbara Palmer. They'd schemed to kill her before and she had no reason to think they'd hate her any less when she suddenly reappeared. From above her, on the deck, she heard Philip shouting orders and was reassured. She'd fought Nichodemus and Barbara alone last time, and lost. But this time, this time Philip would be beside her and she felt no fear.

# FIDELITY'S FLIGHT

## Sandra DuBay

---

### *GLITTERING PALACES,*
### *HEATED PASSIONS!*

Lovely Fidelity Fairfax aroused the desires of every man she met. Her search for a lasting love led her from one forbidden romance to another, earning her the enmity of the most powerful women at the French and English Courts.

Though nobleman and commoner alike attempted to win her, Fidelity's heart belonged to dashing Philip Wilmington, the bold highwayman whose ardor had enflamed her senses. But Philip was torn from her arms and forced into exile, unjustly accused of a crime he had not committed. Despite the adoration of Louis XIV, King of France, who offered her his protection, Fidelity had but one end in view—to join her fate to that of her beloved wherever he might be, no matter what the cost!

**LEISURE BOOKS**                    **PRICE: $4.25**
                                     **0-8439-2031-9**

# Thrilling
# Historical Romance
## by
# *CATHERINE HART*
## Leisure's
# *LEADING LADY OF*
# *LOVE*

# Make the Most of Your Leisure Time with
# LEISURE BOOKS

Please send me the following titles:

| Quantity | Book Number | Price |
|---|---|---|
| _____ | _____ | _____ |
| _____ | _____ | _____ |
| _____ | _____ | _____ |
| _____ | _____ | _____ |
| _____ | _____ | _____ |

If out of stock on any of the above titles, please send me the alternate title(s) listed below:

| | | |
|---|---|---|
| _____ | _____ | _____ |
| _____ | _____ | _____ |
| _____ | _____ | _____ |
| _____ | _____ | _____ |

Postage & Handling _____

Total Enclosed    $ _____

☐ Please send me a free catalog.

NAME _____
(please print)

ADDRESS _____

CITY _____ STATE _____ ZIP _____

Please include $1.00 shipping and handling for the first book ordered and 25¢ for each book thereafter in the same order. All orders are shipped within approximately 4 weeks via postal service book rate. PAYMENT MUST ACCOMPANY ALL ORDERS.*

*Canadian orders must be paid in US dollars payable through a New York banking facility.

Mail coupon to: **Dorchester Publishing Co., Inc.**
**6 East 39 Street, Suite 900**
**New York, NY 10016**
**Att: ORDER DEPT.**